THE THOUSAND DEATHS OF MR SMALL

The Thousand Deaths of Mr Small

GERALD KERSH

FABER & FABER

This edition first published in 2013
by Faber and Faber Ltd
Bloomsbury House, 74–77 Great Russell Street
London WC1B 3DA

Printed and bound by CPI Group (UK) Ltd, Croydon, CR0 4YY

A CIP record for this book is available from the British Library

ISBN 978-0-571-30458-5

To

Florence Sochis

Preface to the 2013 Edition

> At his death in 1968 Kersh had left us with a dazzling gallery of criminals and artists, characters filled with love and loathing, and carrying the seeds of their own destruction. It's a mystery that he is not regarded as a great British writer of the twentieth century.
>
> Christopher Fowler, *Independent on Sunday*, 18 September 2011

Forty-five years after he left us Gerald Kersh still suffers from little better than the 'large, vague renown' Orwell famously ascribed to Thomas Carlyle. He is remembered chiefly for *Night and the City* (1938), one of the great novels of London's Soho, driven by its shabby anti-hero Harry Fabian. Jules Dassin's 1950 film version starring Richard Widmark has certainly helped that book to endure. But Kersh's novel lives on by itself because it teems with adroitly observed forms of (low) life, and it still feels like the real thing. Readers who come newly to Kersh usually sense quite soon from his salty, word-rich presence on the page that this was a writer who lived fully, and who never missed a trick. Evidently all he saw was of interest to him, not to say fair game.

Kersh does have his notable and steadfast champions today: Harlan Ellison has vigorously sought to promote awareness of a man whose talent he considered 'immense and compelling'; Michael Moorcock is the 'sometime executor' of the Kersh estate and has kindly made possible Faber Finds' reissues of a selection of Kersh's finest works; while cinema-book specialist Paul Duncan has also been an avid advocate for Kersh, and is understood to have been at work awhile on a biography. What general readers may know of Kersh for the moment is largely down to the information these men have placed in the public domain.

Kersh was born in Teddington on 26 August 1911. Writing as a meaningful pastime came quickly to him, such that he soon sniffed a vocation. He quit schooling early, and raced through a succession of jobs as if seeking to go one better on Hemingway's maxim that a novelist ought to have a friend in every occupation. In 1934 he published a *roman-à-clef, Jews without Jehovah*, but it wasn't on sale for very long, since three uncles and a cousin of Kersh's made out unflattering renderings of themselves within its pages, and sought legal redress – apparently a lasting source of tension at Kersh family occasions.

Following the outbreak of war Kersh joined the Coldstream Guards in 1940 and seems to have been rated a decent soldier. His first stint of leave was during the Luftwaffe's Blitz, whereupon he narrowly escaped fatal injury but was thereafter reassigned to desk duties. In 1941 he drew on his Guardsman experience to write *They Die with Their Boots Clean*, a classic fictional account of basic training, and he enjoyed a surprise bestseller with a work that is richly illustrative of his gift for refining into print things you can well imagine he actually heard. (Finds offers the book, bound up with its sequel *The Nine Lives of Bill Nelson*, under the title given this pairing by their US publisher: *Sergeant Nelson of the Guards*.)

Thereafter Kersh would be phenomenally productive: a writer not merely of novels and stories but of journalism, sketches and columns, radio and documentary film scripts. After the war he settled in the US and there made himself a fixture in popular magazines that paid well for stories and brought him to huge readerships: the *Saturday Evening Post, Esquire, Collier's, Playboy*. Kersh's stories are the most accessible demonstration of his protean gifts: the strange and fantastical tales are especially cherished, and may be sampled in Finds' reissues of *The Horrible Dummy and Other Stories* as well as a broader selection chosen by Simon Raven entitled *The Best of Gerald Kersh*. At the height of this productivity came three of his most admired novels: *Prelude to a Certain Midnight* (1947), *The Song of the Flea* (1948), and *The Thousand Deaths of Mr Small* (1950).

Kersh wrote so much, his printed output was so compendious, that one might suppose he never had time to blot a line. And yet his sentence-making is remarkably strong. He was both a singular talent and a hard grafter: a crafter of sentences, spinner of yarns, scholar of human follies. His living by the pen, however, seems to have been rarely better than precarious, for a variety of reasons: he had money troubles, personal troubles, health troubles, and over time these tended to come at him in battalions. Amid this turmoil he could still produce *Fowler's End* (1958), judged by Anthony Burgess as 'one of the best comic novels of the century'. Burgess was also a champion of *The Implacable Hunter* (1961); and *The Angel and the Cuckoo* (1966) earned Kersh more high praise. But by then he was very nearly through: he died in New York on 5 November 1968, aged fifty-seven. He remains one of those writers perpetually in need of revival, admired by near enough all who read him, awaiting still his golden hour of evangelism. The reader, if not already a convert, is warmly invited to start here.

Richard T. Kelly
Editor, Faber Finds
July 2013

AUTHOR'S NOTE

Desdemona's taste for outlandish stories led her to an untimely end, suffocated under a pillow by the spinner of untrue tales. She died as she lived—breathless.

She asked for it, and she got it. She was the pulp magazine reader of her day. Nothing but outlandish monsters could satisfy her. Her imagination craved the unnatural, the supernatural, and the freakish. If Othello were alive to-day he would probably write for the pulps; and if he published a book his publishers would put in a piece to the effect that all characters therein were fictitious and had no relation to any living person, etc.

Yet the fact is that there is no horror or fantasy or fairy tale conceivable by man that has not its roots in his neighbour's house and back garden. For example: look at the illustrations to the startling stories in the sensational magazines. The illustrators, some of whom are capable artists, strain every fibre of their imaginations to outline the Nightmare. They can't. The monster from Mars turns out to be nothing but an exaggerated ant. The dreadful apparition that haunts the house is only a man distorted. If nausea is to be inspired the illustrators must fall back on slime, such as oozes out of any box of fish. The predatory cannot be expressed except in terms of teeth and claws and tentacles. Everything that every writer writes about must in some way have relation to something or somebody, living or dead.

Try it and see. Describe me, say, a butcher, without scraping together memories of all the butchers you have seen and known. Draw me the character of somebody hateful without remembering everyone you ever disliked. It can't be done, because you are not God Almighty, you see, and cannot create life. As a part of all that you have met, you must use things seen and remembered. No character can be fictitious.

So I come to the characters in this book. For the character of the flabby-minded Mr. Small I have drawn on all the flabby-minded fathers I have ever met, taken them apart and put the choicest bits together. I have met at least fifty Mrs. Smalls, whom I have squeezed into the skin of that monstrous woman . . . and so on. The characters in this book are not portraits of individuals, dead or alive; but they have relation to innumerable individuals all over this sad world wherever children suck their mother's milk and mothers suck their children's souls.

GERALD KERSH
New York, 1950

The Thousand Deaths of Mr. Small

CHAPTER I

IT used to happen only once or twice in three or four months. But now, when he is a dozen years older, and the poison has worked its way into him, Charles Small has what his wife calls a "mood" twice a week. (She tells the children that he has a "pain".)

Small locks himself in, throws himself on the bed, pushes his knees up to his chin, grasps his ankles, closes his eyes tightly, and tries to understand himself. His eyelids are not thick enough to black out the daylight. He sees, first of all, a redness that grows smoky. *What is it about? Tell me, what is it all about? Answer me at once!* he shouts—but the shouting is all inside himself. His anxious family hear nothing. *Come out, come out!* he screams, silently, until he is purple in the face and his heart beats painfully.

The time comes when his eyes seem to turn a somersault in the cloudy darkness, so that they are looking into his sloppy skull as a gypsy fortune-teller looks into the dregs of a teacup, and there he sees a spattered accidental pattern, something like a hieroglyph which must somehow make sense but which he cannot translate. By this time he is drowsy: the flaky leaves run together to make a brown blob, whereupon he remembers a ridiculous old story: the story of the little boy who went into raging hysterics at the sight of *kreplach* . . .

It seems that once upon a time there was a little boy who, at the age of nine, was a perfectly normal child. He looked you between the eyes, and spoke his mind. In school he was second in the class, and he was good at games. He had never been beaten or frightened. His mother loved and cherished him, and he lived a clean, happy life. Looking at this child everyone said: "Here is the perfect type of the clean-cut, fearless, uninhibited boy." Yet he had one mad, unreasoning fear—of *kreplach!* You could put him in a cage with a tiger, or live rattlesnakes, and he was unafraid. But if you showed him a dish of *kreplach* he would scream until he burst a blood vessel.

The boy's mother, naturally, was worried. She explained to him that *kreplach* was only another word for *ravioli*. Still, nothing would reconcile the boy to the sight of *kreplach*. At last she consulted a psychiatrist, who told her that *kreplach* in themselves were not objects calculated to inspire fear. Obviously, if the boy knew the meaning of *kreplach*—that is to say, if he understood all the processes that went to the making of *kreplach* —this blind terror would be washed out of his mind. The psychiatrist said: "Now go home, and bring your little boy into the kitchen, and demonstrate to him stage by stage how *kreplach* are made. Then, I wager a pension, his little trouble will pass away. . . . Not at all, not at all, glad to have been of help. That will be twenty dollars."

The mother went home and called her little boy, saying: "Isidor, I want you to watch me making something nice for dinner."

"Sure, Mom."

"Now look, Isidor, you see what I am doing?"

"Sure, Mom. You're putting an egg in some flour and beating it all up."

"That's right, Isidor, quite right. Now what am I doing?"

"Why, Mom, you're squeezing it all together and rolling it out with a rolling pin. . . . Why, what's the matter, Mom?"

"Now what am I doing, Isidor?"

"Why, Mom, you are rolling it out thin, and thinner and thinner. . . . What's the idea, Mom?"

"Now what am I doing, Isidor?"

"Why, Mom! You *know* what you're doing! You're taking a glass and cutting out little round pieces from all that stuff you rolled flat. . . . What's the matter, Mom?"

"That's all right, son. Now look and tell me what I'm doing now, Isidor darling."

"Aw, gee, Mom, you're getting little bits of meat and putting them in the middle of them round pieces."

"Good boy! And what am I doing now?"

"Well, Mom, you *know* what you're doing now! You're covering that meat up with another round piece, and pinching up all the edges. Aren't you, Mom?"

"That's a clever boy. And how many of these pieces have I got here now?"

"Five . . . ten . . . twenty."

"Quite right. Now I want you should watch carefully, Isidor, what I'm going to do now," said the mother. She scooped

2

up the completed pasta and threw it into boiling water. "Do you see?"

"Sure I see. Why? Is anything the matter, Mom?"

"Isidor, I want you should wait right here. I want you should see exactly what I'm doing."

"But Mo-om! I've seen it! I got a date——"

"Isidor, wait!"

"But what for?"

"For your own good, Isidor. . . . Now look . . ."

She dipped a spoon into the pot and fished out a plateful of *kreplach*, saying, triumphantly: "There you are now, you see now, Isidor—what was there to be afraid of?"

The little boy looked at her with wide uncomprehending eyes. Then he looked down at the plate. Pink foam gushed out of his mouth and his eyes started out of their sockets. *"KREPLACH!"* he screamed, and went into convulsions.

* * * * *

It is at this point that Small tries for the thousandth time to think calmly and reasonably of his mother. For thirty-odd years he peeped and pried and sniffed and squinted through chinks and keyholes into the sooty half-light of the family kitchen, and he knows pretty well how his mother was made.

He has seen the flour that was heedlessly ground out of a million subtly different seeds, carelessly dipped up in cupped hands and thrown down on a board. He has heard the clapping of the floury hands beating away loose particles, and the dull clicking of the piled eggs under the fumbling fingers.

He has seen the little hillock of flour beaten into a crater; heard the sharp crack of the eggshell against the edge of a basin, and the quick sniff of the cook when she convinced herself that the egg was not bad. He knows how the egg went into the crater with a tiny thud, followed by the double-rap of the thrown-down halves of the empty shell; and he has not forgotten the glutinous slap of the fork that beat the egg into the flour . . . under a cloud. Oh, he knows the operation, process by process!

Soon the sloppy live egg, companying with the flour, grows stickily obstinate. The quick, fierce fork becomes slow and uncertain in its movements. The soft glutinous stuff is resisting the steel. The egg is the ringleader of resistance in the crater. Very deliberately the fork pushes in the sides of the mountain.

3

The yellow stickiness becomes heavy, sluggish. Crag by crag the mountain falls. The dough still resists. There is a pause. Then, from a rack, comes a big stick, a rolling pin. It descends with a smacking sound and cuts a chasm in the stiff dough. Before the dough can recover, the rolling pin is down again with a crash. The hill becomes a plateau. A few more blows and the plateau becomes a rolling steppe. The steppe becomes a plain. The plain becomes a lawn. The stubborn dough has been thrashed into a limp sheet. There it lies on the board, thin as paper; yellow, beaten.

So far so good. Now it is necessary to cut the enemy into shape. The cook takes a thin glass, powders the rim with flour, stamps out circles; snatches up the residue of the dough, which she beats and rolls again, and stamps again into circles, adding the little extra bit of dough that must inevitably be left over to one last extra-large disc.

On the stove a pot boils and a saucepan lid rattles. The cook's face seems to burst into flame as she drags the pot aside, and then there is a blast of heat, a puff of dark smoke, and a red light in which Small can see her winking sweat out of her eyes while she puts upon each disc of dough a spoonful of left-over meat, chopped up fine and cunningly seasoned, which she covers with another doughy circle, pinching the edges together.

Oh, Small knows how his mother was made! The odds and ends are used up; the life is beaten plastic and submissive; the left-overs of the family are salted and peppered to taste, and imprisoned.

So, before the iron pot crashes back over the fire, a lurid light fills the dark kitchen. The water boils, and in go the *kreplach*. Soon the lid is lifted. It rattles down while the steam comes up. A spoon goes down into the boiling water, and out of a cloud a voice says: "I made this specially for you—eat it all up—all up!"

"I'm not hungry."

"But I made it specially for you."

"But I can't eat it."

"What's the matter with you? Do you want to kill me? Look at me! Look at me! See how tired I am! Feel how wet I am! For what do I sweat? For whom? Why? . . . *Eat it up!*"

"But Mama, please! Please, Mama!"

"I've killed myself for you. To please me, eat, for God's sake!"

"I'll be sick, Mama."

4

"To please *me* . . . please?"

A great lump of hot, wet dough is stuffed into Small's mouth, while the voice says: "There, there, nice, nice, there, nice. . . . Mmmm!"

The hot damp dough is in his nostrils—Small's head must go backwards before he can breathe, and then he is compelled to eat *kreplach*, the sort they make out of curd-cheese . . . there is a taste of sour milk, and he is sick. "'There there, there," says the voice; and he is floating over a mountain, upside-down —he is dizzy, because he has been swung and swayed here and there. He knows that the mountain had a cratered peak. It is an ancient volcano in eruption. Swung high and low, he grabs with clutching hands. "Drink it, then," says the voice; and his mouth is full again.

Sucking milk, and gasping between breathless swallows, he sobs: "*Ma-ma.*"

"He's talking!" says the voice.

"So soon! It can't be!"

"I should live so sure—he said mama."

"*Maa-maa!*"

"Would you believe it! Bless him!"

He is struggling desperately, striking out with an impotent square inch of hand. He has no strength: he is enraged. They have pinned him up in something rough which chafes the tenderest parts of him. Moistening itself to cut more efficiently, this rough thing is filing away the soft skin between his thighs. He shuts his eyes, opens wide his toothless mouth, and empties his lungs in one terrible cry.

"Quick! Quick! For God's sake, quick! He's holding his breath! What shall I do? Send for the doctor!"

"Give him to me, Mrs. Small."

He is picked up like a straw on a high wind, thrown on his belly upon a canopy of stinking black cloth, and beaten in the ribs. Drawing breath again, he weeps. His head is down, his heels are up, and since he has no muscles to hold what remains of the sour liquid stuff inside him, he is sick again—whereupon everything spins and he is passed from hand to hand, until he lands on his back, exhausted.

"I had such a fright. . . ."

"It's nothing."

"I thought it was convulsions."

5

"Convulsions! All your life you should have such convulsions! Change him, go on."

Something clicks and the coarse wet stuff peels away. For a second or two—only for a second or two—he feels free and cool, so he croons a little, while they dry him and powder him before imprisoning him again. But now he is completely empty, empty with an emptiness that hurts. Feeling pain, he cries out, and gropes for something to make him feel better.

"You should feed him now, Mrs. Small."

Jerkily, buttonhole by buttonhole a darkness is split by a great white triangle, out of which bursts another mountain, from the purple summit of which a reticulated pattern of blue rivers runs down into the dark. *Maa-maa* he bleats.

"*K'nehora*, already he understands everything. *Imbeshrier*, he's talking!"

The mountain falls. Charles Small's mouth finds what it has been seeking. A gentle warmth fills his belly. Now he is content; he will sleep. But the voice says: "He hasn't had *anything!* For God's sake, look! Look! He's closing his eyes! He brought everything up, and now he won't eat! What've I done! What've I done to deserve it?"

"He'll eat, he'll eat, please God, he'll eat, Mrs. Small. Believe me. Encourage him, and he'll eat."

The purple-summited pale mountain darts at him as a terrier attacks a rat. He claws the air with nails that are soft as films of transparent pink varnish, and screams, throwing his head back. This head of his is covered with black fluff: in the centre of the crown of it there is a boneless quadrilateral hot and soft, beneath which the brain, full of blood, throbs and grows. He is caught by the hard, round back part of his skull, and pushed, in spite of resistance, to the mountain. Hot milk is forced into his mouth. Charles Small must drink or suffocate. He drinks, and at last he is put to bed. He would keep that which was forced into him if he could, but he cannot: his overloaded stomach rejects the milk. Then he is comfortable and happy, and would gladly sleep. But the rough stuff about his loins and in his crutch has moistened itself again to lubricate its jagged teeth. It bites.

Charles Small cries. The voice cries: "Oh my God, Oh God, he's got convulsions!" Then he is picked up, pounded, rubbed, kissed, undressed, wiped, powdered, and pinned up again. After that the mountain comes to him out of a long white nightdress,

6

and at last there is the dark. He sleeps a little and, awakening, sees nothing. He is alone. So he cries. Springs squeal. Someone moans. Still in the dark he feels the embrace of powerful arms, and inhales a familiar smell—which he hates. Still, it is better than nothing; and alone, Charles Small is nothing. Soothed, he allows himself to be put down again, and then, missing the protective warmth, he cries again. A flat paraffin-wax night-light makes a hole in the shadows—a hole no bigger than an orange-pip. "My little dolly! What do you want then? Let Mummy sleep a little, then!"

Charles Small weeps desperately. The voice says: "*Sha! . . . Sha! . . .*" Out comes the mountain. As a man nibbles a blade of grass, chews a piece of gum, or smokes a cigarette—so he sucks. ". . . Was he hungry? There, little dolly, was it then? There then, there then. . . ."

. . . Charles Small starts out of a dyspeptic doze with a vile, sour taste in his mouth. He feels crop-full of curds and awash with a gurgling bilge of whey. "What a life, what a bloody life!" he says, grinding his teeth and tenderly pressing his throbbing temples. His head is neither aching nor not aching. He grips it hard in his damp hands, and shakes it until it rattles like a money-box, wishing that he could tear it off, dash it to the floor, and stamp on it. *Damn you, ache or don't ache— don't threaten to ache!* bellows the exasperated inaudible voice inside himself; and he hits himself hard on the forehead. The blow drives the indeterminate headache into some hole or corner in the fog. Obedient but always malignant, it slips into a secret passage, wriggles around his cheek-bone, and finds a back tooth, where it sits sulkily picking at the nerve, while it says:

All right then, if you don't want me I'll go away!

Damn you, damn you! Oh, if only I could get hold of you! screams the noiseless voice of Charles Small, and he snaps his jaws together, baring his teeth. At this the vague ache hunches its shoulders, curls up, and becomes a concentrated pain. Charles Small cries "Ow!"

Smugly nodding, and sending home a new pang with every nod, the Pain says, with hypocritical bewilderment, strongly tinged with hysteria: *What's the matter? What d'you want of me? Didn't I do what you told me to do? Don't I try to please you? Whatever I do is wrong. If I stay, that's not good. If I go away, that's not good. What am I to do? Die, to please you?* The Pain begins to cry: the nerve in the tooth seems to shudder, hiccup, and twitch. Charles Small strikes it with his fist; whereupon it cowers, and runs to a safe place, behind his left shoulder-blade, not far from the base of his neck, where it swells big and glows bright and says: *Well, does this suit you?*

He groans aloud, and puts out his hand for something cold to drink. The sour curds inside him have become a great ball of soapy cheese floating in burning acid. His unsteady hand finds the glass his wife has put on the little table by the bed. Greedily, he swallows two great mouthfuls: then he sits up retching, with a shudder, and sees that the glass was full of milk. Milk! He makes as if to throw the glass away but, remembering that he is thirsty, drinks the rest of the milk; and then hurls the empty glass across the room and sees it smash and hears the pieces fall. Charles Small is angry with himself. As the little Pain prods his shoulder he asks, angrily: *What the hell do you want?*

Control yourself!

Then, of course, someone knocks at the door, and he must shout: "Oh, come in, come in!" His ten-year-old daughter Laura is there, asking if he is all right.

"Yes, yes, yes, yes, yes, yes, yes! *Yes!* Can't you let me rest?"

Laura looks at him with round, startled eyes. Charles Small perceives that her feelings are hurt, and he loves this little girl, he believes, more than she deserves. He wants to apologise, to say: *I'm sorry, Laura, my little darling, if I sounded as if I was angry with you. I'm not, you know—I couldn't be angry with you. I was angry, darling, but not with you, and I knocked a glass over. Come in, my sweet, and let me tell you a story. . . .*

Something makes him say: "What the hell do you want? What do you take me for, your slave? I work my fingers to the bone for you and I can't get a minute's peace in my own house, is that it?"

Laura says: "Mummy told me to come and see if you were all right and ask you if you'd like a nice glass of hot milk."

"No!" shouts Charles Small, right into the child's face. "Go away!"

She goes downstairs, trying not to cry. In an ecstasy of remorse he stretches his right arm so that his knuckles can strike the painful place by his left shoulder-blade. The Pain

8

runs back to the place it came from and settles down in his head, while his insides grow more and more sour, and a soft, invisible hand squeezes his belly like a sponge until bitter water comes out of his eyes.

To-morrow he will buy Laura a present. He will take her to the best toyshop in town and say: "Choose whatever you want." Whatever her heart desires, or her fancy dictates, she shall have, if it costs fifty pounds. But he knows that fifty thousand rocking-horses with crimson nostrils and snow-white tails could not drag out of her recollection the memory of the last ninety seconds.

He feels that he has hurled a brick at a priceless vase.

If wishing could make it so, Charles Small would drop dead: twenty thousand shot-guns would blow him into a fine spray. The Pain in his head laughs a laugh, that shakes every nerve in his body. *What for? Why? What's the use?* he asks himself. *Die, die, you idiot, die!*

He goes to the bathroom, takes from its oblong box one of his big hollow-ground German razors, and bares his throat. The broad blade sings under his thumb. One quick slash under the ear and then, shadowy jet by jet, comes the dark . . .

. . . Downstairs he hears voices. He must know what is being said. Silent on his stockinged feet he goes to the bedroom door, closing the razor and replacing it in its box as he goes. What he is doing is shameful, and he knows it. He is spying, prying, eavesdropping; secretly listening to the private conversation of his own flesh and blood. Of all the despicable things to do, this is the most despicable. His mother and her sisters did such shameful and disgusting things—but still he listens, holding his breath and trying to gulp down his stomach, which is sticking in his throat. Laura, that wet-eyed little sneak—the spitting image of her damned mother—is snivelling again: "Mummy, Daddy shouted at me, Daddy grumbled at me!"

Laura's mother, Charles' wife, says, in her tinny, monotonous voice—oh, that voice, that voice like a tap with a worn-out washer dripping into an enamel basin in a kitchen sink in the dead of night!—she says: "There, there, Laura darling, Daddy didn't mean it, Daddy isn't well. Daddy's got a pain!"

At this, of course, the child cheers up. Good news: Daddy has a pain. Excellent! "What kind of a pain, Mummy?" she asks. She hopes that it is a bad pain.

9

"Daddy's got a pain in the tum-tum. A naughty pain in his little tum-tum."

"Why has Daddy got a pain in his tum-tum?"

"Daddy is worried, and it gives him a pain in his tum-tum."

Now "tum-tum" is more than Charles Small can bear: he must protest. But how? If he were an honest man he'd go downstairs and thrash the matter out. But an honest man would not have listened to this conversation in the first place; and he knows it. Curling a contemptuous lip at himself he reaches backwards, finds the door-knob, rattles it, and pushes the bedroom door open so violently that it rebounds from the wall with a quivering bang. (The people downstairs will believe that he has just thrown it open.) Then he roars: "What's the matter down there? *Tum*, tum, tum—*tum*, tum, TUM! What's the idea? What's going on? Tum, tum, *tum!* Where is this? Africa? Can't I get five minutes rest? *Tum, tum, tum!* Hire a hall if you want to practice the drums and let a man have a little peace!"

There is a terrible silence. He goes back into the bedroom, slamming the door. He knows, now, that Laura, his accursed daughter, and Hettie, his damned wife, are whispering together. His wife's eyelids, over her prominent blue eyes, are pink with a sickly pinkness. It is a psychological certainty that the whites of those disgusting eyes are going red at the corners, and that there is an exudation of tears. Charles Small can see it all. A big tear rises and stands, like a water-blister, between her white mouse's eyelids—it wobbles tantalisingly, so that you want to take a stick and knock it off, or stick a pin in it. Then it seems to go pop, and a foolish little trickle runs to the bridge of her absurd nose. The bridge of this nose is situated less than an inch from the tip—it is an admirable distribution-centre for idle tears. Plip-plop, bloop-bleep—down fall the lazy, colourless drops. Laura, of course, blubbers in sympathy. *Let them cry their confounded eyes out!—— And put red pepper on them and swallow them like oysters, and drop dead!* says Charles Small, lying down again.

His face is hot, his ears are burning, and between his breastbone and his spine he is aware of an unhealthy glow. From deep inside him struggles a puff of gas in a wriggling bubble which nudges itself away up through the sour curds, flutters through the acidulous whey, and bursts. Something like a branding iron burns his gullet, and in his mouth again is the taste of sour milk, milk so sour that it is wrinkled like a brain and powdered with grey-green mildew between the convulsions.

Then, of course, he hears the thunder of a little boy's feet. Jules, his son, has come home from school. The weather is warm; the boy is wearing rubber-soled shoes; and yet he manages to clump about the place like a Suffolk Punch stallion . . . . From somewhere inside Charles Small shoots something like a sky-rocket, which bursts under his left collar-bone in a shower of gold and silver sparks that emerge, brilliantly glittering and burning like hot needles, from every pore of his skin. As the sparks die they grow cold, and their coldness freezes the sweat brought out by the burning heat. Wet and shivering, abnormally sensitive in the ears, he waits for what he knows must come. In some indefinable place, not far from where his neck joins his shoulders, there is the over-wound mainspring of a great clock, which, at a touch, will fly open with a whirring noise.

Here it comes—a terrible hiss, as of compressed steam from a boiler at bursting point—a noise that makes him cower in expec-tation of an awful bang. Hettie is whispering "Hush". How like his mother she is—how well she thinks she means, and how ill she does! Little Laura is whispering now, and her whisper is like the noise of pent-up breath being blown into a toy balloon which swells tighter and tighter until you shut your eyes and cringe away with your fingers in your ears, dreading the inevitable *pop* . . . as if a toy balloonful of baby's breath could hurt you, dirty little coward that you are! . . .

The inevitable pop. The inevitable Mom and the inevitable Pop. There was Pop, there was his father to the life—a toy balloon, a bubble, a pennyworth of membrane puffed up with sour-milky baby's breath, an inflated nothing obedient to every idle wind; but capable of inspiring idiot fear, fear that he might burst! The more you shuddered away from him the bigger he grew; until at last, poor skinful of wind, he deflated himself and became the shrivelled little empty bag that he was . . . so that out of sheer pity you lent him the breath of your life wherewith he might reinflate himself and feel like somebody again . . . whereupon, sucking your breath, he grew big to frighten you once more. He was dangerous as a toy balloon is dangerous—only if the baby swallows it.

He used to come home, flabby and empty, to be pumped up by his family after the world had taken the wind out of him.

Thus he made ready for another day . . the nobody, the nothing, the dead-beat, the sound-and-fury-signifying-nothing, the failure.

Charles Small's son Jules is maturing early. He is only thirteen years old, but his voice is already breaking. Of all the irritating noises in the world—knives scratching plates, uninhibited soup-drinking, the gasping of Hettie's father when he is drinking hot tea; the sucking noise Hettie's brother makes when he gets a fibre of meat from between his teeth after a meal and, having held it up on his finger-nail for examination, swallows it with a smacking of the lips; Hettie's whimpering glottal stoppage when she says: "Buts I didn't meann it"; the adenoidal sing-song of Nathan when, opening his muddy eyes and slippery mouth, he reaches out with a shiny red hand to take the pot a second before he turns up the Ace King Queen Jack Ten of hearts, saying: "*Give me the money*"—of all these noises the sound of his son's voice is the most unbearable.

Jules starts to talk like a human boy. Then, somewhere in Jules's stomach an invisible finger plucks one of the strings of a bass-viol, whereupon Jules roars like a bull. The instrumentalist who is practising on his larynx picks up a mandolin, then, and plinks a high note for a little while, before experimenting with a fret-saw on a dancing master's fiddle—after which some apprentice breaks in, experimentally, with a piccolo, while an uncontrollable amateur pecks at the parchment of a kettle-drum. Then it is all given to the 'cello and the flute.

"Tum-tum?" Jules roars and squeaks.

"*Ssshhh!*"

The over-wound spring breaks—not that there is more than enough of it to fill a boot-polish tin. Something touches it now, and it goes shrieking out of a tight blue disc into an inextricably tangled heap of shivering steel ribbon.

Charles Small feels that his bowels have come up to strangle him. Then he remembers the gramophone . . . and up pops Daddy, that gassy, vacillating little popper. Pop! Pop!

Oh, that windbag, that squeaked when it emptied itself; that ball of breath! He was full of sententious talk about a penny saved being a penny earned. As bums loaf around the stoves in doss-houses solving problems of state, so this man squatted on a heap of unpaid bills and talked big business. There was money in this, money in that, money in the other—old man Small had it at his finger-tips. One day, after he had been roaring and writhing and groaning about the unpaid rates and taxes, a pasty little man came into the shop carrying a great black box by a heavy leather handle, and said: "Want a bargain?"

Up jumped I. Small the big shot, keen as mustard; watchful, cautious, cunning, ready to out-Machiavelli Machiavelli. The pasty man, lifting the box with difficulty—it must have weighed between thirty and forty pounds—put it on the counter, knocked down several clip-locks, and opened one of the first portable phonographs that was ever made.

The lid of this fantastic box contained something like a nickel-plated wash-basin into which was clipped a tone-arm as big and heavy as a footballer's leg, at the end of which hung a mica sound-box of a peculiarly club-footed shape. The basic half of this contraption was heavy with machinery. There was a turntable to which was glued a disc hacked out of one of those green plush tablecloths that used to be fringed with pom-poms.

Old man Small, his hands locked behind him, watched Napoleonically, rocking to and fro on his heels. The pasty man unclipped a crank-handle that terminated in a sort of trephine, which he cunningly inserted into a hole in the case, and turned. There was a stink of oil. The cogs of the machine alternately begged for mercy and gnashed their teeth. The pasty man put on to the turntable a phonograph record a quarter of an inch thick. He pulled a big lever, and the disc began to spin. Then he dislodged the arm with a blow of his fist, put the needle on the record (which was rocking like a see-saw) and out came the *Zampa* Overture.

Shouting to make himself heard above the din he said that this was a most remarkable invention. Take your ordinary gramophone—it was a heavy affair, unwieldy. It had a great tin horn on it, so that you could not take it anywhere. But this remarkable device—this was portable. The metal bowl constituted a horn. Everything clipped into place, so that all you had to do was close it . . . like that . . . snap home the clasps —so—pick it up by the handle (he almost dislocated his shoulder trying to do it) and walk off with it. Could Mr. Small not see what an acquisition this was? No? Ah, but say one called on friends. Well, one said hullo, and how are you, and how is so-and-so, and how's business . . . and then there was nothing else to talk about. There one was, twiddling one's thumbs with a whole evening to get through. But if one happened to be lucky enough to possess such a machine as this, one opened it, and said: "Let's have a little music!" Amid cries of astonishment, one became a social success. It was a genuine American machine, and had cost twelve pounds when it was new. But he, the pasty man, was prepared to part with it for four guineas.

Charles Small knows that his father was not interested in music, and was terrified of machinery of every description: he could not wind a watch without holding his breath, and had sternly forbidden his son to play with his most beloved birthday-present, an ingeniously-contrived German clockwork frog that jumped with a clatter while a key in its belly turned anti-clock-wise to a standstill—I. Small had locked it up in a cupboard, asserting that it was dangerous.

But if a salesman showed him something, he did not know how not to buy it. He had no arguments. Shamefully conscious of his ignorance, he nodded and muttered, stroking his chin, cleared his throat, and said that he understood. In any case he was hopelessly vulnerable to a direct attack.

When the pasty man said "four guineas", he said: "I wouldn't give you more than thirty shillings for a thing like that"—hoping, of course, that the pasty man would shake his head, pick up his machine, and walk out of the shop.

But he replied: "All right then, I'll let you have it for thirty shillings." He would gratefully have accepted ten. He threw in twenty-four assorted records, somewhat the worse for wear, but when he was gone Charles Small's father looked at the machine with hate. The infant Charles, hopping with excitement, said: "Daddy, can we play it?"

Now the old man was strong and authoritative. He shouted: "You? What are you doing here, what? Didn't I told you you should keep out from the shop?"

He loomed large, dark, and dangerous. Charles lied: "I just came in . . . Daddy, can I play it?"

"Play it? *Play* it? Play what? Play it! What do you mean, play it? That's all I've got to *do*, play? Get out from the *shop!*"

His father put the portable phonograph behind the counter. His mother did not see it until she stumbled over it two days later.

"What's this?" she asked.

"What's what? What do you mean, what's this? . . . Oh that, that! A novelty—a gremophone."

"Gramophones! *Gramophones!* That's all he's short of—

gramophones! Gramophones, now! A new madness—gramophones!"

"A poor devil came in, so he's got this gremophone. So his wife, she's being confined. It was a *mitzvah*. What's five shillings?"

"Five shillings he's got to throw away, the millionaire! Gramophones, *gramophones* he wants!" But she let him show her how it worked, and was nearly placated. Little Charles, luckily for him, forgot to correct his father and say: "You made a mistake, Daddy, it wasn't five shillings, it was thirty shillings" —he was so passionately interested in the machine.

He shudders when he thinks of what might have happened if he had impulsively blurted out the truth at that moment. He would have been completely undone. He would have been slapped on several counts: (1) For contradicting his father. (2) For having lied when he said that he had only just come into the shop. (3) For having told the truth when his father chose to lie. (4) For upsetting his mother. She would have been dreadfully upset. "Thirty shillings he's got to throw away on such rubbish! For *this* he's got to go out and borrow! What've I done to deserve it? What've I done, what've I done?"

With a sidelong look of bitter hatred at little Charles the old man would have shouted: "Millie, I swear by my life and yours too, I should fall down dead on the spot where I stand, I didn't give more than five shillings for this here gremaphone!"

Charles Small can see it all. . . .

"By your mother's life?"

The old man's eyes grow wet as he says: "She's dead and gone, God bless her, she should rest in peace! Leave her alone. My mother, God rest her soul, she's got nothing to do with gremaphones."

"Swear by your child's life!"

"By my child's life, I didn't give a farden more than five shillings for this bleddy gremaphone!" I. Small is violently excited, now, and full of strong words: "So sure should I do good, and you too! May I bleddy well beg in the streets like a bleddy bugger——"

"*Beggar!*"

"Beggar, *schmegger!* That child should drop where he stands!"

At this Charles Small's mother snatches her son to her bosom and sprinkles him with tears, while the gramophone runs down with a reluctant squeak, and the old man, shouting down the crescendo of the *Zampa* Overture, howls: "May I be paralysed and you too! May I die! When I say five shillings, it's five *shillings!* Five bleddy shillings! Or may I be buried alive!"

There is a pause for breath. The old man—he will never learn—becomes calm, so that he sighs with relief. His puny rage is exhausted, now that he believes that he has sworn his lie out of existence. Then, with a slow ominous nod, she says: "So, that's what you are, eh? As long as I know. All right, as long as I know. Thirty shillings he rushes out and spends on rubbishing gramophones. I'm ashamed to look the family in the face. I should go and borrow money from Father, so this one can go and buy gramophones for thirty shillings like a millionaire. All right—now I know what you are. As long as I know. It's all right."

The old man shouts again: "By your life and mine and the bleddy child's! Five shillings! Didn't I told you?"

"Didn't I *tell* you. You're in England now—talk English. . . . Thirty shillings! Well, go on—play. Play gramophones. Put it on a pram, and go into the streets, and play—hold out a hat for pennies—that's all you're fit for! Go on, what are you waiting for? Musician! Myeh!"

Then, day after day and night after night little Charles hears nothing but gramophone, gramophone, gramophone. If his deservedly unhappy father, depressed and discouraged, sits down without appetite, fiddling with his knife and fork and staring blankly at his plate, it is: "What's the matter now? What do you want to do with it? Put it on the gramophone?" When luck sends him a few pounds and he rushes feverishly to the bank, one jump ahead of an uttered cheque, he is admonished: "Don't come back with a grand piano, you and your gramophones." If he suggests that it might be useful to have a telephone installed, there is an outcry: "If it's not gramophones, it's telephones. Musician!"

CHAPTER II

THIS is what would inevitably have happened if Charles Small
had blurted out the truth on that occasion. But he had already
learned not only to lie, but to deal in lies. Hating himself for a
sickening little sycophant he remembers that when his father
said "five shillings" his mother looked at him quickly for confirmation, and he repeated: "Only five shillings." She liked
music: it was genteel. They played that horrible phonograph
every day. He squirms when he thinks of it. The records were
worn out, the clockwork was old and tired, and although one was
specifically instructed to use a needle once only the old man,
thunderously didactic and portentously informative, bellowed:
"Once! *Once!* Fools believe it—so that's how they sell needles,
and make fortunes! Take no notice!" This old fool who couldn't
find his bottom if he wanted to wipe it, this gull of the world,
this mark, this fore-damned victim of the clumsiest rogues in
town, was prudent when it came to pins and profoundly wise in
the matter of gramophone needles at a shilling a hundred. The
shop shut and the supper table cleared, he became great; he
called for music. Charles Small remembers, all too clearly, how the
rickety turntable rocked and swayed, and how sometimes, in the
middle of some scratching, indeterminate ecstasy, something in
the guts of the black box went *prrut!*—and the glory slid in a slow
glissando until working hard on the handle and driving home the
blunted serrations of the trephine he made the disc spin fast
enough to wind the music back.

One evening his parents went out to talk to someone about
some business premises that were to let, leaving Charles alone
in the house with the servant, Mollie. Creeping down from the
attic, or tiptoeing up from the basement (he forgets which), she
said: "What about a bit of music?" Charles dragged out the
phonograph, although he was under oath not to touch it, and
put on a husky record of a bass-baritone singing *In Cellar Cool.*
He will never forget that dreadful evening. In the middle of the
line:

Drinking, drinking, drinking . . .

17

there was a quick, thick snap, and the needle snarled and sneered in the worn grooves of the record which spun slower and slower until it stopped. He turned the handle in a frenzy of terror, but it swung loose. His most furious efforts elicited nothing but a tired squeak from the inside of the black box beyond the chafed hole where the crank-shaft went in. The worn mainspring had snapped. "Now you've been and done it," said Mollie.

Pale with fright but stiff with resolution, Charles got a screwdriver and took out the top of the phonograph: he believed that he could put the machine right by tightening a screw, loosening a screw, or banging something. The only tools in the house (the old man could not knock a nail into a bit of wood without smashing his fingers) were a screwdriver, a hammer, a pair of pincers, and a mushroom-shaped cold chisel which some workman had left behind. With these tools young Charles prepared to go to work.

The interior of the old phonograph bewildered and scared him. It did not take him long to learn what happened when one wound it up: a great flat cylinder set upon a cogged wheel four inches in diameter turned, controlled by a stubborn bit of blue steel that clicked doggedly into its teeth. These teeth met and locked with the teeth of another cogged wheel. The whole machine was made up of toothy steel wheels, sticky and stinking with oil and black with graphite. Somewhere to one side of it there was a "centrifugal governor"—a vertical bar crowned with three lead balls on little hinged rods, that whirled in a blue-grey blur if you touched something. The trouble, Charles divined, was in the cylindrical box; so he unscrewed the screw, prised with the screwdriver, levered the lid off, and discovered a coiled oily spring. The innermost part of this spring had been attached by a screw through a cut slot to a steel bar. The slotted portion of the spring was still screwed down, but a quarter of an inch beyond the slot there was a hideous gap. In his innocence Charles Small said to himself: *All I have to do is, take out that bit of spring, make another hole in the broken end, screw it all down again, and there we are.* How he pities himself when he thinks of it! Confident that he could cut through the blue steel with the sixpenny hammer and the eightpenny screwdriver, he went to work on the coiled spring. It stuck. There was no use trying to loosen it from the periphery, so he went to work from the centre, where he could get leverage. The clock struck nine. It was necessary

18

to get everything done in half an hour. He threw his weight on the handle of the screwdriver, and then, with a triumphant scream that he will hear to the last day he lives, the spring sprang free. It shot up into the air, spattering the ceiling with black oil and came down shivering, as it seemed, in delight at its liberation.

"Mollie, Mollie, Mollie!" he cried. Then he and Mollie tried to re-coil the spring and put it back, but it was as slippery and strong as an Indian wrestler in a pit of mud. Mollie with her strong, stupid red hands and Charles with his soft and sensitive white fingers struggled like the very devil, sweating and straining, forcing the spring inch by inch into its box, working from the circumference to the centre. God knows how long they worked. Charles Small knows that after twelve or fifteen attempts they got the spring half-way back, when familiar footsteps sounded in the street. There was no mistaking his mother's brisk, busy trot—she always sounded as if she had six legs, and was hurrying to call a doctor in a matter of life and death. (Thinking of her, Charles Small thinks of an ant wearing boots.) His father, though, walked portentously, like a policeman pounding a beat. Hearing him coming round a corner you stood aside, expecting to see some big-booted brute as heavy as Hackenschmidt. You were astonished when you saw a man of average size and nondescript shape, wearing respectable shoes, size eight. Their voices were audible, too. A foreigner, trying to understand what they were saying by the way they were saying it, would have clutched at his heart and turned pale. She might have been saying: *Police! Fire engines! A doctor! An escaped madman has broken in, set fire to the house, and slashed us with a butcher's knife! My baby's head is hanging by a thread and I am burning and bleeding to death! Help!* And the old man might have been saying, in his voice of thunder: *Call out the Guards—every man to his post! One hundred and twenty rounds of ammunition for every man. Fix bayonets! Stand back to back, in the name of God and the King, my lads, and fight it out to the bitter end.*

But his mother was saying: ". . . Yes, it's in a good position, but look at the neighbourhood!"

"What's the matter with the neighbourhood? Piccadilly, you want?"

"I'm not used to such neighbourhoods."

"The neighbourhood's good enough for Woolworth's, the

neighbourhood's good enough for Thomas Lipton's, the neighbourhood's good enough for Lyons's—so for you the neighbourhood's not good enough!"

"—And the kitchen—a hole! Pitch-dark——!"

The key had rattled angrily and the door was closed. They were coming upstairs, and now their voices were turned on full. . . .

". . . Kitchens she wants! All right. So I'll take the, the Savoy Hotel with the Ritz, so she should have chicken!"

"—*Kitchens!*"

"Kitchens, *schmitchens!*"

"I'd be ashamed to ask anybody to a place like that!"

"You want I should get a place to *ask* people to? I'll take Park Lane. Buckingham Palace I'll take. The Tower from London I'll take, so you can *ask* people. The British Museum I'll take——"

—Charles and Mollie threw all their strength into one last effort; whereupon the spring leapt up again with a thin shivering shriek, and Mr. and Mrs. Small opened the door of the sitting-room and saw them standing, grey with sweat, white with fear, and black with dirty oil, over the wreckage of the gutted phonograph on the table.

For two or three seconds his father was silent, paralysed with wrath; but his mother was triumphantly calm. She nodded gravely, compressing her lips. It was quite all right. She had known it all along. Everything was exactly as it should be. She said: "You see? What did I tell you? Go on, run round the corner and buy a few more gramophones. Go on, what are you waiting for—run out, buy!"

The old man found his voice. It came out in an ululation: "Bleddy murderer! Snotty-nose! Stinker! Robber! Bleddy pig!"—and struck Charles with a rolled-up evening newspaper.

"Not on the head!" screamed Mrs. Small, "for God's sake, not on the head!"

The newspaper—it was the *Star*—came down again. The old man's teeth were bared, his cheeks were crimson, and his eyes were full of blood, sweat and tears. Yet, striking out with all his strength, while he shouted: "Beggar his bleddy head!" he could not hit hard enough to bend the evening paper.

Charles Small, frightened by the gramophone rather than by the impotent rage of his father, and not a bit hurt, burst into tears; whereupon his mother, squealing like a bleeding sow, snatched him up, tore the newspaper out of her husband's hand, and cried: "Madman! Stop it, or I'll jump out of the window and call for the police!"

Then Mollie said: "Oh, it's all right—I done it. Didn't I, Charley?"

Charles Small hammers at his skull with his knuckles as he remembers that he did not say *no*, but shrugged his shoulders, and snivelled, wiping his nose with his right forefinger. Why the devil couldn't he simply have said: "No you didn't do it. I did it!" and take the consequences—a breathy admonition, a windy threat, and a slap that would not have knocked the skin off a rice pudding?

But he was silent, God forgive him, and no cock crowed, while Mollie said: "I'll pay for it, don't worry. I'll get it mended."

Mollie was as good as her word. There was a sturdy young mechanic who worked for the plumber in the next street—a fine young fellow named Lygo who could turn his hand to anything. He did the job for five-and-sixpence, the bare cost of a new mainspring, and put the entire machine into perfect order. When she brought it back to the house, old man Small shouted: "Take it away! I want you should never show me it again!"

"What d'you want me to do with it?" she asked, roughly. (In spite of his menacing expression and his tinpot thunderings, the old man never managed to get a respectful word out of anybody—even the skivvyish Mollie, illegitimate offspring of a gas-fitter's mate and a kitchen maid, conceived in the shadows of a broom cupboard and born in Marylebone Workhouse—even she couldn't take him seriously.)

"Keep it!" he cried. "Let me not see it again!"

"Coo, ta very much, Mr. Small!" she said, and took him at his word for once. On her next day off she carried it back to young Lygo, who, as luck would have it, knew an old lady who was looking for a phonograph of that sort, and whom he coaxed into buying it for three pounds, not a penny of which he kept for himself, although he was entitled to a little commission. Mollie went shopping and came home in a black straw hat wreathed in blue and yellow roses, a violet plush dress cut rather low at the neck, and high-heeled black-and-white boots; all picked up for next to nothing in a Ladies' Wardrobe shop—a sinister establishment near Praed Street, where Paddington tarts, down on their

21

luck, used to sell their spare finery. To make matters worse, she had got a soiled white umbrella with an ivorine handle and an astonishing necklace of huge orange-coloured beads which hung on her like a marigold garland on a sacred cow, and she had crammed her massive fists into white gloves striped with black over the knuckles. From her stiffly-bent left arm dangled one of those silly little things called a "Dorothy Bag". There is no fun in being well dressed unless you can show yourself to people who appreciate nice things. Mollie showed herself to young Lygo, who at once invited her to go with him, at her earliest convenience, to a music hall. Then she let herself be seen by Mrs. Small.

. . . Now, Charles Small starts telling himself that fundamentally his mother was of a sweet nature . . . twisted, like barley-sugar, but positively sweet. But on reflection he curses himself for a fool, for a lying fool, a foolish crook with a bit of grit in his conscience, trying to high-pressure himself into believing his own lies. . . . Sweet! Is this a recommendation? Of course she was sweet—sweet like sugar cane. Strip her, peel her, crush her, smash her between irresistible iron rollers, and from out of the splintered husk oozed sweetness, if you like—dirty, muddy, pulpy, sticky sweetness that spoiled your appetite for solid things—sweetness that rotted your teeth so that you writhed in torment until they were pulled out; when you fell back, a suckling babe again, limp and defenceless—to hell with such sweetness! Such sugar is symptomatic of disease, a pathognomonic sign pointing to coma and death. True sweetness, healthy sugar, is transmuted into energy and strength. This happens only when it does not stay sweet.

Charles Small punches the pillow.

If he lives a thousand years—and he feels that he has already lived five or six hundred—he will not forget what happened that day. His mother sweetly said: "Very smart, Mollie, very nice! What a pretty hat, and what lovely boots!" She said this in a half-bantering way; leaving a loophole through which she might wriggle if quoted, or overheard; only joking, of course, but giving the girl a few kind words, just to cheer her up. What had Mollie to look forward to, after all, the poor girl? Who was she, what was she? A nothing, a nobody, from nowhere. "What lovely boots! And those beads—where did you get them? Mm! Gloves too, eh? Somebody must have left you a fortune."

Then Mollie said, all in one eager breath: "You know that

broken gramophone Mr. Small give me? That young man Lygo what works for Mr. Looby, 'e ment it for me, an' when Mr. Small give it me I took it to 'im, an' 'e took it to a party—she lives up Maida Vale—an' she sez a pound, an' 'e sez four, and she sez thirty shilling——"

"—Hm!"

"—She sez thirty shilling, mum, an' 'e sez four-pun ten, and she sez two quid, an' 'e sez four-pun, an' she sez two-pun ten is my last offer, an' 'e sez three-pun ten's my last word if I was to drop dead this minute, and she sez three quid—take it or leave it. So 'e sez done, and that's 'ow I got the money."

"Gramophones, eh?" said Mrs. Small; and suddenly an arctic cold filled the house, although it was sweltering in the July heat. "Gramophones. Very nice. Very nice!"

His mother appeared to be curiously contented. She had the air of a theoretician who, let out of a lunatic asylum after twenty years of unjust incarceration, pinches the corners of his mouth and eyes into a knowing smile for the demoralisation of his apologetic persecutors.

At supper time she said naïvely to her husband: "Oh, by the way, what happened to the gramophone?"

The old man changed colour. His eyes flickered. He dropped his fork with a clatter, picked it up with a growl, blew his nose like a foghorn, made a knot of his eyebrows, and thundered: "Gremaphones, schmemaphones! Dancing, singing, they want already! Gremaphones!"

"Where is it then?"

"Where *is* it? A rubbish—*where* is it! Ask this bleddy little murderer!"—he threatened Charles Small with the crust of a slice of soft bread. "——You want gremaphones? Ask your, your, your, your little murderer! Gremaphones!"

Charles Small knew that something dreadful was going to happen because his mother was speaking calmly, saying: "You threw it away?"

"What did you want I should do with it?"

"Well, it's a pity. It could be somebody could have made use of it."

"Use of it, schmoose of it!"

"To give thirty shillings, and then throw it away. All right. You're the master. You know best."

Straining his lungs until the veins in his temples became blue,

23

his father shouted: "Five shillings! Once and a thousand times for all, five! *Five!* FIVE!"

"Listen. Srul! Why did you do it? What made you do it? What for?"

"What, what for? What do you mean, why did I do it what for?"

"Did I ever do anything to you?"

"What does she mean, what? Do, do, do, schmoo, bloo! What do you mean, what?"

"Srul, tell me the honest truth. Did—you—give—that—gramophone—to—that—girl?"

"Girl?"

"Yes, Srul. Girl."

"Leave me alone with your gremaphones!" the old man shouted, pounding the table with his fists. "Niggle, niggle, niggle—nag, nag, nag! Gremaphones!"

The louder the old man bellowed, the more plainly he was defeated. The more emphatically he swore, the more obviously he was lying. Now he let out a yell that made the glasses dance on the sideboard, while the windows rattled and the house shivered, as he called upon God to strike him dead if what his wife said had the least grain of truth in it. He tore his hair, cried, brandished a fork, picked up a glass of water and put it down again; gripped the edge of the tablecloth as if to drag all the dishes down clattering to rack and ruin about his knees, at which his wife cried *No!*—so he tore a slice of bread to pieces instead. He brandished his fists over the head of his son, called him a "neglectful pig"—God knows where he had picked up that expression—and struck him with an envelope he had not dared to open because he knew that it enclosed a bill for water rates.

"Can you look me straight in the face and tell me that you didn't give that girl that gramophone?" she asked, when he paused for breath.

"What do they take me for, what? A millionaire, I should give gremaphones? This piece of bread should choke me if I gave gremaphones!" His trembling hand found a bit of crust which he dramatically thrust into his mouth and tried to swallow but fear had dried his mouth, and the crust was dry too. So it choked him. Then the uproar was really terrible. He tore at his collar, knocked over his chair, and seemed to dance, while his

24

wife threw her head back and screamed, until Mollie came running in from the kitchen with a glass of water. The old man drank, and the crust was washed down.

"A nerrow escape!" he gasped.

"You see? It serves you right—you shouldn't swear false."

"False? May I——" he caught Mollie's eye, winked, made a face, shook his head and said: "Mollie, I didn't gave you no gremaphone, did I?"

Mollie said: "Of course you did!"

"Deliberate bleddy liar!"—*deliberate* was another word he had recently picked up and found a use for in every conversation —"deliberate bleddy liar! I told you to chuck it out—to chuck it out I deliberately told you!"

"Chuck! Chuck!" said Mrs. Small, scandalised. "Who says chuck? *Throw* it out!"

"Throw, schmow!"

"You give it to me," Mollie persisted. "After I got it ment you give it me, and Mr. Lygo sold it for me for three pound."

"She makes me out a liar? A liar she makes me out? Kick her out from the bleddy house!"

"Oh, oright, I give a week's notice. I may be in service but I'm not going to be made out to be a liar. I might as well be in Bedlam," said Mollie, and stamped out of the room slamming the door.

All that had been said that evening amounted to nothing more than a hurried, whispered outline of what was now to come. It was a mere tuning and warming-up of instruments. First, Charles Small's mother turned to her son and said: "You see? A liar is always found out!" Then, rapping the table with a tea-spoon, as a conductor raps the music-stand with a baton, she started the overture to a mad opera.

Charles Small, in other, comparatively good-humoured periods of reminiscence, tells himself that if he could have been a musician, he might have got the inspiration for a terrible comedy out of that scene. He would have needed the London Symphony Orchestra, some bagpipes, the Mills Brothers, the Duncan Sisters, a dinner-gong, several bombardons, a fishwife, a sergeant-major, and a Cuban band complete with maracas and ass's jawbones rattling with loose teeth. Technically, it would have been difficult to put over as it deserved. It would have been necessary to discover a pair of versatile geniuses who could sing down all

25

other noises for three hours and forty minutes in duet, dancing at the same time. It would take Chaliapin, the Marx Brothers, and Henry Irving to play the part of Mr. Small. The Prima Donna, Mrs. Small, would have to be compounded of Sarah Bernhardt, Koringa (the lady sword-swallower), Dorothy Parker, Little Orphan Annie, Tillie The Toiler, Catherine de Medici, and Gertrude Stein.

As for the libretto, he could write that himself:

—You did, you did!

—I did not!

—Swear! Swear by your life!

—I have swore! I swear by my life! See?

—Hah!

—*You* say Hah? *I* say Hah! *Hah!* What's a joke?

—Hum!

—Speak or don't speak! Don't *hum!* Bleddywell——

—Srul, Srul, not in front of the child!

—What *not* in front from the bleddy child?

—Don't say "bleddy", for God's sake, Srul!

—Don't say "God", then. Then I won't say "bleddy".

—He'll grow up with "bleddy" in his mouth.

—Better the bleddy murderer should grow up with "bleddy" in his bleddy mouth, than "God". God, schmod! Let him bleddy-well bleddy, the dirty rotten stinkpot!

Mr. Small strikes his son on the head with envelope containing final demand for water rates.

—For God's sake, Srul, not on the head!

—Beggar his bel-el-el-eddy head so he should know in future! Bleddywell beggar the bleddy beggar, so in future he should beggarwell bleddy know!

—He's gone mad, mad!

—Mad, schmad! . . .

—Srul, in England, speak English!

—Hm! Nice bleddy English *your* bleddy father bleddywell spoked! Ha!

—Spoked. Spoked! *Spoked!* I'm so ashamed I could kill myself.

—She's here with her killing! Murderer!

—Foreigner!

—Englisher!

—Oh, I'm so ashamed, so ashamed, so ashamed!

—Ashamed from what? From what ashamed? So from where did *your* father came from, where?

—*Come* from! Not *came* from. In England, talk English.

—From Samovarna, your father come from. Deny it!

—And you, gramophones? Where did *you* come from? Cracow! A Galicianer! A Galicianer!

—Is already a *place*, Cracow! Samovarna—*phut!*

—Go to your Mollies. Go to your prostitutes. Finish!

—I swear, I swear! I tell you I swear.

—Liar.

—I swore, Millie. Millie!

—Sha! You're not with Mollie now.

—Who said Mollie? Who said?

—You did, you did—deny it!

—I did not! May I rot! May I die!

—You swear?

—I should drop——

—Ssh!

—She wants me to swear, so she shushes me! What for, why? I swear by my life I said Millie.

—Mollie, you meant.

—No!

—You did, you did!

Then it started all over again. Having thundered in the voice of Chaliapin in *Ivan the Terrible*, the old man, black in the face, opened big white hands and called upon his mammy in the voice of Al Jolson; while she, on Mimi's deathbed, came up with a double-take, and went into a Desdemoniac frenzy, before she passed away in convulsions like Cleopatra. It went on into the small hours, breaking young Charles's sleep. When he came down to breakfast at eight o'clock next morning his mother was red-eyed but triumphant. His father had gone downstairs sullenly to open the shop. He could not eat any breakfast; food would choke him; the sight of it would make him sick; he couldn't touch a thing. Little Charles was worried, but he ate everything that was put before him. His mother refused to speak to Mollie, even to give her an order, so she sighed while she carried down a tray loaded with eggs, smoked haddock, hot rolls, and tea in her own martyred hands. The voice of the old man came up: "Take it away! Away! Didn't I told you, I'm choked?"

Yet between two sighs the plates were emptied.

Charles went to school while his father, walking up and down the shop, waited for business.

It is all very well, all very well, and all very funny, says Charles now, kicking his left foot with his right, *all very fine and large. But damn my eyes, why didn't I admit that it was I who broke the spring? For God's sake, what was I afraid of?*

He is far from well. The bed rolls and the bedroom spins. The neat coils, nicely packed in his abdomen, are sliding loose. He winds them tighter with a tremendous effort. Still they slide. He throws his weight upon that which should control them, but there is a dull snap . . . and then he is hopelessly entangled in something blue, slippery, and interminable—struggling with his own guts.

CHAPTER III

His father called himself a "gentlemen's hoser". He never missed an opportunity of giving you one of his cards upon which, heavily printed in Old English type, was the inscription:

M. & I. SMALL & SON
Stylish Gents' Hosiery
9, Milk Street
Grosvenor Street
(Nr. Buckingham Palace)
S.W.1.

Thinking of this card Charles Small becomes alternately red with shame and white with anger, until his face feels like an electric sign. It was his mother's idea, of course: who else could have thought of such a thing? Oh, that woman, that woman— if only he could get his hands on her throat, he would shake her as a terrier shakes a rat! He knew it all now: crumb by crumb, shard by shard, splinter by splinter he has picked up the bits and glued them together into something so nearly whole that he thinks he knows the shape, size, and pattern of it. And having stuck this rubbish together, what has he got? A lead-glazed, big-bellied, narrow-necked, crockery pot, neither useful nor decorative that had better not have been made. He wants to send it back to the dust with one savage kick.

His father's name was Yisroel Schmulowitz. He left Cracow in Galicia in the 1880s, before he was twenty years old, because he was about to be called up to serve his time in the Army. His mother, wailing and moaning, tearing to pieces her *shaitel*, had begged him to leave her and go, because in the Army he would associate with rough men and eat the flesh of dead swine. (A *shaitel* is a hideous wig, parted in the middle, which orthodox Jewesses, having shaved their heads, were supposed to wear after they were married in case they became appetising to strange men. Charles Small's grandmother, at her best, could not have looked much more attractive than a plucked chicken. He had never seen her, but on the strength of a flattering photograph you wanted to tie her up with a piece of thin twine and throw her into a pot of boiling water, the old fowl.) So Yisroel Schmulowitz ran for his life, and reached England with a few *groschen* in his pocket. He was not without a trade: he had been apprenticed to a bootmaker in some Cracovian suburb. A man named Noman, a philanthropist, picked him up and found him a job with a cobbler, for whom he sweated for several years, earning an honest living. He spent most of his money on clothes—cutaway coats, fancy waistcoats, tight patent-leather boots, spats, hats. Every Sunday he dressed himself up and walked in the park with his friend Schwartz. Twirling their moustaches and swinging their walking-sticks they strolled through Mayfair and Regent Street, where they made eyes at all the girls. Later, perhaps, they went to a music hall. Crime does not pay—murder will out. Charles's mother had dragged out of her husband the scandalous story of the offering of a cup of cocoa to a loose gentlewoman, a "sport". This beautiful anonymous one said that she thought him "quaint and charming", and drank the cocoa with gusto. (The subsequent battle raged for three days, after which no cocoa was ever brought into the house. Once, when the old man employed an assistant named Cadbury, Mrs. Small screamed: "So you can't get her out of your mind, is that what you are?" —so that Cadbury had to go.)

The time came when a marriage broker told Yisroel Schmulowitz that he was good-looking, well-dressed, self-supporting, and marriageable, and that a beautiful young woman of good family was willing to look at him.

"What's she like?"

"An Englisher gel—lovely!"

"Dark? Fair?"

"Medium."

"Tall? Short?"

"Middling. What do you want? Jersey Lilies? Lily Lengtry? If I say a beautiful gel, it's a beautiful gel. Look, see, and if you don't like her, I'll hang myself!"

So he introduced young Schmulowitz to Millie, the least marriageable of six daughters. She was a screaming coquette. Four of her sisters were married, and she hated them with a bitter, deadly hate. Her unmarried sister had a queer leg, and she limped, so that Millie loved her. When Yisroel Schmulowitz came into the house, healthy and handsome and eminently presentable, Millie's heart melted. She had five hundred pounds of dowry, and the young man had fallen in love with her. She made conditions. First and foremost, she could not marry a man who would impose upon her the name of Schmulowitz.

"So what's the matter mit mein name?"

"*With!* With your name! Not *mit*. Not *mein*. *With my* name!"

"Mein father's name was Schmulowitz. Should I be ashamed from it?"

"Ashamed from it! *Of* it! *Of!*"

"Of. Let it be of. If my father's name——"

"——You are not your father."

"Schmul was a great man. In the bible read—read in the bible! Hannah was married to Elkanah, so she lies down and gives a son——"

"——So that's what you are! Hm! A nice way to talk!"

"So what's what I am? What did I said wrong?"

"What did I said wrong! What did I *say* wrong?"

"Say. Hannah brought Schmul to Eli, so it was he got to be a prophet."

"You are not a prophet now. You are not in Palestine now. Millie Schmulowitz! I'd be so ashamed! Millie Schmulowitz—never!"

"What do you want I should call myself, what?"

She thought of Smiles, Wits, de Witt, and Mule; but finally decided on Small.

"But what are you ashamed of, what?"

"Who's ashamed?"

"What's *your* name? Moses."

"Moss!"

"What's the matter with Moses? Moses was good enough to lead you out of the land of Egypt, out of the house of bondage, wasn't he?"

"You're not in Egypt now. Schmulowitz! I should call myself Schmulowitz! Small!"

"Let it be Small," he said, heavily.

"It sounds like the same thing, really. And Yisroel. It's not . . . it's not . . ."

"——It's not what? What, it's not?"

"Listen, you're in England now."

"So I'm in England—so what's the matter, what?"

"Yisroel! It makes people laugh. Yis*roel!* Rollo! Make it Rollo—that's a nice name. Rollo Small."

"My name isn't good enough, so I'm not good enough. Good day! Go find a Rollo, a Schmollo! Good-bye!"

She did not care whether he came or went, lived or died, but she had told all her friends that he was desperately in love with her. He, for his part, was sick and tired of the whole affair, and she could see it. One syllable, now—one brusque *Go* might have sent Yisroel Schmulowitz stamping away. Sensing this, she cried, and said, through her tears: "It's not what you're called, it's what you are that counts!"

She had got this out of some novelette, no doubt. It was a little too deep for Schmulowitz, who in any case was powerless in the presence of a weeping woman. He cried himself when he saw a woman shedding tears, thinking of his mother, so this fool, missing a heaven-sent opportunity of giving himself a better wife, and Charles Small a different mother, pulled out a silk handkerchief, saying: "Rollo, Schmollo, Wollo, Bollo, call me what you like!"

"A rose by any other name would smell," she sobbed.

So they were engaged. He had to give her a ring, of course, but he had very little money to spend. Millie's youngest sister Lily was married to a prosperous photographer who had given her an engagement ring that cost £85—the whole family had seen the receipt; after which young Lily had acquired a maddening habit of touching her hair, adjusting her blouse, and emphasising her lightest word with a queenly gesture of the left hand, so that wherever Millie looked she saw the diamond flash.

"Stop showing off with your rubbishing bit of glass!" she screamed, at last.

"Bit of glass, eh? Ha-ha! You wouldn't say no to such a bit of glass. What's the matter, are you jealous, or what?"

"Ha-ha! *I* should be jealous of a rubbishing bit of a thing like that?"

"Oh yes. We all know. We all know all about that, Millie. We all know all about the rings your young man gives you."

Trust Lily to be a bitch! Every one of those damnable sisters was a bitch: three of them were born bitches, two had achieved bitchery, and one had had bitchery thrust upon her. They had to be so in order to survive. They were perpetually feeling one another for a fresh sore spot—which it was never difficult to find —they were sore to the core, those hysterical fools. They enjoyed being hurt: it gave them something to cry about. If, by some miracle, you managed not to hurt them they would tread on their own corns to make themselves scream. They would stop at nothing, to put you in the wrong. Charles Small once saw his Aunt Sarah scraping her eyes with a match-stick in order to draw tears that might wring the heart of his mother with remorse for having hurt Sarah's feelings by saying that a certain sky-blue woollen jumper "showed off her figure too much". Sarah had a bosom like a pair of overblown pomegranates, and made the most of it—in the end it got her a tobacconist with three branch shops and a motor-car. But when Millie, who was flat-chested, expressed righteous indignation and virtuous disgust at her pride in these peerless globes, these conspicuous founts of motherhood, Sarah, having said a few never-to-be-forgotten things about "it being better to have a proper figure than something like pimples on your chest" rushed into the kitchen and poked herself in the eye with a match to get in the first weep. What a battle there was then!—complete with forced marches, dark strategies, dirty tactics, espionage, attack, counter-attack, entrenchment, night assaults, sieges and sorties! It lasted three months—in which time Lily and Pearl, having formed a secret alliance, carried a blitzkrieg to Becky because she had said that Ruth was the best cook in the family.

However when Millie remembered Lily's ring she wanted one like it, which the cobbler Schmulowitz could not afford to buy. He had his eye on a bargain priced at £15—a wretched little cluster of chip-diamonds around a flawed sapphire no bigger than a split pea. Millie had hysterics. . . . So she should be the laughing-stock of her friends! So she should be ashamed to look anybody in the face for the rest of her life! Oh, oh, oh what had she done to deserve it?

Schmulowitz said that later on, please God, he would give her pearls, and diamonds, and rubies, and anything she fancied. In the meantime, why spend money on rings when there was a living to make?

"Rubies! How comes, rubies! Who wears rubies? You're in England now! And sapphires—oh, how they'll laugh!"

Yisroel Schmulowitz, who was already beginning to hate the

33

sight of her, and who still had a little spirit left in him, said "Give me back the ring and finish!"

Then she wept heartbrokenly until she had a clever idea. She went to her father and said: "You're giving me five hundred pounds. Now look—a diamond is as good as money. Buy me a ring, now, for a hundred pounds."

Mr. Moss, her father, said: "Was fur meshuggass is dis? Fur a hündred pfund a diamant? Ich, soll a——"

"I won't marry him without," she said.

At this, Mr. Moss, who had been gathering himself for a devastating charge, pulled himself back on his haunches and became thoughtful. Then he said: "Nu, nu vell, a diamant is already wie gelt"—and he took her to Black Lion Yard, where she chose a diamond ring that cost £92, which he gave to Schmulowitz, who later at a little engagement party took it out of a square, velveteen-lined box, and put it on the third finger of Millie's left hand. Healths were drunk. Everyone admired the ring. Lily bit her lips with envy, and Millie was as happy as she could be. Schmulowitz was proud to be associated with such fine people, but he was unaccountably miserable. He admired the brilliants set in the ring, but he would have looked with greater pleasure upon the cracked sapphire that he had bought with his own money. He gave it to Millie, but she did not like to be seen wearing it. Who wore sapphires? Diamonds were the thing.

This was the beginning of the end of Yisroel Schmulowitz. He had sacrificed his father's name, and let himself be called "Small". To his first name, Yisroel, he clung with desperate stubbornness. Millie reddened her eyes a dozen times with weeping, begging him to call himself Rollo. But he held out until, at last, Millie went to Nathan, the Photographer, a clever man, and (she never forgave him for this) asked him to reason with her fiancé. Nathan, the Photographer (she never stopped hating him), went and wrestled with Yisroel Small. He said:

"Now look here. When in Rome, you've got to do as Rome does. Honest, this is England."

"What's the metter, what?"

"Nothing. But what do you want to be pig-headed for? What do you want to call yourself Yisroel for? Think, and you'll see! Yisroel!" the photographer laughed. "You're going to get married. Am I right?"

There was an alarming pause, which Nathan, the Photographer, did not fail to note, before Yisroel Small said: "So?"

"Listen. English people can't pronounce, they can't *say* all these names. When you're in Rome, do as Rome does——"

"—I'm not in Rome."

"That's just it. You're in England. When in England, do as England does."

"What's the metter from mein name, what?"

"It's foreign. You're going into business."

"Is already in the King's pelace a person called Battenburg. I put new heels yesterday on a proper gentleman from the Russian Ambassy—Protopopoff. Protopopoff!"

"Now look here. This is England."

"England, Schmengland—what's the metter with mein name?"

"There's a prejudice against Joosh people. *Yisroel!* Everybody'll laugh."

"Let 'em laugh!"

"Now look. Yisroel is only another word for Israel."

"So?"

"Israel is a name like any other name. Israel, Rollo—what's the difference?"

"All right then, Yisroel, Israel—let it be Israel!"

"No, wait a minute—'Israel' only makes matters worse."

"Enough, already!"

"Of course," said Nathan, the Fhotographer, who saw that his man was obdurate, "for the painting of your fascia you could just put *I. Small.*"

"I., schmy, pie—enough!" So the old man clung to his Yisroel. But people called him "Srul" or "I". Renamed Small, he was called "Big" in the family, because he was a wretched failure and everything he touched fell to dust and ashes.

CHAPTER IV

Now he had nothing but his trade to lose. He had intended to set up shop as a shoe repairer, but Millie drew the line at that. She had seen him at work once or twice, and hated the sight of his nails, black with cobbler's wax, and the smell of leather and old boots. Working, he wore no coat; his shirt-sleeves were rolled up and his arms were bare to the elbow while he impolitely spat out of his mouth shiny iron brads which he banged into the soles of common men's boots. This, in itself, was repulsive. There were women's boots, too, and it seemed that he caressed these instead of handling them with proper severity. He wriggled his fingers, tickling their tongues below the laces, and repaired their soles and heels with the tiniest, tenderest, softest nails. A nice business, this, in which a man humbly mended the dirty boots of working men and the footwear of God knows what female scum of the streets! Besides—to be married to a man in such a trade, and to have to admit the fact! *My hubby is a tobacconist,* Sarah could say. . . . Pearl could boast: *My husband is a dealer in electrical goods.* Lily, that bragger, was already telling the world that she was married to a photographer. . . . *Thank God I'm not married!* Becky would say, please God, laying herself open to a couple of savage stabs. . . . Ruth, the accursed one, had married herself to an estate agent, if you please: *Izzy is in the office,* she might say, on the slightest provocation.

Was Millie to be reduced to apologising to her friends for having married a black-handed, waxy-nailed, sweating, knife-wielding, hammering, slashing cobbler? The whole world knew already that she had paid for her own ring. Someone had dropped a word: the whole town was ringing with the story. Now was there to be more shame and humiliation?

A family conference was called.

I. Small suggested mildly that, after all, people couldn't go around on their bare feet. People had to have boots. Not being Rothschild, the man in the street had to get soled and heeled just like everybody else. There was a living in it; it was a trade. He couldn't make boots and shoes, but he knew how to repair

36

them. He suggested the establishment of a cobbler's shop. It was not likely that there was a fortune to be made out of it, but a man who was not afraid of hard work might make a good solid living.

The family looked up, exchanged glances, and smiled. Teeth were sucked and heads were wagged until Lily kicked Nathan, the Photographer, who made diplomacy, saying, in an ambiguous voice: "There's money in boots and shoes. Look at Randall's. Look at Freeman, Hardy & Willis. Buy from a reliable wholesaler, push your stuff, and sell it. Like that you can make good. Now ask yourself a question——"

"—Listen to him," said Lily.

"—How long does it take to sole and heel a pair of boots?"

"It depends——" began I. Small.

"—Don't interrupt—you're not at home now," said Millie.

Nathan, the Photographer, continued severely: "Excuse me. How long does it take to mend a pair of boots? Half an hour? An hour? An hour and a half——?"

"—Well, it depends——"

"—Please! Call it half an hour. How much do you get for it? Two, three shillings?"

"Now that depends——"

"Manners, manners, Rollo!"

"I don't know what you mean by Rollo."

"—Call it two-and-six. From this deduct the cost of the leather, the cost of the nails, and your rent, because it takes time. You've got to be sensible. You pay, say, a pound a week rent. What does that mean? It means that every minute that passes is worth money. A pound a week you pay, and you keep your shop open maybe ten hours. That makes two shillings an hour working time gone in rent. On top of that comes gas, leather, nails, raw materials, tools. Then there's an assistant. He's got to be paid. Call your overheads four shillings per working hour. Yes?"

Everyone nodded. Nathan, the Photographer, continued:

"You can sole and heel a pair of boots for two-and-sixpence in, it might be, a half an hour. This means to say you make, if you are lucky, one shilling an hour. You make, if you have got the business, ten shillings a day if you work ten hours a day. That makes three pounds ten a week. From this you must deduct all day Sunday and one half day. Five and a half days, at one shilling an hour for ten hours a day makes fifty-five shillings. With this fifty-five shillings you must support a wife and family with heat, light, wear-and-tear, clothing, and something to eat. It can't be done!"

Millie burst into tears, and I. Small struck himself on the chin in bewilderment and said: "What do they all do, then? Die? Me and my friend Schwartz, we got an idea. From America comes a machine——"

"He's here again with his friend Schwartz," said Millie, kicking him in the ankle.

He was silent. Nathan, the Photographer, continued: "If a man has got a trade, he should follow that trade."

I. Small said: "Quite right! My frand Schwartz and me, we thought what . . . in America, so they make a machine. So by this machine you can do hend-sewn work, *ein—zwei—drei*—in two minutes. Here a veel—there a veel——" the young man made enthusiastic gestures, building the American boot-repairing machine in the air. "Everything is done miv veels. Me and mein frand Schwartz, ve tinked vot . . . vot . . . vot . . ." In his excitement he mislaid his English. He wanted to put forward the suggestion of his vigorous and imaginative friend Solly Schwartz, a keen, progressive young fellow whom he loved and admired. Schwartz, who had a club-foot, a hump on his back, a tallowy Punch's face, whose glittering little black eyes moved so fast that they seemed to be watching the floor, the ceiling, the four walls, your face, and the back of your neck—Schwartz, one of the ugliest men in London, was quick and cool as a lizard, and full of ideas.

Like a lizard he was perpetually darting after the invisible; he was always on the watch for something that was not there. He had no money, of course. Solly Schwartz had come out of some Stepney slum. Born out of shape, he was his father's shame, and therefore his mother's joy. His father could not bear to look at him; so his mother lost no chance of kissing and cosseting him. No one ever beat this marred brat that might fall dead at a slap, but he would not have cared if they had laid into him with a copper-stick from dawn to dusk: he felt within him a greatness. At the age of fourteen he was sent to do all that he was fit to do. His father apprenticed him to a tailor. He and Yisroel Schmulo-witz became friends. The hows, the whys and wherefores can wait, One day, telling Srul (short for Yisroel) Schmulowitz about the new American machine that sewed, buffed, rasped, and finished the soling and heeling of a pair of shoes in just a few minutes, Schwartz said: "What's the matter with you? *Schuster-kopf!* go on sit on your arse and hammer and sew and sew and hammer and where are you? Where you began back where you started. There's a machine does it all for you in a couple of seconds and you don't need to lift a finger only get a couple of bloody fools for a couple of pounds a week to press a button here and pull a bit of string there and put their foot on a pedal. Hand-work is a thing of the past you should learn everything is done nowadays by machinery you stitch and stitch and stitch and stitch and stitch until you make holes in your thimble and along comes a sewing machine and *tra-la-la, tra-la-la, tra-la-la* there's a seam. Let's get an American machine where there's a wheel here and a wheel there. With this machine it's *tratata—tratata—tratata* and what it would take you to do in an hour this machine does in a minute. A feller like you. Find yourself a girl with a few hundred and marry her and get a machine and make a fortune. *Schuster-kopf*—fifty pairs of boots and shoes you can have on the shelves to be finished in a few minutes each and cut the price and . . . and what for bang with a hammer when any Tom Dick and Harry can run a machine?"

"Where should I get a machine, where?"

"Marry and get a few hundred pounds and get credit and be a man!"

I. Small, as he had begun to call himself, was thinking of all this when his English ran through his fingers. Millie and all her family spoke fluent Yiddish, but he would have been ashamed to slip back into the jargon. Millie whispered: "Be quiet. Do you want to make a poppy-show of me?" Then Nathan, the Photographer, continued:

"Let's look on this side of it. Say I'm in the boot and shoe repairing business. Right? I bang away and sweat, I sew, I work myself like a fool and knock my guts out for an hour . . . what for? A couple of shillings. Still, all the same if my business *is* boots and shoes, it should *be* boots and shoes. *Now* look on *this* side of it. I take premises. I go to a wholesaler and I take a line of goods, gents' boots and shoes, that I pay eight shillings a pair for. In five minutes I sell a pair of gents' boots and shoes for ten-and-six. In five minutes I've made half a crown, and at the same time I walk up and down in a coat and I'm a somebody,

39

a *mensch*, a man! If I sell a pair of boots for two-and-six profit
every five minutes for ten hours I've made thirty shillings an
hour. Thirty shillings an hour is fifteen pounds a day. Fifteen
pounds a day, five and a half days a week . . . well, to be on the
safe side call it twelve pounds a day five days a week, that makes
sixty pounds a week clear profit. And you're a gentleman. You
come, you go. That's better than banging and banging with your
mouth full of nails—sixty pounds a week clear profit. The thing
to do, in this life, is let other people do the dirty work. Give them
a living wage, yes. But what for bang your guts out? Do I make
myself clear?"

"It's a trade. It is an honest living," Small persisted
stubbornly.

"Certainly it's a trade, an honest living," said Nathan, the
Photographer, suavely. "So is sweeping the streets. So is being
a dustman an honest living. A navvy makes an honest living.
A chimney-sweep makes an honest living. Agreed, Schmulowitz!"

"Small," said Millie.

"—I beg your pardon, Small. But you're young, you're
inexperienced, and if you don't mind my saying so, you don't
realise that you're marrying a well-brought-up girl from a nice
family. You've got to give her the . . . the *surroundings*"—
he was proud of this word, and said it again, rolling it on his
tongue—"the surroundings she's used to. A friend pops in for
a cup of tea. What does she see? She sees you sitting in an apron,
with your sleeves rolled up klupping hobnails into some toe-rag's
boot. Ask yourself, Small, ask yourself a question—how would
you like it?"

At this point Millie's feelings—whatever they were; she was
full of woe-begetting "feelings"—burst into tears and said: "For
my sake! For *my* sake! To please *me!*"

All the English had been washed out of his memory by this
torrent of eloquence and flood of tears: groping and scrabbling
in the wash for a few words, I. Small stammered but said nothing.
He was ashamed to break into Yiddish in the presence of Millie's
sisters.

Nathan the Photographer, who was a man of intuition, sensed
this and said, in fluent Yiddish with a strong Ukrainian accent
that made Becky giggle (whereupon Lily bit her lips and stored
up another grudge): "Srulka, how much do you make?"

I. Small said, excitedly: "Tree pound a veek!"

"For a single man it's a very good wage. A single man can live on twenty-five shillings. I pay my assistant—my assistant, mind you—thirty shillings. But circumstances alter cases. Now look. Listen to me just for a minute, and take advice from a fool."

Nathan, the Photographer, paused, and I. Small nodded, deeply impressed. In this family there were two infallible formulæ by the application of which it was possible to compel anyone, however distantly related, to do something foolish. Formula One, the Feminine Formula, was: *Do it, do it to please me. Just to PLEASE ME do it!* Formula Two, nearly irresistible, consisted in five words spoken in a plaintive voice after a violent quarrel: *Take advice from a fool.* If one said: "I will not do this, that, or the other, against my inclination, to please you or anyone else," the woman had grounds for hysterical recrimination and the exhumation of dead and rotten scandals and martyrdoms for a period of three to six months.

If, in the other case, one asked: "Why should I take advice from a fool?" Or said: "If you insist that you are a fool, who are you to tell me what to do?" up popped the devil.

The lover of peace, in the family, did violence to all his feelings if someone said: "To please *me*, do something that you'd die rather than do," or: "Take advice from a fool—don't do what you've always wanted to do."

Nathan, the Photographer, said: "Take advice from a fool. There's a few hundred pounds. Find a place in a good position and go into business. Do you want to be a *schuster* all your life?"

The company nodded, groaning. A *schuster* is a man who works with shoes; and this, they thought, was a very degraded thing to be.

I. Small shook his head. The estate agent laughed, "Ha-ha," so contemptuously that Millie got his face in focus through a couple of eyefuls of tears, and put into cold storage a little vitriolic something to throw into his eyes one of these days when he might be off his guard.

"It's as good as nailing up boards outside dirty old empty houses!" she cried.

"I'd rather deal in property than stick my nose into every Tom Dick and Harry's great big *ferschtinkener* feet!" said Ruth.

This was not well found: Ruth had big feet. Millie said: "Look who's talking about feet! Who takes size seven?"

"My feet she throws into my face! I know certain people

who'd take size eight, if they didn't go about like Chinamen, all squeezed up! I'd rather have big feet than bite my nails!"

All the Moss girls had big feet, but Sarah's feet were biggest, and her husband the tobacconist bit his nails. He was a passionate nail-biter. He bit his nails as a drunkard drinks, so that he went in for secretive economies. He exercised a sort of self-indulgent self-control, like a terrified alcoholic who keeps an inch or two of gin in the bottle overnight to keep him going until the bars open next day. He bit nine of his finger-nails until they bled, making them last until Sunday morning. But he never touched the nail on the little finger of his left hand: this was his cellar, his secret hoard, his plantation. In six days it grew an eighth of an inch. He hurried through breakfast on Sunday morning and then locked himself into the sitting-room with the *News of the World* and, with a shudder of ecstasy, nibbled off the first sliver.

Pearl shouted: "Sha! Sha!" To I. Small she said graciously: "Sisterly love. It's only sisterly love."

"I don't know, what's the matter with a shoemaker?" said Becky, in her leering, sneering way.

I. Small nodded, smiling at her, and said: "Qvidel right! What's the matter, what?"—at which old Mr. Moss felt his beard and looked at Becky through half closed-eyes. Becky had a nose like a squashed pear and irregular eyes. Her ears were set at odd angles. She would have married anything that wore trousers. But as soon as she had said what she said Millie wept again.

Then the tobacconist shouted: "Whose nails are they? Do I ask *you* for nails? Do I bite *your* nails? If it isn't one thing it's another. Now it's nails! What d'you want me to bite, screws? Mind your own business! I'll bite what I bloomingwell like! Leave me alone!"

Ruth shrieked at her husband: "You let a creature like that talk to me like that? And you call yourself a man?"

The estate agent, half-heartedly, said: "Talk like a gentleman!"

The tobacconist cried: "First teach your wife to talk like a lady."

"So now I'm not a lady," said Ruth, in tears. "If I was a man I'd tear him to pieces."

Then the estate agent rose abruptly, knocking over his chair, and said: "I didn't come here to be insulted. I wish you goodnight." He started to leave the room, but his wife clung to his coat-tails, sobbing:

42

"Stay, stay!"

"Stay to be insulted?"

"To please *me*—for *my* sake!"

"Let us be quiet," said the photographer.

"You see what you've done?" said Millie to her fiancé, "do you see? *Now* do you see what you've done?"

I. Small, taking himself by the ears and shaking himself, shouted: "I didn't done nothing, I didn't said a word! Let it be a boot and shoe shop, a shmoot and boo shop—for the sake of peace, anything!"

So at last it was decided that I. Small was to become a retailer of footwear. There were passionate arguments about suitable premises. The photographer suggested one of the expanding north-western suburbs. Millie took this as a slight. Having listened, nodding in agreement, until the photographer was gone, she foamed at the mouth with resentment. . . .

So! Now she knew. She knew it all now. He was jealous already, that twopenny-halfpenny photographer—he wanted the West End of London all to himself, the glutton! So that was the kind of man he was: thank God she had found out at last! She tore a handkerchief and cried. So that was the idea, was it? To get them out of the way. Just because he talked good English, he was ashamed of his future brother-in-law. So that was it, was it? Who was *he* to be stuck up just because he was a photographer—all he had to do was put a bit of black cloth over his head and say: "Smile please," or "Look at the dicky bird." Him and his dicky birds—he looked down on her Intended because he was a high-class shoemaker, did he? What was the matter with a shoemaker, anyway? A high-class shoemaker was as good as a photographer any day, in fact twenty times better than certain photographers she could mention. In any case, I. Small was not a shoemaker—he was in ladies' and gentlemen's shoes. . . . But everybody wanted to get them out into the suburbs, that was it. . . . Millie carried on in this vein until her father drove his clenched fist into a soup tureen full of hot borsch and screamed like a maddened horse in a burning stable, saying: "I want you should be calm!"

In the end she set her heart on business premises with an upper part in a side street off Oxford Street. (The place the photographer had suggested was in Golders Green. He bought it himself, freehold, for £300 and sold it twenty years later for

43

£7,350—which made Millie's blood boil again.) But at present, at least, she could say that her husband was in the ladies' and gentlemen's boot and shoe business in the heart of the West End. Mayfair! From Oxford Circus you turned westward, walked three hundred and fifty yards, turned left, walked four hundred yards, crossed the street, took the turning by the antique shop, and there was I. Small's establishment, in Mayfair —a five minutes' walk from Park Lane.

Charles Small, who has inherited a tendency to sit on tacks to give himself something to cry over, walked one evening to look at that shop in Noblett Street, W.1. Of all the streets in London this was the least frequented. It had no right to call itself a thoroughfare. There was no earthly reason why any human being should ever set foot in it. Noblett Street was an unnecessary street, a sort of dried-up fjord, ominously quiet. The motor horns in Oxford Street sounded half a mile and a hundred years away. It was the sort of street to which a misanthropic Londoner might retire in the twilight of his life, to brood in woolly silence, out of the sight of mankind. There he could walk up and down of an afternoon, and be certain that he would not encounter any living creature, except cats. To borrow an image of James Thurber's, Noblett Street had cats as other places have mice— the cats knew that no one would disturb them here. They wooed their mates in the open road and had honeymoons in the doorways, while bloated, verminous pigeons cooed and strutted in the gutters with such smug self-satisfaction that you wanted to cuff their heads. Noblett Street was full of empty peace. It had had enough of life, and settled down to a well-earned rest—it could never have amounted to anything in any case. Once in a while an old beggar-woman who picked rags out of the dustbins and lived on potato peelings, kipper bones, the residual juice in salmon tins, and orange peel went there to relieve herself. In Noblett Street, even at high noon, she was assured of privacy. If there had been any people worth mentioning living in it, even if they had had nothing better to do than loaf on their thresholds, it would not have been so bad. But when Charles Small visited Noblett Street it was dead and derelict. There were only eight shops and outside seven of them hung agents' boards saying *To Let* or *For Sale*. The only open shop was described as a "Pets' Beauty Parlour". He glanced inside and saw a lumpy-faced woman parting the hair of a petulant Yorkshire terrier—probably

44

her first customer in weeks, and a discontented one at that, to judge by the sound of its voice.

The houses on the other side of the street were being demolished to make room for a block of flats. Work was finished for the day, but a miasmatic haze of dirty dust still hung in the foul air over the ruins. The standing brickwork looked so rotten that Charles Small would not have been much surprised if someone told him that the workmen were pushing the houses down with their shoulders. Trust his mother to pick on a street like this—oh, trust her! Mayfair! He spat, partly in anger, and partly because his mouth was full of dust.

There was a gloomy little pub, "The Noblett Arms", on the far corner. Charles Small's curiosity was something like the gnawing hunger of a dyspeptic who must indulge his craving for sour pickles although he knows that there will be the devil to pay. He went into The *Private Bar*, where an aged man looked up from last Sunday's newspaper and stared, round-eyed with hope, until Charles Small ordered a shandy—a mixture of ginger-beer and mild ale that used to cost threepence. Obviously, the landlord, seeing a well-dressed gentleman, expected to get rid of at least tenpennyworth of brandy. Mowing and gibbering, and looking as if he was about to bite him, he squirted a little ale from a beer engine that creaked and groaned at being awakened out of a long sleep; wrung the neck of a ginger-beer bottle; filled the glass and pushed it across the bar with a snarl. Charles Small said: "Will you take something yourself?"

"Drop of brandy."

Putting down a ten-shilling note he said: "Help yourself."

"Haven't you got nothing smaller? Where d'you suppose I'm going to get change? It's one-and-four. Haven't you got one-and-four?"

"Here's one-and-four. . . . Is your clock right?"

"It wouldn't be 'ere if it was," said the publican.

"Have you been here long?"

"A bloody sight too long."

"May I ask how long?"

"Thirty years. Thirty years too long."

"Business good?"

"It looks like it, don't it?"

"Well, good health!" said Charles Small, sipping his shandy, while the landlord snorted and swallowed his brandy. . . . "You say you've been here thirty years. I wonder if, by any chance, you remember some people called . . . let me see . . . yes, Small, that's it, Small, who used to have a shoe shop in this street?"

At this the muscles twitched in the landlord's face—he was trying to smile, but he had lost the knack. While his face was twitching and quivering, he blew air through his nostrils; he was laughing. Then he said: "Shoe shop? I remember *them*. They came here and opened a shoe shop. They must have been off their heads. They didn't last five minutes. They went broke in no time. That's how it is with them Jews, here to-day, gone to-morrow. Give 'em an inch and they'll take a yard. It's your money they want. That's how they rule the world. What's the idea of a boot shop in Noblett Street? If you want my opinion, there was dirty work going on somewhere. Boot shop! I'm too old a bird to be caught with chaff. There was more in that than meets the eye, but I never got to the bottom of it. . . ."

CHAPTER V

THEY put the Noblett Street shop in order. Millie wanted it
painted white. Why? Because white was a nice clean colour.
The estate agent suggested varnished brown, grained to look
like walnut. But Millie insisted that white was the only respectable paint. One speck of dust, on white paint, showed up like a
fly in a glass of milk, so that if a woman kept the place clean
(she looked sideways at Lily) there was no question about it.
Who went in for brown paint? What sort of a colour was brown?
White!

So the woodwork was painted white. The shop was fitted and
stocked. The family called a secret conference and it was agreed
that everyone should buy a pair of boots or shoes from the Smalls
of Mayfair, if only to give them a little encouragement. Sisters,
brothers-in-law, uncles and cousins came and bought boots,
shoes, dancing pumps and slippers. Millie insisted on their
paying no more than the wholesale price. It looked bad, she said,
to make money out of your own flesh and blood. So they emptied
eighteen shiny oblong boxes in the first week—at cost price.
After that business fell flat. Millie, who had large ideas, and had
conversed with people who had brains, knew something of the
strategy of modern commerce. She said: "We must advertise!"

"What advertise? Where advertise?"

"What's the use of talking? Oh, what's the *use?*"

"Then don't talk!"

"So now he wants to shut me up! What marvels have *you*
done? . . . Advertise! For God's sake, advertise!"

They bought six lines of space in a local newspaper. Nothing
happened.

"Ha! A bargain we got!" said I. Small, angry but satisfied.

"Then send out circulars!"

"Who to?"

"What's the use of talking if he's ignorant?" cried Charles
Small's mother. (She and her husband had already acquired the
habit of quarrelling in apostrophe.) "Send out letters. Who to,
he says. Everybody!"

"Go on then, send out letters, send! To everybody send letters. *Na—Nadir* a pen, *nadir* a bottle ink—go on, to everybody write letters, quick! Tell them they should come at once, quick!"

"What's the use of talking to him? He's ignorant."

"What does she mean, he's ignorant?"

"You're ignorant!"

"All right. Take the pen, take the ink, write letters to everybody. Go on, educated woman, *schreib!* Write!"

Yes, the business was a failure, and Millie was ashamed. They were in debt, and after the next quarter's rent had been paid there would be less than two hundred pounds in the bank.

I. Small was bored because he had nothing to do. Noblett Street was too quiet. He missed the hammering and the grunting of the cobblers in the workshop. He was unhappy. So one day when somebody's manservant came into the shop and asked him if he did repairs, he said: "Well, why not?"

"Well look, let you and me have an understanding. I work for a certain gentleman who's got a whole lot of boots and shoes for repairs, do you see? Only it's got to be first-rate work, top-notch first-rate, every stitch by hand—understand?"

"Every stitch by hend."

"Now look: this is how it is: my gentleman's stuff has been going to Trumpet's for repair. Trumpet charges eight-and-six. I've come to an understanding here and there, see? So if you see eye to eye, you and me might come to an understanding for six-and-six."

"Six-and-six?"

"All right, call it seven bob. I can put a whole lot of work in your way, only you understand, it's not for love. If I bring you a receipt that I can make a few pence on, you sign it. That's only fair, isn't it? If you don't think so, say so. Eh?"

"So what is it you've got you want I should do?"

"To start with, there's eight pairs of boots and shoes. And I've got friends, see? I can make it worth your while, understand? Eh?"

"Bring 'em."

I. Small went to the cellar and opened a packing-case in which he had nailed down his tools. But when he told his wife that he proposed to take in repairs, she had hysterics. At last she knew what he was, at last she knew the creature she had married! She had tried, oh God, she had tried so hard to drag

48

him out of the gutter—but now he wanted to go back to it, back and back, dragging her down and down into the mire! That was it. Had she but known. She had known it all along. She had been warned, more fool she, by her sisters. Now it would be necessary for her to admit that they were right and she was wrong. Such, indeed, was the truth. But to admit that truth—oh, shame, shame! Let the fact be faced: she was married to a dirty little cobbler. And there she was, and woe was she.

"Then what do you want I should do, what?"

"Be a man! *Do* something!"

"Do what? What do you want I should do? What? Say, speak, tell me what!"

"All right, go on, go and mend boots," said Millie.

"So what am I doing?"

"That's all you're fit for. Go on, mend boots. What's the matter with you, what are you waiting for? Go on, mend boots!"

"You should have a good hiding! A good hiding you should have!" shouted I. Small.

"I'll call a policeman!"

"*Bah!*"

There was an armistice, and it was arranged that I. Small should set up his last in the basement. If any member of the family popped in it was to be understood that he was hammering away to oblige a nobleman. She looked after the shop while he worked in the cellar, and so they managed to keep their muddled heads above water for a few months. Then she announced that she was pregnant.

Thinking of this, Charles Small shuts his eyes tight and pinches himself, because it seems too horrible. For many years, now, he has been trying to close his mind against the idea of having been begotten by his stupid father upon his stupid mother, and carried around for nine months in—of all things—of all unimaginable things—his mother's womb. What business had she with a womb? As for how he got there, that is not to be thought of. When he remembers hearing his mother boast of the trouble she took to breast-feed him his weak, nervous stomach, turns over again. He heaves, he nauseates, his face becomes wet and cold. So he drinks a glass of water. The ostentatious silence of his hushed household gets on his nerves, and in his mouth, always, is that sickening taste of sour milk.

* * * * *

49

Oh, what a liar, coward, bully and cheat his mother must have been! Truth wasn't in the woman. She lived by false pretences. Every other word she said was uttered with intent to defraud. She was constantly endeavouring to create some convincing falsehood complimentary to herself. Everything she did and said was for the sake of appearance, and she really thought that her appearances were deceptive. Obviously she imagined that everyone was a bit of a fool. At the same time, she was ignorant and gullible as a Congo savage: she believed everything but the truth, and was influenced by everything but reason. There was no way of plumbing the abyss of her stupidity.

As soon as she knew that she was pregnant she behaved not like a woman with child, but like a woman possessed by a devil that had to be cast out. She went for advice, first of all, to her married sisters, who were as ignorant as she was and just as spiteful. They had all had children, without much difficulty, but had done their duty to their sex and glorified themselves in the process. Having heard from other lying wives that it is only natural for a pregnant woman to have strange fancies, they had had strange fancies. It was conveyed to Millie that the more strange fancies she had, the better; Sarah boasted that she had awakened at four o'clock in the morning with a craving for hot rolls and butter. Her husband, who was the best husband in the world, had got up immediately, run to a bake-house where men were working all night to turn out the next day's bread, and bribed the foreman to let him take away half a dozen rolls so hot that you could hardly touch them.

Thereupon there was a controversy. Pearl, red with anger, asked Sarah what she meant by "best husband in the world". When she was big with her little Arthur she woke up at one o'clock in the morning and said: "I fancy a pickled herring." Now where was a pickled herring to be procured at one o'clock in the morning? Her husband jumped out of bed like a shot, ran half a mile, knocked at the door of a delicatessen shop until the proprietor came down and gave him pickled herrings. She laughed triumphantly.

At this Ruth sneered: "Didn't he wait to put his trousers on?"

"Go on, make a mockery, just because a man has consideration. Did your husband get up at one o'clock in the morning to get you a herring?"

"No, Pearly, no," said Ruth, with a quiet smile. "He got home at one o'clock in the morning, from a big deal."

"Ha-ha—big deal! Was she fair or dark?"

"I only wish that you and your husband should have such deals every day of your life, fair, dark or medium," said Ruth, with dignity. "He was so tired he could hardly stand. He was so tired, he was too tired to eat. All he wanted was to sleep. All of a sudden what do I fancy? Cream-crackers with butter and strawberry jam. There isn't a cream-cracker in the neighbourhood. But he gets up, goes out in his slippers, and comes back at three o'clock with cream-crackers. And may I never move from this chair, he was so tired he fell asleep with all his clothes on. . . . It's no use talking, when you get a fancy, you get a fancy."

But Lily, the unnatural creature, smiled smugly and said: "Very nice too. But when I was five months gone I woke up in the middle of the night and said to Nathan: 'Nathan, I fancy a bit of gingerbread.' Nathan sat up in bed and so he said: 'You fancy a bit of gingerbread, Lily?' I said: 'In the cupboard, Nathan.' So Nathan said: 'If you fancy gingerbread, have gingerbread—go and get it out of the cupboard,' he said, 'my mother had twelve of us without fancying gingerbread.' So I went back to sleep, and I didn't fancy gingerbread any more. That's how I like a man to be. Nathan's a rock, a brick, a stone! Catch *my* Nathan running for *herrings* in the middle of the night!"

"Where there's no sense there's no feeling," said Ruth.

"That's what she calls a man!" cried Pearl.

"What's the use of talking?" asked Sarah.

But I. Small was told that if the mother's craving was not instantly satisfied the baby would be born deformed. Two days later, at five o'clock in the morning, Millie shook her husband and said: "I fancy hot rolls and butter." He got up, groaning, and went out to find hot rolls. Then she wanted pickled herrings at one o'clock, salted herrings at three o'clock, red herrings at four o'clock, soused herrings at five o'clock, cream-crackers at two o'clock, water-biscuits at two-thirty, and gingerbread in the middle of the night. When I. Small came home with gingerbread, she pretended to be asleep. Millie had hoped that he would say: "Go and get it." . . . Oh for a rock, a brick, a stone!

So, in the last six months of her pregnancy, she sucked down all the foolishness of her gossiping acquaintances—

51

gurgling drain that she was—*cloaca maxima* of femine slops!

If one old fool said that she ought to eat for two now, Millie ate herself sick. If another said that if she ate too much she would make the baby too big, she starved herself. Someone said that bottled stout made milk, so she drank stout. Someone else said that if she drank stout the child would be a drunkard. She stopped drinking stout. Her nipples became swollen and sore. Aha—cancer! Her belly swelled. Wow—— something horrible, unbelievably horrible, was going to happen. I. Small was informed that she was about to be torn to pieces. She would have to be sewn up after having burst. It was all because men were selfish. Their own pleasures was all they thought of. They took their pleasure, and then their wives went *bang* and exploded in a shower of torn entrails, screaming in ineluctable torment, in the middle of a dancing ring of shrieking martyrs, all tugging and pounding and kicking and pulling and digging and dragging. . . . I. Small thought of Millie as a thoroughfare about to be taken apart with pickaxes, and he pulled out handfuls of his hair. Once, when she said: "Srul, quick! It's kicking!" he screamed: "Murderer! I'll break his bleddy neck!"

I wish to God I'd kicked her out of the window, thinks Charles Small.

But at last he managed to be born. His father ran up and down in an ecstasy of self-accusation, beating himself on the head and breast and calling himself by insulting names: *Lobbus!* Snot-rag, toe-rag, uncivilised madman, murderer, pisspot, cannibal, rotter, turd, bandit, loafer, bugger, beast!" He tried to tear off his ears. "Piddler, manure, cad, nogoodnik, *scheisspot*, foreigner, *lapatutnik*, nothing, fartnik!" He banged himself about the head. "Muck! . . . *Makkes!* . . . *Schlemazzel!* Rubbish, bastard!"

One of the women came to him and said: "It's a boy."

"Boy, boy! How's Millie?"

"Please God she'll be . . . I don't know, please God."

"Let me go up, let me go!"

"Wait yet!"

At last they let I. Small go upstairs. His wife was asleep. They showed him something like a lump of raw liver wrapped in cloth. "What d'you call this?" he asked.

"Ssh! Your son!"

"*This? A son?*"

"What then?"

I. Small looked at it with loathing. So that was how it was!

52

Millie's insides *had* fallen out. There was some of her offal loosely wrapped in a towel, still pulsating. This was what came of being a beast.

(Millie, grudgingly yielding to his puppyish amorous advances with a tremendous affectation of disgust, had managed to make him feel horribly ashamed of himself. She somehow conveyed the impression that in *her* family there had been no sexual intercourse for many generations. Respectable people never even thought of such things. Pfoo!—filthy! . . . The hypocrite: she enjoyed nothing better than a prurient, sloppy love romance; she used to walk a mile and a half to a threepenny circulating library where she could pick a book off the shelf, so that she would not have to soil her lips by whispering the lewd, unmentionable name of Monsieur Paul de Kock.)

I. Small, that puny little fool, felt like a raging, ravening, blood-drinking rapist. He was terribly shocked, and perhaps a little proud, of the blood ruin he had wrought. When he started to cry they hustled him out of the bedroom. In the sitting-room the doctor, ostentatiously putting great glittering instruments into a black bag, said affably—it had been a perfectly easy delivery— "That's all right, control yourself, take it easy man. I pulled her through all right."

Pulled her through! I. Small saw his wife being pulled through something with sharp spikes on it. If everything else was not enough, they had to *pull her through*. He moaned: "Terrible terrible, terrible, oi!"

The doctor, not wanting to belittle himself, said: "Oh well . . . it's her first, you see, and in the case of a primipara it is sometimes hard. I only had to put a stitch or two in the sphincter. I'll look in to-morrow."

Then I. Small ran about like a chicken with its head cut off. Stitches! He saw the women, red to the armpits, wrapping up Millie's liver and pushing back all that was left of her while the doctor, with bradawl and shoemaker's needle, sewed her up with wax ends, hammering a mouthful of nails into the hips to make everything safe and watertight. It was more than he could bear.

Lily, Ruth, and Pearl came in from the bedroom, alarmed by his outcries. He said: "It's finished! She's got a case of primepera! She's hard! She's got to have stitches in the spink!"

The doctor paused on his way out, laughing, and said: "Don't be a fool. She'll be all right. It was not at all a difficult delivery."

53

"Der liver!" cried I. Small, and fainted.

They revived him with brandy. On the whole they thought well of him for having fainted: it showed that he had feelings.

But Lily said, with her triumphant smirk: "When my pains came on my Nathan went to a music hall. He said: 'What's the use of sitting and waiting? What can *I* do? What comes, comes. There's enough crying and worrying in the house already. Will it make matters better if I walk up and down and get in everybody's way? I'll come back later.'"

"Heartless!"

"Disgusting!"

"Unnatural!"

"What do you mean? *Would* it have helped if Nathan'd mooched about the house fainting? Answer me, tell me the honest truth—what good would it have done?"

Since the only answer to this question was *No good at all*, the others became furiously angry. They made disparaging noises, ironically humming and sardonically hawing while they rummaged in their muddled heads for something conclusive to say; until Ruth said: "Who said anything about doing good? It shows feeling, that's all. Feeling!"

Lily went on, malevolently calm: "I started to be confined at six o'clock in the evening when Nathan had just come back from the office. The office. He put on his hat, and he put on his coat, and he went out and had something to eat at a restaurant, and after that he went to the Alhambra, and by the time he came home my little Stanley was born. Nathan wanted a boy. So it was a boy. So it was a boy. When *my* Nathan says he's going to have a *boy*, *he* has a *boy!*" She looked triumphantly at Sarah, who had a daughter.

If Millie had not been asleep there would have been a battle of words, a battle royal. The sisters did what they could in whispers—an unsatisfactory way of quarrelling, but sufficiently audible to bring Millie's mother out of the bedroom. Threatening them with a hard, familiar right hand, the old woman said, in Yiddish: "Noisy rattles, silence; or old as you are I'll give you such a *putsch* that you'll stick to the wall."

So Millie slept her sleep for twelve hours and awoke, feeling lighter and healthier than she had ever felt before—but moaning piteously for her husband's benefit. Eight days later, Charles Small—whose blood had run into its proper channels from his surface, so that instead of looking like a piece of liver he resembled a piece of tripe—was ceremoniously circumcised, as the Law prescribes, in the flesh of his foreskin. Everyone gave him gifts. Izzy, the estate agent, gave him a magnificent rattle with a mother-of-pearl ring to cut his teeth on, and a dozen jingling silver bells. It had been given to his own child, but Izzy had locked it up in a drawer because it was dangerous—the bells were certain to come loose so that a baby was bound to swallow them, sooner or later. Millie was deeply impressed by the magnificence of this gift. She put it away because it was, as she said, "too good to use". She was like that: anything new, or freshly cleaned, was too good to use. She only half-blew her nose into a freshly laundered handkerchief. Years passed before the dust-covers came off the chairs and you made yourself comfortable. It was a pity even to sharpen a new pencil.

The tobacconist (trust him to show off) gave him a silver drinking cup with a five-pound note inside it. Becky produced a new golden sovereign. Millie's mother and father offered a neat black case containing a child's knife, fork, spoon and napkin ring, with a fifty-pound note. The photographer, that hateful creature, said that he would take the child's photograph free of charge. So one day they went to Nathan's "studio" and Charles Small was photographed in the nude, lying on his belly on a soft cushion, looking disgustingly helpless. Nathan threw in, free of charge, what he called a Cabinet Study of the Family Group. It has been preserved for forty years, and Charles Small has it still.

There is his father, in a black coat, obviously afraid of the camera—no doubt he expected it to go off bang—looking angry, therefore. There sits his mother, noticeably in a state of lactation, holding a sort of cretin dressed in long, complicated, frilly clothes with a laced bonnet stuck on its stupid head, and a general air of discomfort. That was Charles Small. The camera caught him half a second before he burst into tears because he was uncomfortable, having wet himself. His mother hated that picture, but she did not have the nerve to say so. She would not tear it up, because she believed that it was unlucky to tear up photographs. Whenever Charles Small sees it he wants to destroy it. Once, in a rage, he started to tear it up, but something stronger than himself made him desist. And there it is, somewhat faded, an embarrassment. He loathes it. His father is a scowling guinea-

55

pig with a moustache, his mother is a little monkey in a floral hat, and he is nothing on earth pinned up in a diaper-full of egested maternal milk.

Here was the beginning of his misery. Here was the record of the beginning of the end of Charles Small.

CHAPTER VI

THERE was trouble from the start. His parents quarrelled over him constantly. *Here was something worth quarrelling over!* he thinks, striking himself on the chest, partly because he has heart-burn, and partly because he despises himself; and he shudders at the thought of himself as he was when that picture was taken.

What was there worth quarrelling over? Do reasonable, civilised human beings quarrel over bags of corruption begotten in guilt and shameful darkness, gestated in fear, and born in mess and panic? Into his tortured mind comes a disgusting image: he sees himself as a nightmarish bagpipe. You tucked this bagpipe under your arm, but you did not blow into it: it was ready-filled with human breath. Day and night, night and day, day in and day out and night after night it squealed and screamed. With all your soul you hated its nerve-racking music, and yet you were compelled to walk up and down with it in the middle of the night in the hope of silencing it. It paused in its shrieking only as long as it took to discharge vomit from one end and dung from the other . . . and something compelled you to cherish this filthy instrument and hold it in your arms until it sprouted wicked little white teeth so that it might bite you. Trust *his* father and *his* mother to have words over such an object! They did not argue about the best way of killing it and disposing of it, but about what label they ought to tie upon it: in other words, they wrangled bitterly over the baby's name.

It was customary to name a child after some close relative who had more or less recently died. I. Small's father had been dead for several years, and his name was Khatzkele. One day, while he was crooning and yearning over the baby, tickling its slimy chin, and actually kissing it, he said—with tears in his eyes—"Liddle Khatzkele, mein liddle Khatzkele!"

"*Khatzkele!* What do you mean? What are you talking about? Where do you think you are? Khatzkele! Who's called Khatz-kele?" said Millie.

"What's the matter miv Khatzkele?"

"You want to make the child a laughing-stock? How can

57

you call a child Khatzkele? In front of strangers you want me to
say: 'Come here, *Khatzkele*,' I suppose. Is that the sort of man
you are?"

"Why not?"

"Why not. Why not! . . . What's the use of talking to people
if they're ignorant? What's the use?" Millie said, in agony, to the
ceiling.

"Khatzkele was good enough for mein father. It should be
good enough for mein son. What do you want you should call
him, then?"

"He should be called Dudley after my Uncle David."

"How comes Dudley to David?"

"What's the use of talking if people are ignorant?"

"Ignorant, schmignorant. Dudley, Schmudley . . . *Khatzkele!*"

"Never!"

"Is your bleddy uncle more important than mein bleddy father,
God rest his bleddy soul?" cried I. Small, in anger.

"A nice way to talk in front of the child," said Millie, snatching
the week-old baby to her bosom.

I. Small roared: "Certainly mein father, God rest his soul, is
more important by me than your bleddy Uncle Dudley. Dudley!
Schmudley! Hah!"

"Khatzkele! When he grows up people will say: 'What's your
name?' and he'll say 'Khatzkele,' and then people'll say 'A Jew
boy!' "

"Is there any shame in that? Shame in that is there any?
Is Rothschild ashamed? Is Sessoon ashamed from it? Is Monte-
fior ashamed? Is—is—is—is Shakespeare ashamed? He should
be ashamed to be a Jew?"

"Not a Jew—*Jewish!* Talk English! You're not in Cracow
now."

"What's the matter with Cracow? Is Samovarna better? No
Dudleys. *Soll ich——*"

"—I swear by my life and by yours too that my child will
never be called Khatzkele. There!"

"By your life, by my life, and by the child's life too, if I should
fall dead this minute, that bleddy child won't be called Dudley!"

"I swear by my health, *not Khatzkele!*"

"And I swear by *my* health, and *your* health, and *his* health
and *every* bleddy health, no Dudley!"

"Oh, I'm so ashamed, so ashamed!"

58

"She's ashamed. *She's* ashamed. All right—*I'm* ashamed, *I'm* ashamed. She's ashamed, I'm ashamed. No Dudley! I should have mein son a Dudley! Hah!"

"*His* son? What does he mean by *his* son?" said Millie to the overmantel.

I. Small, addressing the washstand, cried: "Whose son does she think it is, already?"

"Isn't it my son?"

"And isn't it mein son?"

"*I* don't have Khatzkeles."

"I don't have no *Dudleys!* Mein son is going to be called after mein father. Your bleddy uncle can go and beggar himself. *Na!*"

"I'm so ashamed, so ashamed, so ashamed!"

I. Small was magnificent (for him) in this situation. He stamped a foot, folded his arms, and said: "Khatzkele or nothingk!"

Millie began to cry. The baby was asleep but she gave it a sly pinch so that it cried with her. A nurse, still in attendance, who had been listening at the door, came running in and said: "You'll sour her milk. Have a little consideration. Selfishness —there's men for you!"

"Sour, sweet, long, short, big, little, large, hot, cold, *no Dudley!* Khatzkele. Beggar their bleddy uncles!"

Then the baby threw up a stomachful of half-digested milk, and Millie, calling for a doctor, was consoled by the nurse, who said that everything was quite all right because everyone knew that men were beasts. Later it was necessary to come to some arrangement. The photographer was called in as arbitrator. He said:

"You are both right. But what is in a name? On the whole, Srul is right. His father's name was Khatzkele, and the father comes first."

Since the discussion took place in Millie's father's house, she said nothing at that time: but she gave the photographer a terrible look, catching which, he continued: "On the other hand, the mother's wishes must be obeyed. Now, take the name Khatzkele. A good name, an honourable name, a perfect name. But when in Rome you do as Rome does. Say for example that your father's name was Habakkuk. Therefore would you call your son Habakkuk? No. Why? Because you're in England now. If you called your son Habakkuk everyone would laugh at him. People would say: 'Why don't you go and have a Kuck.' Every time he left the room people would say 'He'll be back in a minute, he's just gone to Habak*kuk*.' . . . Now you've got to call somebody after somebody, so you'd call your Habakkuk *Habakkuk* actually, but in English you'd call him *Henry*. Why? For his own good! Take the name Khatzkele. I've got a cousin called Khatzkele. He calls himself Charles, and what's the matter with that? Now Millie wants a Dudley, and Srul wants a Khatzkele. Well? What's the matter with two names? I say, call the boy Charles Dudley. Charles Dudley Small—isn't that a name? Charles Dudley Small."

All Millie's sisters and brothers-in-law applauded this suggestion. Her mother had no fault to find with it. Her father, scratching his beard in perplexity, muttered: "Duddler? Duddler? Who was Duddler, who?" For as far as he knew there was no one in the Pentateuch who begat a Duddler.

But the photographer said: "Dudley, Dudley is short for Dovidel."

"Then let it be."

I. Small was defeated again. The brat was named Charles Dudley, but for thirteen years he did not know exactly what his name was. When his mother hated his father more than usual —two or three days in every week—she would call her son Dudley; with extraordinary subtlety and courage (for him) I. Small put a stop to this by waiting until they were all together in a public place and then saying in a loud voice: "Khatzkele, mein liddle boychik."

This made Millie so ashamed that she settled on the name of Charley. The photographer, who loved his little joke, called him Chudleigh. Lily, who missed no opportunity of annoying her sisters in general and Millie in particular, and liked nothing better than a suggestive word or smutty story called him Habakkuk. The last syllable of the name of that fierily poetic prophet had, in jargon, a fæcal significance, so she laid heavy emphasis upon it. But that was Lily all over; that was the way her mind worked. (If she admired your room she developed an inability to pronounce her R's, so that she was talking about your womb; and if you could have heard her talking about male chickens, you would have died laughing.)

Habakkuk, Dudley, Khatzkele, Chudleigh, Charley. . . . The child was confused for years until the jokes wore out, and everyone called him Charley. I. Small grew to like the name: it was a handy name to shout when he wanted to let all the air out of his lungs—Char-LAAAY!—— He made it sound as if he was selling Charlies by the sackful off a coalheaver's cart, at two-and-twopence a hundredweight.

But when, at the age of thirteen, the boy was according to Jewish Law proclaimed a man morally responsible for his own sins—on the momentous occasion when, wearing his first long trousers, he was called up to read a portion of the Law in the local synagogue, did they call Charles Dudley Small? No. They called Khatzkele-ben-Yisroel: and then old I. Small disgraced himself by making a sucking, popping noise like a wet cork drawn out of a rubber bottle and letting his feelings overcome him to such an extent that tears ran down into his moustache and were sniffed up into his nostrils, from which they were expelled in a whirling spray by a terrible sneeze; whereupon he had to use his handkerchief, blowing a ram's-horn blast that might have brought down the walls of Jericho. But they were not in Jericho. They were in synagogue. The whole family was there. By this time Khatzkele-ben-Yisroel, alias Charles Dudley Small, had half a dozen male cousins who had already been initiated, thus, into full manhood. It had been conveyed to him that all the world was waiting for him to make a fool of himself. When his father blew his nose the Portion of Law which he had learned by heart, word by word, fell through a hole in his head. He had stage fright. Something like a hard-boiled egg was stuck at the back of his throat. Then the great scroll unrolled, and a voice hissed the first word, which was *Kee*, and it all came back in a rush, and came out in a rush, delivered in a voice so piercing that several people in the audience could not hear themselves speak for half an hour after.

When it was all over his mother kissed him and said: "Dudley! Dudley!"

"Khatzkele," said his father, shaking him by the hand, "Khatzkele, now you are a man!"

"Come on, *Dudley!*"

"Do what your mother tells you, *Khatzkele*."

He was aware of an interlacing, a reticulation of forked lightning not far above his head: looks were being exchanged. But there was no quarrel that day, because Millie was in a genial, expansive mood. She smiled and nodded, as if to say: "To-day is

61

a holiday, for to-day let me put aside my tools—my rack, my thumbscrew, and my pincers. Let me turn my four wild horses out to graze for a few hours and refresh them. I will make a fresh start and tear you asunder first thing to-morrow morning."

For on that day her son had become a Man. . . .

Ha-ha-ha! says Charles Small, looking at the photograph that was taken to commemorate the occasion. It is a magnificent photograph, expensively mounted and signed (if you please) like an Old Master—*Nathan*, with a flourish. There is a high-class-looking inscription chastely printed in elegant type: *The Studio Nathan, Old Bond Street, West One*—not a common or garden W.1. but *West One*. This was the kind of man Nathan, the Photographer, had turned out to be: Bond Street, *West One!* He had picked up (such creatures have all the luck; there is no getting away from it) a wonderful Belgian photographer, a refugee who had fled from Brussels when the Kaiser's Army was on its way in. So now Nathan was making a fortune. He was patronised by the nobility and gentry. Society beauties had their photographs taken by Nathan of West One. Foolish people who did not know what Millie knew about the immoral lives Society ladies led, illiterates unacquainted with the works of Miss Marie Corelli, stood and gaped at framed photographs of famous beauties in the vestibule of The Studio Nathan. Millie, who was a keen observer of women, and who could be relied upon to find their weak points —she had brought a charwoman around to her opinion that Lily Langtry was ugly as sin and that Ellen Terry had a face like a horse—could not bear to look at such portraits. If Lady A. was blonde, she bleached. If Lady B. was dark, she dyed. If the Duchess of C. had a fine bosom, it was because she stuffed her dress with newspapers or handkerchiefs. Millie was very much down on bosoms. She thanked God that she had never gone in for any such filthiness. But as for Nathan, the Photographer, all *he* thought about was bosoms. Millie said that she would rather see her husband sweeping the streets than messing about with Duchess's bosoms.

Be it as it may: Nathan's present to Charles Small when he became a Man was a picture, again. Naturally: it cost Nathan nothing. He said that his normal charge for such a picture would be "in the region of twenty guineas." When he suggested a date for an appointment Millie said that she did not know how to thank him. As soon as he was out of earshot she laughed without mirth and said: "It just shows you. That's the way to get rich. I'd rather sell bootlaces in the street than get rich that way. But there you are—what can you expect from a *Litvak?*"

I. Small said: "Nathan comes from Jmerinka, Millie."

"What's the use of talking? He's a foreigner, he's ignorant —him and his Jmerinka. Oh, what's the use, what's the use of talking? A photographer. Oh, I'm so ashamed, so ashamed! Do you call yourself a man? He stands there and he calls himself a man."

"So what do you want I should do, what?"

"Photogrephs! A photogreph!"

"Every five minutes she wants to go out to get a photogreph taken. So now all of a sudden by her is a misery miv photogrephs! If she didn't wanted a photogreph, she should said she didn't wanted photogrephs. What for does she wait, what for, till anybody's here to make mein life a misery miv her photogrephs? What does she want from mein life?"

"What's the use of talking to him if he's ignorant, ignorant! He wants his son to go to a place where such a class of people go? That's the way you catch diseases. All right! *I'm* not *used* to that sort of thing."

"Diseases? What diseases? Who is?"

"It's all right, Srul. It's all right. As long as I know what you are it's quite all right. Go to your Society Beauties!"

I. Small howled: "Then if it's all right it's all right, so what is there to make an *all right* about?"

"Another man would have a little pride. Another man would tell a photographer to keep his twopenny-halfpenny photogrephs. . . . Where is he going?"

"Where's he going? He's bleddywell going to tell Nathan to bleddywell keep his bleddy photogreph," said I. Small, reaching for his hat.

"No, wait," said Millie, terrified. "I don't want trouble. Wait. This is better: when Nathan gives us the photogreph I'll tear it up and throw it in his face."

And for twenty-seven years she has been boasting that this photograph has come out of the same camera that caught the likenesses of Lords and Ladies and Honourables. The Belgian, De Groot, knew how to take a picture. He was an artist. He listened carefully to Nathan's directions, expunged them from his consciousness, formed his group, and clicked his camera—it was all over in two or three minutes. For the look of the thing he exposed several more plates and made the sitting last half an hour, but what his eye caught first, that was the picture. Nathan stood in the background appearing to direct the operation.

There it hangs, expensively framed, the detestable photograph. On one side stands Charles Small's father dressed in cutaway coat, light waistcoat, and striped trousers. An instant before he pressed the bulb, De Groot cried: "*Ha!*"—so that I. Small's eyebrows are aristocratically arched, his eyelids droop, his mouth appears to be about to open to issue a desperate word of command, and his shoulders are tense.

The poor downtrodden imbecile has been photographically trapped in a moment of terror, yet looks remarkably like D'Artagnan. When De Groot cried "*Ha!*" Millie's intestines convulsed, and wanted to empty themselves, so that she tightened her abdomen and instinctively turned her face to the doorway behind which, she knew, the toilet was; so that she appears genteelly detached. Between them stands Charles Small. Got up in a winged stiff collar, bow tie, black jacket and waistcoat, striped trousers and patent-leather shoes, and gripping his first bowler hat in his left hand, he resembles the young Napoleon. He didn't want to have his picture taken, and was on the verge of rebellion, even when his father threatened to break every bone in his bleddy body. His mother pinched him, and De Groot's camera, neatly picking out the expression that comes into a face between surprise and resentment, made him look imperious. The pain of the pinch made him relax his grip on his hat: you would think that he was about to point towards a new world.

In his way De Groot was a master. His work has survived him: Charles Small cannot bring himself to burn it. Even if he could, it would do him no good; the image is with him. He will continue to say to himself: *Four years to make a good, thoroughbred dog . . . Four years to make a fine glistening race-horse . . . One year to make a lovely wheat field . . . And thirteen years to make that thing with the bowler hat! . . . Forty years to make me! . . . In forty years a tree gets big and strong . . . Oh, miserable creature!*

He is shocked and bewildered when he realises that it took thirteen years to make him what he was when he was declared a Man. Like everything else they said, it was a confounded lie. Man! They told him that he was a man, and gave him manly

64

gifts—gold watches, cigarette cases, dressing cases, and all that. After dinner he made a speech, saying: "My dear Parents, Grand-parents, Relatives and Friends! Now I have become a Man . . ." But next day they took away his presents and locked them up, and he was nothing but a thirteen-year-old boy, stuffed with a sense of dragging time, and wondering how people lived to the age of forty. Thirteen years was quite enough.

It took me thirteen years to be that, says Charles Small, looking at the framed photograph. *That!*

CHAPTER VII

IT must be remembered that Charles Small's thirteenth birthday was celebrated fourteen years after his parents were married. Several of his relatives were dead and two or three of his father's friends were estranged, notably Solly Schwartz. Millie hated Schwartz. She might have forgiven him for his club-foot, for his puniness, and for the curve of his back, but I. Small seemed to love him. So she hated him. Sometimes Schwartz paid them a visit. He was received by I. Small with enthusiasm, and greeted courteously by Millie. As soon as he was gone there were quarrels.

"Well, he can eat, your friend!"

"What do you mean, he can eat, *my* friend? Can't *your* friends eat?"

"That's right. Go on. Pick up every word I say. Show your ignorance—pick up every word."

"All right, I'll show my ignorance—every word you say I'll pick up. . . . What did you say?"

"Never mind."

"What's the matter miv Solly Schwartz?"

"Nothing."

"What does she mean *nothing?*"

"Now he wants to bring cripples into the house. So that's what he is. I haven't got enough. So he wants cripples in the house," said Millie, with resignation. "As long as everybody is happy, let it be cripples in the house. There's a man up the road with no arms and legs, who plays a barrel organ with his mouth. Go on, bring *him* into the house! What's he waiting for? Let him put on his hat and coat and bring a few *more* cripples into the house."

"What's the matter with cripples?"

"Nothing. Nothing! Who said there was anything wrong with cripples? Wrong, *wrong*—with cripples? I only ask that you should bring them into the house. Didn't I say so? Didn't I say 'Bring cripples into the house'? Then bring them."

I. Small, muddle-headed and angry, shouted:

"So what's the matter miv Schwartz?"

66

"Who said anything about Schwartz? But go on, get Schwartz. That's all I'm short of, Schwartz. Do me a favour, will you? Get Schwartz, and the man that turns the organ with his mouth. You know I haven't got enough trouble, don't you?"

"Is it Schwartz's fault he's got a bed foot?"

"Well, no . . . no, not *his* fault."

"*Whose* fault then, whose fault?"

"Nothing. Who said anything about anybody's fault? Let him come, let him live here. I've got nothing better to do than wait hand and foot on your humpy angels. Threehalfpence-twopence, threehalfpence-twopence, threehalfpence-twopence," said Millie, referring to Schwartz's club-footed limp.

"He comes in to say hullo. Siz a friend of marn!"

"Now he wants *friends*. His family isn't enough."

"What's the matter miv friends, what? Because I've got a family, I mustn't have a friend any more? Is that what you want?"

"All right, as long as I know! So that's what he is. He's had what he wanted, and now it's 'Goodbye, I'm going out to run after prostitutes with my cripple friends.' Very nice!"

"What does she mean, what?" cried I. Small, in a frenzy of bewilderment. "I say there's no harm I should said hullo to Solly Schwartz and she's here with her prostitutes. Why must you always have your mouth full miv prostitutes?"

"That's all right. It's quite all right. *I* know!"

This injustice hurt I. Small. Prostitutes! She spoke of prostitutes to him! When other men winked and whispered about their amorous triumphs—their various five-shillingsworths of waste in shame picked up around Leicester Square—I. Small boasted of his purity. He could honestly say that he had never "been with" a woman until he was married: this was all he had to be proud of. His pride was wounded; his honour was touched; he lost his voice for a minute or two, and when it came back he screeched like a grackle: "If I have the name I'll have the game! Wait and see!"

Then Millie became savage. She behaved like all kinds of predatory creatures—she slavered like a jackal-bitch, bared her teeth like a hyena, and in the manner of a hungry caracal sharpened her claws upon the air. (They never touched each other, that couple, even in anger: she bit, slashed, scratched, and tore her husband to pieces in fantasy. He strangled her, broke her back, and trampled her dead body in pantomime. Willing to wound and yet afraid to strike as the poet says, they fought at a distance. Remembering them in their little tantrums Charles Small remembers a visit to the Zoological Gardens, where he saw two wretched little furious monkeys trying to get at each other through a fine-meshed wire partition.)

"Siz wicked to make a mockery from cripples!" I. Small shouted. "Wicked!"

"So now I'm wicked, is that it?"

"Certainly," said I. Small.

"Go on then, go away, go to your cripples, go to your Solly Schwartz. Go on!"

"You told me to go," said I. Small, putting his on hat, "so good-bye."

At this, Millie was afraid. It was not that she would not know what to do if her husband left her. She could go home, where, as she imagined, she would be welcome; where she would buzz around like a blue-bottle, flapping at imaginary dust and moving pieces of furniture that were best left alone and stirring pots that did not need to be stirred, offending everyone by repolishing into dullness mahogany furniture in which you could see your reflection, saying that she hated dirt, hanging out of windows to smear panes of glass professionally cleaned and polished an hour before, lifting up heavy objects and putting them down again just for the sake of lifting them up and putting them down, begging comfortably-seated people to get up while she shook up chair cushions, and driving everyone to the verge of madness so that at the end of the day she could pant through parched lips: "*I'm* not afraid of a little hard work, like *certain* people I could mention." Then there would be, she thought, something like the shout that tore hell's concaves while father, mother and the rest said: "Millie is here. Thank God, no one could call *her* dirty and *she*, at least, is not afraid of work. Look at her, worn out. Why doesn't she stop it, why doesn't she go to bed and rest? Every five minutes she gets up and moves everything and takes up the carpets and polishes all the furniture. She'll kill herself with work."

Then she would come groaning out of her chair saying that she had forgotten the carbolic. Certain people, no doubt for reasons of their own, liked to have disease in the house. Not Millie. To her, water was something into which people who were not absolutely filthy poured carbolic, so that it could be scattered about the house. . . . She would fill the lavatories with carbolic, she would scrub the saucepans with carbolic, she would sprinkle the clocks with carbolic; disinfect the soap with carbolic, pour carbolic on the evening newspaper, and gargle with carbolic. Oh, she would be welcome if she went home; she constantly worried about how they were getting along without her. If her husband left her she would not be without a place to go.

But there was something disgraceful in being left by a husband. Millie knew exactly what people would say—she had said it herself on several occasions. Like her sisters, she had cast-iron opinions on the subject of Separation. When the Duke and Duchess of Battersea separated, the sisters all said: "*She's* no good, that's what it is. She carries on with every Tom Dick and Harry." When Mr. Nussbaum ran off to America with a milliner, they said it again of Mrs. Nussbaum. When Dr. Crippen was sentenced to death for the murder of his wife, they shook sad, wise heads and said: "He's not to blame—she drove him to it, carrying on with every Tom Dick and Harry, leading him a dog's life. Such women deserve all they get. Believe me, he had his reasons. It serves her right." Of Ethel le Neve, again, they said: "It serves her right, for carrying on with Doctor Crippen—a married man! She should be hung too." And when they came again to Crippen, it was: "Serve him right—a married man carrying on with girls. Hang him, and a good job too!"

If, on the other hand, a wife separated herself from her husband, their anger was terrible. They denounced both parties. "What was she in such a hurry for, her? Somebody waiting to meet her at the station—she was afraid of being late—some Tom Dick or Harry. . . . And him, he drove her to it—*him!*—carrying on with everything in petticoats, beating his wife, never satisfied with the cooking, smoking day and night, lazy. . . . But if she hadn't left him, believe me, he'd have left her—her, with her nagging; and she couldn't boil an egg. Her house was a disgrace —you could write your name in the dust on the mantelpiece. She was too busy carrying on with every Tom Dick and Harry. . . . Let's hope it'll be a lesson to him, the rotter, when she dies in the gutter, the common woman. . . ."

No, truly respectable married people did not separate. Respectable wives and respectable husbands did not leave and were not left. Such goings-on were good enough for the riff-raff, the rabble, the costermongers, the dukes and duchesses who committed adultery on tiger-skin sofas and then tore out their hair and went home and drank poison and killed themselves. The Moss sisters had read all about them—it was all down in black and white—and they rejoiced that they were good girls, not duchesses. No scandals for them, thank you. If husband and wife didn't agree, the proper thing to do was exchange smiles in public for the look of the thing, and fight it out at home; fight in silence like pit-dogs locked belly-and-throat so that nothing but death could part them. This battle of dog and bitch, since it was, so to speak, illegal, had to be fought at night, in secret. It might go on until the opponents were utterly exhausted—only old age brought a lethargic, weary, disgruntled peace—as in the case of a certain Mr. and Mrs. Good, of whom Pearl said, with a sidelong glance at her husband: "Certain people not far from here ought to take a lesson from those two—fifty years they've been married and they still say please and thank you to each other." Millie, remembering a passage in some novelette that had moved her to tears, changed her tone and said: "If you're not happy with me I want you to go, Srul. I want you to have your freedom. Don't worry about me, I'll manage somehow. I don't want to know where you're going. I only want to know that you'll be happy. Go, Srul!"

"Didn't I told you," said I. Small, who had not enough sense to keep his mouth shut and walk out of the house, "didn't I told you I'm going out for an hour with Solly Schwartz?"

"You mean, 'didn't I *tell* you'. For God's sake, at least, Srul, for the child's sake, tell me—where are you going?"

"I thought you didn't want to know."

"I should want to know where you're going with your friend? Friends, he wants friends! I should want to know where he's going with his *friends*, ha-ha!"

I. Small shouted in his deafening bass voice: "Don't *you* got friends?"

"Srul, don't change the subject. If you don't want to tell me where you're going, don't tell me where you're going. Go. Go on, go. If burglars break in I'll call the policeman. Please, Srul, I want you should go."

"All right, I won't go!" He threw his hat into the fireplace, from which it rebounded with a hollow sound.

Millie said: "For *my* sake—to please *me*—I *want* you to go to your humpback. Don't worry about me, I can't help it if you hurt my feelings. Go!"

"Look, Millie, if you're not careful I'll go."

"Go!"

"I should go when she makes poison of it."

"Now I'm poisoning him. All right. What can you expect?"

"From what, what can you expect?"

"It's my fault," said Millie shaking her head. "I was warned, I didn't take advice, so I suffer. It's all right, Srul, go on, go. Go with your humpy. How comes your wife with you? What for? What does he want a wife for? What does *he* care if his wife isn't well? No, he's got to go out with threehalfpence-twopence, drinking with prostitutes. It's all right, as long as I know what he is. As long as I know, it's all right. I only want to know. Go on, go. I've got a headache. Thank God there isn't a stone floor in the kitchen, Crippen!"

"Oh, bleddywell beggar yourself!" shouted I. Small, putting on his hat back to front and stamping his feet.

"That's just what I expected. Go on, go."

"You asked me to go, you told me to go, you said *go* when I asked you if I could go weeks ago, and now in that tone of voice she says go."

"First learn to talk English, Srul, then talk about my tone of voice. If my tone of voice doesn't suit you, find another tone of voice. Go! Should I mind being let alone? I'm used to it."

"You're a bleddy story-teller! You can have a hundred friends in and out of the house all day long, and so me, so I mustn't go out five minutes miv one friend!"

"Don't say *miv;* say with . . . Do I go out at all hours of the night with humpbacks with a leg and a half, running after goodness knows what rubbish to get myself diseased? Do I go out drinking in dirty rotten common public-houses?"

"All right, I'm not going."

"Srul, to please me, go!"

"May I drop dead if I go!"

"So sure should I live, you'll go!"

"Honest? You want I should go?" asked I. Small. "What's the matter, Millie, I should go out miv a friend for a walk, and a chat, and for sixpence a glass lager beer? Tell me, what's the matter with that, Millie?" he asked, in a heartbroken voice.

"A chat. What secrets has he got with his humpy little Punch and Judy show?"

"Millie, once for all, stop talking about humps! Is it Solly's fault he's got a liddle hump? Did he said to his father und mother: 'Please, mummy-deddy, do me a favour, give me a hump—for my sake, to please me, mummy-deddy, for mein birthday a hump give me.' Eh?"

"I don't know. He's your friend, ask him. All right, go on, creep out, go and *chat*, what are you waiting for? What do they want to talk about that I mustn't hear? Dirt, filth, women. As long as I know what he is. Oh, I'm so ashamed, so ashamed. The whole town'll know. He's had my money; that was what he wanted; and off he goes dressed up like a Piccadilly Johnny with a walking-stick—a walking-stick if you don't mind!—to roam about the West End with humpbacks. Goodness only knows what they get up to."

She had never allowed her husband to forget that when they married he was penniless, and she had five hundred pounds. She had rubbed it in so thoroughly that he was sore and tingling from head to foot with shame, so that now, when she referred to her money he wanted to go and hide. He took out his purse and emptied it on to the table. There was a golden sovereign, a half-sovereign, three half-crowns, two florins, four sixpences, and a threepenny piece. With something like calm, almost with dignity, he said: "I earned it. Look—I take a shilling, one shilling. Is it too much?" She did not answer. He threw down the shilling and picked up sixpence. "*Na!* That suits you?"

"Certainly, Srul. How much more do you want to buy cups of cocoa for your Society ladies?"

Millie's allusion to her exhausted dowry had demoralised him. He did not roar with rage, but said humbly, holding up the sixpence: "A glass lager beer."

"Very nice. The last sixpence in his pocket Piccadilly Johnny's got to rush out and spend on beer. Now I know what he is. It's all right as long as I know. He can't buy a bottle of beer and drink it in the house like a man. Oh no. He must go out and about, Piccadilly Johnny with a walking-stick! Go on, hurry up, you'll be late for humpy."

"Leave humps alone, I told you!"

"Don't hurry back. Stay out all night. Don't worry, I'll be waiting with a nice cup of tea and something to eat."

"Millie, for goodness' sake, why should you *be* like that?" said I. Small, tearfully.

"Like what? He wants me to be like his fancy women—is that what it is? So that's what it is! Well, I'm sorry, Srul, I can't help my nature. I'm not going to be a fancy woman, even to please you. But don't let me get in your way. Go on, Piccadilly Johnny, take your walking-stick. Ha-ha, a walking-stick he wants.

This enraged I. Small. He bellowed: "What's the matter, what, with a walking-stick, what?"

"Let his children starve. What does he care, the millionaire, as long as he can buy walking-sticks!"

"Deliberate bleddy story-teller! For ten years I had this stick!"

"Then take it, Piccadilly Johnny, go on, go out and show off with it—him with a walking-stick!—I never heard of such a thing!"

"Oh, beggary!" cried I. Small, and broke his stick over his knee. Throwing down the splintered halves he said: "*Na!* Ten years I had that stick. It was in your way, was it? Right! Now you should be satisfied. There, take the stick, put it in the fire —in the fire put it! Now am I a Piccadilly Johnny?"

"So that's what you are! So this is what he's come down to! Breaking up walking-sticks to light the fire. It's all right, I don't mind, as long as I know, Srul. I only want to know the truth. Once I know——"

"Beggar yourself! Beggar the bleddy truth!" shouted I. Small, and went out.

When she heard the street door slam, Millie was sad. She looked at her husband's saddle-shaped purse open and empty on the table, at the few gold and silver coins gleaming among bronze pennies in the gaslight, and she wept. She was ashamed and unhappy. *What is the matter with me?* she asked herself, pushing the loose money about with a fork on the tablecloth. (She could not bring herself to touch it with a finger.) *He does his best, poor man. He'd run to the devil for me. He's a good man—what do I want of him?*

Still weeping, she remembered that she too was not without virtue: she remembered a December afternoon when she had taken off her overcoat and hung it on the shoulders of a blind beggar woman who was pretending to sell matches in Oxford Street. She was like that. All that she had was anyone's to take;

73

and she could be sympathetic for hours on end while neighbours talked of their troubles. But, confronted with people she loved, she felt as a gun might feel—if it could feel—when the hammer clicks back, the cartridge is rammed tight, the finger is upon the trigger, the eye is on the sights, and the spark is waiting that will scatter the charge.

Then there was a bang. The one nearest to her got hurt.

CHAPTER VIII

AFTERWARDS she was always sorry, and she cried. But even as she cried she knew that her tears were in their way missiles, because she had been born and bred like that. Sometimes she wept alone, as she wept then, while her husband, sick with guilt and completely discouraged, slunk westward to meet his friend, Solly Schwartz.

His evening was poisoned.

. . . The dull ache in Charles Small's right side is subsiding. A certain congestion in that region takes itself away to somewhere lower down, so that by God's grace he can sigh and, in sighing, lift an awful weight off his breast-bone. Having sighed he thinks again . . .

A lot of people aren't so bad, if only they are left alone. But people won't leave you alone. Oh no! They've got to fiddle with you, interfere with you, mess about with you. They say they love you. Well, if they love you, why can't they let you be? What do they want to try and make you like themselves for?

. . . The pain is coming back, and so is the sour taste of curds and the hopeless gurgling washiness of the whey. He punches his pillow, every feather in which seems suddenly to have become a thorn, and thinks again:

Whose fault is it? Your own, no one's fault but your own, if you are squeezed out of shape and made miserable by weaklings. Would they bruise their fingers on a piece of iron? No. More fool you, then, for letting yourself stay soft. More fool you, for letting your mother get a scissors-hold on you before you had wriggled clear of her womb! Oh, rottenly unfair game played by abominably matched opponents! . . . You weigh seven pounds; she weighs a hundred and fifty pounds. "Now you can suck me dry, on condition that later I may suck you." Maaa-maaa-maaa! . . . You thought you were pretty clever to have gulped a bellyful of sour milk. Later you were reminded that it was your opponent's turn. Then out came your heart, your brain, your guts, your liver and the marrow of your bones; whereupon she gets back with a ladylike belch and says "Good son, good son"—like

75

a satisfied customer in a restaurant saying "Good custard."

Oh why was not everyone like Solly Schwartz? Charles Small loved Solly Schwartz.

* * * * *

Model the figure of an average man, and then, while the clay is still wet, put a heavy weight on its head and leave it to settle down and harden, and you will find yourself possessed of an oddly deformed statuette. Its head will be sessile, pushed down into its shoulders. Between the flattened cranium and the almost invisible throat you will see a queer, lowering face that seems to be nothing but a dog-like grin, an immense nose and a chin like the toe of a boot. Anything may happen to the torso, but in all probability the shoulders will come up as the head sinks down, the back will hunch itself, and the legs will become short and thick and curiously curved while the feet are splayed. Only the arms harden in their original shape, and then they appear disproportionately large. Such was Solly Schwartz. ——in fact he was even less than that. There had not been enough clay to complete his left leg, so that since it was six inches shorter than his right he wore a surgical boot with a steel frame—what they used to call an "iron foot". His father considered him as an affliction rather than a child, and so indeed he must have appeared when the midwife, in Kutno, held him up for inspection on a towel. Every mother shuddered at the thought of Solly Schwartz newly born, and thanked God that no such monstrosity had been born to her. He, laughing heartily, used to tell his friends that when he was circumcised his father cried: "For God's sake, keep the little piece and throw the big one away!" What was there to do with such a creature? "It gives me the sick to look at him," said the father, who was a tailor, watching the hunch-backed child playing with an empty cotton-reel. "*Gott sei dank* he doesn't get it from *me!*"

"Nor from me," said the mother, meekly. "Leave him, leave him—it's not his fault, it's his misfortune. Let him be, Avrumkele, leave him. . . . Ah, my darling little dove! Ah, my pretty little doll! Bless him, then!"

"Yes," said the father, "let him sit on his *tukhess* and stitch, and stitch, like me. That's all he'll be good for. Let him be a tailor like his unlucky father."

So as soon as Solly Schwartz was old enough to learn how to

work the child went to work. By that time his parents had emigrated. He hopped about the workshop, damping rags for the pressers and sweeping the floor until he learned how to sew. But he was clumsy. His father cursed himself for having begotten such a son, who could not even "threadle a needle". The fact had to be faced: little Solly Schwartz was maladroit. But he was strong in the arms and had large, sinewy hands—disproportionately large, extraordinarily muscular hands, to which the tailors in the sweat-shop referred as *luppes*. The end of it was that he became a presser. Singing cheerful songs in a voice which was audible above the thunder of the heavy sewing machines, he hopped from the pressing-stove to the bench and back again, clownishly juggling the hot, ponderous irons. It was generally assumed that he was not in his right mind; he was happy. Malformed, hunchbacked, incurably lame, sentenced to hard labour for life with no earthly hope of earning more than thirty shillings a week, he sang. On one leg, he danced. When his father died and his colleagues offered condolence, Solly Schwartz said nothing but: "Good."

An old cutter, pausing with his mouth and his scissors wide open said: "What did you say? *Good?* By you is good if your father dies, God rest his soul?"

Young Solly Schwartz replied: "Certainly is good. Ain't God good?"

"Who's talking about God? Honour thy father and thy mother."

"Who said so? Moses said so. Who said so to Moses? God. Who gave the Law to Moses? God. If you live, it's good. If you die, all right, it's good. Did you want he should live for ever? Let him be, he's dead and done with. What do you care? Cry over your own father."

"A bladdy good hiding, that's what he wants," said the cutter, picking up a yardstick; for Solly Schwartz was only fifteen years old.

"Come on, give me a good hiding. But put one finger on me and I warn you, that's all—I warn you!" said Solly Schwartz, picking up a hot pressing-iron and holding it effortlessly like a Roman boxer with a cestus.

"What's the use talking? Where there's no sense there's no feeling. And so that's how we go," said the cutter going back to work; while some of the other workers in the sweat-shop

77

glanced at Solly Schwartz and, winking at one another said: "He's a *riach*, a proper devil!"

His mother died soon after his father. He did not observe the eight days of mourning prescribed by ritual, but came back to work as soon as she was under ground, whistling a vulgar tune entitled *Poppety-Poppety-Pop*, and wearing a pink tie.

The cutter, a large man of violent temper, shocked by such callousness, picked up the brass-tipped yardstick and shouted: "Look at 'im! Cossack, epicurean, murderer! His father and his mother, dead in their graves they are lying, and he's here whistling like . . . like . . . like an Irishman, in a check jacket. Haven't you got no respect for the dead, may they rest in peace?"

"No!" said young Solly Schwartz. "Respect for the dead? What for?"

"What *for?* Because a son should *have* respect! Your *mother* is lying dead—so you should *have* respect! Think, think, you . . . you . . . you humpty-dumpty, your mother, she's lying dead! *Dead!*"

"What do you want me to do? Just tell me, Mister Berkowitz, say the word. Have her stuffed? She's dead. Well? And so?"

"Show respect. Respect show!"

Taking off his coat and rolling up his sleeves in preparation for the day's work Solly Schwartz said: "Mr. Berkowitz, don't talk about her. She's my business, not your business. She's dead, and a good job too. Better off!"

"Honour thy father and thy mother!" cried Berkowitz, the cutter.

"Honour them? What for? Did they honour me? They're gone—let them go. What d'you want me to do, cry? I'm glad they're dead. What did I want *them* for? *In der erde* with my father. *In der erde* with my mother, and a good job, too! Now I'm nobody's son. Now I'm Solomon Schwartz. Good!"

Brandishing the yard-measure the cutter said: "What you want is——"

"—*I* know what I want. Give me what *you* think I want," said Solly Schwartz, clenching his fists. "Come on."

Then the master of the workshop came in, took the cutter aside, and said: "What's the matter with you? Why can't you leave the boy alone? He's an orphan. It's a *mitzvah*, Berkowitz, to be kind to an orphan. Stop it, Berkowitz!"

78

"Mr. Cohen, can you stand there and talk to me like this? Stop it? Stop what? He threatened me already with a red-hot iron. With a red-hot iron this humpty-dumpty threatened me. A nogoodnik, a rotter! His mother still twisting and turning in her grave, God forbid, and in he comes in a check coat whistling already *Poppety-Poppety-Pop. Tfoo!* Mr. Cohen, enough! *Oder* he goes, *oder* I go. *Na!* What, am I here to be . . . be . . . be blackmailed by this, this *scheisspot?* Me?"

"*Sha!*" said Mr. Cohen. "Berkowitz, *sha!* A cripple, an orphan —may it never happen to you—it's written, it's a *mitzvah* to do good to an orphan. Let him alone. No mother, no father, leave him be!"

"If that *rotzer* stays, by my life and yours too, and may I drop down dead, then I go, Mr. Cohen."

Mr. Cohen said, wearily: "Oh, let it be, Berkowitz, go! What do you take me for, I should throw out into the streets orphans already into the streets, what? Go! Go, for God's sake, leave me in peace and go!"

Berkowitz said: "So that's how it is. You wanted to get rid of me and you couldn't say so like a man. Look at the way he gets himself up, that *schtinker!*"

"Are you going, Berkowitz?"

"Hm! For such a little loafer, for such *scheisspots* I should take away my living, is *that* what you want? A *krenk* on the——"

"—Berkowitz, no curses in my workshop! May the man be paralysed with a rotten fit and take a black cholera who makes curses in this place! Is that clear?" said Mr. Cohen, in Yiddish. "May worms devour him and a fire in his *kishges!* And a week's notice. No cursing, Berkowitz, or may my hands drop off. . . . What, are you making me rich with your dribbing and drabbing? Look at you, *stuck narr*, look at you, *stuck ochs*, you . . . you . . . whatever you are, go, work, you *stuck pferd!*" Mr. Cohen was getting angry, and enjoying it. "*Parkh!*" he cried. That meant *scab.* "*Lozerducke hund!* Herod! Lazybones! Pisstank, loafer, aristocrat, go back to work—a grown-up man fighting with boychiks!"

Berkowitz, pale with anger, went back to work, but thereafter he tried to make himself offensive to Solly Schwartz. He did not dare physically to threaten this ugly boy who had the arms of a weight-lifter and the eyes of a detective-inspector: he used his tongue.

79

"Look at the way it dresses, that thing," he said to the assistant cutter. "Hm! Look at humpty-dumpty! Shepherd's plaid he's got to wear, with a *hoika* on his back like Primrose Hill. Pink shirts, give him. Patent boots, to button up; nothing is too good for it. . . . They've got no *khine*, Pressburger, no bloody *khine*. How comes for a presser to dress himself up like a . . . a . . . door-knocker? There you are, that's what it is. They want to make a show of themselves, these pressers. What can you do with people like that? Eh, Pressburger? Ask yourself the question. Answer me."

Pressburger, a good-natured man, whispered: "Ah, come on, Mr. Berkowitz, be nice, please! What do you want to hurt his feelings for? If it gives him pleasure, why shouldn't he wear a check suit with a pink shirt? What's the matter with you, Mr. Berkowitz? When I was a boy all I could think about was I should have a moustache with a fancy weskit." Pressburger laughed. "Well, so I got a moustache—look, feel the quality, all hair, a nice shade of grey. By me, this was ambition. You can have it for eighteenpence." Pressburger was trying to sweeten the atmosphere of the workshop; to cleanse it of acrimony and spite.

But Berkowitz went on and on until Solly Schwartz said: "*Achtung, stuck schneider.* Listen!"

Now this was fighting talk. It is always dangerous to call a man what he is—it is insulting because in doing so you imply that you are different, and therefore somehow superior. It must be because most men are ashamed of what they are. There is a tacit understanding that one is superior to one's trade, however respectable it may be. Call a plumber an idle thievish, incompetent dog, and he will reason with you; shout: "You plumber!" and he will hit you with a wrench. Tell your bank manager that he is a heartless robber, a parasitic bourgeois, and a rotten cheat, and he will try to explain matters: call him a banker and he will probably have you thrown out of his office. There is no surer way to irritate a man than to tell him coldly that he is what he ought to be proud to be. It must be because men have lost their pride in their work. Perhaps they have been listening to too many fairy stories about Vanderbilt and Rockefeller, or reading too many columns of Society Gossip and looking at too many shiny rotogravure supplements in the weekly magazines. The fact remains that for fifty years, now, all anyone has needed to do, if he wanted a punch in the face, has been, in effect, to say to any man: "You are what you are."

Berkowitz, passionately angry, said: "What did you call me, what?"

"*Schneider*. Tailor. Well? What are you? *Schneider*. Go on *schneid*, you *schneider*."

"Did you heard what he said?" screamed Berkowitz, picking up his terrible cutting-shears. "Apologise, or——"

"Or what? Are you trying to frighten me, *schneider-tukhess*, you with your little pair of scissors? Put them down," said Solly Schwartz. "What d'you think you're going to do with them? Cut my head off? Hit me with them? Do you want a fight with me?"

"Why can't we have peace in the workshop?" said Pressburger. "Berkowtiz, Mr. Berkowitz, leave the boy alone for God's sake. An orphan, a . . ."

He was going to add *a cripple*, but stopped himself. Solly Schwartz, quick as a woman, said:

"All right, Pressburger. A hump on my back, a funny leg. Say it. What do I care? A hump, a limp, I'm no beauty. Eh? Is that it? All right. Look at him, this Berkowitz, this *stuck* elephant! You want a fight, Berkowitz? Touch me and you'll get it, you and your scissors and all. Start something, I want you to start, *schneider-tukhess!*"

"You dare say that word again!" said Berkowitz.

"*Schneider-tukhess*. And listen to me, if this bloody hump on my back was as big as a camel, I'd still wear a jacket like the King of England, you *lump*, you rubbish. Come on, fight, have a go!"

Berkowitz was afraid of this terrible little hunchback, but he had his pride, so he put down his great shears and advanced.

"Come on, bring your scissors," said Solly Schwartz, standing on tiptoe to shout right into the big man's face.

Somebody moaned: "For God's sake, can't somebody stop them?"

"*Genug*, enough," said Pressburger. "Shame, shame, Mr. Berkowitz, shame!"

The sewing machines had stopped so that the whole place was still and everyone's ears were ringing with the silence of it. The tailoresses had turned on their stools, and were watching. One of them, an anæmic girl, came near to fainting, and had to be supported by another girl. Mr. Cohen, who was breakfasting in a back room, feeling the impact of the silence, came into the workshop with a buttered roll in his right hand and stood, inarticulate, gagged by a mouthful which he was trying to swallow. He heard several voices say: "Shush! Here's Mr. Cohen! Stop it!"

Then Solly Schwartz said: "I'll shush when I want to shush, and one of these days I'll put you all in a sack, you stinkers, and tie you up. . . . Pressburger, I don't mean you; you're a nice man. But *you*, Berkowitz, *you* I'll smash! Leave me alone, big as you are."

"What's the matter, what?" asked Mr. Cohen, who had swallowed his mouthful. "No fighting! Make friends, shake hands, do you hear?"

Solly Schwartz offered his hand. Reluctantly obedient to the master of the workshop Berkowitz took it. Everyone sighed with relief. Then Berkowitz screamed: "Let go! Let go!"

The hunchback seemed to have squeezed up the cutter's hand like an empty glove, in his powerful fist.

"That feels nice, Berkowitz?" he said. "My head you'll knock off? How do you like that, eh? I got a funny leg. Do you think I want to run races with you? I got a hump back, yes? Eh?"

"Let go. You're breaking my hand."

"What's the matter? A great big man like you, begging of a *schnip* like me I should let go his hand? What are we coming to?"

"Mr. Cohen," said Berkowitz, in agony, "tell him he should leave go."

"Schwartz, leave go!"

"With pleasure, Mr. Cohen. Just a minute . . . I tell you, Berkowitz, I got more than what you got. You got no hump. I got a hump. You ain't got a funny leg. I got a funny leg. And I got a hand, here, feel it?"

"Enough, enough!"

"Then say you're sorry."

"Say it, say it," said Mr. Cohen to Berkowitz.

"If Mr. Cohen says 'Say it,' I'll say it: I'm sorry."

"Who talks like that? Say: 'I'm sorry, Mr. Schwartz!'"

"All right. I'm sorry, Mr. Schwartz. Let go."

"*Na*, then, take your hand back," said Solly Schwartz releasing

82

his grip. Berkowitz's right hand was squeezed white and wrinkled. ". . . You told me to shake hands, Mr. Cohen, so I shook hands."

Berkowitz went and put his hand in one of the buckets of cold water in which the pressers moistened their linen pressing-rags, saying: "I can't work to-day. My hand is broken."

Cohen's first impulse, then, was to tell Berkowitz and Schwartz to go to the devil, but that would have been inconvenient. Berkowitz was a first-rate cutter, and in dealing with cutters one must take the rough with the smooth, because they are, in their way, artists, and rather temperamental. Little Schwartz, too, was an excellent workman, and a cripple, and an orphan as well. So Mr. Cohen said nothing more. Berkowitz, in awful silence, picked up his shears and wrapped them up in brown paper. This meant that he was sending in his resignation. But Pressburger, the man of peace, Pressburger, the diplomat of the sweat-shop, took him aside and persuaded him to stay. ". . . A fine man like you, Mr. Berkowitz, a lion! Why should you run away from a little boy, an orphan, a cripple? A man like you, Mr. Berkowitz! Have pity on him, the poor boy."

So Berkowitz unwrapped his shears and shouted: "Just this once—but never no more again!" and went back to his table. The tailoresses pedalled out their thunder while, in clouds of malodorous steam, the pressers banged the sweat that dripped from their foreheads into the finished and the half-finished clothes. Old Mr. Cohen listened to the din. He heard the uproarious machines, the raucous scrape of the iron gooses sliding out of the slotted stove, the heavy clangour of their return, the hiss of wet linen under hot iron, the voices of men screaming in order to be heard, *Quick, lazybones, damp me a rag! . . . Fill me up with water this basin, stinkpot, or else . . .* Sometimes, in some coincidental lull, he heard the chirping and snapping of busy scissors; at which he smiled as some men smile when they hear birds singing. He was happy. He asked for nothing but a little peace in the workshop.

He put on his hat and coat and went out to see a man about cloth. On the whole he was not displeased by the brouhaha of that morning. He chuckled when he thought of big, blustering Berkowitz squeezed into submission by the hand of a hunchback boy. He did not like Berkowitz. Mr. Cohen did not chuckle when he thought of Solly Schwartz: he smiled. It was impossible

not to admire that little monkey who was not afraid of hard work
—who was, indeed, magnificently indifferent to hard work—
who, banging his guts out, kept his sharp eyes fixed on something
out of sight, while he sang some strange song with only one word
and only one note:

> *Rer rer rer rer*
> *Rer rer rer rer*
> *Rer rer rer rer rer rer rer RER!*

Mr. Cohen felt a tenderness for Solly Schwartz. He wanted
to do something for him. One day, when work was done, and the
hunchback, having washed his hands and face, put on his winged
collar, satin tie, fancy waistcoat, and check coat, and was about to
limp away on his ivorine-handled cane, Mr. Cohen said: "Schwartz,
come back a minute. How old are you?"

"Nearly seventeen, Mr. Cohen. Why?"

"You're a presser. Look, Schwartz, why don't you learn the
cutting?"

"What for?"

"What *for*? To *be* something, to be a *somebody*. A good cutter
is like diamonds. What's the good of being a presser? What do
you make from it? Now a good cutter, he can make . . . anything he likes he can make, a good cutter. Learn the cutting,
Schwartzele"—Cohen used the diminutive; he was a fatherly
soul—"learn the cutting."

"You're a nice man, Mr. Cohen, and I won't forget it. But
I don't want to learn no tailoring, thank you."

"What's that?" asked Mr. Cohen, astonished.

"I don't want to learn it."

"What's the matter with it? Wherever you are in the world,
if you're a practical man, a good tailor, you can get a good
living."

"I know, Mr. Cohen, and so I don't want it. What's the good
of it? Look . . ." said Solly Schwartz. "I don't know how
to say it, but . . . say I'm in London or Timbuctoo, and I'm a
schneider. What'll I do? Get a living—sit down on my *schneider-
tukhess*, and stitch. Once a tailor always a tailor. You say to
yourself, you say: 'Well, well, I got something to fall back on.'
So you fall back on it. Mr. Cohen, I don't want to fall back, I
want to fall front. I know all about cutting."

84

"So you know!" said Mr. Cohen, half amazed and half angry. "You know already?"

"All I want to know, I know. I don't want nothing to fall back on."

"It could be one day so you might get married. Why not? And then what? I'm telling you this for your own good, Schwartz."

"I don't want to marry anybody. But even so. What if I did?"

"On twenty-five shillings a week, yes?"

"Mr. Cohen, tell me something, will you? If I'm no good as a presser, say so, tell me to get out."

"God forbid, Schwartz!"

"Why God forbid, Mr. Cohen? Are you afraid you won't find another presser? Don't be silly, Mr. Cohen. Pressers! *Schmattes!* God forbid you should kick out a lousy presser? You're keeping me for this—and this"—— he touched his hump, and made his iron foot ring on the floor. —"I appreciate it. I don't want no pity, Mr. Cohen, but I appreciate it. And one of these days you won't be sorry."

The old tailor raised his arms and let them fall again so that his hands bounced on his hips, and said: "If you want to press, press, I don't understand you, may I never move again if I drop down dead this minute, I don't understand you."

"Why should you? *I* understand me—what more do I want?" Tapping his employer's starched false shirt front with two strong fingers he added: "You mean good, so I'll tell you something. One of these days I'll make you a rich man."

Then he hobbled away, while Cohen, looking after him, touched himself on the forehead and sighed. If everything else was not enough, this poor creature was wrong in the head. The first time he saw Solly Schwartz, Cohen, a pious man, said under his breath the Hebrew Blessing that should be pronounced when one sees a monstrosity. And so now this abortion was going to make him rich. But Solly Schwartz went boldly on his way, his iron foot clanking, his cheap flashy cane rapping the pavement. As he went he hummed his weird tuneless song—*Rer rer rer*—dauntless, imperturbable, unabashed.

CHAPTER IX

SEVERAL months after this, one of Mr. Cohen's customers went broke three days before he was to have accepted delivery of twenty-four dozen pairs of trousers at five shillings a pair; dark trousers—the kind of trousers that city clerks and drapers' assistants could buy, in those days, for six-and-sixpence a pair. The slop-shops of the suburbs were choked with such merchandise. Trousers of that sort—sad, dark, coarse, respectable trousers— could be seen hanging like bunches of bananas under the gas- brackets and naphtha flares in every quarter of London. One big retailer in Tottenham cut the price of these trousers to five-and- ninepence, and gave every customer a glass of beer into the bargain. Shopmen and clerks wore them for everyday work in the office, and churchgoing artisans wore them for Sunday.

Cohen, therefore, found himself with two hundred and eighty- eight pairs of superfluous trousers, for which he was to have received seventy-two pounds. He cried to heaven, and then, taking a pair of trousers for a sample, went out without much hope to try and sell the lot at a cut price to some other dealer, but came back an hour or two later saying that he was ruined and threw the trousers into a corner of the workshop. Solly Schwartz picked them up and said: "Listen, Mr. Cohen, these trousers . . ."

"Trousers, schmousers—don't talk to me about trousers!"

"Mr. Cohen, do you want to sell this two gross pair of trousers?"

"What do you think I made two gross pair trousers for, to wear? I'll take sixty pound for the lot—fifty-five pund I'll take, for the lot, quick. What's it got to do with you?"

"Mr. Cohen, if I got rid of this here two gross trousers for you for fifty-five pound, would you give me a commission?"

"*You?* You get rid of these trousers? Don't be silly."

"What'll you give me, Mr. Cohen?"

Mr. Cohen, with a bitter laugh, said: "Look, Schwartz, get me these trousers off mein hands to-morrow and I'll give you a ten- pun-note. Trousers!"

"Done!" said Solly Schwartz.

Cohen looked at him, shaking his head. "Done. Done! *Done!*
I *been* done! I *am* done! . . . Get on with your work, less talk!"

"Done then," said Solly Schwartz, wielding the twelve-pound
goose.

One of the tailoresses whispered to her neighbour: "You wait
and see—he's got something up his sleeve."

So he had. That evening, before he dressed himself in his not
inconspicuous coat and put on his indecently showy necktie,
Solly Schwartz carefully pressed the pair of trousers that Mr.
Cohen had hurled into the corner and put them in a box. Then he
went brazenly to a gentlemen's clothing establishment in Clapham.
In those days shops were open until midnight. Refusing to take
no for an answer he was at last admitted to the little room in
which the proprietor sat in the hot glare of a hanging gaslight and
brooded over a litter of scribbled bill-heads and rows of hooked
wire files full of spiked sales-chits.

"Pardon the intrusion. You know me, I think. You remember
me? Or have you forgotten me?" said Schwartz.

No one forgets a lame man or a hunchback: the proprietor was
hesitant. He had, in fact, seen Solly Schwartz in Cohen's workshop, having had occasion to go there in connection with a large
order of boys' Norfolk suits. "Well, what do you want?" he
asked.

"I want to make a deal with you, Mr. Monopol. I want to
make a deal with you in the strictest confidence."

"Well, what is it? What d'you mean, confidence?"

Schwartz opened the box, smoothed the trousers on the table,
and said: "Now look, Mr. Monopol, look at this trouser. You're
in the business, I'm in the business, we're all in the business.
What I want you to do is, look at that trouser. Feel it. What
do you think of it?"

"It's a pair of trousers," said Mr. Monopol. "What do you
want me to do, dance a jig?"

"Now look. To a sensible man a word should be enough. I've
got twenty-four dozen pairs. You understand?" said Solly
Schwartz, winking.

"Well?"

"You can sell such trousers, Mr. Monopol?"

"I sell them, yes, I sell them. Where d'you get them?"

"Mr. Monopol, for God's sake, let us ask no questions and not
tell no lies. Listen: I can let you have this trouser for five-and-

threepence a pair, two gross, delivered to-night. Tell me one thing," said Solly Schwartz, hunching his shoulders and glancing furtively right and left, "tell me quick—are you interested?"

Now Monopol became strong and sly. He said: "Five-and-threepence? Madness! For this kind of stuff I wouldn't give you a penny more than three shillings."

"Five-and-threepence, Mr. Monopol, delivery to-night. Take it or leave it."

"Independent, eh?" said Monopol, with menace.

Simulating embarrassment, Solly Schwartz said: "All right, five shillings a pair."

Now Monopol began to feel that he had the affair in hand. He said: "Three shillings. Take it or leave it."

"Five shillings."

"Three shillings a pair," said Monopol, with a hard, tight smile. "You think I don't know where that stuff comes from?"

Only a thin matchboard partition stood between them and the busy shop. Their conversation, therefore, had been in undertones. Now Solly Schwartz raised a voice that rang from Monopol's office to the other side of the street. He shouted: "You know where it comes from? So do I! Stolen property, is that what you want for your dirty three shillings? What? You accuse me of selling stolen property so you can buy stolen property for three shillings? Aha, a receiver of stolen property, yes? To make extra profit out of your customers you want to sell them stolen property, eh? Answer me!"

"Shut up, you bloody fool, shut up!"

"You can't shut me up! Five shillings!"

"Ssh, ssh, take it easy."

Solly Schwartz said: "Look. Do you want these trousers for five shillings or don't you want these trousers for five shillings?"

"Lower your voice. Listen to reason. For five shillings I can't do it."

"All right, look, Monopol; make it four-and-nine, and done. And I can let you have the stuff to-night. I'll be along the back entrance quarter to one in the morning. Have £68 8s ready in cash. And you've got a bargain. Well?"

"No. It looks bad. Better send it to-morrow by Carter Paterson. Like that it looks better."

"No, better still, nine o'clock to-morrow morning I bring the stuff in a cart. If you like I'll give you my receipt, properly stamped. So you bought open and above board. Will that satisfy you?"

"No, look, I'll tell you what," said Monopol, "here's my address. Bring it to my private house to-night, in a cab, and do it like that. That way it's better."

"You got a bargain, Mr. Monopol, and I congratulate you. I'll be there."

That night Solly Schwartz arrived at Monopol's house in a four-wheeler, out of which a big man with a kicked-in face dragged twelve packages, each containing two dozen pairs of trousers. Monopol handed over the money in gold and silver. Solly Schwartz gave him a stamped receipt on one of Mr. Cohen's bill-heads. After the cab had rattled away Monopol looked at the trousers he had bought, and hung his head. They were exactly like the trousers Solly Schwartz had shown him so secretively in the shop. Unquestionably they were up to sample, only they were nothing but ordinary trousers such as he might have bought in broad daylight in the open market for four-and-sixpence a pair! Mrs. Monopol, hearing her husband's voice loudly requesting God Almighty to strike the hunchback dead, came down in her nightdress and found him standing on one foot, and holding up a pair of trousers by one leg, saying through his teeth: "Four-and-nine, four-and-nine, four-and-nine!"

"What is it, for God's sake?"

"Nothing. I've been swindled by a crook, that's all. Go back to bed."

And he sat smoking cigarettes and brooding until four o'clock in the morning. How could he have been such a fool? Monopol had been in the gents' outfitting business forty-five years, and knew the value of a garment to a fraction of a penny; he was one of the shrewdest buyers in the trade. Should he go with his wife to Bournemouth for a week or two? Should he sell the business and retire? Since he had enough put by to live in luxury for the rest of his life, was there any sense in driving himself mad with work? If he was going crazy, losing his grip, he would ruin himself if he carried on. Tenderly pressing his aching head he saw himself buying workmen's socks for eightpence three farthings a pair and paying four-and-six a dozen for celluloid collars.

He had to unlock the sideboard and pour himself a glass of brandy to steady his nerves. After that he began to reason.

The hunchback had cheated him. If he had come in the daytime offering his trousers for sale, Monopol would have known what they were worth. Furthermore, he would have guessed that these trousers were superfluous stock left on the hands of some manufacturing tailor who was glad to get rid of them at any price; and he could have got them for as little as thirty-six shillings a dozen. But this devilish hunchback had bewitched him with his furtive gestures and subtle whispers under the hissing gaslight —tricked him into believing that he was buying a bargain in stolen property. Monopol had made many such bargains in his time, and no doubt the hunchback knew it. "I deserve it. It serves me right. God punished me," said Monopol, and went to bed.

* * * * *

Solly Schwartz kept thirteen pounds eight shillings for himself and, next day, offered Mr. Cohen fifty-five golden sovereigns with a great flourish. Cohen, who was at breakfast, asked: "Who did you sell them to, who?"

"I sold them to Monopol," said Solly Schwartz.

"Monopol? For fifty-five pounds to *Monopol* you sold them trousers? No jokes?"

"There's the fifty-five pounds, in cash, Mr. Cohen. What about my ten?"

"Take it, take it!" said Mr. Cohen, with a bewildered gesture. "But Monopol! That *khazza*, he'd . . . he'd . . . he'd shave hair off an egg. He paid you fifty-five pounds cash?"

Balancing his ten golden pounds in his hand, Solly Schwartz said: "He paid me four-and-ninepence a pair, Mr. Cohen."

"What? And where's the rest of the money?"

"You said you'd be glad to take fifty-five pound for the rubbish, Mr. Cohen; you said it'd be worth a ten-pun-note to you if I sold it for you. I sold it, you got your fifty-five pound, I got my ten-pun-note—what more do you want?"

"Then twenty-three, twenty-four pounds you put in your pocket, eh?"

"That's right, Mr. Cohen. What difference should it make to you if it was a thousand? I got you what you asked for."

"*Gonof!*" cried Mr. Cohen. "Thief!"

Solly Schwartz laughed. "Why *gonof*, Mr. Cohen? How do you make me out a thief? What did I steal from you? I sold your *schmattes*, your rags, I took my commission, and that's that. How can you call me a *gonof?*"

Shrugging helplessly, Cohen said: "What I want to know is, how did you get four-and-nine a pair from Monopol, how—tell me!"

Smiling the smile of Scapin, Solly Schwartz replied: "Mr. Cohen, there are ways and means."

The news ran through the workshop. A voluptuous button-hole-maker, a notorious coquette, said: "Take me out to-night, Mr. Schwartz?"

He answered scornfully: "What do you take me for? I should waste time taking you out? What good'd that do me? Take you out—what for? Do I work to entertain you? Don't make me laugh. Supposing I took you out . . ."

"Well, and supposing?" the buttonhole-maker asked.

Solly Schwartz's laugh was clear and free from bitterness as he replied: "Ask yourself a question, dearie: did you want me to take you out yesterday? No. Why do you want me to take you out to-day? Don't be a foolish girl. For a bit of hokey-pokey ice cream and a bit of rubbish in a music hall you want to be seen with *me?* And then when everybody laughs at you you've got to tell them you did it for a joke? You don't want *me* to take you out, me dear, you just want to *go* out. . . . Here, Samuels," he said, throwing a half-sovereign to a stalwart young presser with fine wavy hair, "take her out. Eat a hokey-pokey, sing, dance! Me, I'm busy."

Samuels balanced the little gold coin on the tip of a finger and looked hesitantly from Solly Schwartz to the buttonhole-maker. She, forcing a laugh, said: "All right," and stooped low over her sewing to hide her red face.

Then there was some laughter, and a machinist called Fat Gittele, an ugly woman who was notorious for her poisonous tongue, said: "See what it is to have *mazzel?* He makes all the money, and then all the pretty girls run after him. Let me touch him for luck," and she touched the hump on his back. At this everyone in the workshop got up and touched Solly Schwartz for luck—everyone except Pressburger, who, with an embarrassed smile and an apologetic gesture, said: "They don't mean no harm, Solly, take no notice."

But Solly Schwartz, calmly jingling a handful of gold, said: "Much obliged, Mr. Pressburger. Much I care what they mean. Let 'em touch. I should worry."

An old tailoress whispered: "It's a shame to make a mock of the boy."

Solly Schwartz, who had the ears of a dog, heard her and said, with an easy laugh: "That's all right, Mrs. Ashkenazer. I may not be a beauty like all these Sandows, all these Hackenschmidts, all these Ellen Terrys, these Jersey Lilies. But I'll be riding in my carriage in Piccadilly when they're still scratching bug bites on their *tukhesses* in Back Church Lane. Wait and see, Mrs. Ashkenazer. . . . Quick, catch! Buy sweets for the children!" He flipped a sovereign across the workshop with such nice aim that it fell into her lap. Then he put the rest of his money in his pocket and went back to work singing *Rer rer rer rer, rer rer rer rer, rer rer rer rer rer rer rer RER.*

So young Samuels took the voluptuous buttonhole-maker to a music hall, but they did not enjoy their evening. The gay gaslit streets seemed to swarm with little men and hunchbacks. All conversation crept around to Solly Schwartz, with whose money they were uneasily trying to enjoy themselves. Solly Schwartz had taken possession of the city. When Little Tich hopped on the stage, they exchanged guilty glances: that comical, deformed dwarf was wearing a fantastic coat and a glass diamond as big as a walnut. When, later, they walked in the park in the moonlight and the shadows, even the grass wore black-and-white check, and was afflicted with humps, and Marble Arch was bow-legged. The yellow moon was a gold coin contemptuously tossed into the sky. A humpy cloud leaned for support upon a tree that reminded them of Solly Schwartz's walking-stick. They parted glumly before midnight. Twelve months later they married, and went to South Africa. There was no news of them until 1936. In the spring of that year one of Mr. Cohen's tailors who had also emigrated and grown prosperous, sitting in the dining-room of the best hotel in Johannesburg, overheard a petulant exchange of words between a man and his wife at an adjacent table.

The woman said: "Why shouldn't we have proper champagne for a change?"

The man said: "What do you want of my life? The soup's too thin, the meat's too thick, the sugar's too sweet, the pepper's too peppery, and now the wine doesn't suit you. Why don't you go and ask your humpback to take you out?"

The visitor started, stared, and cried: *"Samuels!"*

*   *   *   *   *

Schwartz put his money in the bank, keeping only two pounds for his immediate use. He spent fifteen shillings on a fashionable hat and bought a pair of lemon-coloured gloves for five shillings; gave a two-shilling piece to each of his landlady's five children, and then went out to squander ten shillings in the West End. He ate wienerschnitzel and drank two seidels of dark Munich beer at Appenrodt's; drank coffee and liqueurs at the Café Royal; rode in a hansom cab to Hyde Park Corner, and walked in the park for an hour, admiring, without envy, the great straight-backed guardsmen who strutted, glorious in scarlet and magnificently moustachioed, each with an eager girl clinging to his arm. The shadows under the trees were full of amorous noises. Near the bandstand a woman accosted him, offering herself for a shilling. Solly Schwartz gave her a shilling and said: "If I want to make myself ill I can go and sit in a draught free of charge. Here you are, there's your shilling. Do you want another shilling?"

"Of course I do."

"All right. Tell me how much you make a week."

"That depends," said the woman, cautiously.

"What does it depend on?" She did not know, so he continued: "Take a good week. What do you make in a good week?"

"It's hard to say."

"All right. What did you make in your *best* week?"

"Once a gentleman gave me a sovereign in mistake for a shilling."

"What for do you do it? Why?"

"I was unlucky——"

"Nobody's unlucky. Here's another shilling. Go and rot."

Taking the shilling she said, resentfully: "You don't realise— a girl *can* be unlucky."

"Go away. Go to hell. . . . Wait a minute, here, take another shilling," said Solly Schwartz.

She took it and, quickly calculating the length of his arm and his walking-stick, walked a couple of yards backwards and said: "Humpy bastard!"

"Good-night," said Solly Schwartz, and went to sit on an empty bench by the Serpentine, because he found peace in contemplating the cool moonlight touching the tremulous water.

Later he went home in an omnibus, hopped off a hundred yards from the "Three Nuns", Aldgate, and walked through several dark and dangerous streets before he reached the house in Laurel Yard where he lived in a room for which he paid three-and-six-pence a week.

He took off his new hat, smoothed it with his sleeve, and put it where he could see it when he awoke in the morning; wiped his walking-stick with the palm of his right hand, and balanced it in a corner; took off his iron boot and cooled his deformed foot in a basin of cold water. Then, singing *Rer rer rer rer, rer rer rer rer, rer rer rer rer rer rer rer RER*, he undressed and went to bed. The mattress was full of hollows. He fumbled for the deep indentation that fitted his hump, eased himself into it, and relaxed. From a distance came a clatter and rattle of hoofs and wheels. He thought of carriages, and grinned. The lady in the next room made noisy use of a chamber-pot. *And from this we come*, said Solly Schwartz, with a scornful smile. The Irishman who lived in the house next door came home, drunk, melancholy, and musical.

A bedbug bit Solly Schwartz in the softest part of his left ankle. But he, smiling in the dark, did not feel the bite. Half a minute passed before he became aware of it, and then he said: "I should get up from my comfortable bed for *you?* If I chase you away you'll come back the minute I drop off to sleep. I should lose a night's sleep for a farthing's-worth of blood? Get away with you—do you take me for a fool? Good appetite. Good-night."

And he fell asleep smiling.

Several years later, Solly Schwartz of Stepney swaggered out with five pounds in his purse, to meet I. Small of Mayfair, who was nervously feeling one thin sixpence.

CHAPTER X

WITHOUT his walking-stick I. Small felt naked and defenceless.
With only sixpence in his pocket he felt humble and hopeless.
He was thoroughly depressed. Before he had walked fifty paces
—poking at the pavement with an imaginary stick and pausing,
embarrassed, to imprison his refractory right hand in his trousers
pocket—he was also attacked by an overwhelming sense of guilt.
He was going out like a Gentile, like a common navvy, to drink
beer with male friends while his wife languished in his absence.
If burglars broke in and murdered the woman and the child, how
could he forgive himself? At the corner of the street he turned
back, went home again, and unlocked the side door. Millie
screamed: "Who is it?"

Then I. Small, weak irresolute little man, impulsively locked the
door again and crept away, keeping close to the wall; for he had a
great yearning for friendly male company. Emotion choked him
when Solly Schwartz greeted him at their meeting place in
Piccadilly Circus; he shook hands fervently, with a lingering
grip, and his eyes filled with tears of delight as he cried: "Shloimele!
Solly! Boychik! Pleased to see you! You look well—smart!"

Solly Schwartz was, in fact, magnificent; visible from a considerable distance. He was dressed in a jacket-suit of black,
white and grey plaid check that seemed to be both deafening and
blinding like a thunderstorm. His collar was so high and stiff
that a newspaper boy had told him to look out for himself—if
he fell down it would cut his ears off—and his emerald-green
satin cravat was threaded through a gold ring half an inch wide,
set with a bloodstone as big as a shilling. A pearl-grey trilby hat,
excessively curled at the brim, was cocked over his right eye.
The glossily-starched cuffs of his shirt touched the balls of his
thumbs, and he was carrying an extraordinary walking-stick of
rich malacca with a gold band under an ivory head carved in the
shape of a naked woman. He was smoking a cigar. Passers-by,
too polite to turn their heads and stare, made elaborate detours
for the sake of another glance at him.

He said, easily: "Hello, hello, Srulkele! You're putting on weight already. You're getting fat. How comes?"

"Married life, Solly."

"How's the wife?"

"She's fine, bless her."

"The boy?"

"Bless him, he's lovely."

"How's business?"

"Slack. How is with you, Solly?"

With the thumb and forefinger of his right hand Solly Schwartz delicately picked up an imaginary grain of sand, cocked the little finger, smiled, and said: "Like that!'

"You deserve it," said I. Small.

"You wait and see, Srulkele, I'll show you a thing or two. Now, what would you like to do? I'll tell you what we'll do. We'll have a drink in the Criterion. Then we'll go and have a snack at Appenrodt's. Then we'll go to the Alhambra. That's what you'd like to do. That's what I'd like to do. So we'll do it. Come on."

I. Small's face was red and hot as he fumbled his sixpence and stammered: "I . . . I . . . a glass beer, a little chat. . . ."

"Don't be silly, Srulke, come on."

I. Small confessed: "I can't afford it, Solly."

"Who asked you to, *schlemihl?* I can. Come on."

"I came out in a hurry. In a hurry I came out, so my purse I left behind."

"Don't worry, Srulke, I didn't leave my purse behind. What's the matter with you? How many times did you treat me when I was young?"

"You're an old man already?" said I. Small, half laughing.

"Twenty-three last birthday. No arguments. Come."

They went to the Criterion, and drank brandy and soda. Looking at them, other customers wondered why such a handsome, erect young man should associate with a preposterously-clothed leering hunchback. Solly Schwartz gesticulated and bounced in his chair, while I. Small sat, calm and pale. One waiter whispered to another: "I bet you the Hump is trying to sell the Gent a few photographs."

Solly Schwartz was saying: "Pull yourself together Srulkele. Be a man. What do you take me for, an idiot? Look at you—look at yourself. You put on weight from good cooking, you liar.

You've got a fat belly and a miserable face. How old are you?
Twenty-seven. What is it? What's the matter? Tell me."

"Nothing. Nothing's the matter. Can't you leave a man alone?"

"Is it the wife? Yes, it's the wife—she gives you a nice time of it, no?"

"She's a good wife, Solly, and don't you daren't say a word!"

"Right you are, Srulkele, not one word. . . . Waiter, the bill!"

They walked to Appenrodt's, and I. Small, dragging himself out of a sucking quicksand of misery, came up with a sort of spiritual *pop*, and said: "What's with you boychik? Tell me. You're like a son to me."

"Thanks all the same, Srulke, I don't want no fathers. I had one. What's with me? You want to know?"

"You still with Cohen?"

"I left. I'm going into business."

"Business? What business?" asked I. Small alarmed.

"Tin cans," said Solly Schwartz.

"For God's sake, Shloimele, what do you mean, tin cans?"

"You'll see. Don't worry. Here's Appenrodt's. A snack, Srulke, a snack."

The brandy was working in I. Small's head. He said, almost tearfully :"Like old times, eh, Solly? But . . . but I left my purse . . ."

"Again purse, purse, purse? You know where you can *shtip* your purse? Come on." When they were seated he asked: "What do you fancy? Don't tell me, I know. You fancy a nice plate of ham—that's what you fancy."

I. Small giggled. This was his secret lust, his guilty Passion. He loved to eat the forbidden flesh of the swine. Solly Schwartz had corrupted him to this vice. Whenever he closed his lips over a furtive forkful his mouth filled with saliva, his eyes closed in ecstasy, and a pleasurable shudder ran from the base of his skull, all the way down his spine—he felt as a fallen Christian might feel, who cuts the throat of a black goat at midnight, says the Lord's Prayer backwards, and offers homage to Asmodeus.

The ham intoxicated him more than the great pots of Munich beer with which they washed it down. They sweetened their mouths with apfel strudel, and drank more beer. Then Solly Schwartz called for brandy, and they solemnly drank each other's health. An invisible hand had pulled a warm woolly film over

97

I. Small's eyes and ears so that he saw and heard as it were through downy fluff. He was very happy. "Tell me, Solly-leben, what was you talking about, what? Tin cans! What for a joke is tin cans?" He laughed uproariously.

"I met a man with a new process. I'm going to handle it."

"Process? What's process? Solly, I'm older than you," said I. Small, solemnly, "so take advice from me. No process! A man should stick to a steady trade."

"A *schneider* can stick to his bench until his trousers stick to his *tukhess*. I'm finished with the workshop from now, I'm on my own. Another brandy?"

"Not another drop, I swear."

"Waiter, two brandies! . . ."

"I mean for your good, Solly, believe me. You're young, you've got a lot to learn yet. Processes . . . tin cans . . . keep a steady job. Settle down."

"Look who's talking!" said Solly Schwartz, contemptuously. "What marvels have you done? Look who's giving me advice. If you'd taken my advice, *stuck narr*, you'd be doing all right now. Why didn't you get one of those machines, like I told you? But no, they want to be gentlemen on their two *groschen*—shop-keepers! Gah! Have you lost your memory? *I* told *you* to stick to *your* trade. Me, I've got no trade, I'll make a trade, I'll make a million pounds. Do me a favour, Srul, don't give *me* advice."

"I was going to get a machine," said I. Small unhappily, "I was. But . . . one thing, another thing . . ."

"Don't upset yourself, Srulke," said Solly Schwartz, pinching I. Small's cheek and smiling. "Drink up."

"What do people want of me? What do they want of my years? What do they want of my life? What do they want me to do? Leave me alone, for God's sake, you and your, your, your tin cans!"

"Can I get you anything more, gentlemen?" asked a waiter.

"A brandy for me and two black coffees," said Solly Schwartz.

I. Small had stumbled clean over the rim of sobriety: he sat unsteadily, rolling his eyes, stroking his moustache, and twirling his glass. Talking as a child talks to a doll, Solly Schwartz said: "Srul, Srulke, Srulkele, I'll put the whole bloody world in a tin can and solder it down. Wait and see."

"I should go home. . . ."

"Drink your coffee first."

"When I think . . . when I think . . . a little boy with a . . . a . . ."

"Hump?"

"Was it *his* fault he had a little tiny hump?" asked I. Small angrily. ". . . And he puts down a golden sovereign and . . ."

I. Small drew himself back into one piece and said: "Excuse me, Solly. Excuse me. I must go home. The wife and child are alone."

Under the hot white lights he felt himself spreading, evaporating like a cast-up jellyfish in the sun, and had to pause while he scraped himself into shape. Solly Schwartz paid the bill, helped him to climb the stairs, and sat beside him after he had fallen into a hansom cab.

I. Small came home, unsteadily, at half-past eleven. Millie was waiting, rocking young Charles in her arms, while a simmering tea-kettle whispered on the stove. A carefully prepared meal was ready on the nicely-laid table.

"I'm glad he's enjoyed himself. That's all I wanted to know," she said.

"Ah, Millie, Millie!"

"Go on, eat—*fress*—that's all he thinks of!"

"I'm not hungry. I'm sorry."

"So now my cooking isn't good enough for him," said Millie to the kettle.

I. Small staggered and fell heavily into a chair, feebly murmuring: "Millie, Millie. . . ."

"The minute he left the house burglars came and opened the door, and I had to frighten them away, while he—and he calls himself a man—was roaming about with humpbacks and prostitutes, spending every penny on——" She paused, horrified; sniffed, raised her streaming eyes to the gas-bracket, and wailed: "—This is all I'm short of! He drinks!"

But I. Small had fallen asleep in his chair. When he awoke at dawn Millie was still sitting, looking at him with inflamed eyes, twisting a tear-soaked handkerchief. The evening meal, untouched, was still on the table. Starting awake, he leapt up; but something that felt like a red-hot poker hissed through his head from ear to ear, and he sat down again, moaning. His remorse was terrible, but even if he had known what to say he would not have known how to say it; so he pulled out his handkerchief and began to weep. With the handkerchief a fork came out

99

of his breast pocket, and fell to the floor with a rattling noise
that awoke little Charles, so that Millie ran away to soothe him.
She returned five minutes later with the two-year-old child in
her arms and said in a voice that lifted the hair at the nape of her
husband's neck: "Good-morning, Srul. I hope you're all right.
I nearly called the doctor. Have a cup of tea. I was waiting for
you to wake up—I kept the kettle on all night."

"Millie . . ."

"It's all right. As long as I know what you are, it's all right,
Srul. Well, I made a mistake, that's all. Who am I to interfere
with his pleasures?" she said, weeping. ". . . What difference
does it make if burglars break in and murder his wife and child,
as long as he's got his friends?"

"Millie, I——"

"—But another man wouldn't have the heart to leave his wife
alone and go out drinking, in the state I'm in."

"What state, what?" asked I. Small, in terror.

"Nothing. What does he want to know for?"

"Tell me, for God's sake!"

"You know. Don't pretend you don't know."

"I *don't* know! Say!"

"It's nothing much. I'm going to have another baby, that's all."

I. Small roared: "What? Since when?"

"Three months."

"Millie!" said I. Small, smiling until the points of his moustache
touched his cheek-bones.

"Go on, laugh. Now I know what he is—I kill myself for him
and he laughs in my face."

"May I be——"

"—Ssh! I've had trouble enough with *this* one all night while
the drunkard was snoring away like a house on fire. What fork
is that?"

I. Small picked it up and turned it over saying: "Millie, so sure
should I live, I don't know."

"*Appenrodt's*," she said, reading the name stamped on the
handle. "So that's it. So now we know. He gets blind drunk
and steals forks. He'll end up in prison——"

"—Forks, shmorks—to bleddy beggary miv forks, Millie!
Tell me, no jokes—*are* you? Honest?"

"Jokes? For him it's a joke. They get all the pleasure; it's
the woman who pays," said Millie, quoting one of the pithiest

apophthegms of the heroine of *Broken Hearts*. "Go and steal forks!"

"No, Millie, listen," said I. Small, cautiously stroking her shoulder. "It would be nice, p'raps, this time a liddle girl?"

"Girls. That's all he thinks of. If you want girls you know where to find them. You don't want my help."

"Millie, Millie, don't be like that."

"Get away from me. Stealing forks. Any minute, now, we'll have policemen in the house. Oh, I'll be so ashamed!"

"It was a . . . a . . . a accident, I made a mistake. What for do I want a fork, what for?"

"Yes, that's what he is. In Cracow they'd rather eat with their fingers, like uncivilised beasts."

"Who said fingers? What for would I steal forks? Isn't there forks in the house, I should go steal forks?"

"Forks in the house. That's what they are. Give them half a dozen forks, and they think they're rich. Go on as you're going on, and you'll see if you've got forks in the house. Drink them all away, go on, much I care!"

"It was a misunder, a mistook!" cried I. Small, throwing the fork into the fire. Millie took it out with the tongs and said:

"He steals forks to throw into the fire. A drunkard, a burglar, a madman—it's all right, as long as I know what he is."

She wiped the fork carefully, saying something about catching diseases from it, and put it in a drawer. Later, she washed it in carbolic, boiled it, and used it in the kitchen. It was a very fine fork, made to last for ever. Sometimes it found its way on to the dining-room table. When Charles Small enquired how one of Appenrodt's forks had come into the house, his mother shook her head and said: "Ask your father." His father, brushing up his moustache with the knuckle of a forefinger, smiled enigmatically and said: "Ask your mother." Young Charles used to dream of that fork: he liked to play with it when his mother was not looking. When she caught him, she took it away, and said cryptically: "That's who he's taking after. So that's what he's growing up to be."

Nearly fifteen years passed before Charles Small learned the history of the fork. Not once, in all those years, had I. Small dared to go out alone in the evening. Then Ruth fell ill. She lived in an elegant villa near Hove, where her husband, the estate agent, was supposed to be making money hand over fist, selling real estate in the neighbourhood of Roedean.

One fine day in July Millie, who had gone out to exchange a few hateful pleasantries and sisterly acrimonies with Becky, came home, quaking with shock, and cried: "Srul! Srul! Quick!"

"Millie, quick, tell me—what is it, what?"

"*Ruth!*"

"What's the matter, quick!"

"She's been taken bad."

"What am I, a doctor already?"

"Heartless. So that's what you are."

"God forbid. But what is it?"

"She's been taken to a nursing-home to have her womb scraped."

"*Oi!*" said I. Small, grey with horror. "Scraped?"

Charles Small was listening and he, too, was appalled. Scraped! He imagined Aunt Ruth's womb as something like the bowl of a pipe, a choked tobacco pipe as big as a pumpkin, being decarbonised with hammers and chisels by men in dungaree overalls; while I. Small thought in terms of vices and shoemaker's lasts gripped between hard knees, wooden-handled inward-cutting knives that seemed to beckon, and hoarse, coarse rasps—and his stomach turned

"Scraped!" he said, "scraped!"

"You see? Now, perhaps, you'll appreciate."

"But . . . scraping! Scraping—oi!" He thought of knives on the surfaces of glazed plates, dentists' instruments on teeth, files on iron. It was too much. He had to drink a glass of water.

"I must go at once," she said.

"But why go at once, Millie? What can you do?"

"You see, that's what they are. What can I do, he wants to know? I can . . ."

"Well?"

"I can . . . Oh, what's the use of talking to them? Isn't she my sister? What should I do, let her lie there?"

"What then? Pick her up? She's in a nursing-home. So she's not being looked after?"

"By strangers. But what's the use of talking if people are ignorant. She's my sister!"

"Then go."

"He's quick to say go. He's anxious to get rid of me. It's quite all right."

"Then don't go."

"I must go. God forbid, if anything happened, how would it look?"

"Is anybody else going?"

"Becky's coming with."

"Scraped," said I. Small, wincing at the thought. "Scraped! It makes you sick to think of it."

"Well, there you are. Men are selfish, what can you expect? That's what comes of selfishness."

"Hm. Well, God forbid I should stop you going to your sister. I'd like to come, but what about the shop? And the expense? You go with Priscilla. I'll stay here with Charlie."

"It's not for my pleasure I'm going," said Millie, defensively. "Only it's my duty. Blood's thicker than water."

I. Small nodded, and measured off half a yard of air in a gesture that seemed to say *at least that much thicker;* while his forehead wrinkled and his eyes half closed in an expression of intense spiritual anguish.

"And the child needs a bit of fresh air, Srul. She's not eating, she looks pasty. A girl of her age needs fresh air. . . . Don't look so miserable, I'll be back the day after to-morrow, please goodness."

"What must be, must be," said I. Small, sighing, "only I want you should take care of yourself."

Then Millie became so friendly that her husband was almost sorry that she was going. She prepared cold chicken and laid out as much salad-stuff as two hungry men might consume in a week, together with tinned salmon, sardines, and stewed fruit. She gave her husband and her son instruction in the art and mystery of frying an egg, and explained in detail the means whereby a kettle of water may be brought to boiling point on a gas-stove so that (if one had the knack, and the experience) it might be poured over a handful of tea in a teapot to make a liquid which, served in a teacup and mixed with sugar and milk, might turn out to be a cup of tea. . . . This thing here was a bread knife; that thing there was known as a loaf. All you had to do was, put the edge of the knife—the sharp edge, not the blunt edge—on the loaf, and keep on cutting until a piece of the loaf fell away. Then you had a slice of bread. It was simple, if you knew how to do it. The spreading of butter she had not time to explain, since her sister was lying in bed being scraped; but in an emergency it was permissible simply to take a little butter on the end of a knife and smear it over the bread, to make the crude likeness of bread-and-butter. . . .

At last she went away with the girl Priscilla, and Charles Small was alone with his father for the first time in his life.

At first they had little to say to each other. I. Small fidgeted uncomfortably, while his son moodily fingered the *Westminster Gazette*. At last the father said: "Well, Charley, what's the latest?" When Charles told him that most of the news was of Lloyd George, President Wilson, and Clemenceau, he nodded knowingly and said weightily, "Now there's clever men, politicians. Take a lesson from them. Read the paper and . . . and . . . read the paper. A Welshman. But he worked his way up to be Prime Minister. See, Charley?"

. . . Remembering this Charles Small understands, now, that his father, then, was trying to light the way to glory. And he thinks of a tired man before dawn, less than half awake, who has lost his bearings in his own bedroom, groping after a box of matches. . . . Somewhere in two thousand cubic feet of darkness there is a matchbox, and in that matchbox one last thin match. He gropes and fumbles, reaching for the light, until, having stumbled and hurt himself, he grows angry and rages impotently against the dark—the dark that keeps still and waits. . . . Charles Small understands this now.

But then, when I. Small said: "He was a Welshman, but he wanted to be a somebody. So he studied for a solicitor and look at him now—Premier. The Premier is bigger than the King. You see? When Lloyd George was a bit of a boy, and his mother and his father said: 'Lloydel, it's already time to think of a trade'—d'you think he said: 'Mummy, Daddy, I want to be Prime Minister?' Don't you believe it! He said: 'I'll learn a proper trade and take up the politics, p'raps, as a side-line.' "

"Oh, stop it!"

"Believe me, Charley, you're young yet—you got to learn yet," said I. Small. "You heard of Disraeli? Take a lesson from——"

"Father, talk about something else," said young Charles, screwing the *Westminster Gazette* in two, and throwing the twisted pieces on to the floor.

Now if his mother had been present then there would have been trouble. She would have given his father a knowing look and said: "You see what he is? A madman! Who does he take after? Thank goodness he doesn't get it from me."

Then I. Small, black with rage, would have shouted: "Who then from does he get it? From *me?*"

So, like a couple of dabchicks hunting worms in a shallow, stagnant pond, Mr. and Mrs. Small would have scratched up mud until everything was black.

Charles Small waited for something to happen. When his father said: "I mean for your good, Charley," he ran to his room and lay on his bed in the twilight staring at the grey ceiling. A mouse scuffled in the wall. A fly droned. Several streets away a motor-horn honked insistently while a drunken woman laughed in the road below. There was a chirming and cooing and twittering of vulgar, dusty Cockney sparrows and pigeons settling down to sleep. "Dusk," said young Charles, dramatically, "dusk. . . ." Then he quoted:

> So be my passing!
> My task accomplished and the long day done,
> My wages taken, and in my heart
> Some late lark singing,
> Let me be gathered to the quiet west
> The sundown splendid and serene,
> Death . . .

Then downstairs a chair fell over, a plate smashed, and I. Small's voice reverberated through the house: "Dem bleddy beggary! Beggar you, you bandit! Murderer, come here at once! I'll cut you to smidereens, I'll break you off the legs!"

"You can't frighten me," said young Charles, in a dramatic undertone. "Blow, rage, crack your cheeks! I defy you."

"I'll murder you, you bleddy murderer!" cried I. Small, in a voice that shook flakes of plaster from the ceiling. "Wait. Wait there, I'll get a knife. As long as I know what you are!"

"'There is no terror, Cassius, in your threats, for I am armed so strong in honesty they pass me by like the idle wind which I respect not' . . . you old bluffer," said young Charles.

Then I. Small came upstairs, opened the bedroom door and whispered: "Charley, are you asleep? Yes or no?"

"Yes."

"You shouldn't read in the dark. It's bad for the eyes to read if you can't see to read."

Curling a contemptuous lip, the boy said: "If I can't see to read, obviously, I can't be reading."

I. Small lit the gas and Charles saw him standing under the gas bracket holding a plate of chicken. His left hand was tied up in a bloodstained handkerchief.

"What's the matter with your hand, Father? Did you cut it?"

If Millie had been there I. Small would probably have told him to talk bleddy sense, arguing at the top of his voice that if he had not cut his hand it wouldn't be bleeding. But now, in the tones of an ordinary human being, he said: "It's nothing, Charley. That bleddy fowl. The knife was blunt, so it slipped, so I got a proper knife and cut it up. I cut it up all right! You wait and see. Go on, Charley, eat something. Eat, grow, go on—eat it all up."

"But you cut yourself, you're bleeding."

"Take no notice—eat, Charley. A cut here, a cut there, what's the difference? All my life I been cutting myself."

As his father said this an invisible hand came out of the shadows, took young Charles by the throat, and shook a sob out of him. He turned to the wall to hide his face.

'Charley, what is it now? Tell me, now what did I say wrong? Now what did I do?"

"Nothing."

"Charley, it's a terrible thing you should be like this—terrible!" I. Small, exploring his imagination for consolatory words, felt as he had felt one day in a tramcar, when the conductor punched his ticket and he remembered that he had left his purse in his other trousers and sat stammering, wordless, penniless, burning with shame. "Go on, Charley, eat up. To-morrow is also a day."

"To-morrow and to-morrow and to-morrow creeps in this petty pace from day to day to the last syllable of recorded time and all our yesterdays have lighted fools the way to dusty death. . . . I couldn't touch a thing."

"Believe me, Charley, everything is for the best," said I. Small, unhappily, "and . . . and . . . and what is done is done, believe me!"

"Father, please leave me alone," said young Charles, burying his face in his pillow.

He felt something warm on the nape of his neck and caught a whiff of tobacco. His father must have kissed the back of his head.

Later, when I. Small's heavy footsteps died away and the

bedsprings cried themselves to sleep in the bedroom below, he sat up and considered the chicken and bread-and-butter on the table. The fowl was neatly but unconventionally carved. On the left-hand side of the plate lay the Appenrodt fork; on the right, a cobbler's knife. This struck young Charles as humorous. He thought of the old man throwing down the blunt carver, taking up the tool to which he was accustomed, sitting on a hard chair in the kitchen and shaping a cold chicken which he was gripping between his knees. The thought made him laugh. There was a spot of blood on the gold rim of the plate. He wiped it off with a bit of crust; ate heartily, turned out the light and slept dreamlessly.

Next day, when he had carried the plate down to the kitchen, and they were eating burnt and broken fried eggs and drinking underdone tea, he said: "Come on, Father, tell me—as man to man, where *did* you get that fork?"

It was Sunday morning, and I. Small was in a carefree mood. He was wearing his best clothes, his lowest collar, and his gayest tie. His eyes were bright; a certain cheerful contraction of the muscles in his face had sent his coppery moustache springing up in a fine curve, so that you felt that if you plucked at it it would give out a resonant golden twanging note.

He laughed, and said: "Aha, boychik—swear not never to say a word, and I might p'raps tell you. It was when I was young and foolish. Thank God I know better now. It was when you was a child in arms, Charley . . . Oi, was that a night! I'm lucky I'm here now alive to tell the tale. The madness you get up to, when you're young and don't know no better! There was nearly Scotland Yard detectives in the house. Your mother, bless her, she doesn't like to think of it—and quite right too. It was something terrible, Charley, I tell you. To tell you the honest truth, then I was wild like a wild beast, like a mad dog, like . . . like a lion in the zoo. I was young, Charley, foolish. I was uneducated. You've got an education, so there's no need you should be a madman like I was. Oi, what we got up to!"

"Go on, tell me."

"P'raps I better not."

Charles Small, sixteen and a half years old, said: "Oh, come on, Father—man to man—tell us."

If Millie had been present then, I. Small would have thundered: "Man to man? What, so he's a man already, that *schnip*? The bleddy cheek of it! Let them learn to wipe their noses before they call themselves men!"

But now the phrase pleased him. He gave his son a suggestive, intimate dig in the ribs, and told him in fantastic detail the history of Appenrodt's fork. Into this history he threw all he had ever heard of high life and dissipation. The story started somewhat sheepishly:

". . . Well, as man to man, it was nothing much. It was nothing much, as man to man . . ." Seeing that his son looked disappointed, I. Small scoured the stockpot of imagination and scraped the bones of fancy. In a solemn, dramatic voice, he went on: "Me and my friend Mr. Schwartz, we went one night to the Criterion. You, Charley, you were not born or thought of. Well, born, yes. Thought of, you wasn't. No, wait a minute— I didn't had your education—you was thought of, day and night. That was the days! So Mr. Schwartz and me, we went to the Criterion, in Piccadilly. And you should have seen who was there!" I. Small pursed his lips and whistled. ". . . Actors, with actresses, artists, gentlemen, designers, politicians, lords and ladies, Rothschild, everybody you can think of. Do you hear, Charley? Boxers, Hackenschmidt, T. E. Dunville, dukes, duchesses everybody!"

"As man to man, Father, was Mother there?"

"As man to man, Charley, no. Your mother, bless her, was at home with you, because you was a baby in arms. You wasn't born or thought of, practically. You was a backward child. You was still teeding—day and night you screamed murder with your teet. They wouldn't come out from your gunks, Charley. It wasn't your fault, it was your misfortune. Your poor mother——"

"I've heard all that before about ten thousand times, Father. Go on about the fork."

"This should be a lesson to you, Charley," said I. Small, solemnly. Then he proceeded to give an account of that unforgettable evening. He suggested that he and Solly Schwartz had practically sacked the West End of London, leaving no window unbroken and no maiden unravished. He exposed himself as a drink-crazed hooligan abominably devoid of conscience—a sort of Mohock who had gone roaring and ravaging from the Criterion to the Quadrant and back again, scattering torn-up policemen in his wake as a runner in a paper-chase scatters paper. Maddened with liquor he had destroyed restaurants, uprooted lamp-posts, whistled after girls and made a perfect beast of himself. He made it clear that if the mounted police had not been called out he might have put an end once and for all to law and order. But luckily for him, seventeen or eighteen strong men subdued him. They may or may not have tied him with ropes—these details slip out of memory.

One thing is certain, and that is that I. Small came home and found one of Appenrodt's forks in his outside breast pocket.

At the conclusion of his terrific narrative he began to laugh, and his son laughed with him. When they stopped laughing he said: "Eat another egg, Charley."

"No thanks, I can't eat more than two."

"Then shall I tell you what we'll do?"

"What?"

"I'll tell you what—you and me, let's go to Kew. Go on, Charley, put on your new suit. Your other suit put on, and we'll go to Kew Gardens. Hurry up."

Young Charles Small dressed himself in a pepper-and-salt Norfolk suit, and they took a tramcar to Kew. Young Charles discovered, with astonishment, that he was beginning almost to like the old man.

They walked in the Gardens for an hour, visiting all the hothouses. Large white flowers aroused in I. Small a strange, strong, tender emotion: his eyes filled with tears when he looked at a Victoria Lily; and when he gazed up at the feathery head of a stately palm tree he struck himself on the chest and sighed— "Look at it, Charley. Look and . . . and . . . and take a lesson." He stood several minutes before the bronze statue of the bowman, and started to say something: "That's a . . . that's a . . ." Poor man, he had no words. At last they left the Gardens. The teashops outside were advertising strawberries and cream.

"Do you fancy a strawberry, Charley?"

"I wouldn't mind," said young Charles haughtily; and so they went and ate strawberries and cream. I. Small pushed his portion over to his son. After the bill was paid they walked over Kew Bridge and stopped at a little fair-ground where there were swings and merry-go-rounds.

I. Small said: "What about a ride on the roundabout?"

Charles Small, at sixteen and a half, was above such frivolity, but it was obvious that the old man was dying to go up and down and around and around on the saddle of a spotted wooden horse; so he said, scornfully: "All right, Father, if you like." Then they rode four times on the roundabout, and swung three times on the swings.

"Foolishness," said I. Small, laughing. "*Kinderspiel*—baby-games! Tell me, Charley, are you hungry?"

"Well . . ."

"Let's eat something, let's."

There was a superior sort of public-house across the road. They went in, sat down, and looked at the menu.

"What do you fancy, Charley, boychik?"

"Well I don't know, what do *you* fancy, Father?"

"What does it say?" asked I. Small, whose eyes were getting weak.

"Well, there's soup, cold ham and tongue, there's——"

"Ham? I wonder what ham tastes like? *Ham!* What sort of a thing *is* ham, I wonder," said I. Small. "I tell you what, just for a joke, shall we taste it—just a taste—just to see?"

"Why yes, I don't mind."

"Man to man? Not a word, eh? Just to taste?"

"By all means," said young Charles.

"It's nice to know what people see in it. . . . Ham! What'll we drink? A nice glass lemonade? Or I tell you what—what's the matter with a glass beer? Man to man, Charley, what do you say—a glass beer? In moderation everything is good. Even deadly poison in moderation is good. Too much of a good thing can be poison. Everything in moderation. A glass beer." When the ham was served he said: "It looks like smoked salmon. What does it taste like to you, Charley?"

"Like ham."

"It's funny, but by me it's like smoked salmon."

They ate their ham, drank their beer, and became friends. When they had finished eating and had, between them, drunk a pint and a half of beer, young Charles said: "Father, tell me something about yourself—tell me something about your life."

"My life," said I. Small, startled. "What d'you mean?"

"Things must have happened to you. After all you're middle-aged—more than forty years old. Why don't you tell me all about yourself?"

Time passed before I. Small said: ". . . My father made boots for a Graf. In English, that's the same as a Lord. Well, one day I had to take a pair boots to this Graf, and he got hold of me by the hair and shook me up and down and backwards and forwards, and I started crying, and he gave me a silver rouble . . . And . . . and . . . What do you mean, Life?" said I. Small, irritated. "Life! What time have I had for Life? What do they take me for, a Piccadilly Johnny, Life I should have?"

Then he said: "Charley, don't take too much notice of every word I say. Would you like I should tell you? Then take a lesson from me. Listen: I'm ignorant. Man to man"—I. Small had taken a fancy to this expression—"man to man say nothing to nobody, man to man. I'm ignorant. You know more than I know. I know more than my father knew, rest his soul. And so it goes on, Charley, so we go, and there's the world. Look at me. What am I? A nobody, a nothing. A nothing from nothing. A *schuster*."

I. Small said this with deep humility.

"I wanted you to go to school, Charley, so you should *be* something, not a nobody. Life! What do you mean, Life? What time have I had for Life? Didn't I never have nothing more important to do? Life! *You'll* have Life, please God. My child," said I. Small, thrusting out his weak hands with their broken and blackened nails, "these hands I would work to the bone for you, man to man."

Then the breast of young Charles Small contracted and squeezed his heart into the back of his eyes, so that he had to run away to the lavatory and cry.

When he came back he was sorry for his father when, furtively smiling, he said: "Listen, Charley, supposing your mother should turn round and say: 'So where you been? What you done?' What'll you say?"

"I'll say we went to Kew Gardens."

"Yes," said I. Small, uneasily, "I want you should always tell the truth. A liar is worse than a thief. A thief, he'll steal your money, but a liar, a liar will swear your life away. Quidle right —I only want you should be honest. A liar is always found out. A tram for a few pence we took to Kew Gardens. Why not? What's the matter with Kew Gardens? . . . Flowers, trees, water lilies—it's good to keep in touch so a boy should know what's going on in the world. What's the matter with Kew Gardens, what?"

"Nothing's the matter with Kew Gardens."

"Tell the truth, Charley, and nothing but the truth. Only one thing I ask—don't tell your mother, bless her, *don't tell her I went on the roundabout!* To please me!"

"I shan't say a word."

"That's right, Charley-boychik," said I. Small, with relief, "never tell a lie. A liar is a rotter. You can never trust a liar. But there is no need to . . . talk too much. Man to man, we went in a tram to Kew Gardens. Enough is enough."

"Oh all right, all right!" said young Charles, impatiently.

"What's the matter, boychik? Didn't you enjoy yourself?"

"Yes, yes, I enjoyed myself . . . I wish you wouldn't call me boychik."

"I won't, if it hurts your feelings, Charley."

"It doesn't hurt my *feelings!*"

"Charley-boychik, are you still fretting about that other nonsense and rubbish, eh? Man to man?"

The expression on the old man's face was such that his son saw him, then, as a dog unjustly beaten, lifting a placatory paw in supplication. He wanted to stroke him, comfort him, fondle his ears and soothe him to sleep; but the best he could do was, touch his arm and say: "Don't worry. It's all right. I'll be quite all right."

"It was all for your own good, my little boychik. Believe me, your mother and me, we're a little bit older than you. Your mother knows best."

"Don't worry," said young Charles.

I. Small was dismayed to find his wife at home when they got back to the house.

"So soon?" he asked.

"Why, what's the matter, am I in the way?"

"Tell me, how's Ruth?"

"You should think yourself lucky *I'm* not the kind of person to make a fuss about nothing. If *I* rushed into nursing-homes with every twopenny-halfpenny ache and pain—ha-ha! . . . They want to be pitied, that's what they want. All right, as long as I know what they are."

It appeared that Ruth, wrapped in a quilted sky-blue dressing-gown trimmed with swansdown, was sitting in a rocking-chair, eating chocolate cream, smelling flowers, and reading a novel by Charles Garvice which she was reluctant to put down. Trained nurses were dancing attendance on her and calling her "Madam". There were dishes heaped with peaches and grapes; a bottle of Invalid Port. Crammed with the fat of the land she was lolling in the lap of luxury, pretending to be ill. Her husband had given her a pair of bedroom slippers made of white fur—probably rabbit. Ruth had not been seriously ill, and had told her that she didn't need to be looked after—Millie was humiliated, angry and disappointed.

"But *scraped!* They scraped her?" whispered I. Small.

Millie indicated that Ruth had not been what *she* would call scraped. A spoiled fuss-maker might call it being scraped. She suggested that Ruth's womb had been varnished and polished. "But where have you been?" she asked.

"Where have *we* been, Charley?"

"We took a tram to Kew Gardens, Mother."

"I hope you enjoyed yourselves."

"Well, Millie, it was such a lovely day . . . what does it cost, sixpence on a tram? What's the matter with Kew Gardens?"

"What did you have to eat?"

I. Small said quickly: "We went to a tea garden, eh Charley? So we had tea, we had bread-and-butter; jam we had, with water-cress."

"Is that all?"

"Strawberries and cream," muttered young Charles.

"Quidle right—I forgot—strawberries and cream."

"What else did you do?"

"Nothing, Millie, nothing at all—eh, Charley?"

Young Charles nodded.

"A bit of bread-and-butter and a strawberry—is that all they've had to eat all day long? Kill yourself to fill the house up with food for them, and the minute you turn your back they rush out to restaurants to eat goodness knows what, and goodness knows who's been touching it. Leave them alone for five minutes and they neglect themselves. Them and their water-cress! Water-cress!"

I. Small said: "We had a sandwich—eh, Charley?"

"That's right."

"Where? What sandwich?"

I. Small said: "Where? What do you mean, where? In Kew, where else should I eat a sandwich?"

"What kind of sandwich?"

I. Small pretended to forget. He squeezed his head between his hands, slapped his forehead, and said: ". . . A, a, a *sandwich*. Eh Charley? What sandwich, Charley? Man to man?"

"Oh, smoked salmon," growled young Charles, naming the first pink-coloured eatable that came into his mind. But he gave his father a contemptuous look that was meant to say: *You coward—can't you even carry the weight of your own little lies? Must you chuck your muck into my conscience?*

I. Small blew his nose.

He had become a tremendous nose-blower. Confronted with a problem he took out a great handkerchief, shook it out of its folds, and blew into it, making a noise like a trombone. This stunning noise generally put an end to discussion. On such occasions, when I. Small paused for breath, he cautiously opened his handkerchief, peered into the folds, shook his head, and blew and peered again. *What did he expect to find—pearls?* Charles wondered.

On this occasion he trumpeted so violently that he sounded a sort of Call to Arms. Millie, that seasoned warrior, leapt into battle, crying: "What class of people makes a noise like that when they use their handkerchiefs? Who blows like that into a *clean* handkerchief? He's got to blow straight into a clean handkerchief, this millionaire!"

Millie and I. Small had been quarrelling, off and on, for seventeen years about handkerchiefs. She had got it into her head that it was wickedly extravagant to blow one's nose into a perfectly clean handkerchief. Then, as surely as the bang follows the flash, I. Small roared: "Then tell me, tell me then —what for *is* a clean handkerchief? What does she want I should do with a clean handkerchief—have it framed?"

Charles went to bed. He had begun to feel affectionately about his father; and at the same time resentful.

He remembers that he thought: *Damn him, if the old man wanted to eat ham why couldn't he just have eaten it and said so? If he didn't want to say so why couldn't he tell his own lie instead of sticking it into my mouth? . . . He's not so bad. But oh, damn, damn, damn—why did he have to wait all these years until Mother's back was turned before he let me begin to understand him?*

Then compassion and contempt fought a tug-of-war in Charles Small's soul until, after a short, sharp tussle, both sides let go in the same instant, so that he relaxed with a snap and went to sleep.

Oh, if only I could sleep like that now! says Charles Small, with a groan. *What wouldn't I give, to sleep the way I used to sleep when I was a boy of sixteen . . . sixteen from forty. . . . Good God, twenty-four years ago. . . .*

It is good, to sleep as a healthy sixteen-year-old boy can sleep, but looking back Charles Small decides that he would not relive his first sixteen years for an eternity of sleep—paradisiacal sleep full of erotic dreams in technicolor—not for any consideration!

CHAPTER XI

Now, naturally, just as he is hanging trembling on the edge of sleep like a raindrop on the point of a leaf, Charles Small is disturbed by a stealthy sound. His wife is cautiously turning the knob of the door. Instantly he comes back, worse than conscious, to an exacerbated state of nervous tension. It is as if he has taken hold of the handles of a shocking-coil. An agonising shudder runs from his wrists to his shoulders and down his spine. He is sorry for his silly wife. But, having taken his two handfuls of self-pity and dropped his penny, he cannot control the mysterious current that shakes him—the strange, uncontrollable, quivering current of hate. He listens, closing his eyes and pretending to be asleep. The lock of the bedroom door, although it is well oiled, makes a little chirping noise. Hettie, with all the goodwill in the world, cannot move without making a noise—some silly little noise—she will swallow, gurgle in the stomach, hiccup. Even when she blinks her eyes her lashes seem to scratch the air like so many slate pencils. Now, by way of a change, she is overtaken by a need to sneeze. Opening his left eye half an inch, Charles Small sees her pressing her left forefinger against her upper lip. She is shaken by convulsions; yet she manages to make no more noise than one makes when one draws the cork of a medicine bottle: *Bip!*

Charles Small sits up, shouting at the top of his voice: "What's the big idea? For God's sake, what have I done to deserve this? When *you* don't feel well do *I* deliberately come and make disgusting noises in your ear when you're trying to get five minutes rest and peace?"

Hettie's tremendous effort to hold back the sneeze has forced tears into her eyes. Now they run down her face.

"I didn't——" she begins.

"—If you didn't who did? And *now* what are you crying for?"

"I didn't know if you were asleep, Charley. I——"

"—So you came to wake me up, to find out, eh?" Even as he says this Charles Small knows that he is being despicably cruel and unjust; but something stronger than himself has taken possession of him.

"Charley, darling, I brought you an egg beaten up in milk," says Hettie. "And I wasn't crying, Charley. I know it annoys you if I cry. Honestly, I wasn't, because I know how it gets on your nerves. I got something in my eye. Please drink this milk. There's a new-laid egg beaten up in it, and a little sugar. Come on, Charley darling, dear darling Charley, it'll do you a world of good."

Charles Small glares at her angrily, but not without pity. He sees that she is looking at him with yearning under her pink eyelids, and he says to himself, with a hard, short laugh: *Aha, aha, here it is again!* He knows what that look means: it means that she wants to make love to him.

In every imaginable way, however, this woman is repulsive to him. He is bored and irritated by her sloppy adoration. He loathes her because she agrees with every word he says, however preposterous. He is sickened by the lingering touch of her humid hand. His heart sinks when he embraces her. On such occasions, it was necessary to close the eyes tightly and . . . one, two, three . . . back to everyday indifference and normal distaste.

She puts the glass by his bed, saying: "I'm sorry if I disturbed you, Charley. I tried to be as quiet as I could. Drink it if you can. I'm sure it'll do you good. I won't disturb you again."

Then, after she has opened the door, he wants to call her back and say: *Hettie, Hettie, my poor dear Hettie! Please forgive me. I'm not very good to you. You are very patient with me, and I don't deserve it. I beg your pardon with all my heart and soul. Excuse me—I am not really a pig, although I behave like one. . . .*

He actually begins to say it: "—I say, Hettie."

Startled by the changed tone of his voice, she stops, rigid, and says: "What is it, Charley?"

He pauses and, after a short struggle with himself, says: "Try and keep those children quiet, will you?"

"Yes, Charley. Have a nice rest."

I suppose I shall go to bed with her to-night says Charles Small. Sighing in anticipation of this fortnightly function, he lies back and, searching his tired memory, decides that he will think of Lya de Putti. . . . He is rather partial to that woman of blazing passions who cannot shake hands, on the screen, without an orgasmic wriggle . . . he has never forgotten the way she kissed

Emile Jannings in *Vaudeville*—it was like a woman, dying of thirst, sucking an orange. She is one of his small, select harem, which includes Cleopatra, Eleonora Duse, a lady with remarkable buttocks who once jostled him in a bus, and Mary Queen of Scots. But Lya is his favourite. He imperiously calls her into his imagination once a month. But he knows that if he found her in his arms in the flesh he would probably faint, or pretend to have a stomach-ache, or say that he had to go and see a man about a dog, or say "Let us just be good friends," or cry for his mummy —in any case, nothing would happen.

Nothing Charles Small desired ever had or ever could happen.

CHAPTER XII

IT was the same with poor old I. Small. He was marked and fore-doomed to perish squealing, like a stuck pig. One Sunday morning he said to his wife: "Millie, the time has come—we got to face facts."

He had picked up this phrase from an old shoemaker whom he occasionally employed—an argumentative Freethinker, an audacious revolutionary who talked in such a manner that he made one's blood run cold. His name was Lizzard, and he had devoted some fifty of his seventy years to what he called "Meet-ings". He had all sorts of jargon on the tip of his tongue, and was always ready with some startling proposition, such as: "There are two classes in society, Mr. Small. One produces but does not accumulate, and the other accumulates but does not produce.' And: "There is such a thing as Evolution." And: "The time has come to act, not to talk." And: "A fact is not called a fact for nothing. Therefore it must be faced. Let us face facts!" He went on like this all day, his lips bristling with bright iron brads under his grizzled beard, talking, spitting out nails, hammering them in, gasping, misquoting and singing all at the same time, lively as a leprechaun. ". . . The spectre of war is haunting Europe!"—*bang bang bang*—"You have nothing but your chains to lose, Mr. Small, and all the world to gain!"

"Chains?" asked I. Small, looking about him. "What do you mean, chains? What chains? Where chains?" He touched his watch-chain to satisfy himself that it was not yet lost. Then, somewhat sadly, he said: "You're bleddywell right. I got nothing but my chain to lose. And what's *that* worth? Three pounds?"

Banging so furiously that he had to shout to make himself heard, Lizzard shouted: . . . "Common ownership of the means of production!"

Remembering that if you were "common" you spat on the floor, picked your nose, scratched yourself, and slept with your socks on, I. Small said, firmly: "Means, yes! Common, no!"

"The social system——" said Lizzard, scraping away with a rasp, "the social system——"

119

"—Listen," said I. Small, gravely. He had a hazy memory of policemen with big moustaches arresting Socialists. "Listen, Lizzard, don't use that word in this house."

"What word? Repeat it to me!"

"Social," whispered I. Small.

"Another lackey of the bourgeoisie, eh?"

"Say it in English, Lizzard. I haven't had your education. I don't talk French. You're in England now, not in France."

"The ruling classes——"

A bell tinkled upstairs. I. Small put on his coat and hurried out of the underground workshop, pausing only to say: "Mind you, Lizzard, you're not bleddy far wrong about my chain to lose, but did I asked you to poke your bleddy nose into my business? It's *my* chain. Get on with your work!"

Yet he was influenced by the erudition and the eloquence of Lizzard. Sometimes, after supper, reading the evening paper, he looked up and said portentously: "Aha! So that's what they are, the ruling classes!" Or: "Um-um! The skepter of war is haunting Europe already!" Or: "More taxes! My last chain they want to take away from me! The time has come not to talk, Millie, *not* to talk the time has come!" Once, reading a headline: *Facts In The Mexican Case*, he shouted: "Do you see? Facts! Face them!"

Now, throwing down a wire spike-file of bills, he said, "Face facts, Millie, whatever else you do."

Then he twisted and pulled his coppery moustache until it was taut as a telegraph-cable and said: "Well, Millie, I'm sorry to say I done my best. I done my best, I'm sorry to say. Now what I'm going to do goodness only knows. Rent, rates, taxes, gas, milk, bread, and here's for £8.10s. leather. And stock—stock! Oi! The plumber, 25s.——"

"—And whose fault was that?"

"Beggar the bleddy fault, you, me, him, her, it, that—whatever it is—a pipe bursts, so what does she want I should do? Drownd myself?"

"So that's what he is."

"So what's what he is, beggar it? Listen, Millie, the business is a failure."

"Whose fault is that, Srul, answer me—whose fault?"

"Face facts," said I. Small.

Tragically, Millie said: "It's my fault, it's all my fault, I made a mistake. I thought I could make something of you. It's my fault. It was a mistake. You can't make a purse out of a sow's ear. Well, you can't lie down and die. You must *do* something. What do we owe?"

"Nearly a hundred pounds."

"And what have we got?" asked Millie, with terrible calm.

Loosening the fourth button of his waistcoat, I. Small pulled out his massive gold watch-chain—the sort of chain they used to call a Double Curb Albert. It was an impressive chain, worthy of a ponderous repeater; but one end of it was clipped to a five-shilling Waterbury watch, and from the other there hung a little gun-metal matchbox. Having detached the watch and the matchbox I. Small let the chain fall on to the table and said: "*Na!*—I got nothing but my chain to lose."

"What are we going to do? To have to go and ask Father for money—I'm so ashamed!"

"Who's asking her father for money?" screamed I. Small kicking the sofa.

Millie wept copiously. Her body was shaken by sobs of such violence that I. Small thought of a careless washerwoman shaking a half-wrung sheet. She writhed and twisted, with a dull slapping and a slow intermittent hissing, while drops of dirty water seemed to sprinkle the table, as she cried: "I knew it would come to this. . . . I knew it would come to this. . . . Oh what are we going to do, oh what are we going to do? What is going to happen to the children?"

Now, I. Small, humiliated and angry, started to say *Beggary!* —but, being of a compassionate nature, and seeing that his wife was genuinely wretched, he stopped himself short at the first syllable, so that he said: "Beg——"

"That's all he's fit for. To beg," said Millie, gathering to her bosom her five-year-old son and her two-year-old daughter. "Get him a barrel organ—buy him a monkey—that's what he wants! Here——" she held out little Priscilla at arm's length. "Take her, go on, take her out into the street, hold your hat out and cadge for coppers. Oh oh, oh!"

She cried out so dolefully that the children, already terrified, began to scream. Charles, in spite of his puny stature, could make a noise like a klaxon. Priscilla, when she cried—which was almost all the time—raised a scratchy, intermittent shriek reminiscent of bats in the twilight; a sound so high-pitched that it was felt rather than heard; but it sent its vibrations into every nerve.

As for Millie, who could put the passion and agony of Ruth and Naomi into the search for a mislaid matchbox and the sullen rage of Jonah into a dissertation upon a misplaced crumb of cigarette ash—she surpassed herself. She began by emitting a noise such as one might make by squirting a fine jet of water, under enormous pressure, into a resonant zinc pail, and ended by going off like a geyser. If she had made noises as horrible as this over a broken egg-cup, what unexplored heights and depths of sound would she explore now? Even the honking and squeaking of Charles and Priscilla made I. Small's scalp tighten so that the hair at the nape of his neck stood on end. And this was nothing. The orchestra was merely tuning up.

It was more than I. Small's weak flesh and thin blood could bear. He ran out of the room, snatched up his hat, put it on back to front, went, panting, into the street and walked aimlessly, lashing about with an imaginary walking-stick, until the heart in his breast, like a well-battered punching-ball, rattled itself quiet. By then he found himself in Langham Place. He pushed his hat away from his forehead, shoved his hands into his trouser pockets, and walked on, slowly and resolutely, trying to think, to make a plan.

When he reached the other end of Portland Place he realised, with a horrible sinking of his knocked-about heart, that if it came to thinking he had nothing to think with, and that he could no more make a plan than a monkey could make a watch. So he turned and walked back, and all that he could say to himself was: *I wish I had my stick.* Without his walking-stick he did not know what to do with his right hand; he liked the feel of that stick, and found pleasure in the smart tap of its ferrule on the paving stones, but he dared not buy another—he would never hear the end of it. Twice he had been tempted; once by a snakewood stick with a silver band, and once by an elegantly polished stick of pimento wood. But, standing with his nose almost touching Cox's window in Oxford Street, like a hungry urchin at the window of a pastry-cook, he heard a voice saying: *So, that's what he is, Piccadilly Johnny! There could be no bread in the house, but he's got to rush out and spend his last penny on walking sticks. Why doesn't he go and get an eyeglass, while he's about it? What does he care if his children go in rags?* . . .

Indignantly framing something beginning with *bleddy*, I. Small stepped off the kerb opposite the Langham Hotel, and then a large motor-car stopped with a strained outcry of brakes while, above the *parp-parp-parp* of an exceptionally powerful horn, an imperious voice shouted: "Why the hell don't you look where——"

I. Small, who had not been alarmed by the proximity of the car or the blasts of the horn because at that moment he did not care whether he lived or died, turned with a great start at the sound of the voice, and cried, half sick with emotion: "Is it you? No, it can't be! Can it?"

"Why don't you look where you're going, does your mother know you're out? Why, you—— Why, may I drop dead if it isn't Srulke Small! Srul, *wie geht's?*"

"Shloimele—Sollyle—to see you is . . . is . . . is . . . *oi!*" I. Small was strangled with joy. Half incoherent in his most lucid moments, he stood in the gutter, gibbering, trying to find something good to say.

"Get in, *schlemihl*," said Solly Schwartz, opening the door.

"In a motor-car he's riding?" stammered I. Small "Whose motor-car?" And he touched with the tip of a finger the polished brass of one of the headlamps, and felt the machine quivering and straining like a thoroughbred horse before a race. It was a large, luxurious Renault, brilliantly enamelled, high and roomy, coquettishly bonneted.

"It's mine, *schmerel*," said Solly Schwartz. "Get in, Srul. Have a ride."

I. Small, who had never ridden in an automobile, climbed into the car with trepidation. When, after three fumbling attempts he closed the door, and found himself sitting next to his old friend, a great happiness came up from somewhere inside him so that he caught the hunchback's neck in the crook of his arm and kissed him three times on the cheek, saying: "Schloimele . . . my little Solly! This is . . . this . . . I got no words!"

"Ah, it's nice to see you again, Srul, you old *schlemazzel!* Where would you like to go? I bet I know where you'd like to go."

"Where?"

"You'd like to go and have a snack and a glass of beer at Appenrodt's, that's where you'd like to go," said Solly Schwartz, pulling levers and busying himself with little knobs. The car began to move. I. Small, terrified but curiously exhilarated, sat tense. His heart was beating painfully, but he was happy.

"Solly, are you sure you know the way you should work it?"

he asked, when they missed a four-wheeler by half an inch at the corner of Great Titchfield Street.

Solly Schwartz laughed scornfully, and in a few minutes they were in Piccadilly.

"I know you'd rather go to Appenrodt's for old time's sake," said Solly Schwartz, and I. Small sighed and said:

"That's right, Solly, old time's sake, no?"

"A snack, a drink, a chat—yes?"

I. Small was silent. He had so much to say, but, when he came around to trying to find a way to say it, he felt as a lawyer might feel who, called upon for documents, discovers that some blind idiot has shaken up the contents of his filing cabinets in a big black sack—miserably enraged, impotent, apologetic. When they sat at a table, face to face in the light, he gripped Solly Schwartz's hand again and said affectionately: "How smart he looks! What did you pay for that suit?"

"Eight guineas."

"What do you mean, eight guineas? For God's sake, Solly—motor-cars, suits for eight guineas, pearl tiepins, kid gloves, silk veskits. . . . How comes, tell me?"

"It's nothing," said Solly Schwartz, with an impatient gesture. "How has it been with you?"

"So-so," said I. Small; but it would have taken a stronger will than his to hold his misery under the surface of his face.

While they were eating their ham and drinking their big, comfortable mugs of Munich beer, Solly Schwartz said: "Come on, Srulke—give it a name. What's the matter with you? You're in trouble? Tell an old friend. You're worried. What is it?"

"Who said so?" said I. Small.

"Out with it, Srulke—come on, what's up?"

"Nothing. . . . That's a nice stick you got, Solly. Where do you get it?" He picked up from between Solly Schwartz's feet the most wonderful walking-stick he had ever seen. It was cut out of some rare wood that resembled red ivory, and the head, secured by a ring of gold, was cunningly carved out of the monstrous tooth of some aquatic beast. The craftsman who had shaped it had carved it into the likeness of a crocodile. The stick could not have weighed less than three pounds.

"Like it, Srulke?"

"Who wouldn't?"

"Good. It's yours, Srulke. Take it."

"What do you mean, take it? I couldn't take a thing like *this!*"

"Don't be silly, I've got plenty of sticks—I've got seventeen walking-sticks," said Solly Schwartz. "I want to make you a present. Take it, Srulke, and hold your jaw. Hoi, waiter, let's have some more beer. Drink up, Srulke, and tell us what's the matter."

There were tears in I. Small's eyes as he stroked the crocodile on the walking-stick and said: "Nothing. You mustn't give me a stick like this. By my life and yours too, Solly, I won't take it!"

"Shut up. Don't argue with me, Srulke—I don't like people arguing with me. Take it and be quiet, or are you trying to annoy me? . . . Now I asked you a simple question, *schlemazzel*, and all I want is a simple answer. What's the matter with you? Things are bad?"

"They could be better, Solly, and they could be worse."

Solly Schwartz had grown masterful in the past three years, and his temper had not sweetened. His Punch's-face was almost malignant as he said: "Give me a straight answer, will you? Everything could be better, everything could be worse. You're short of money, that's what it is, isn't it?"

"Who said so?"

"Well, you're in Mayfair, aren't you? What more do you want?"

"Beggar Mayfair," said I. Small.

"You wouldn't take my advice, would you?" said Solly Schwartz, appearing, with his tight, sunken mouth, to bite a mouthful of beer and drink a forkful of ham. "And I should have patience with you!"

"Solly, what's the matter?" said I. Small, miserably, bewildered, "what did I say? What did I do wrong? What are you so annoyed with me for? The business is a failure: all right, don't we all make mistakes, Solly? For God's sake . . ." Suddenly I. Small became angry: ". . . Wherever I go must it be always the same thing? In the house, out of the house, upstairs, downstairs; what do they want with me?" The beer was creeping into his veins. "What do they want me to do? Grow wings? Fly?"

Solly Schwartz said to the waiter: "Bring two more beers," and gripping I. Small's wrist in his swarthy right hand squeezed it until the bones seemed to crack, saying: "Don't get excited."

"He's got a hand like a pair of pinchers," said I. Small, rubbing his wrist; and he seemed to fall into a reverie. Arranging his moustache with the back of a forefinger he looked straight in front of him in his bewildered, thunderstruck way, at six empty glasses on an adjacent table. He gazed so intently that his eyes crossed and the six glasses became twelve, the twelve became twenty-four, forty-eight, ninety-six, a hundred and ninety-two, three hundred and eighty-four, seven hundred and sixty-eight . . . they multiplied, shifting, iridescent like soap-bubbles in a loose lather until they filled the restaurant. He stared, hypnotised. Then a waiter whisked the glasses away, and all the bubbles burst, and there was Solly Schwartz grinning at him out of a blue drift of fragrant cigar smoke.

"Excuse me, Solly; all of a sudden it went to my head."

"Head! You haven't got a head, *schusterkopf!* Come on now, I'm asking you a simple question. You're in debt. How much?"

"What difference does it make? What's the use of talking about my troubles? Let's talk about old times, Solly."

Solly Schwartz snapped like a dog as he said: "Keep your old times. I'm finished with old times. I want new times. I was asking you a question. Don't answer if you don't want to. But listen, Srul, there's a saying: the shoemaker should stick to his last."

"My last what?"

"You should have stuck to your trade," said Solly Schwartz. "You didn't, did you?"

"I'm different. You, you were born a *schuster* and you'll die a *schuster*. So you ought to live a *schuster*. You ought to have taken my advice when I told you to get a machine and go in for the repairing on a proper scale. But no, the *schlemihl* has got to take a shop in such a back alley that even the policeman on the corner never heard of it. Who goes into a back alley to buy a pair of boots? . . . Mayfair! If you'd done what I told you you wouldn't be chewing there like an ox, worrying your guts out about—*how* much is it?"

"A hundred and two pounds seven-and-six," said I. Small, taken off his guard.

"A hundred and two pounds seven-and-six, good God! Oh, you *schlemazzel*, oh you . . . put that beer away and have a brandy, for God's sake."

While they were sipping brandy, Solly Schwartz said: "A hundred and two pounds seven-and-six. . . . Isn't your wife's father well-to-do?"

"I'd rather beg with an organ and a monkey in the streets," I. Small muttered, moodily twisting and turning his glass. "Why?"

I. Small stammered: "It . . . I . . . From the first they . . . what with one thing and another, a person doesn't like to, to, to make himself look—look——"

"—Small?"

"Yes, what is it?" said I. Small, jumping as if he had heard the tinkle of the shop-door bell.

Solly Schwartz looked at him, smiling and shaking his predatory head. "Srulke," he said, "if you live a thousand years you'll never learn enough to blow your nose. A hundred and two pounds seven-and-six! Get away with you!"

The needle-point of his contempt penetrated the woolly blanket that was enveloping I. Small's consciousness and touched a nerve, so that, prodded to alertness, he shouted: "Who's this, Mr. Bandervilt? By him a hundred pounds is nothing? Go on, laugh at me. Go on, why don't you laugh?"

Then his lowered eyes saw the crocodile-head of the walking-stick, through two tears. Stroking the exquisitely-carved tail of the crocodile he said: "Well, the time has come to talk, not to act. We must face facts. . . . You're young, Shloimele, one of these days you'll learn there's two classes in society. You, already, you got a motor-car . . . already you are in society . . . Enough. Enough is as good as . . . enough. What are you writing?"

Solly Schwartz said: "This," and scaled a little oblong of blue paper on to the table. "A present for you. It's open. Don't lose it. Take it to the bank to-morrow morning and they'll give you the money across the counter."

"What do you mean? What's the idea? What's this?"

"Put it in your pocket."

"It says here two hundred pounds," said I. Small, trembling. "What's this for?"

Almost dreamily, Solly Schwartz said: "*Schlemazzel,* I've got a long memory. Do you remember nine years ago when you went to Cohen's to try on a jacket?"

"I was always fussy about my clothes," said I. Small. "I never wore ready-made. A man I know, I forget his name, took me to Cohen and made me to measure for a special price."

"Pressburger, that was——"

"—Quidleright! That was where I met you, Schloi! You was a nothing, then, a bit of a *schnip*."

"You pay a penny to see things like me pickled in a jar, in a sideshow on Hampstead Heath," said Solly Schwartz, dispassionately. "You remember where we met, Srul?"

"I went to (excuse me) make water, and you were in the laventory. Crying, Solly."

"Crying my eyes out," said Solly Schwartz, calmly, but through clenched teeth. "And you said: 'What is it, boychik?' "

"And what *was* it, boychik?"

"Never mind. Then you said: 'Come on, boychik, wipe your nose and come out with me and let's eat a sausage.' "

"And why not?" asked I. Small.

"Well, stick *that* in your pocket," said Solly Schwartz, pointing to the cheque.

"But what for, tell me—why?"

"Why not?" said Solly Schwartz, with all the pride of Lucifer in his eyes, striking his chest so that it thudded like a muffled drum. "Schwartz does not forget a friend or an enemy. Put that in your pocket, *schlemazzel*, drink up and I'll drive you home in my motor-car."

I. Small, dumbfounded, stunned as surely as if he had been struck on the head with a club, could only say: "We . . . we . . . we went to . . . to Isaacs, and we had for a few pence a Frankfurter with a bit potato sellid. I don't . . . I can't . . . what do you mean, tell me, what? Speak!"

Smiling, Solly Schwartz said: And we had a glass of ginger-beer apiece."

"Ginger-beer, schminger-beer—a penny glass of . . . What difference, ginger-beer! To my worst enemy I give a glass ginger-beer, for God's sake!"

"Put that in your pocket and drink up," said Solly Schwartz. He added contemptuously, but not without sadness: "And *I* said to myself: 'That such a fine man with an eighteen-carat gold moustache should treat me to Frankfurters and ginger-beer!' Good God!"

"No jokes? About *me* you said that?" said I. Small, with tears on his cheeks.

"Come on, come on, Srul."

So I. Small was rushed in a daze through the roaring streets until he found himself standing alone outside his own door in

Noblett Street, leaning on a wonderful walking-stick; sobered by shock but so astounded that he wondered whether he had been walking in his sleep.

When Millie saw the walking-stick, she screamed: "What's this? Haven't I got enough——"

"—Shush, Millie, I found it."

"Where did he find it?"

"Where? In a bus."

"What bus? That's all he's got to do with his money, ride about in buses all day long. What bus, Srul, what bus? Where were you going on a bus? Much he cares what happened to his daughter while he was riding up and down in buses."

"What happened? To the little girl what happened—speak!"

"While he's been joyriding in buses, that Piccadilly Johnny with his walking-stick, I've had to have a doctor in the house."

"Why? Millie, for God's sake, what for? God forbid a doctor!"

Millie managed to convey to him that after he had stamped out of the house like a wild beast little Priscilla had picked up a shirt button and stuck it up her nose. Now a shirt button, stuck up the nose, is likely at any moment to reach the brain, and the consequences are terrible. Millie did her duty as a mother—she screamed. A doctor was called in—a very good doctor—a physician and surgeon. With extraordinary skill he had inserted the fourth finger of his left hand into the little girl's nostril and, exercising all his strength, pulled out the shirt button in half a second; for which he had charged five shillings. But it was quite all right, as long as I. Small had enjoyed himself riding in buses.

"How is she, where is she?" asked I. Small, appalled.

"I put her to bed. Please God——"

I. Small went to their bedroom, where the baby's cot was. Priscilla was lying on her back, kicking her legs, and trying to screw a pillowcase-button into her left ear. She was delighted by the sensation she had made and hoped that the nice-smelling doctor would come again and poke his soft finger into her ear. Cooing and gurgling, she smiled at the ceiling as an astronomer might smile at the stars, delighted by the infinite permutations and combinations of the cosmos. She had stuck a button up her nose; but this was only a beginning. It seemed to her, then, that that nostril was only one of many delightful holes with which she was perforated: she was an unexplored world.

But I. Small, seeing her screwing the button into her ear, yelled: "Halp! Millie, halp!"

Then everyone made such a noise that a policeman on his beat stopped and gazed steadfastly at the door until the noise subsided. Some loiterer who had nothing better to do than walk in Noblett Street asked, eagerly: "What's up?"

"Just a little family affair," said the policeman.

"Me, I send the God-forbids to Sunday school, so me and the missis can 'ave a bit of a cuddle in peace and quiet."

"There's a lot to be said for religion," said the policeman, weightily, pounding his way on his beat.

As he had lied about the walking-stick I. Small said nothing about the cheque, because he was afraid to tell Millie that he had spent the afternoon with Solly Schwartz. Besides, the cheque might not be good—it could not be. His enigmatic silence drove Millie through three stages of rage, but he said nothing. At nine o'clock on Monday morning he went to the Strand branch of the Belgrave Bank and pushed the cheque under the grille. The teller examined it closely, and I. Small remembered a tub full of crawling, live black lobsters packed in ice in a fishmonger's window in Victoria. He felt that the contents of this tub had been poured from the back of his collar into the seat of his trousers. He said: "Is it all right, is it?"

"Oh, quite all right, sir. How would you prefer it?"

He left the bank, his pocket heavy with two hundred pounds in banknotes and gold, and his feelings overcame him so that he had to stop at "The George" for a glass of brandy. He was hopelessly bewildered and haggard with anxiety in spite of his tremendous relief.

He walked home slowly, gnawed by a fresh worry. When Millie asked him where he had got the money, what could he tell her? He was irresolute and incompetent in lying, as in everything else—although, as in everything else, no one could accuse him of failing to do his best. He had the wild idea of telling her that he had found the money in the street; but let it drop. Coming so soon after the tale of the walking-stick, that might be a little too rich for Millie to swallow, and even if she believed him she might insist on his taking the money to the police station. If he told her the truth he would be compelled to admit that he had been loafing in Appenrodt's with Solly Schwartz while the baby had a button up her nose, and although this confession would be letting him in for no more than a week or ten days of sharp reproach which would soften into innuendo after a further period of niggling recrimination—call it a month in all—I. Small shuddered away from the thought of what Millie might say about Solly Schwartz. He did not like to mention his name in her presence because she hated him and he loved him and would defend him with his last breath . . . and so one word would lead to another, and there would be no peace in the house. Then he thought that he might tell her that he had had the money all the time, put away for a rainy day; but he knew that he would never get away with this, for Millie could nag the cork out of a bottle, natter the lock off a door. He decided, at last, to say nothing at all; brushed up his moustache with his forefinger, squared his shoulders, and gripped his new stick resolutely, mentally rehearsing the next scene.

MILLIE: Srul, tell me, where did you get it?
I. SMALL: (*with deliberation*) Millie, the time has come to face facts. Where, when, what, who, how, why—this is neither here nor there. Actions speak louder than words. I got it—*na!*
MILLIE: Has he been borrowing?
I. SMALL: That is my own bleddy business. I didn't thieved it, don't worry! P'raps I was keeping it all the time for a little surprise. P'raps not. Not another word! Finished!
MILLIE: He's showing off, he's acting. Stop acting!
I. SMALL: (*in a voice of thunder*) The bleddy time has come to act, and not to talk! Not another word. What, is she a Scotland Yarderler, I should be blackmailed like a magistrate in a Court Law? Quiet!
MILLIE: (*weakening*) Srul, for my sake, to please me——
I. SMALL: (*icily*) Millie, you heard what I said. What is neither here nor there is neither here nor there. Don't waste breath. Take the money. Enough.
MILLIE: So that's what you are!
I. SMALL: Yes!

He walked faster now, so that he was at home in ten minutes. Millie was in the shop, clinking disconsolately at the shelves full of white boot boxes. She said: "Oh, so there he is, Piccadilly

Johnny with his walking-stick. Where's he been all the morning?"

"And what's the matter with my walking-stick, what?"

"A bill came in for water-rates," said Millie.

Then I. Small, who had the money clutched in his hand threw on to the counter a buff-coloured banker's paper bag containing twenty five-pound notes and a hundred golden sovereigns, and said: "*Na*, Millie—two hundred pounds."

She looked up with a twitch of the eyebrows that appeared to toss over her head the weight of a dozen years, and smiled as she said: "No!"

I. Small, happy to see her smiling, pinched her cheek and said, laughing: "No? Look and see."

"But, Srul, where'd you get it?"

"From Solly Schwartz, and what do you think of that?" Then, having spoken, he uttered a sharp cry because he knew, to a word, what was coming.

Millie said, incredulously: "What, that little humpty-dumpty? I don't believe it."

"Oh, beggary!" shouted I. Small, "oh, oh, beggary!"

"A nice tale. Where could your humpty-dumpty get two hundred pence, let alone two hundred pounds?"

"Is it a man's fault he's born with a little hump?"

"Don't change the subject, Srul. Make a clean breast of it——"

"—Aha! Breast! *Now* who's using dirty talk? Two hundred pounds, two hundred pence—hah! In motor-cars Solly Schwartz is riding about—all your life you should be riding about in such motor-cars! And she's here with her humps and her pence, already!"

"What did he want to give you two hundred pounds for?"

"For . . . for . . . a, a, a sausage, a glass ginger-beer," said I. Small. Then, realising how incredible this must sound, he gesticulated limply and said: "Honest truth, Millie."

"And where did humpty-dumpty get two hundred pounds?" asked Millie. "You liar!"

At that, I. Small struck the counter with his beautiful stick, knocking off the tip of the crocodile's tail, and, roaring: "Enough of her humpty-dumpty," went into battle.

CHAPTER XIII

THE Monopol deal was the first of a dozen such adroit little manipulations. Solly Schwartz did conjuring tricks with surplus waistcoats, juggled with buttons, and disposed of misfit coats, taking profit with his left hand and commission with his right.

He went to his room only to sleep; was never at rest between half-past six in the morning and midnight, never still. He lived in a kind of cold fever, an intelligent delirium, a patient frenzy, a deliberate desperation, a calculated hurry. He could carry on two conversations and listen to two other conversations at the same time. In three years he wore out two of the steel surgical appliances called "iron feet".

His great hooked nose poked itself into the inwardness of things as a parrot's beak gets into a banana. He talked as if he were haunted by a fear that he might fall dead before the end of every sentence, gesticulating like a threshing-machine, stamping his iron foot like a trip-hammer, and banging the floor with his stick, hammering home his ideas, right or wrong. One grey morning two years after he tricked Monopol into buying the trousers, old Cohen, who was somewhat weary, and whose grip was loosening, said: "The prices, the prices they're cutting till they bleed. They're ruining me."

Now he had been talking like this for thirty years, so that everyone who heard exchanged winks, nudges, and smiles—everyone but Solly Schwartz. He knew the difference between a grumble and a groan. Following his employer into the little back room he saw the old man pouring a second cup of coffee, while his rolls and butter were untouched, and he was certain that the business was in danger. Then he said: "Mr. Cohen, listen. An idea."

"Another idea?"

"Yes. A West-End tailor-made suit, with two fittings, for thirty shillings."

"*Meshuggene!*" said Cohen. "Let me at least drink a cup of coffee in peace in mein old age. You're so clever you're going mad. Get out! A West-End tailor-made suit, two fittings, for

133

thirty shillings he wants! And a bottle champagnier wine thrown in?"

"A West-End tailor-made suit, two fittings, thirty shillings —that's what I said. *West-End Tailor-made*. It's a name. Look at eau-de-Cologne. Does it comes from Cologne? They make it in Stepney. Look at Vienna sausages—do they come from Vienna? Brick Lane! *West-End Tailor-made*—in nice gold letters on a big label, with a little white part on the bottom, so you can write in the customer's name and the date, live in Savile Row. There's a fortune in it. Take every penny you've got, borrow—your credit's good—every farthing you can lay your hands on. Strike out! It's as easy as ABC, Mr. Cohen, on my word of honour. Take shops, branches, anywhere, everywhere. Two or three to begin with, in good positions—the Strand, Oxford Street—never mind if it costs you the shirt off your back. Fit them, stock them, advertise in the papers—stick bills on the walls—*West-End Tailor-made suit, Two Fittings, Thirty Shillings!* In the meantime, bigger workshops, a factory, machines. Button-hole machines, cutting machines—these pasty-faced *scheisspots* stitching and stitching, they're a thing of the past, Mr. Cohen. I'd put twenty of them on to a coat, not two or three. You can make five shillings on a suit, easy, if you play your cards clever. . . . Wait a minute, Mr. Cohen, let me speak, please! Machinery, premises, stock, advertising, all that will run you into thousands? Good, let it! The more you spend the more credit you can get. If you organise," cried Solly Schwartz, slapping the table with his hand, "in two years, three years, four years, you can sell half a million suits a year and two hundred thousand overcoats. That would bring you in £175,000 a year. Are my figures wrong? Seven hundred thousand times five shillings is £175,000, isn't it? Make allowances, say I put down profits too high. Call it a lousy half-crown on a suit of clothes. Even then you've got £87,500 a year profit. The thing to do is go in, hit hard, what can you lose?"

Old Cohen, spellbound, had let his coffee get cold. Now he sighed himself back to life and said: "No. . . . Thirty years ago, twenty years ago, ten years ago; yes. Now, no. When you're my age . . ."

"—All right, Mr. Cohen, I understand," said Solly Schwartz, with pity. "But look. Listen. The idea about the labels. What about this—make up some smashing samples and get orders for West-End tailor-made suits, to sell to the retailers. Alterations guaranteed, eh? As good as made to measure. I'll go on the road —what about that? Ten per cent commission. All right, Mr. Cohen?"

"That, I don't mind," said the old man.

"Right!" said Solly Schwartz, and went out. After he had banged the door behind him, Cohen smiled. The little hunchback had the power to inspire hope, and stimulate appetite. He drank his tepid coffee and ate his roll and butter, thinking: *I'll make that boy a partner in the business, so help me God!*

*   *   *   *   *

Now Solly Schwartz had followed the old man into his little sitting-room merely with the intention of persuading him to buy some fancy labels, because he knew a struggling label-manufacturer who had said to him: "You get out and about, don't you? Well, if you come across anything in my line, put it in my way and I'll give you four shillings in the pound commission."

But suddenly, the devil knows how, he had stumbled upon this tremendous idea which, in an instant, had taken hold of him. It was as if he had sprung a wolf-trap. It had him in a painful, relentless grip. Writhing, agonising, raging at the senile stupidity of Cohen who could not see the pure splendour of his vision, he scornfully flicked from the astronomical reflector in his brain the wretched little dust-motes of two or three pounds of commission, and gave himself to the steady contemplation of the galaxy of millions. He wanted millions; millions and millions. Cohen, obviously, could not help him: he was too old, too tired, too timid. Solly Schwartz wanted a keen visionary with the heart and nerves of a good gambler who prefers to play neck or nothing to the last penny. At the same time this gambler, speculator, investor, capitalist—call him what you like—must have complete faith in Solly Schwartz. But he must not be too clever.

Tapping his iron foot with his heavy stick he tried to think of some man of substance whom he might approach. At last he snapped his fingers and said: "Monopol!" And this is how he reasoned: *He knows I tricked him once with those trousers. Monopol isn't an easy man to play tricks on. He's one of the trickiest tricksters in the trade—I tricked him. Therefore he respects me—he knows I'm no fool. He's a good businessman and a bit of a chancer, or he couldn't have got where he is to-day. At the same time, he's not quite so smart as me, because if he were he wouldn't have bought those trousers, the way I sold them to him. He'll be suspicious of me, naturally. But I'll talk him over, I'll manage him. Yes, Monopol, by God! Monopol, that swindler, will work with me just because I swindled him. Because after all is said and done the man is a bit of a fool.*

He went to Monopol's place in Clapham—the "Main Branch", it was called now, for Monopol was opening shops in every busy street north of Camden Road. On his way he had another dazzling inspiration. He remembered a three-line notice in the morning paper concerning the bankruptcy of the aged Duke of London —an indescribably dissolute old nobleman who had squandered three fortunes and had nothing to live on but his name. *Now here*, thought Solly Schwartz, making his iron foot ring with an impetuous stroke of his stick—*now here is the very thing. The Duke of London! The Duke of London! For a couple of thousand pounds and a few shares in the company, my word, what wouldn't he do? "Duke of London". What more could anybody want of a suit of clothes? Recommended by the Duke of London* . . .

Solly Schwartz had a morbid craving for news, news of any sort. He read the newspapers ravenously, to the last crumb, so he knew all about the Duke of London, and the knowledge made him stronger. He had not the least doubt that now he could mould Monopol like wax.

Now, Monopol had a secretary who politely asked Solly Schwartz his name, begged him to be seated, and went into Mr. Monopol's office. Then Solly Schwartz heard Monopol's voice shouting: "That twicer? Kick him out, throw him downstairs! He wants to see me again, does he? What a nerve! Pick him up by the scruff of his neck and chuck him out—*him!* What sauce!"

There was a noise, which Solly Schwartz recognised as the sound of a paperweight hurled against a wall. Then the secretary, a frail little old lady, returned, trembling, and said: "I'm afraid Mr. Monopol is out at present, but——"

"—There isn't any but," said Solly Schwartz. "Excuse me, miss," and, putting her aside with a gentle push of his powerful arm he limped past her, opened Monopol's Private Office door, went in, slammed it behind him, and, wildly excited, struck his iron foot with his stick so that it seemed to toll like an alarum bell while he shouted: "Monopol, keep calm! I'm not here to sell you anything. Nothing! Calm, Monopol—I've come to do you a favour."

"You? You——"

"—Ssh! Ladies present. I've come to make you a millionaire, Monopol."

"What *you?* You make *me*——"

Solly Schwartz said: "Monopol, why don't you wipe your face? You're sweating."

Monopol stopped, took out a handkerchief and wiped his face, and Solly Schwartz knew that he had beaten him to his knees. "What is it?" asked Monopol.

Then Solly Schwartz, drawing a breath that seemed to suck the very papers on the desk into his great mouth, began to talk. His idea about the Duke of London within ten minutes engendered a hundred fresh ideas in his fecund brain. He made it sound like a poem. Spraying words left and right, with eloquence so compelling that Monopol was unable to move from his chair, Solly Schwartz described his scheme. As he talked the face of Monopol, which had been purple with anger, became pleasantly pink, and he began to smile. His smile started with a slight upward flicker of the eyes. After that his eyebrows, as if he were trying to hide his eyes, while his mouth came down as if to snuff out a smile of the mouth and he nodded agreeably, saying: "Ha! That's good, that's clever!"

Then Solly Schwartz knew that he had won the man. He ejaculated another thousand words between four lungfuls of air and arrived at his peroration. By which time Monopol was smiling broadly and rubbing his hands. Something in his manner made Solly Schwartz stop and ask:

"What's the joke?"

"It's funny, that's all. It's funny. If it's funny, why shouldn't I laugh?"

"What's funny?"

"All you've been saying to me."

"What's funny about it, tell me."

"Well, Mr. Schwartz," said Monopol, grinning like a fiend, "what you've been telling me is the best idea I ever heard of. But the fact of the matter is, I thought of it myself yesterday morning."

Solly Schwartz looked at Monopol, let out the rest of his breath in a tremendous hiss through his nose, and compelled himself to smile.

"Is that all you've got to say?" said Mr. Monopol. "Or perhaps you want to sell me a few pairs of trousers? Eh?"

"All right, Monopol," said Solly Schwartz, still smiling, "it's quite all right, Monopol. Wait and see."

"Well, so good-bye, eh? I would gladly have considered your suggestion if I had not already thought of it already myself."

"Yes, you're quite right," said Solly Schwartz, holding out his hand. "More fool me. Serves me right. Shake hands."

Monopol said, with a chuckle: "Live and learn, live and learn. Good-bye, good-bye—— Hey! Let go! What are you doing?"

"You'll remember me when we meet again, eh, Monopol?"

"For God's sake, let go my hand!"

Solly Schwartz released Monopol's hand and said: "You bloody crook, one of these days this hand will choke you. Good-bye till we meet again, Monopol. God help you when we do." Then he left the office.

It had never occurred to him that anyone like Monopol could outwit him. The rest of the world, yes; naturally. Monopol was welcome to the rest of the world. Not to Solly Schwartz. He was not angry with Monopol, but with himself. He was ashamed; he could have wept. In the foullest terms he cursed, insulted, and upbraided himself for having let himself make a fool of himself, as he stamped and clanked away, pushing himself forward with his walking-stick like a resolute skier on a dangerous slope, who must at all costs rush down fast before he can rise and soar like a bird.

Soon he became calm. Monopol had won a trick, but the game had only begun. Solly Schwartz began to be convinced that Monopol, not he, was the fool, because anyone but a fool would realise that in a gigantic adventurous enterprise of this sort a Monopol without a Schwartz was like bread without yeast, like a balloon without gas. He foresaw Monopol's ruin, and smiled. Thinking of ruin he remembered Cohen, and scowled. If the old fool had the nerve of a mouse, Solly Schwartz would not have been subjected to this humiliation. He was finished with Cohen, once and for all, doddering old *schneider-tukhess* that he was, with his tea and coffee and rolls and butter.

It was necessary to make a plan. But the brain and the nerves need food, and Solly Schwartz was ravenously hungry. He could throw ten shillings in gold to a Samuels or stand treat to an I. Small in Appenrodt's, but when he was alone he was parsimonious. Not unlike one of those jolly fellows who splash their money about among boon companions but begrudge their wives and children a mouthful of bread, Solly Schwartz, when he came home to himself, treated himself with severity; grumbling at himself, accusing himself of wanton extravagance for every penny that he spent on himself; shouting to himself: *What? You stuff yourself with steak while the bank account goes hungry?* . . . Until, exhausted, he forgave himself, took himself to bed, and, affectionately kissing himself good-night, slept peacefully with himself.

When he dined alone, which he generally did, he dined for sixpence, or even less, off boiled beef and pease-pudding and a glass of ale or, preferably, fish and chips in a lowdown fish-shop. He loved, above all things to eat fried fish and chips out of an old newspaper. The flavour of discarded newsprint and the subtle aroma of stale printer's ink really do blend with the combined savours of fish and potatoes fried in nut-oil, to make something exquisite. Sometimes he took a parcel home; devoured the food with his fingers, and read every word of the paper it had been wrapped in. But generally, having his dignity to consider, he sat down in the shop and ordered a fourpenny piece of fish and twopennyworth of chips (no mean order, in those days) to be served on a plate, with a roll and butter and a bottle of ginger-beer, or a cup of tea.

Now, his mouth watering at the thought of these good things, he went to a fried-fish shop in a side street off Vauxhall Bridge Road, where he forgot everything in the contemplation of a blackboard upon which the proprietor had chalked:

NOW FRYING!!!
PLAICE!
ROCK SALMON!
HADDOCK!
SKATE!

Then there was a decorative scroll and, in extra large letters:

NEW POTATOES!!!!!

He went in, sat down, and ordered: "A fourpenny plaice, two penn'orth, roll and butter, cup of tea."

Making music with a fork and the marble top of the table, he looked about him. His brain was cool but swollen like the belly of the spawning codfish that lays a hundred thousand eggs so that ten may hatch. At an adjacent table a man with a wine-coloured face who was eating haddock with the abrupt voracity of a drunkard spat out a bone, which landed upon the brim of Solly Schwartz's hat; but he did not notice. He was listening to other things.

He heard a voice cry: "Dick! Taters!" A tiny shutter opened with a slam, and a gnome-like man appeared, bawling: "Taters, guv'—right you are!"—and out came a wire cage packed with cut potatoes, which the proprietor, sweating like a horse, plunged into a great pan of steaming oil so that every chip hissed like a snake in a cloud of steamy smoke, under a sputtering shower of bubbles. A little boy with congested nostrils asked for "Dapoth o' crackligs"—halfpennyworth of cracklings, which are the detritus of fried fish that have been dipped in batter—and Solly Schwartz beckoned him to his side and gave him threepence, saying: "Cracklings won't do you no good, get yourself a tuppeny-and-a-penn'orth." The fryer, with bared teeth, shook his wire basket as a terrier shakes a rat and tossed out of the pan another heap of chips—then, snatching at the handle of another basket, shook into a hot container a quarter of a stone of skate, while the proprietor, beating the little shutter with his fists as if he was trying to knock it down and escape into the open air howled: "Dick! Haddock! Are you asleep?"

Solly Schwartz thought: *Look at that—look at this bloody mess. All this could be done properly. Those stinking frying-pans I'd put behind glass, with chimneys, or something, to take the smell away. Those fryers I'd put into white coats and white hats. Look at that woman behind the counter wiping her face with her hand. In any place of mine, that would be: 'Out, with a fortnight's wages, at a minute's notice!' . . . And fish and chips to be taken away in newspaper, eh? God knows how many Tom Dick and Harrys have plastered dirty hands all over old newspapers. There's a point! It's unhealthy. Hygienic paper bags for fish and chips. Hygienic. Branches all over the country——*

He was about to have another idea, but the harassed waiter threw down his plate, saying: "Eightpence," stamping and blinking impatiently. Solly Schwartz gave him tenpence, and prepared to eat. But when he looked up to find the salt, he saw the great tin salt box in the hands of the most repulsive-looking individual that ever offended the eyes and nostrils of the world, who had taken a chair on the opposite side of the little table. Solly

Schwartz, dreaming his dreams, had not noticed him. If he had, he would certainly have said: "Excuse me, if you don't mind— that chair's engaged." For, although he had observed and despised the scum of the slums—pickers of poor men's dustbins and eaters of unclean things so heavily bodyguarded by lice and stench that no policeman dared arrest them—he had never seen a man like the man who was playing with the salt box. He was as dirty as it is possible for a living creature to be. The frock-coat in which his tall, stooping, skeletal body was wrapped was not merely disintegrating: its fibres were so impregnated with animal and vegetable matter—soup, beer, meat, fish, vomit—that it was in a state of putrefaction. But this was nothing. He wore a celluloid collar white and shiny as a false tooth, fastened with a brass paper clip, and a necktie which showed evidence of having been used as a pocket handkerchief, but no shirt, and his finger-nails, which were thick and fluted like oyster shells, were full of black dirt. This, again, was nothing. It was the face of the man that caused Solly Schwartz to drop his fork with a clatter. It was like an artist's conception of Death—there was no flesh on the bones, only skin, in a pimplous patchwork, stretched so tightly over the bones that the mouth and eyes, seemingly lipless and lidless, were pulled wide open. It was a head-hunter's smoked trophy with the rictus of the last agony miraculously preserved. Of his teeth, only the four canines remained, long and orange-coloured. He made you think of what you would look like and smell like when your time came and you had been a little while underground.

Solly Schwartz drew back his chair with a start, at which the macabre stranger started too and put down the salt shaker.

"I'm so sorry, I beg your pardon," he said, in a strange, high, peculiarly sweet and gentle voice, "do forgive me. May I pass you the salt?"

The salt was damp. Solly Schwartz had to bang the sprinkler on the table, and afterwards slap its bottom vigorously before he shook out a few reluctant grains. The stranger watched him with his bloodshot yellow-green eyes and said: "Is it not incredible? In this year of grace we still cling to these archaic devices!"

The very sight, let alone the proximity, of such a creature would have killed an ordinary man's appetite. But avid Solly Schwartz, hungry for everything, replied: "What do you mean?" Then, when another fishbone rattled upon the crown of his hat he turned and said to the man behind him: "Keep your bones to yourself, can't you? Spit them out on to your plate like a gentleman!"

When he turned again the hideous stranger was drawing with a pencil on the marble top of the table. Even the pencil was dirty, but Solly Schwartz saw that guided by the stained forefinger and the filthy thumb it described beautiful lines, pure curves and shapes as clear as daylight, while the stranger, talking to himself, said: "It is childishly simple really. It is perfectly obvious. That thing there, that absurd thing punctured with open holes—it is barbarous, it is unhygienic, not clean. I have seen flies swarming about the tops of such bronze-age devices. A salt sprinkler is good, necessary. Given salt cellars, in a place like this, people whose hands are not necessarily clean—artisans, mechanics, engineers, etcetera—would plunge their fingers into the salt. Or their knives, which would be just as bad, since people who are reduced to eating in these establishments generally eat with their knives." All the time he was drawing with marvellous speed and accuracy. ". . . I remember an occasion in a cabmen's shelter when some poor hungry fellow, eating steak-and-kidney pudding, thrust his knife into his mouth with such unrestrained violence that he cut his uvula, yet with that same knife he took salt from the salt cellar, and who can say what harm might come of this, assuming the man to have had an infected throat, and that the silver—I mean, cutlery—were not thoroughly washed? . . . On the other hand these sprinklers, while they are advantageous in that they keep the salt from contact with the human hand, which, as you must know, is not necessarily hygienic, have a certain grave disadvantage . . . the humidity of our climate and the deliquescence of salt tend to combine—as you have just demonstrated, sir—to . . . in effect, make salt damp and therefore difficult to pour. Now what could be simpler than this—a salt sprinkler with a moveable air-tight cap motivated by a spring and operated by a simple movement of the thumb? There it is," he said, pointing to his drawings on the marble. "The cap, spring, mechanism, and container could all be manufactured for sixpence. People who buy such things would gladly pay a shilling. But what is the use of talking, what is the use of talking?"

Solly Schwartz, chewing a mouthful of chips, stared at the table. In a few seconds the stranger had drawn three beautifully accurate diagrams marked A, B, and C, with neat arrows pointing to D, E, F, G, and H. "When did you think of that idea?" he asked.

"Oh. just now. A triviality, a nothing. *Think*, my dear sir— *think* of *that?*" he smeared the diagrams away with his cuff. "Pah! I have thought of a thousand things better than that. But my real work, ah, that!"

"Have something to eat," said Solly Schwartz, panting. "Have whatever you fancy. Go on, have . . . have a large piece of plaice. Have some chips. Ginger-beer, lemonade, kaola, a cup of tea— whatever you like."

"Thank you, sir, I believe I will," said the stranger. "You are very kind. I might take a little of that excellent fish which you seem to have relished——" Solly Schwartz's plate was full of chewed bones "—and, perhaps, a fried potato. *Ginger*-beer no. Beer yes. Ginger, no. I do not agree with those who insist that ginger is an excellent stomachic. I am infinitely obliged to you——"

Then the waiter came and said: "What's this? You again? I told you once before, we don't want you around here. Go on, clear off—I won't tell you again. Out you go!"

Solly Schwartz said: "Leave him be. He's my guest. What do you mean by insulting my guests?"

"I'm sorry, sir, but it's the guv'ner's orders."

The stranger said: "I accept your apology——"

"—I wasn't talking to you."

"—I accept your apology and if my presence embarrasses your governor I will relieve him of my presence."

"He drives customers away," said the waiter to Solly Schwartz, who was following the stranger to the street.

When they were outside Schwartz said: "Do you live any-where?"

"Why, of course. I have rooms in Wilkin Street. Could I live nowhere?"

"Then I'll tell you what," said Solly Schwartz, "if those dirty dogs want to be independent—and I can tell you I won't spend a penny in *their* place again—what say I get some fish and chips and a bottle of beer and we go back to your place to drink it, and you can tell me all about machinery and all that. Eh?"

"I could wish for nothing better, sir, but I warn you that neither I nor any man can tell you all about machinery. I can tell you only what I know, which is the little that is known. Did you mention beer?"

"What sort do you like?"

"I am indifferent. I patronise, impartially, Barclay Perkins,

Watney Combe Reid, Meux, Guinness . . . but I have observed that there is no brew that cannot be improved by a judicious admixture of gin, in the combination known as Dog's Nose."

Solly Schwartz bought a bottle of gin, two quarts of beer, and a shillingsworth of fish and chips. The stranger waited outside the public-house saying: "Eh . . . the last time I came here they treated me with discourtesy. In fact they threw me out. Will you forgive me if I do not accompany you?" When Solly Schwartz came out with the bottles he said: ". . . However, I will, since you are so pressing, drink a little of the excellent gin which you have been so good to offer me"—and, uncorking the bottle and putting it to his lips, he swallowed about a quarter of a pint of the neat spirit before recorking it, and saying: "There never was such Heliogabalian hospitality! I am deeply obliged to you, sir. Pray allow me to return it. My rooms are yours."

CHAPTER XIV

As the lock clicked and the rusty hinges groaned, the basement room seemed to open a square black mouth in an asphyxiated yawn, sighing out a hot, stale breath. Then a match flared and Mr. Goodridge, followed by his horrible shadow, made his way through the narrow lanes between shadowy piles of mysterious lumber, and then became invisible until, with the noise of a man spitting out an orange pip an antiquated gas-burner relieved itself of a jet of yellow flame shaped like a duck's foot. The unhealthy light of this feeble flame seemed to be shivering with cold in spite of the stuffy heat—and as Mr. Goodridge turned the gas higher it made a chattering noise as it tremulously slapped and scratched the great black face of the night. "Do come in, my dear sir. This is not exactly the palace at Versailles, or Windsor Castle; Versailles and Windsor, after all, are open to the general public. This place is not. His Majesty the King receives. I do not. So, although I cannot offer you velvet arm-chairs or Gobelin tapestries——" Mr. Goodridge conducted his guest into the room and shut—and double-bolted—the door.

By then Solly Schwartz's eyes had adjusted themselves to that wired, gaslight-haunted half-dark, and, hugging his beer bottles and holding his packet of fish and chips in such a manner that the oil it exuded would not stain his cuff, he looked about him. There was a window to the right of the door, but it was shuttered and barred, and the bar was secured with a great padlock. Close by this window stood a long table with a sloping top, covered with great sheets of cartridge paper and littered with drawing instruments—ivory-handled compasses and dividers, ivory slide-rules, ivory T-squares—worth a nice few pounds, Solly Schwartz observed. On the floor, to the left of the desk, there was a heap of torn up and crumpled paper, enough to fill two bushel baskets, and by the size and the shape of this heap Solly Schwartz knew that for many weeks past his host had been writing at that table, throwing away what he had written, and kicking it impatiently aside. The fireplace on the other side of the room was choked with the ashes of burnt paper. Draughts from the door of a chimney had scattered a good bucketful of these ashes over the floor, which was dangerous with heaps of iron and brass cut into bewildering shapes. An engineer's bench filled a third of the room, and when he looked at it in the light that flickered through the fog in the basement Solly Schwartz felt as he had once felt when he had walked into a lamp-post in a black fog. He knew that the big iron thing was a hand-lathe, and that the smaller one was a vice, but all the rest of the paraphernalia—callipers, files, bits of brass, saws, spanners, screwdrivers, hammers—burst like the shower of sparks that the lamp-post had knocked out of his head. Instinctively, he looked towards the gas-jet, and one of the fingers of flame, tipped with a long black nail of shadow, pointed to a pile of books so that he read the word *MATHEMATIC*— before the gas-jet quivered away, raising its webbed hand to the ceiling, as if in supplication, chattering. It seemed to be saying: "I am so tired. Please send me back to my pipe. I am afraid of the dark. Please let me go out."

Mr. Goodridge, in his urbane way, said: "It is possible that you may find it a little untidy here."

"Not at all," said Solly Schwartz.

"Yes, I admit that the place is not quite as tidy as it might be, but what can I do? I could get a woman to come and clean up, but she would put this here, that there, the other somewhere else, until . . . in short, I could not trust a woman to leave things alone if she tidied up. Myself, I have so little time away from my work. But do sit down, Mr. . . . Mr. . . ."

"Schwartz, Mr. Goodridge."

"Do forgive me. I am . . . distrait. Do sit down." The only chair in the room was the chair by the sloping desk. Solly Schwartz balanced himself on the edge of it, while his host sat on the bench, saying, in a vague, amnesiac way: "I think I had some plates, and glasses—cups, at least—but for the life of me. . . . Oh yes, yes, the cups I used when I mixed——"

"That's quite all right, Mr. Goodridge, I've had my supper. You eat that up before it gets cold."

"You really are very kind. With your permission, I will. Working, one forgets the demands of the body. Oh dear, how badly designed is man, who must waste valuable time eating, sleeping, and so forth! I tried to reduce my sleeping and eating time to three hours. I couldn't do it. Try as I will, I must sleep six hours. Think of that. I'm fifty-two years of age. For fifty-two years I have been sleeping six hours a day. I have therefore slept thirteen years of my life away. So much time lost—but you are not drinking, my dear sir! Naturally, you have no glass. Perhaps this will serve?" He offered a tin can.

"Certainly," said Solly Schwartz, filling it with beer, although he intended not to drink out of it. Then, looking at the can he said: "This is a funny tin, isn't it?"

At that moment there was a sharp metallic snap and a shrill squeak of terror, and Mr. Goodridge leapt up, baring his four orange-coloured teeth in an awful grin, and said: "I've got another one!" He plunged into the shadows under the sloping table and came back with a wire contrivance shaped like the toe of a Dutch wooden shoe. It was a tiny cage that imprisoned a trapped mouse. The bait, a piece of cold fried potato, was still clasped in the mouse's forepaws. "I am overrun with mice," said Mr. Goodridge. "I have been at a loss to know what to do —or at least I was, until I devised this little trap. I detest those barbarous contraptions of wood and springs that they sell in the ironmongery shops. They break the mouse's back. This catches the mouse alive."

Solly Schwartz, watching Goodridge, shuddered. It came into his mind that Goodridge ate live mice, but he said: "What do you want to catch them alive for?"

"My dear sir! Obviously, in order to let them go." Then, addressing the mouse, Mr. Goodridge said: "Now I have warned you. If you invade my privacy and devour my property you are liable to imprisonment or death. Is that clear? Be warned, and go about your business!" Then he opened the trap and let the mouse fall to the floor. The mouse, stunned, sat still. Goodridge blew at it, saying *Shoo*, and it ran away. "I beg your pardon," he said, "the mice here are sometimes very troublesome. I try to reason with them, but, upon my word, they are occasionally more refractory than you might believe. My dear sir, will you not partake of your own bounty? Are you quite sure?"

He had been eating voraciously with his fingers, and there were five chips left.

"No thanks," said Solly Schwartz.

"Oh well," said Mr. Goodridge, eating four of the chips. He was about to eat the fifth, when he paused, took it out of his mouth, and baited the mousetrap again.

"What's the idea of catching mice just to let them go again?" asked Solly Schwartz.

"Oh, I catch them to teach them a lesson, and I let them go in order that they may perhaps do better."

"And then they come back?"

"Oh no, I think not."

"But if they don't come back to you, they'll go to someone else, won't they?"

"I really don't know, Mr. Schwartz. I give them time to mend their ways. I really am not interested. I have so many other things to think of. . . . I think I will avail myself——"

"—Do, do!"

Mr. Goodridge drank out of the bottle and said: "It was Ralph Waldo Emerson, I believe, who said that if a man can write a better book, preach a better sermon, or make a better mousetrap than his neighbour, though he builds his house in the woods, the world will make a beaten path to his door. Do I misquote?"

"I imagine not," said Solly Schwartz.

"I have a great admiration for Mr. Emerson. A fine writer, a profound thinker. But . . . as you see, in the little matter of mousetraps, not infallible. But it doesn't matter, does it? Mousetraps are not important, are they?"

"Oh I don't know. If you want one you've got to buy one, and it costs you tuppence."

"Oh that, oh yes, yes. Tuppence, yes, I grant you. But of no real importance to mankind, I think you will admit?" said Mr. Goodridge, trying to scratch an unreachable part of his back. "After all, there is no real harm in a mouse. It is a little naughty sometimes—it eats one's things, and when it makes its nest in one's waste paper it makes an irritating noise that can break the thread of a thought, if one happens to be thinking. But they mean no harm. They do not march in armies against their own kind. They do not go out and shoot inoffensive elephants. Do they?"

"Well, I suppose not," said Solly Schwartz, humouring him. "But they're dirty."

"Dirty? Are they? Oh well, I dare say they find it difficult to keep clean in the conditions in which they are compelled to live. But what of it? The landlord of the public-house in which you purchased this excellent gin in which I am about to drink your very good health said that *I* was dirty. It is true that I have little time to devote to a pernickety toilet, and little money to spare for fripperies—perfumes, toilet waters, soaps, dressing-cases, towels, sponges, all that kind of thing, but would you therefore bait a snare with, say, a glass of gin and break my back? I sincerely hope not. In fact I am sure that you would not."

"Of course I wouldn't. Why don't you have another drink, Mr. Goodridge?"

"Since you are so pressing," said Mr. Goodridge, drinking out of the bottle, "I don't mind if I do. . . . We were speaking of mousetraps. I assure you, my dear Mr. Schwartz, that the world has beaten no path to my door for the sake of my mouse-trap. I am reminded of an occasion when, being in urgent need of the wherewithal to purchase a little platinum wire, I offered my mousetrap for five pounds to a firm that manufactures such things, and they slammed the door in my face." He laughed, as a man laughs at himself in comfortable reminiscence.

"Did you get your wire?"

"Oh yes, yes. The platinum wire? Of course, I got *that*—it was necessary for me, you see."

"You managed to raise the money, did you?"

"Eh? Raise the money? Well, yes, because I have, you see, a regular income of a hundred and fifty pounds a year. It was necessary only to curb my appetites for a few days, and there was the five pounds. But the flesh, you know, is weak, and once in a while—as, for example, to-night, this weak flesh cries out for a mild debauch, and——" Mr. Goodridge took another drink of gin.

Solly Schwartz asked: "So you didn't sell your mousetrap. And what about your salt-shaker, eh?"

"I beg your pardon? Salt-shaker? . . . Oh, that silly little thing!" said Mr. Goodridge, laughing. "You are referring to the suggestion I threw out in that fish shop, is that it?"

"Yes, what about that?"

"I shall certainly never patronise that establishment again and, in drinking your health, my dear sir, may I thank you for the loyalty with which you stood by me?"

"Don't mention it. Good health," said Solly Schwartz, pretending to touch the tin can with his lips. "You were telling me about that salt-shaker—with the spring."

"Pay no attention to it, my dear friend, don't give it a thought.

If you take such things seriously you'll break your heart. You must understand," said Mr. Goodridge, "that a man of active mind sometimes relieves that mind of a weight by turning it to a triviality; just as, it might seem, the North Sea amuses itself in the Norwegian fjords. So I, when the tide of my mind ebbs—when my moon wanes—so I play with a trivia. I amuse myself with cruets, gas-brackets, pots and pans, locks and bolts, anything that catches my eye. How many times have I made a sort of *voyage autour de ma chambre*, devising improvements upon this, that, and the other. Ha-ha-ha! Childish, you may say—unprofitable—yes. But a man must find some form of recreation especially when he finds himself in an impasse. I have not the slightest doubt, my dear sir, as a man of intellect, you have found yourself in one of these intellectual blind alleys after a protracted period of labour. Oh dear me, the silly things I have thought of!"

"What silly things?" asked Solly Schwartz, eagerly.

"Oh well, that silly salt-cellar, for instance. And—you'll laugh at me, and I don't blame you—that tin out of which you are drinking, and which, incidentally, I should be happy to replenish. . . . You are not a mathematician, by any chance?"

"I'm afraid not. Tell me about the tin."

"Hah, the tin—that tin! Well, my dear sir," said Mr. Goodridge between two gulps, "less than three months ago I found myself hopelessly mystified by the unaccountable action of a certain device that was intended to control the movement of a certain wheel. You must forgive me if I do not offer to go into details. Let us say simply that I was mystified. Of course, it was simply that my mind was tired, because the work upon which I am engaged is of the first magnitude, and no one can possibly help me, so that I must work all alone. However, I stopped work in despair and, having prudently laid in some bread and a tin of salmon, I forced myself away from my work and sat down to refresh myself a little. In opening the tin I cut my finger. It occurred to me, then, that while it is an excellent thing to pack meat and fish in tin cans, the method of opening these cans is barbarous. To get at one's Pink Salmon, I thought, one had to risk life and limb. It was necessary for the housekeeper to carry tools, ironmongery, tin-openers. In a Utopian state, I thought, tins would open themselves. Then, having put some cobwebs on my cut finger—there is nothing better than a cobweb for a cut finger—I lay down and thought all night, worrying at the possibility of a self-opening tin can; or at least a safe tin can so devised that there would be no need for women and children to risk their life's blood for a bit of salmon or a preserved peach. By daybreak I had discovered the very thing—and believe me, the intense thought I had given to this silly, trivial thing had so completely taken my mind away from that which had been baffling it that I went back to work delightfully refreshed and solved my problem within five minutes."

"But what did you do with the can? Eh? Eh?" snapped Solly Schwartz.

"Oh that," said Mr. Goodridge, laughing, "the tin can. Let me see. Oh yes, I remember. It occurred to me that such an invention might be of real use in the world——"

"—Use? My God, I should think there would be! There's bags of money in it."

Mr. Goodridge, who was not listening, went right on: "—And I thought, moreover, that one of the great companies that go in for such things might be willing to pay a few pounds for the idea. I was rather short of money at that time, because I had spent all I had on certain intricate and delicate brass castings. So, having drawn a fairly accurate diagram I constructed two models and, as soon as I had the time, put on my hat and went to see . . . now who was it? It wasn't Crosse & Blackwell . . . it wasn't Applin & Barrett . . . it is neither here nor there. I went into the office, and civilly asked to see the proprietor, the manager, anyone in authority. Would you believe it—they told me to go away!"

"No!"

" I assure you, yes, sir. They were quite rude. I made it clear that I did not expect necessarily to be conducted into the office of Mr. Crosse, or Mr. Blackwell, or whoever it was—that in fact some general manager would do. They laughed in my face. I wonder why. It really was very foolish of them."

Solly Schwartz said boldly: "Maybe your appearance, perhaps?"

"Do you think so? Perhaps you are right. I am not a Beau Brummell, it is true; I do not dress even with the informal elegance of His Majesty King Edward. I have neither the time nor the money. I am not interested in such things in any case. Life is so short, sir, and there is so very much to do. The work I have in hand would tax the endurance of a Hercules. Indeed, his labours are nothing in comparison with mine. What, after all, was the carrying off of the golden apples of the Hesperides? A mere nothing. As for the cleansing of the Augean Stables, without boasting I may say that I could have done the job better myself. Hercules, as you will remember, wrestled with Death for the body of Alcestis. Ha-ha! Every hour, sir, I wrestle with death for my own body—I struggle with Time for my work. If I told you of the problems with which I am confronted believe me, you would be appalled."

"Could I have a look at that tin can?"

Mr. Goodridge was slapping his pockets. "Oh dear, oh dear, oh dear, I have no tobacco. Have you, by any chance, a cigarette-case?"

Solly Schwartz had, but it was empty. He said: "I'll tell you what: I'll pop round the corner and get some. What do you smoke?"

"I roll my cigarettes out of a mixture of equal parts of black shag, bird's-eye, and red shag. You are very obliging, my dear sir."

"That's all right. You stay here and finish that gin, and I'll be back in two ticks. Oh, by the way, while I'm gone you might dig out that tin can of yours."

"I can refuse you nothing. It is so seldom that one meets with a sympathetic and enlightened companion with whom one may enjoy intelligent conversation. The can, certainly."

"I shan't be a quarter of a second," said Solly Schwartz. He hurried to the nearest tobacconist and bought a quarter of a pound each of black shag, red shag, and bird's-eye. Then, on an afterthought, he got six big Corona-Coronas and a large box of fat-headed wax vestas. Returning, he paused at a public-house and bought another bottle of gin; fiery old Tom. He was back in the basement in five minutes. Mr. Goodridge had dug out of one of the piles of junk on the floor a large tin can and a sheet of paper. When he saw Solly Schwartz's purchases he cried: "What, cigars? Heavens above, can I believe the evidence of my eyes? Corona-Coronas, as I am a living sinner! And what is this? Another bottle? Oh, but my dear sir, you shouldn't! No, really. This is munificent."

"A pleasure, I am sure," said Solly Schwartz, striking a match and offering a light. Mr. Goodridge's eyes flickered with drunken delight and a great cloud of smoke poured out of his nostrils while his lips puckered about his cigar. Meanwhile Solly Schwartz was examining the tin can.

"I don't quite see this," he said.

"Beg pardon? See what? Oh, that silly thing! Why it's perfectly simple. All you need do is, roll that little wheel that you will observe on the rim of the lid with a simple movement of your thumb, and the entire top is accurately and scientifically cut off. Better than that, the raw edge of the tin is at the same time neatly folded over. A child could use it, without cutting his little fingers."

"And does it really work?"

"Oh, infallibly. But do you really mean to tell me that a man of your intellect is interested in such toys?"

"I'm interested in its business possibilities, same as you were. Why don't you have another drink?"

"Thank you. No, but I assure you, you had better profit by my experience. There really aren't any business possibilities in that piece of nonsense. They simply won't have anything to do with you, you know—although perhaps you, an elegant man, a well-dressed man, a man of commerce who is not otherwise preoccupied; you might induce one of these inaccessible magnates to take an interest in it. In which case . . . allow me to make you a present of it."

He thrust the tin can and the diagram into Solly Schwartz's hands. The hunchback could hear the beating of his own heart, but he said, calmly enough: "Well, thanks very much. If I can do anything with it, rest assured you won't lose by it, Mr. Goodridge. Is it patented?"

Mr. Goodridge laughed heartily. "Patented? Oh, but, my dear sir, do you think that I have money to waste taking out patents for things of that sort? The taking out of patents is an arduous and expensive business, you know, and when I tell you that when my real work is done I shall have to patent no less than seventy-two new devices for a single machine you will realise that I have neither money nor time to waste on tin cans.

"What machine is that, Mr. Goodridge?"

"There are not many men in this city, I may say in this world, with whom I would talk of the matter. But with you . . . look."

Somewhat unsteadily he struck one of the wax vestas and, after three fumbling attempts, lit a great green-shaded reading-lamp. ". . . I'll show you."

"Watch out for those matches," said Solly Schwartz, stamping one out with his good foot, "you can't be too careful with them."

"Look at this," said Mr. Goodridge, pulling away an oily cloth that covered a shapeless object on the work-bench; and in the bright light of the lamp Solly Schwartz saw a wonderfully intricate and delicate assembly of wheels, wires, and springs. It could be likened to a steel spider's web spun to catch tiny, elusive brass insects—at regular intervals, apparently enmeshed, there lay bright, polished fittings shaped like dead ants, with legs and antennae of fine, strong steel—it was a machine out of a dream. There was something about the look of it that filled Solly Schwartz with unaccountable excitement. "What is it?" he asked.

Mr. Goodridge did not answer this question; he said, playfully: "You may look, but you mustn't touch. Only I may touch." Then he forced down a lever which must have tensed a powerful spring, for when he touched a button after that the machine seemed to come to life. With an appearance of deliberation, almost terrifying in a notched disc of lifeless metal, a large wheel turned and nudged awake another wheel, which, with a movement strongly suggestive of an understanding nod, gently pushed forward three subtly-bent bars that resembled thin, sensitive fingers. They explored three hidden places, and set some mechanism in motion that whirred, buzzed and hummed. Mr. Goodridge pressed the big lever again, and then the machine seemed to be trying to sing. "Watch closely, now, but do not touch," he said. Solly Schwartz saw something reminiscent of the keyboard of a typewriter, neatly inscribed with letters of the alphabet, numerals, and mathematical symbols. "Watch this closely. I press these four symbols—A, plus, B, square." As he did so, wheels began to spin and the dead brass ants awoke and moved their antennæ—whereupon, above the drone of the machine Solly Schwartz heard a gentle but insistent rhythmic rapping as some concealed metal parts fell, he supposed, into certain grooves. And this noise, metallic as it was, had a disconcertingly human quality: it was like the noise an impatient man makes when he drums with his fingers on a table while he is making some trivial but annoying calculations. There were nine taps in less than a second, and the machine was still; and then it was as if a heart had stopped beating.

"See," said Mr. Goodridge. He reached for a slot and pulled out a little oblong frame containing nine tiny squares of gunmetal, each bearing a symbol neatly painted in white, so that Solly Schwartz could read: $A^2 + 2AB + B^2$.

Mr. Goodridge continued: "$(A + B)^2 = A^2 + 2AB + B^2$—a simple quadratic equation. I am perfecting the one, the only real calculating machine."

"I don't understand those As and Bs and all that. I . . . well, I haven't had your education," said Solly Schwartz.

"You are not a mathematician, I see," said Mr. Goodridge, fondling the machine with one skinny hand while with the other he raised the bottle to his lips. "It is not important, many men of talent have no taste for mathematics, although for the life of me I cannot understand why. Let me demonstrate in a simpler way—although goodness knows what can be simpler than a quadratic equation. Give me some jumble of figures—something that would take you several minutes, with pencil and paper, to add up and check."

Solly Schwartz said: "9-8-9-2-3-7-9-0-3-4-5."

Mr. Goodridge tightened the spring and depressed eleven keys. The machine sang again, and tapped its fingers twice. Mr. Goodridge pulled out another frame containing two numbered metal wafers. "The total is 59," he said, and Solly Schwartz who was stilly busy with a pencil on his cuff cried out in astonishment. Covering the machine again, Mr. Goodridge said: "If I am spared for another ten years, I hope to complete this work. But will you not take a little of this excellent gin you have been so generous to provide, and for which I am so very grateful? Most of my little income goes to feed my little baby——" he caressed his machine through the cloth—"and I seldom have the opportunity to indulge."

"No, thanks all the same. But go on, what were you saying? Finish it? Haven't you finished it already?"

"Oh far from it, so very far from it, I assure you! What on earth is the use of a machine that can merely work out a problem in simple arithmetic or algebra that a schoolboy in the fifth form could solve in five minutes?"

"Can it add up pounds shillings and pence?"

"Eh? I beg pardon? Pounds shillings and *pence?* Why, of course it can. At least, it could, if I took the trouble to fit it properly. But I am not concerned with that. My little hungry baby here has passed in simple arithmetic and elementary algebra. I have higher hopes for her. She is destined for the higher mathematics . . . my poor backward child. . . . What, little one? Your father and mother have given their heart and soul to you and the very bread out of their mouths, and thirty-five years after you were conceived you are still only eleven years old. . . . But never mind, never mind, a little patience and all will be well. Slow and steady wins the race, my dear. Soon you shall have infinitesimal calculus, conic sections, and the higher trigonometry. At the touch of a finger you shall lisp logarithms. . . . Have no fear, my dear, Papa will never send you unfledged into a merchant's counting-house, but into the studies of mathematicians. Great astronomers shall cherish you and stroke you with their wise hands, and if they are kind to you you will tell them in a moment what they could not work out in a month. And if you are good the whole world shall dance attendance on you, my life, and clean you and cosset you and anoint your head with oil. . . . And you shall be queen of them all. . . ." He drank again and gasped: "This is remarkably rich and full-bodied, sir. But I mustn't take any more of it. I have work to do."

Instinct warned Solly Schwartz that this was not the moment to talk of commercial possibilities. He said: "I'm afraid I'm detaining you. I don't want to intrude."

"Oh, no in-in-instrusion, I'm (excuse me) sure. But . . . but . . . perhaps, perhaps . . . as a man superior understanding you will . . . perhaps excuse . . ."

"Can I see you to-morrow?"

"Not . . . not so luxurious as . . . or spacious as the Kremlin, or . . . Diocletian's palace in Dalmatia, but welcome." Mr. Goodridge put down the lamp on his drawing-table and, shaking himself like a spaniel, became coherent. "You have been most kind. I do not receive visitors generally, but you are always welcome. Usually I begin to feel in need of refreshment at about six in the evening, when I pause to rest my eyes. At that hour——"

"—All right, thanks very much then, I'll drop in to-morrow about six, and I'll bring a cold chicken—what say?"

"What can I say? I am overwhelmed."

"Oh and I forgot, I got this tobacco for you," said Solly Schwartz, taking the packets out of his pocket. "And I'll leave you the cigars and the matches too."

"My dear sir! I will smoke one of them now to clear my head, bless you. And so, shall we say good-night?"

Turning in the area to wave a second good-night Solly Schwartz caught a glimpse of him in the closing doorway—a macabre figure, holding a big cigar as a trumpeter holds a trumpet, and striking a match on the lintel. Then the door closed, and there was a great clashing of heavy bolts.

Solly Schwartz hurried away. Mr. Goodridge's tin can in the side pocket of his tight-fitting, close-buttoned coat made an unsightly bulge and hurt his hip, but he did not care. In that pocket there was a fortune. Let it hurt: the more it chafed the more certain he was that he had it. He would not undo one button in such a case; he would not give way half an inch.

His head was humming and buzzing, whirring and clattering—and calculating—like Mr. Goodridge's fabulous machine. Behind the barred door of that stuffy, stinking basement in Wilkin Street there was Ali Baba's cave, and he had the Open Sesame. To-morrow he would get the idea of that salt-shaker, properly drawn on a sheet of paper. He remembered the fable of the monkey that thrust its paw into a narrow aperture and clutched too many nuts, so that he got stuck and came to grief. That was not Solly Schwartz's style. A little here, a little there—never more than the hand could easily contain; and so, in the end, all!

Before he fell asleep Solly Schwartz dreamed of enemies cruelly crushed and friends magnanimously rewarded. But when at last his eyes closed, he slept dreamlessly until eight o'clock in the morning, when, as a struck match starts into bright flame, he flared into consciousness and, without even stretching himself, sat up thinking clearly, touching finger-tip to finger-tip gingerly as though he feared that he might burn himself. After five minutes of concentrated thought he got out of bed—in those days he still slept in his underwear—and, having dressed himself in his best clothes, wrapped the tin can in a sheet of brown paper, buttoned the diagram in an inside pocket, and went to consult a solicitor who knew the mysteries of the law appertaining to patents—no shyster-lawyer, no winker and nudger and leerer, but a good hatchet-faced practitioner of the old school, in Staple Inn. He was taking no chances. On the way he stopped at the bank and drew twenty pounds, half in clean bank notes and half in gold. He did not imagine that the consultation would cost him more than a few shillings, but the feel of money in his pocket stiffened his confidence, clarified his mind, and lubricated his tongue. Having pocketed the money he asked for his pass-book and saw that he had more than six hundred pounds to his credit. He had known this before—he knew his resources to a shilling— he simply wanted to see it in black-and-white. It made him feel stronger. Walking to Staple Inn, so vigorously that the iron ferrule of his stick struck an occasional spark out of the paving stones, he thought that it would be a good idea to call his tin can "The Schwartz Safety Can". He had a great desire to see his name in print, or stamped in metal—one bank holiday, when he went to Southend for the day, he put a penny into one of those machines that impress upon a strip of aluminium any twenty-six letters you like, and, punching the handle with all his might, struck out only the thirteen letters of his name, just for the sake of seeing it. He carried that stamped strip in his pocket for years, until it broke. It was his last penny, and he was thirsty, and the great glass receptacles on the lemonade vendors' barrows were full of liquid gold. Yet he had turned away and spent his penny to see, and feel, his own name in capital letters.

He thought: *Better wait a bit. Schwartz: it sounds too foreign —or rather, too common. Besides, The Schwartz Safety Can is too much of a mouthful. I want something they can say quick. Can . . . can . . . can . . .*

Then he remembered a childish rhyme:

A funny old bird is the pelican
His beak can hold more than his belly can

He said: "Pelican! Peli-Can!"

Then he clanked and stamped under an arch, shattering the dignified silence of the Staple Inn, where he sat for an hour with the lawyer and arranged matters to his complete satisfaction.

* * * * *

At five o'clock Solly Schwartz bought a cold roast capon and a quarter of a pound of sliced ham at a cook shop and limped towards the Vauxhall Bridge Road. He was tempted to ride in a cab, because the straps of his iron foot were beginning to chafe his leg. He could easily afford the shilling the cab would cost, and he was hot and tired. But the more his leg hurt him the tighter he clenched his teeth, muttering: "You hurt me, you bastard—now I'll hurt you. Walk, walk!"—hammering the pavement with his heavy stick, and forcing himself to move so fast that he was in Wilkin Street by six o'clock, even though, on the way, he stopped at a crockery shop and bought two three-penny tumblers. He felt the need of a drink, but not out of Mr. Goodridge's utensils. He bought a bottle of gin, too, and a handful of good cigars. This, he felt, was small capital to put into a gold-mine.

But Wilkin Street, normally secretive and empty, was full of people, exchanging knowing nods and weighty conversation. Although there had been no rain for a week, the gutters were running and the drains were gurgling with scummy black water. The air, which ought to have been full of dust, was full of ashes. Solly Schwartz saw a policeman, brushing his tunic with one hand and blowing his nose with the other—and this in itself was extraordinary because he had never before seen a policeman blowing his nose. "What's up, officer?" he asked.

"Fire."

"Where?"

"Number 37B. House burned down, two houses next door seriously damaged. If you want to know anything more read the papers to-morrow—I'm sick of answering questions all day long."

"37B!" screamed Solly Schwartz.

"Anybody you know live there?" asked the policeman, with commiseration.

"Anybody I know? My friend—I was on my way to see him —look, I've got a capon and a bottle of gin for him. He lives in the basement——"

"—No, he doesn't," said the policeman. "Not no more. That's where the fire started. Was your friend a man in the habit of locking himself in with oil-lamps, etcetera, etcetera?"

"Well?"

"Well, I'm sorry to say he set the place alight this morning. The firemen've been at it most of the day. They saved most of the two other houses, but they couldn't do much with 37B except get most of the lodgers out. If your friend lived in the basement I'm sorry to say he's done for. Fire started down there and by the time the firemen broke the door down with their axes—I'm sorry to say your friend locked himself in—the place was a blazing

159

inferno," said the policeman, who read the papers, "a 'olocaust. And there you are."

"Did they get any papers, or any machinery out of the basement?" asked Solly Schwartz, adding: "Have a cigar."

"Thank you sir, but I can't smoke it now . . . and even if I could, I haven't got a light. We just put it out." Pleased by this witticism, he repeated: "No, we just put it out. Papers, did you say? Oh Lord, I should say not. What else was it you said? Machinery? Nothing of the kind, nothing of the kind. There was all kinds of scrap-metal. They shovelled it up. But machinery, not likely. I'm sorry to say even your friend was nothing but charred bones. Must have knocked the lamp over or something—very likely drunk, I should think. Anyway that basement went up like a pinch of gunpowder in a candle, and there you are, that's what comes of losing your self-control."

Beating the macadam with his stick, Solly Schwartz shouted: "Bloody hell!"

"I understand your feelings, but feelings are no excuse for Language in Public," said the policeman.

Solly Schwartz, first looking left and right to assure himself that there were no witnesses, said: "Language? Language——" and snarled the wickedest and dirtiest words he knew. Then he said: "Here you are, here's some more cigars for you;" pushed the cigars into the policeman's hands, and, turning on his iron foot, went hobbling back to the top of the street, cursing himself. He remembered Mr. Goodridge, staggering drunk with his cigar and flaring fusee—a match designed to burn against a high wind —and thinking of the lamp, the oily rags, the waste paper, said: "It serves me right! It serves me right!"

CHAPTER XV

HE felt as a man might feel who has absent-mindedly burnt a thousand-pound note to light a sixpenny cigar. He cursed himself when he thought of all that was lost in the dust and the ashes of the burnt house—the salt-sprinklers, pipe joints, corkscrews, even that queer, chattering piece of machinery that could do the work of a trained book-keeper, infallibly, in half a second, and might even be made to do infinitesimal calculus and logarithms, whatever they might be. A machine such as that, in a great counting house, would be worth more than its weight in gold: it would not need feeding, it would want no wages, it would not fall in love and get married, it would not require even such diplomacy as old Cohen employed in dealing with a temperamental button-hole-maker. Every business house, every bank in the world would pay through the nose for such a machine; and there it was, burnt up and disintegrated, a couple of shovelfuls of fused and twisted scrap-metal, together with the man who had conceived it and given thirty-five years of his life to it. That man Good-ridge had been in himself a gold-mine; and now he was ashes.

In a spasm of rage Solly Schwartz hurled the bottle of gin into the gutter, with such violence that it seemed to explode like a bombshell. Another policeman said, sternly: "Now then! What's the game?"

"It slipped out of my hand," said Solly Schwartz.

"What a shame!"

"To hell with it. Here you are, catch hold," said Solly Schwartz, throwing the roast capon to the policeman, who instinctively caught it, and stood stupidly blinking at it while the hunchback went on his way.

Soon his anger cooled and, remembering that he still had the self-opening tin can, the Peli-Can, he composed himself and sat down to work out schemes, because he felt that it was necessary, now, to be strong, patient, adroit, and extremely cautious.

While his tin can was being examined, before the patent was sealed, he hopped up and down the streets of the city, limping in and out of grocery shops, and feverishly pumping manufacturers.

Not far from the squalid little house in which he lived there was a well-stocked branch of the Provincial Stores, where Solly Schwartz used to buy the tins of sardines and pink salmon that he liked to eat in his bedroom. He took to dropping in at four o'clock in the afternoon, when business was slack. Then the cashier, in her little glass case, knitted a scarf of seven colours for her young man—Solly Schwartz had found out all about it —and the chief assistant, in an alpaca coat and a long white apron, twirled his moustache at the two young ladies who served under him behind the counter. At that time of the day the manager, a subservient but spiteful little man with a snarling Midland accent, went into a matchboard box at the back of the shop and drank a pot of tea. Solly Schwartz became effusively friendly with this manager. His name was Lumpitt, and he was a disappointed man, a failure. Lumpitt greatly admired Solly Schwartz—the clothes he wore, the canes he handled, the way he carried gold and silver loose in his pocket without a purse— above all, his marvellous self-confidence. For Lumpitt was a weak, irresolute man, and that was why he was where he was; finished at fifty-five, running a little branch of a big man's business in a slum; on the edge of the scrap-heap. They had many a pleasant chat. Solly Schwartz deferred to Lumpitt, speaking to him with the profoundest respect for his superior knowledge of the grocery business. "Now what would be the weight of this tin of pineapple?" he would ask.

"That, sir? The nett weight of that would be about one pound four ounces."

"No, really? One pound four ounces? It's no use talking, Mr. Lumpitt, you know your business all right. I'll bet you anything you like there's not many gentlemen in your trade in London who could answer pat like that: 'One pound four ounces.' That's what I admire about you—you know what's what. I admire a man who knows what's he up to. Why don't you come out with me one evening and let's go to a music hall?"

"Ah, that's out of the question, I'm afraid. I'm a married man, you see."

"We'll arrange it, Mr. Lumpitt, on my word of honour, we'll arrange all that, believe me. Don't worry. You're the sort of man I like—a man who knows his business. You and me'll have a night out. We'll go to the Alhambra and see the girls. Me, you know, I'm not much to look at, I'm not what you'd call an oil painting. So I'd gladly stand treat if I could have a good-looking fellow like you with me. And you carry yourself like a gentleman, which is more than can be said for a lot of people I could mention."

"Oh, I wouldn't say that," said Mr. Lumpitt, smiling. "But once upon a time I used to be pretty near as well dressed as you, Mr. Schwartz. I had my own business once, a very nice little business, in the Midlands. In Slupworth. Have you ever been to Slupworth, sir?"

"No, I can't say I have had that privilege," said Solly Schwartz earnestly, "but I've often wanted to go. You were in the provision business there, were you?"

"I dare say if you went to Slupworth to-morrow and said to anybody: 'Do you remember George Lumpitt who had the shop in Royal Road,' they'd say: 'I do!' and here I am, as you see, sir, working as a servant for my own worst enemy, me that was my own master."

"It's a shame, Mr. Lumpitt, it's a terrible shame. A man with your knowledge of——" Solly Schwartz waved an arm in a spiral gesture that included the contents of all the shelves in the shop. "—Yes, you and me must certainly get out one night. But tell me now just for curiosity's sake. You know all about these things, I'm ignorant. You know I've been buying lots and lots of tins of this, that and the other?"

"And paying cash like a gentleman, sir."

"Well, there's something I've been wondering about. I suppose there must be at least fifteen different sorts of tinned stuff in stock here. I mean tinned stuff put up by at least a dozen different manufacturers."

"Eleven, to be precise " said Mr. Lumpitt with pride. "First of all there's——"

"—Yes, Mr. Lumpitt, I can see you know the business from A to Z, from the tips of your fingers. Now tell me something. I ask you because I happen to be curious, and you're the sort of man I like to have a chat with. Now tell me: how many different makes of tinned peas do you stock?"

Counting on his fingers Mr. Lumpitt said: "Five. Yes, we stock five separate and distinct brands of tinned pea."

"Now whose do you sell most of?"

"We sell most of Narwall's Fresh Garden Peas," said Mr. Lumpitt, with a short laugh and a wry smile.

"Now why is that? Because they're better, or what?"

"Narwall's are no better and no worse than any other peas, sir. We sell more of Narwall's for the simple reason that we have strict instructions to push 'em, because Narwall, who puts 'em up, happens to own the Provincial Stores, you see—forty-eight branches, all over the country—*huh!*"

"What's the huh for, Mr. Lumpitt?"

"I don't want to appear bitter, but I've got my reasons, and so have plenty more like me. Narwall!" Mr. Lumpitt lowered his voice and said: "All I can say is, if he was where I wished him . . . Well, he's so mean, he won't have a fire lit in the house until the middle of October. Well, if he was where I wish he was, he'd find that they weren't sparing of the coal all the year round."

"What, you know him?" said Solly Schwartz, keen as a terrier.

"I know him, sir, to my cost. I knew him when he was nothing but a nobody in Slupworth. He used to keep a little General Shop in Paradise Lane—a penn'orth of this, a ha'porth of that, a farden's worth of t'other—when I was my own master in the Royal Road, well-known and respected. It was a lovely little business, sir. I turned over my thirty or forty pound a week. You can ask——"

"—No, is that a fact?"

"—While Narwall was bowing and scraping to the lowest of the low in Paradise Lane. 'Two farden candles, a penn'orth of pepper, a gill o' vinegar, and a penn'orth o' lump salt—and look sharp about it! —— Yes sir, yes mum' . . . that was *his* kind of trade, twenty-five years ago. Why, he was no class. Everybody used to look down on him. And now he's a millionaire, and I'm his humble servant, and if I saw him to-morrow and didn't take my hat off to him I dare say he'd give me the sack. Yes sir, when you're as old as I am—I'm rising sixty—you'll understand that there's no justice in the world."

"Yes, but what d'you mean? How could he? What are you talking about? This man starts selling penny screws of pepper and gills of vinegar, and then all of a sudden—one, two, three! —he opens forty-eight shops and starts making tinned peas? Are you joking?"

"I wish I was. It wasn't all of a sudden. It took time. Nobody knows the ins and outs of it, but one fine day Narwall gives up his dirty little General Shop and starts calling himself a Wholesaler and Retailer, if you please, in the provision business. Wholesaler and Retailer if you don't mind!" said Mr. Lumpitt, with a scornful laugh, "and before you knew where you were he was buying up business premises."

"How? How did he do it, out of a penn'orth of pepper and a ha'porth of candles?"

"I don't rightly know. All I know is, one day he comes into my shop—my shop in Royal Road—looking like I don't know what. You'd think that a man who'd come up in the world like he did would go out and smarten himself up a bit—you know, a clean collar, a new hat, or something like that. Wouldn't you?"

"Very likely," said Solly Schwartz.

"Not Narwall, oh dear no! He was too mean even to get himself a pair of boot-laces. As sure as I sit here," said Mr. Lumpitt, passionately, "the laces in his boots was a mass of knots; and poor as I am I'd be ashamed to be seen dead in those boots. Poor as I am, I've given many a better pair of boots to beggars at the door. Quite apart from all that I was a cut above him then, you know."

"I can well believe it—you're a superior sort of man, Mr. Lumpitt. But go on."

"I said: 'Well, Narwall, what can I do for you?' And he said: 'Good morning, Mr. Lumpitt, I've come to buy your shop.' I burst out laughing. 'You've come to what?'——'I've come to buy your shop, Mr. Lumpitt, lock, stock and barrel and good-will. Tell me what you consider a fair price and if I agree to it I'll write you a cheque. Well?'——'Mr. Narwall, are you out of your mind?' I'd heard that he'd been making money, but I didn't know he was as rich as he really was, and neither did anyone else. Well, he looks at me and says: 'I hope I am not out of my mind, Mr. Lumpitt. I asked you a simple question. I'll repeat it. How much do you want for the business?' I said to him: 'I don't want anything for the business, thank you very much. It's the nicest little business in the best position in the Royal Road, and I'm quite comfortable, thanks all the same.' I said it sarcastic, and looked him up and down, and my good lady who was behind the counter with me gave him one of her looks and said: 'Well, of all the sauce!' Well, so then he said: 'State a fair price and I won't haggle. I'm making you an open offer. If you won't come to terms you must take the consequences.'——'And may I ask what consequences I must take, Mr.-Blooming-Narwall?' ——'Why, Mr. Lumpitt, I'll take those empty premises across

165

the road, and open up a grocery shop that'll put you out of business in a year.'"

Mr. Lumpitt paused, biting the ends of his drooping moustache. Solly Schwartz impatiently snapped: "Go on! What happened next?"

"I showed him the door. I said: 'Damn your impudence, be off!' He said: 'You'd better think it over, you know.' Then I said: 'There's nothing to think over. I'm well-known and respected in Royal Road. I give good value for money, and a little over-weight. Everybody knows that I don't count every grain of rice or pinch of tapioca, and that's why they come to me. You go away.'——'Is that your last word, Mr. Lumpitt?'——'Yes, it is, and good day to you.'"

"What did he do then?"

"What did he not do then? There was a draper called Morgan just across the street whose business was up for sale. What does Narwall do but buy it up, sell in the stock dirt cheap, and the next thing you knew, there was a whole army of workmen tearing down the front and putting in a new one, and up went a fascia—all golden letters and glass—*Provincial Stores*. That didn't worry my fat very much, because business was as usual. Then he took and stocked it chock full with provisions of all sorts, but still I didn't worry, because I sold nothing but the best at the lowest possible price and was well liked and patronised accordingly. And hen, three days before he opened, he sent men with sandwich boards round the town saying that to celebrate the opening of the Provincial Store every customer would get two of whatever he wanted to buy for the price of one—two pounds of rice for the price of one, two pounds of sugar for the price of one, two tins of salmon for the price of one, and so on. What do you think of that for a dirty trick?"

Solly Schwartz stopped himself in the middle of an eager nod of approval and said: "Terrible! But what happened then?"

"Ask yourself the question, sir. The ladies were lining up with their baskets an hour before that shop opened. Two police-men had to keep order. And when the doors opened they rushed in and they emptied those shelves within half an hour. It was a dead loss, of course, but he could afford it, it seemed. He was re-stocked by the following morning, and had another lot of sandwich men up and down the town with notices saying that everything in the Provincial Store was a little bit cheaper than anywhere else in Slupworth. Do you see? He was selling at cost price which, given overheads, means to say he was selling at a dead loss—just to break me."

"Yes, yes, of course, of course!"

"Is there anything to smile about in this? Because if so——"

"—What, smiling? Who, me? I've got a fishbone stuck up here in my gum. Why should I smile? What that man did was wicked," said Solly Schwartz.

"You're right. I'm all for fair trade, fair competition, and none of these dirty tricks. There was no use my cutting back, because I didn't have the capital to hold out, you see. So I tried to hold on. But I ask you: if I'm selling an article for sixpence and a man across the road is selling that selfsame identical article for fivepence, who would you patronise?"

"Regarding you as a friend *I* would patronise *you*," said Solly Schwartz. "But the majority of people wouldn't see any sense in spending sixpence where fivepence would do."

"And there you are, you see. The business went down like . . . like sand out of an egg-boiler. And here I am."

Solly Schwartz asked, eagerly: "And did he break you in a year?"

"Ten months and eleven days," said Mr. Lumpitt.

"And then?"

"Then I had nothing but a few pounds I put aside, and I didn't know what to do. Then, when I'd put up a clearance sale notice before I got out, Narwall comes into the shop. I had a jar of pickles in my hand and I don't mind telling you I came pretty near to letting him have it between the eyes like Cain and Abel. But he said: 'Lumpitt, I'm sorry to see you in this state, but you must admit that I gave you a fair word of warning. If you'd done what I suggested last January all this wouldn't have happened —you'd've been established in another business in some other place. Now look at you.' I said to him: 'Ay, established in another business in another place, to keep it warm for you, I dare say, damn you, you hypocrite!' He's a churchgoer, you know; a thorough-going Christian. Sell all you have and give to the poor . . . suffer little children to come unto me . . . you know, all that kind of thing. He suffered little children to come unto him all right. And, my eye, he made 'em suffer, I can tell you! Got 'em out of orphanages—always the true-blue Christian —put 'em to work in his shops, fed 'em on cocoa and skilly, paid 'em something less than half o' nothing a week, and made a song of it, all about 'the least of these', and 'better a millstone were tied around his confounded neck and he were chucked into the sea', etcetera, etcetera. You know that kind?"

"Only too well," said Solly Schwartz. "But go on, it's interesting. You're a marvellous talker, you know. You make everything seem so real."

"Well, I'll cut a long story short. Narwall says: 'Look here, Lumpitt'—*Lumpitt*, mind you, him as had been thankful if I smiled at him when he raised his hat to me in the street—he says: 'If you haven't made any plans and haven't had the providence to put by sufficient capital to establish yourself elsewhere, being as I know you, Lumpitt, I am prepared to offer you a responsible position in one of my branches.' "

Lumpitt paused, and Solly Schwartz, feeling that he was expected to say something, said: "You don't mean to say!"

"Yes, I do mean to say," said Lumpitt, doggedly. "Naturally, I was going to tell him to go to Hull and Halifax. But then the wife pinched my arm—poor lass, she was worried out of her life —and cut in first and said: 'All right, Mr. Narwall.' Naturally, she was right. What else was there to do? I didn't have enough to start again on my own, and otherwise it would have meant hunting about for a crib, and eating up the little bit that was left. So I humbled myself. And I said: 'All right, but I if work for you for mercy's sake don't let it be in Slupworth where I've been my own master all my life. Send me somewhere else.' Then he said: 'All right, Lumpitt, I will do what you ask since it means so much to you, because as a matter of principle I have always returned good for evil.' And I actually said: 'Thank you very much;' but as soon as he was gone I ran after Phyllis into the shop-parlour and pushed my face into her lap and cried like a baby. And here I am, and that's all about it. So now you know——"

"—Yes, but when did he start canning peas?"

"Eh? Oh, I don't know. He got hold of it somehow or other, don't you worry. You know the saying, We eat what we can and what we can't we can? That's Narwall for you, all over. Nobody knows the ins and outs of Narwall's business."

"And there you are," said Solly Schwartz, shaking his head sadly. "And I wouldn't mind betting that he's worth thousands."

"Thousands? Hundreds of thousands!"

"Living like a lord in Park Lane, the dirty dog I bet you. Eh?"

"Him? Oh no. You won't catch him living in no Park Lane. He won't leave Slupworth, where the factory is."

"I suppose he's got his wife and family there?"

"That's right," said Mr. Lumpitt gloomily.

"If you'll excuse the expression, he sounds like a proper bastard," said Solly Schwartz, "a real swine."

"His wife is fifty thousand million times worse, I can tell you for a fact."

"My word! She must be a tartar! I'd hate to come up against *her*."

"Think yourself lucky you never have. She's the wickedest woman in the world. Her name is Charlotte, but everybody calls her Jezebel. Oh, what a cow!"

"It says on the label, *W. W. Narwall*," said Solly Schwartz. "What does the W. W. stand for?"

"William Wilberforce—you know, the man that freed the slaves. And there's another good joke for you. All this is between you, me, and the gatepost, you know?"

"It stands to reason, Mr. Lumpitt. But it does a man good, it eases his heart, to have a chat once in a while, doesn't it? It eases his nerves, I always think. And you're a bundle of nerves, aren't you? Why don't you let me take you out one of these nights, to the West End, just to get your mind off things; because your work is brain work, Mr. Lumpitt."

"I'm a married man, sir."

"Yes, but a change is as good as a rest. I shouldn't be surprised if you're irritable when you get home after your hard day's work."

"A man does get over-tired, although God knows I don't mean any harm when I drop a hard word here or there."

"And it's all the fault of W. W. Narwall, the swine. Well, I'll never buy another tin of his stuff as long as I live, and that's flat."

"Hey, just a minute, Mr. Schwartz—remember, what I said was between you and me and the gatepost—I've got my living to make, and the more I push——"

"—I was going to say, Mr. Lumpitt, that I'll never buy another tin of his stuff again except from you."

* * * * *

Solly Schwartz left the shop, exultant, saying to himself: *Good. That's what I wanted to know. W. W. Narwall. That's the*

169

*man for me—a pig, a glutton, a crocodile; always hungry, never
satisfied; a fresser-up of everything. The biggest firms are too big.
They think they've got all they want. They think they don't need to
fight . . . as yet. If I go to one of them—me, a nobody—they'll
give me a polite kick in the bum. Narwall. Give me Narwall!*

He might have ridden in an omnibus, or a cab, but he preferred
to walk: thus he defied his deformity. In three-quarters of an
hour he was in Frith Street in Soho, kicking open the shop door
of a metal-worker named Anselmi, a withered, leathery, tanned
Italian who made cooking pots for restaurateurs—copper saucepans, frying-pans, stockpots, fish-kettles; all elegantly finished,
brilliantly polished, and beautifully tinned. He looked as if he
had made himself—dull hammered copper head and tin moustache.

"Anselmi," said Solly Schwartz, "I've got a job for you."

"Please, please!"

"Do you see this?"

Anselmi took Goodridge's self-opening can in his hard, dry
hand, and shook his head, saying: "What you call-a dis?"

"Never mind. What I want you to do is, make me some copies
of it. Oh it's all right, I know you don't make tin cans, Anselmi,
but this is a special thing, see? It's an invention, do you follow
me? Look—this is the diagram. The tin is nothing, do you see?
The thing is, this little business up here with the wheel. Do you
grasp the idea, Anselmi? It opens itself. Does it mean anything
to you?"

"Clever!" cried Anselmi, looking at the diagram. "*You* think-a
this?"

"Don't worry about that. What I want to know is, can you
make me a few samples?"

"Sure, certainly, but-a what for? Better get a tin"—Anselmi,
glancing at his polished copper pots, twitched a contemptuous
lip—"and make only the top."

"You're quite right. But can you do it? I mean, this wheel-
thing, and the way it goes round?"

"*You* make-a *this?*"

"Answer my question."

"Sure, I can make. You bring-a dem tins I make-a top. Howa
many you want?"

"Two dozen," said Solly Schwartz. "How much are you going
to charge me?"

"Five-a shilling each."

At this Solly Schwartz became deathly pale and said: "What the hell are you talking about? What, five shillings? How, five shillings? Are you trying to make a fool of me?"—for a great dread had come down upon him—"Do you mean to say it'd cost five shillings to make a top for a fourpenny tin of peas?"

"No, to *you*, four-and-sixpence," said Anselmi patiently; and when Solly Schwartz stared at him with sick horror he explained, gently, with infinite patience: "Now look, look-a this saucepan. You want to buy-a this saucepan, it'll gonna cost you twenty-five shilling. You can go around a corner to a shop and buy a saucepan to hold so many pints, for a shilling, two shilling. Why? In-a first place is this—look, feel-a weight—copper, solid! And——"

"—To hell with your bloody copper!" cried Solly Schwartz, making harsh music with his stick upon the frame of his iron foot, "who the hell cares about copper? I don't give a bugger for copper! I'm talking about tin cans, you . . . you . . ."

"Mistro please, permit-a me a-finish. This good solid copper cost-a me a few shilling. But-a between the copper and *this*"— he struck the saucepan with his dry knuckles so that it rang like a bell—"is *this!*" He held up his gnarled right hand. "It is this, and the time of my life, that cost-a twenty-five shilling. But my saucepan, your children's children they'll-a use it. It-a last a hundred-a years, because——"

"—Who the hell wants a saucepan to last a hundred years? Who the hell cares about children's children? Let 'em buy their own damned saucepans! Where do you think it'll get you? Making things to last a hundred years? Something to be used once, and then thrown away, that's the idea! Something you can keep on selling and selling and selling, day and night. Take your bloody saucepan away and start talking sense for a change."

Anselmi patted the shining saucepan in a friendly, intimate way, and put it down, saying: "I was-a saying: I make this-a tin, it take-a time. That-a worth four, five shilling. In a factory, a thing comes down like"—he stamped on the floor three times— "and it's-a done for a farthing. Use it, throw it away."

"Sorry, I misunderstood," said Solly Schwartz, secretly ashamed. "For a minute I thought you meant to say that tin would cost five shillings apiece to manufacture."

"Oh no," said Anselmi, laughing. "To make-a by machine, nothing. By hand, for you, well, four-a shillings."

"Right. I'll bring you a dozen and a half tins to get to work on. Do you want the model or the diagram to work with?"

"Model, please."

"All right. Oh, by the way, don't try anything clever, you know, because the patent's applied for, and if you want to be smart there'll be trouble."

Anselmi laughed with a sort of kindly contempt, flipping the tin can with a horny forefinger. "Use it once, throw it away," he said; and picked up the saucepan again, pointing to a stamped inscription below the rivets of the handle. "You see there? *G. L. Anselmi.* In a hundred-a years somebody she'll make a minestrone with this, and she'll read my name and say: 'This-a man Anselmi, that was a good-a workman. Then she clean it, a-polish it, hang 'im up on a nail and sit and look at 'im because the more-a you use 'im the better she shine. Solid-a copper in 'ouse, mister, is better an-agold. A good-a woman, she's proud of 'im. She light a lamp, there 'e is—one two three four five six, all in a row. 'Anselmi done it!' she says."

"But what difference could it make to you?"

"*Me la riderò nella tomba.*"

"What does that mean?"

"I laugh in my grave."

*　　*　　*　　*　　*

Solly Schwartz hurried to the nearest branch of the Provincial Stores and astounded a salesman by ordering eighteen tin of peas —six of Narwall's, and four each of three other popular brands. He put down his money, took his change, and picked up the thirty-pound parcel as if it weighed no more than a box of matches. Then he went to Vespasiano's café in Frith Street to restore his energy with coffee and cake, and to think a little. Something was working in his head, fermenting like a distiller's mash, and he beat a tune with a fork on his teeth while he wondered what that something was. He knew that it had to do with W. W. Narwall, so he tore open a corner of his parcel and pulled out one of Narwall's cans of peas; and then he knew. He turned the can in his hands, looking at it with distaste, saying to himself: *I can well imagine Narwall having to push this muck. If he didn't have forty-eight counters to push it over, it'd stick on the shelves and rot. A starving man wouldn't look twice at it.*

It was obvious that W. W. Narwall had exercised the strictest economy in his packaging. Solly Schwartz with his quick imagination, could see the old man (whom he visualised as something like a locust) standing over some provincial printer and haggling, niggling, nattering, droning on and on, rubbing his back legs together to make a chirping noise while he ate away the morale of his adversary. Looking at that label, Solly Schwartz felt that he was looking into the mind of W. W. Narwall. It was cheap, indescribably mean. This is what it conveyed: that Narwall had begrudged every inch of paper and every drop of ink—even in printing his own name—the typography was reminiscent of the handwriting of a miser who carefully writes small to save paper. As for the paper, its very colour was repulsive—the colour of German mustard with a tinge of green; evidently some wretched job-lot, otherwise unusable, disposed of with a gasp of relief. Solly Schwartz reasoned: *Now if you stick a label on something, what do you stick that label on for? To hit the eye, to draw attention. Otherwise, why waste money on labels? Right. This label of Narwall's —does it draw attention? Yes, it draws attention like dog-shit on the pavement draws attention—just long enough so you can avoid it— that filthy colour! And that's a nice thing to stick on a shelf in a grocer's shop. Apart from the new tin, what that bloody fool wants is a new label. If you're selling peas you don't want to make me think of lavatories. If I'm buying peas I am thinking of peas—you crack a pod and out come nice shiny fresh green peas. In your mind there's a picture. What you say doesn't matter provided you've got a nice picture. A label, a label, a label! The schlemihls—they'd pay six-pence for a tin of dish-water if you put a pretty label on it and called it Nourishing Soup. . . .*

And just as he finished saying this to himself, someone tapped him on the shoulder and said: "Hello, you."

Solly Schwartz looked up and then said: "Mr. Abelard—that's a funny thing, I was just thinking about you."

In the half second between the touch and the recognition, Solly Schwartz had conceived another idea.

Abel Abelard was an artist whom Solly Schwartz had got acquainted with one night when, having prowled the streets and poked his great beak of a nose into many sinister, dimly-lit doorways, he had stopped at Vespasiano's for something to eat and drink , and—always insatiably curious—corkscrewed himself into a little group of men and women, unconventionally dressed, who were talking at the top of their voices about things he did not understand and men he had never heard of. . . . Manet, Monet, Pissarro, Sickert. Here, he felt, was another corner of the sky, something more to learn. It was impossible to know too much. He waited for a loop-hole of silence, and squeezed himself into it, saying: "I beg your pardon, ladies and gentlemen, but if you will pardon the intrusion, I heard you mention a certain name just now. Unless my ears deceive me, I believe I heard that gentleman over there mention the name of Rubens."

"That's right," said a fat, bearded man in a nankeen jacket.

"Is he by any chance any relation of Mr. Max Rubens in the New Road?"

He knew that he was talking nonsense, and that he was exposing himself as pitiably ignorant; but he knew that to the ignorant much is told. He was not a bit offended by the roar of laughter that followed. They made room for him and invited him to sit at their table, where, for two hours, they pitilessly made fun of him:

". . . Rubens of the New Road is a builder. The one I was talking about was a decorator."

". . . You don't, by any chance, happen to know a bloke called Theotocopuli, the one they call El Greco or The Greek?"

". . . Darling, did you hear that? He says he knows a man called The Greek who opened a restaurant in Dalston—isn't he priceless?"

". . . By the way, speaking of Manet, have you any Monet? We could do with a cup of coffee."

He listened to it all, smiling, and ordered coffee and pastries for the company; after which they forgot him. But he kept his seat at their table and went on listening until the party broke up. Then a secretive-looking young man took him aside and said: "I say, I don't suppose you could manage to lend me half a crown, by any chance?"

Solly Schwartz looked at him quizzically, and saw a youthful, nervous face, with a tremulous chin scantily covered by a thin, threadbare beard. "Right you are then, catch hold," he said, handing over half a crown.

"I'm ever so much obliged. I say, you know we didn't mean any harm, ragging you and all that? . . . I suppose you *do* know that we *were* ragging you, or don't you? By the way, my name's Abel Abelard."

"Good-night all," said Solly Schwartz, and limped away, leaving behind him an uneasy doubt as to who had made a fool of whom. He had a rare knack of making people feel uneasy, that hunchback. Walking home, he thought: *Six coffees with cream. Twelve ba-bas. Plus half a crown. They got a coffee and a cake and a laugh from me. We'll see who comes out winning.*

Now, smiling at Abel Abelard he said: "Sit down, I want to talk to you."

"What about?" asked Abelard, nervously fumbling at his light beard.

"Have some coffee."

"Well, yes, if you like."

"A bit of cake?"

"Well, I don't mind if I do."

"Or perhaps you'd like something more substantial—ham and egg, egg and bacon?"

"I wouldn't say no."

"Cigarette? Have a cigarette—they're hand-made."

"Oh thanks awfully. You're ever so kind. I say, look here, I don't suppose by any chance you'd care to lend me a pound until . . . until next . . ."

"That's right. How did you guess?"

"You didn't mind my asking, I hope?" asked Abel Abelard.

"No harm in trying," said Solly Schwartz, jovially. "If it works once in ten times it still shows a profit."

While Abel Abelard was eating his ham and eggs Solly Schwartz said: "I'll tell you what, though—I could put a little bit of work your way. You are an artist, aren't you? How would you like to paint me up two or three samples for labels?"

"Labels? What sort of labels?" asked the painter, who was engaged on a canvas sixteen feet long and eight feet wide depicting the destruction of the Great Library at Alexandria. "Labels?" He made, with his forefingers and thumbs, a tiny oblong.

"Look," said Solly Schwartz, pushing the tin of peas across the table. "You see the label on this here tin."

"I say, isn't it horrid?"

"That's right. Now what I want you to do is paint me a label with peas on it. Do you follow me? Peas. *Garden* peas." Solly Schwartz did not know the difference between a Garden pea and a Common pea—neither does anyone else—but he said it again: "*Garden* peas. Now I want you to paint me up this label so that when I look at it, it should make my mouth water. Listen. At

home, you've helped your mother to shell peas, haven't you?"
Abel Abelard had not, but he nodded, and Solly Schwartz went
on: "You've sat there in the kitchen. It's Saturday. Your mother
has bought half a boiling fowl. She's going to make a lovely
chicken soup with farfel and a few fresh green peas in it before the
boiled chicken. Eh?"—At the thought of this Solly Schwartz's
mouth watered and he paused to order ham and eggs. "Your
mother says to you, whatever your name is: 'Make yourself
useful, do the peas.' So you sit down with a basin and you break
open those pods, and with your finger you scrape out all those
nice cold peas; and when your mother isn't looking you eat one
or two, and they taste . . . they taste . . . they taste *of green*.
Well, that's how I want this label: it's got to *taste* of green peas.
I want pods full of peas, a little basin full of peas straight out of
them pods, and some pods just opened like your mother had just
poked her finger into them, full of peas. I want them shiny-
glossy peas. Up here, on top, I want *W. W. Narwall's Fresh
Garden Peas* in nice clear letters, but not to drown those peas.
Do you understand? A label like this to go round a tin like this.
Do you see? Tell me, yes or no!" cried Solly Schwartz, passionately

"Oh well, yes, I think I can do that. In how many colours?"

"Green! How many colours is a pea? As many colours as you
like—the more the merrier—only I want those peas to look like
peas, to look like they're just coming out of that pod on the end
of your thumb. Never mind colours, *do* it! And can you do me
another label, the same, with tomatoes?"

"Oh yes—they're lovely things, tomatoes. I love them."

"Who doesn't? Imagine—you come home from school hungry
and your mother's making fresh tomato soup with fresh tomatoes,
with a little bit of rice in it, eh?" Solly Schwartz, overcome by the
memory of it, mopped up egg yolk with a bit of bread, and
swallowed noisily; but his eloquence was such that Abel Abelard,
whose diet, between ten and seventeen, had consisted in stew and
pudding at a great public school, felt hungry for green peas in
chicken broth and clear tomato soup with a few grains of rice in
it.

"Well, yes," he said, "but is this a commission, or only a
suggestion?"

"Now look here. You paint me up three good labels, to fit
this tin—you know the lettering. I want—one for garden peas,
one for tomatoes, and one for——" Solly Schwartz thought for a

moment, striking his iron foot with his stick, and then cried—
"Chicken soup! Think of a lovely fat juicy fowl, and a bowl, a
lovely bowl full of chicken soup that looks like gold, with a few
garden peas floating in it. Think of that! Do me those three
labels, by tomorrow this time, and I'll pay you well."

"Could you pay me a little something as it were in advance?"

Solly Schwartz's hand went to his pocket. He knew that Abel
Abelard was hungry, and something told him that the hungrier
he was the more passion he would put into his peas, tomatoes, and
chicken soup. So he put down five shillings and said: "This'll
tide you over till to-morrow. You let me have those labels by
five o'clock to-morrow afternoon, and I'll pay you a pound apiece
for them. Is that fair?"

"Well, I'm agreeable," said Abel Abelard.

"I don't have to tell a man of your education what peas and
tomatoes look like, but have you got that chicken soup clear in
your mind? It's a sort of golden colour—think of melted butter
—and in it there's these little fresh peas, and little tiny square
bits of farfel. You keep on thinking of it and make me a nice
picture with good gold lettering for the label. When I say gold,
remember, I don't mean that sort of gold they paint picture
frames with, I mean——"

"—Oh, *don't!* I know, I know. Hadn't I better take this tin
of peas for the measurement?"

"Certainly, take it."

"By the way, will you want it back?"

"All I want is them labels."

"You see, all of a sudden I've developed a terrific appetite
for green peas. I'll be here by half-past four to-morrow afternoon.
Thank you very, very much. *À demain.*"

When he was gone Solly Schwartz paid the bill and went out
of the café, saying to himself: *My God, what a marvellous salesman
I am! I've sold myself chicken soup!* And he walked as fast as he
could to Fishbone's kosher restaurant in Charing Cross Road.
There, impatiently beating his iron foot, he waited while a waiter
shouted down the shaft: "Von beef vid kasha for a special
customer—and der gentleman says dis time it should not smell
from herring!"

Then Solly Schwartz caught him by the coat-tails and said:
"C'mere—quick, I'm in a hurry! Have you got chicken soup with
a few fresh peas in it, and a little farfel?"

"All your life you should have chicken zoop like ve got chicken zoop," said the waiter.

Solly Schwartz had to swallow a mouthful of saliva before he could say: "Listen. I want a big plate, a great big plate—it had better be a little tureen—with chicken soup, with fresh peas, with a little farfel, the leg quarter of a boiled chicken, and matzo-balls. Quick, I'm in a hurry."

"A leg quarter special boiled chicken in special chicken zoop mit matzo-balls mit fresh peas mit special farfel for a special customer!" shouted the waiter.

Solly Schwartz sat and waited, remembering this dish as his mother used to make it. But when, at last, he was served, the soup was insipid and the chicken boiled to rags. As for the matzo-balls: he bit one, spat out the mouthful with a hideous grimace, picked another out of the bowl with his fingers and flipped it at the waiter's head, as a boy flips a marble, snarling: "You should shoot this *scheiss* out of guns. And what do you call this? Soup? And what do you call *this*, chicken? Ducks should be swimming in such soup—under Westminster Bridge there's better soup. And you call these fresh peas? Eh? They come out of a dirty stinking tin. Don't argue, because you're wrong—don't tell me, I know. This is the last time I patronise this restaurant."

"Vat do you vant from me? I'm der vaiter, not der cook."

"Oh, go away," said Solly Schwartz. He ate his soup and his chicken angrily. He was disenchanted: he had been thinking of the Friday evening meals as his mother prepared them; and thinking of them, even while he was chasing the last elusive drop of gravy around the plate with the last bit of bread, although his belly was full his mouth watered, and he said to himself: *Perhaps, after all, it's a bit of a pity she died. That chicken soup with farfel and peas took a bit of beating.*

(If, just then, someone had offered him a spoonful of the late Mrs. Schwartz's chicken soup, he would have spat it out in a fine spray and called nostalgically for the chicken soup that mother used to make. Mrs. Schwartz was an execrable cook. Solly's yearning was not for her watery, greasy soup: it was for a certain lost second. When he was eleven years old a newsagent and tobacconist paid him half a crown a week for his services as errand boy between four and seven o'clock five evenings a week. He learned to love Friday: it was the last day of school, the last day of labour, it was pay day. One awful Friday afternoon in

November a black fog came down—an icy cold, wet fog that penetrated clothes and skin as water gets into blotting-paper— and in this fog the boy Schwartz was lost. He had one small parcel of papers and periodicals to deliver, but he took the wrong turning and then, when the fog came down he found that he was blind as well as halt and lame, and so he pressed his head against some wet and freezing area railings and, as quietly as he could, for even then he had his pride, cried. Then there were footsteps that seemed to shake the street—whatever street it was—and there was a flash of golden light that concentrated itself into a circle. He found himself looking into a policeman's lantern. A gruff, foggy voice said: "Cheer up, you'll soon be dead. What you crying for? You lost?" The beam of light moved slowly down- wards, and shone upon the boy's iron foot. "Oh, ah," said the policeman, hooking his lantern on his belt, "up you get, come on. Now, where were you supposed to be going? . . . What for? . . . What, to deliver them, eh? Never mind about that. Where d'you live? . . . Oh there, I know: third left, first right, first left again. Come on, son, have a ride home. Hang on, and I'll give you a picky-back. . . . Don't worry about your papers. It's on my beat, and I'll deliver 'em for you. You come on home, my boy."

The policeman put him down outside the tenement in which he lived, and gave him two copper pennies. Solly Schwartz heard him say: "If the Sergeant is about, the odds are he'll never . . ." Then the big, iron-heeled boots clattered away in a hurry, and Solly Schwartz went upstairs. His parents were waiting for him. For once, his father was pleased to see him, and called him by endearing diminutives. They had thought that he had been run over in the fog. There was boiled chicken in soup, farfel, matzo- balls, and peas. They could not, of course, have been fresh peas, but they were delicious. They loaded his plate. Mr. Schwartz pulled a wing from his portion of chicken and gave it to him with a friendly smile. It was the happiest evening of Solly Schwartz's life. The chicken wing was scrawny and tough. But in the second that it took to tear it loose and offer it in that little warm, bright kitchen bolted and barred against the cold, the wet woolly fog, and the terrors of the night—in that second there was born a glory and a dream. . . . For that one second Solly Schwartz was happy. But only for that one second.)

*　　*　　*　　*　　*

He paid the bill, gave the waiter sixpence, and went back to Anselmi, hugging his parcel of tin cans. He was sad and angry. "Here they are," he said, "and I want the job done quick. Before you start, put them in warm water and get those labels off. Keep the labels, I want those labels. How soon can I get 'em?"

"I'm a liddle-a bit slack now, so two, two-three days."

"The day after to-morrow, you mean."

"Oright, day after to-morrow. But-a listen—I gotta open dem tins. What I do with dem peas?"

"Keep 'em, damn 'em—I hate the sight of 'em—I never want to see another pea as long as I live," said Solly Schwartz.

When he was gone Anselmi, turning the tin can in his hands, shook his head, smiled pitifully, and said: "*Ma tu, che capisci, gobbo?*"—Which means "You, what do *you* understand, hunchback?" But he said it in sorrow, not with malevolence.

Abel Abelard went back to his poor little bare studio in Fitzroy Square, where he stood for a long time gazing lovingly at his immense unfinished picture of the burning of the library at Alexandria. Like Haydon, he conceived his pictures on a huge scale. If the studio had been big enough to hold it, his canvas would have been 32 by 16 feet. He picked off a fly that had got stuck in the wet paint on the tip of a Mohammedan warrior's nose, dashed it to the floor and trampled it to death. His lady friend, his mimi, a cheerful slattern with a snub nose and tousled hair, came in and said: "Any luck, duck?"

"Well, I've got five shillings, and if I can turn out some labels for this tin can I can get three pounds. But now that I come to think of it, I don't see how I can. Look at that picture! Then they talk to me about labels!"

"Abel with a label," she said, giggling.

"Can an oak tree grow in a flower pot?"

"It's got to start somewhere, hasn't it, old feller?"

"Oh well. Here, you take this five shillings and go and get me a sheet of cartridge paper and an ounce of coarse-cut Cavendish. You can spend the rest on something to eat, anything you like, and we might as well have a jug of beer."

She took the ewer from the washstand. "Poor old Abel with his poor old label," she said, and went out. He pealed the label off the can and, angrily at first, started to rough out the design as Solly Schwartz had suggested it. Working on a few square inches of paper, he felt like a plainsman in a cellar—he was too big for it. He saw a pea vine as something like Jack's beanstalk. But soon, when the girl came back with the cartridge paper and he had pinned it down and got out his water colours, he became engrossed in the work. He reduced his pea to the size of a pea-and-a-half. He romanticised it, idealised it, shaded and high-lighted it until it resembled a sparkling pea-green jewel. He hung up great pods of polished jade tickled to bursting point by pretty curly tendrils. By the time he came to the tomatoes, he was begin-ning to enjoy himself. He liked tomatoes, too; and the ones he painted from memory were wonderful in their flawless perfection: no one ever saw such tomatoes on a costermonger's barrow. Jewellers put such tomatoes in velvet-lined cases and sell them for five thousand pounds apiece. As for his chicken soup, it was so rich that it might have been ready to pour into 22-carat ingots. Having gone so far he could not stop. "Perhaps he'll take one or two more," he said, and painted two more labels, for a tin of carrots, and a tin of plums.

"Come on, old Abel with a label," said the girl, yawning on the divan, "I can't stay awake much longer."

"Don't bother me now. If you can't stay awake, go to sleep. I've got to finish the lettering."

When Solly Schwartz saw his work he struck his iron foot in an ecstasy of admiration until it rang like an alarm bell, crying: "That's the thing, that's the very thing! The other two? The carrots, the plums? Certainly! How much was it I said I'd pay you? A pound apiece, was it? Right, here's five pounds—and here's a couple of pounds extra for a good job."

"I don't know," said Abel Abelard pensively fluffing out his beard, "now that I come to look at them in cold daylight, you know, they look . . . well, rather too good to be true, I'm afraid."

"That's the whole point, you donkey! That's the beauty of them, don't you see? Write me down your name and address on a bit of paper."

Five days later, carrying a large, brand-new suitcase and dressed in sober pepper-and-salt, Solly Schwartz caught the 8.15 at Euston, bound for Slupworth in the Midlands, where W. W. Narwall lived.

CHAPTER XVI

PEOPLE who were born in Slupworth and cannot afford to go elsewhere are proud of the town which is, they boast, ever so old. Gloomy, dour, sullen farmers working in their fields outside the town have unearthed undeniable evidence of Slupworth's antiquity. In the Museum—three glass cases in the Free Library —there are flint arrow-heads and axe-heads that date back to the Stone Age. It is indicated that Neolithic nomads, weary of wandering, gazed upon the valley of Slupworth and said, in effect: "Here is the Promised Land." There are also some Roman remains, dug up by some busybody of a vicar who fancied himself as an archæologist; several broken pots, a broken bronze buckle, a broken spear-head, a broken sword, several handfuls of scrap metal so deeply corroded that not even the British Museum can make head or tail of them, three copper coins utterly defaced, and a bronze knob. Of this knob one expert has said one thing, and another something else. It has a shelf all to itself. Thus it is conveyed that Slupworth was good enough for the Romans, who were masters of the world. They could have wallowed in the fleshpots of Egypt, rolled on silken carpets in Syria, and made merry in ancient Rome—but they came to Slupworth. A mud slinger who said that some centurion on his way to the Wall had probably halted in the valley to get a drink of water and a bite to eat and give his men a chance to tighten their harness, throw their rubbish away, and empty their bowels before hurrying on, became a social outcast in Slupworth.

Queen Elizabeth stopped there and listened to a quarter of the mayor's oration before she boxed his ears, called him a tight-mouthed ninny, and went on her way. Cavaliers and Round-heads skirmished in the valley. One of King Charles' gentlemen, wounded in the thigh, crawled to the door of a certain Mistress Endless and begged for shelter in the name of Christian charity, because Ireton's men were on his track. She not only took him in; she locked him in, and sent her grandson galloping belly-to-earth on a neighbour's horse to fetch one of Ireton's sergeants whose name was Hip-And-Thigh Edge, whom the Royalist fought, hopping on one leg, until he was brought down by a musket ball. His sword and gloves, also, are in the Museum, under a card upon which the librarian has written their history, and the reason why the main road of Slupworth was called Endless Road until the Restoration, when it was renamed Royal Road.

But Slupworth did not become truly great until 1806, when a man called Horace Hodd, who had managed to secure a contract to provide hides for the government, established a great tannery by the river at the north end of the town. (The central square of Slupworth is still called Hodd Circus.) Drovers whipped in great herds of cattle; for while he was about it Hodd had undertaken to provide the Navy with salt beef—salt being available in abundance from Cheshire, not too far to the north-west. Out of the beeves came tallow, which someone else bought and turned into soap and candles in a manufactory that grew and grew. In 1825 someone discovered a seam of coal less than three miles north of the town, and a local speculator sunk a shaft. He was a lucky speculator. He found iron as well as coal. Since then, no doubt, he has found brimstone. So, up sprang a great foundry, and no one in Slupworth need want for hard work. Men, women and children went crawling down into the pit the coal-and-ironmaster had digged for himself. Hungry men and pregnant women pecked his profit out of the coal face while famished six-year-old children, yelping under the canes of the overseers, pushed the loaded trolleys. Babies were born, and died in the Slupworth pits—and begotten, too, for vile things happened in the dark. But the foundries and tanneries and candle factories thundered and rumbled and blazed, and the smoke of their burning went up to heaven . . . and came down again, rejected by God, to settle in soot upon the town, which grew richer and richer, and dirtier and dirtier. The magnates' wives—one or two very wealthy men had bought young ladies out of impecunious polite society— began to withdraw, politely, from Slupworth. They didn't mind its money but they couldn't stand its breath. Over by Turton, a few miles up the river, where the clay was, a Lancashire man had already established a great brick kiln. Fine red brick houses were put up in walled gardens in a place called Woody Dell, half an hour's carriage drive from the town. Hodd, the tanner, built something like the Royal Pavilion at Brighton. The soap-and-candle-maker, although he was not so rich as Hodd, called in an architect from London and ordered something in the Italian style, with a moat to surround it. The coal-and-ironmaster, to everyone's chagrin and astonishment, demonstrated himself as a modest man of simple taste: his house was a scale model of Buckingham Palace, considerably less than half size.

Slupworth has its show places. Its history is not without dramatic incident. When the invisible King Lud sent out his inaudible word there was the devil to pay in Slupworth, Hell emptied itself. The pits spewed up a legion of gaunt men, women and children, black as devils, armed with pick-axes, shovels and lighted torches. Out of the foundries came a fiendish mob of half-naked, copper-coloured, smoke-smudged men with burned hands and faces, brandishing sledge-hammers. From one of the mine shafts there came a heavy explosion, a dull red glow—as chance would have it, at that moment there was an explosion of fire-damp. The rioters marched into the town, but a man whose name is unrecorded ran in ahead of the procession and warned the authorities, saying that his wife was bad with dust in the chest, and he hoped, God forgive him, that the gentlemen would kindly remember him. The Slupworth militia was called out and broke the rioters with one brief volley of ball, killing three and wounding twelve. Then the mob, throwing down picks, hammers, tongs, and torches, ran off into the dark, hotly pursued by the militia, led by Colonel of Militia Horace Hodd on horseback. Nineteen were caught. Sixteen of these, being grown men, were described as "ringleaders", and hanged at the next assizes. The other three, being ten-year-old boys, were sentenced to transportation for life, and packed off to Australia, where one of them died under the whip, one committed suicide, and one lived to beget children and breed sheep. His great-great-great grandson is not above telling the tale, although he has made a million out of sheep and has a controlling interest in a newspaper. He boasts of his history, talking through clenched teeth, almost without moving his lips, which is the way they speak in Slupworth . . . not unlike old lags who can carry on intimate conversations ventriloquially under the eye of the jailer. But the Slupworthians say: "Ah, see? That's a Slupworth lad. That lad ships tons and tons of mutton to England every week—hundreds of tons. You can keep your London. It's Slupworth as feeds England."

Slupworth is self-consciously working-class and belligerently conservative. Liberal-minded Slupworthians admit that the

British Museum, although it is crammed with foreign rubbish, is in its way a better museum than their own. They even admit that Bond Street in London has more shops than Royal Road; and that after sunset, in London or Paris, one may go out and have dinner in a restaurant. But in admitting this they pump a little more wind into the bloated bladder of their civic pride. They thank God that they are not the kind of folk that have to go to restaurants to eat; they thank God that home cooking is good enough for them; they thank God that the citizens of Slupworth do not waste money supporting dirty filthy night clubs in which fools empty their pockets and lower their constitutions with foreign wines, weaken themselves in the arms of women with dyed hair, and chuck away sixpences to cloak-room attendants. Whenever a wealthy Slupworthian, visiting the Capital on business, meets another Slupworthian with a flushed face in a night club, palpating the thigh of some apathetic blonde, he winks and makes a moue, as if to say: *It's all right, old man, I understand. You've got to know what this sort of thing is, for the children's sake, so that you can tell them what to avoid.*

Then the man with the blonde pretends to brush cigarette ash off her knee while he lifts his eyebrows, depresses the corners of his mouth, and contrives to say without words, with a twitch of his cheeks: *I am trying to reform this young woman, but for goodness' sake don't breathe a word to the wife.*

Certain Slupworthians, after many years of toil, go abroad. In 1928 the soap-and-candle man, whose name is Dong, made a grand tour. Dong visited London, Paris, Nice, Monte Carlo, Florence, Rome, Naples, and Capri. When he returned, and fellow-Slupworthians asked him what he thought of it all, he said: "There were a lot of beggars. There were a lot of flies. They mess up the grub with sauces. You can't understand a word they say. They go in for old-fashioned buildings. The policemen wear funny hats. Otherwise it's nowt different from Slupworth."

This man Dong had married the daughter of the builder and brickmaker, Calvin Lamb, and was, like W. W. Narwall, a great man in Slupworth.

There are cinemas in Slupworth now, and electric signs; motor-buses, dance halls, sixpenny bazaars, and automobile agencies: but still the wind seems to blow from all the thirty-two points of the compass at once; and what with a tannery, the soap-and-candle factory, the colliery, the foundry, and the new fertiliser works, Slupworth still stinks under a smoky cloud that drops black snow, as it did when young Solly Schwartz came in with his great suitcase that looked heavy but felt light because it was full of empty tin cans wrapped in tissue paper.

A porter, with a face like a hangman, looking at him as though he were measuring him for the drop, cocked an eyebrow at the suitcase and, when Solly Schwartz told him to take it to a cab, exerted his strength and fell down—at which Solly Schwartz made music with his stick upon his iron foot and shouted with laughter. Then he gave the man two shillings to buy balm for his hurt feelings, and asked: "What's the best hotel here?"

"Well, that depends on what yow mean by best."

"Where do the best people go, you *trottel?*"

"That depends on what yow calls best," said the porter.

"I see. All right. Then tell me this: what's the most expensive hotel?"

"The Queen Elizabeth."

"Put that bag in a cab and tell him to go to the Queen Elizabeth."

The porter said, querulously: "There's nothing in it. It's light."

"I'm sorry. Next time I come here I'll fill it up with lead. Take it to a cab."

"Gentleman from London wants yow to take 'im and the luggage to Queen Elizabeth," said the porter to the driver of a four-wheeler who crouched on his seat and shivered in the mist.

"Elizabeth? Cost you half-crown."

"Get on with the job," said Solly Schwartz, climbing into the cab.

The cabbie flapped the reins, beat his horse out of the apathy of its misery, and the cab rumbled over the cobblestones. It stopped a hundred yards from the station. "What are you waiting for?" asked Solly Schwartz.

"Yow wanted the Queen Elizabeth, and 'ere yow are," said the driver.

"What! Do you think you're going to charge me half a crown for half a minute's ride, you thief?"

"Oi said half a crown and yow said——"

"—Shut your mouth and stop yow-ing! You and your yow! Half a crown for that? I'll see you in hell first," said Solly Schwartz, gripping his suitcase. "Here you are, yow-yow—take a shilling and think yourself lucky . . . and stop shaking your fist at me, or I'll break your arm. I've got *your* number, cabbie. Go about your business."

Thoroughly quelled, the cabman drove away. His hungry old horse with its hunched shoulders, sway-back, and lowered head reminded him of his passenger; so, having a whip in his hand, he gave it a terrible thrashing. Sweetlips, the horse, took it patiently: the gelder's knife, the breaker's lash, the cold iron bit; the harness, the blinkers, the heavy shafts, the iron-shod hooves, the toil, the wind and the rain, and the whip . . . that was life. At the end of it all, peace: a little oats, a little hay, and, after the delicious relief of the unbuckled harness, a little sleep. Man was God; God was good.

Meanwhile, having established himself in the best hotel's best room, Solly Schwartz was eating steak pie and insinuating himself into the confidence of the waiter.

"Stranger here, sir?"

"I've never been here before, but one of my best friends comes from Slupworth, a man called Lumpitt. I don't know if you know him. He used to have a shop in the Royal Road."

"What, Lumpitt? We all knew Lumpitt's. It's Provincial Stores now, though. They say he went up to London."

"That's right, that's where I met him. We're the best of friends. According to what I hear," said Solly Schwartz, lowering his voice, "he was, as you might say, pushed out of it here by . . . what's his name? . . ."

"Narwall, you mean. Is that it?"

"A bad 'un, by all accounts."

"It's not for me to say, sir."

"A sort of a catch-'em-alive-o, or so I've heard."

"I don't know about that, sir," said the waiter uneasily.

"You can't help admiring the man, though, can you, eh?"

"Yow're right there. Started with nothing and now . . . why, I dare say Narwall could put his hands on half a million pounds."

"You don't mean to say! Put his hands on half a million pounds?"

"Ah. Put his hands on half a million pounds—and keep 'em there."

"Would you believe it! My good old friend Lumpitt told me he started small."

The dining-room was almost empty, so the waiter, glancing left

187

and right, went on: "He started small. Yow're not far wrong there. So does a corn on yowr toe. So does a boil on yowr neck. So does a cold in yowr chest. The Narwalls 'ad a little general shop, and they lived like pigs. They lived on fried potatoes and saved every penny. My cousin on my mother's side 'ad a green-grocer's in Paradise Lane, three doors up. 'E struck a rough patch and went to Narwall for a loan of twenty-five pounds. Narwall got the shop in the end. After that 'e got rich all of a sudden: I never could make it out. We were at school together. 'E was always a bit of a fewel—I helped Narwall with 'is spelling and now 'e's the biggest man in Slupworth. In my opinion it's all because of 'is wife. *There's* a bad 'un for yow, if yow like!"

"What do you mean?"

"Mister, did yow ever go in for dog-foighting? Ever foight tarriers?"

"Why do you ask?"

" 'E's a foighting dog but she's a foighting bitch," said the waiter.

"What's the difference?"

"Whoi, dog'll stop when 'e's killed yow: bitch'll go on till she's got yowr liver out and ate it—that's all. And religious, mind yow, on top on it! Charlotte Nornie, she used to be, prettiest girl in Slupworth. We were all surprised when she took up with Willie Narwall, that shrimp."

"Shrimp?"

"Well," said the waiter, weighing his words, " 'e's not as foine a figure of a man as Sandow, yow moight say. We used to call 'im Sixpenn'orth-o'-Ha'pence. He was good at figures, was Willie, but when it came to spelling 'e couldn't tell an A from a cow's foot. 'E was a bit of a tittle-tattle too. Once, when Oi gave 'im a friendly kick up the backsoide, 'e told teacher, and got me into trouble. 'E'd never lift a 'and to defend 'imself loike a man, Willie wouldn't: it was straight to teacher with a rigamarole. We used to follow 'im 'ome singing:

> "Tell tale tit,
>   Yowr tongue shall be slit,
>   All the little puppy dogs shall 'ave a little bit.

"That's what 'e was. 'Is father kept a chips-and-fish shop and drank."

"You mean a fish-and-chip shop?" said Solly Schwartz, licking his lips.

"That's what Oi said—a chips-and-fish shop. We used to call young Willie The Shrimp. 'Tell yowr father to froy yow'; that's what we used to say to 'im."

"And what about his wife?"

"Ow 'er. Jezebel, they call 'er, after the wicked woman in the boible that the dogs ate, all but the palms of 'er 'ands and the soles of 'er feet—and Oi don't blame 'em. 'Er mother was a widow woman. She came from Milchester. 'Er 'usband got drownded in the docks. That was 'er story, and she 'eld to it. She did sewing. But fair's fair, and Oi will say one thing: young Charlotte was the noicest-looking girl in Slupworth—although we did call 'er Charlotte the 'Arlot."

"What, she was like that, was she?" asked Solly Schwartz, avidly.

"No respectable man would 'ave anything to do with 'er, not seriously, I mean. She went out sewing for some people called Buncup—'e was an engineer as came to put new machinery in a foundry—and she left in a 'urry with a black oiye and went and married Willie Narwall. The baby was born premature, so they said; eight months after."

"You mean it wasn't Narwall's?"

"That shrimp? Whoy, 'e couldn't get a mouse into trouble, let alone a Jezebel."

"That was their only child, was it?"

"Oi wouldn't go so far as to say that, no. They 'ad another one, but it took 'im years to do it. And Oi wouldn't take moy boible oath that that one was Willie's oither. There's rumours, take it from me. And there yow are. She goes about in silk and satin whoile moy woife 'as to make 'er own clothes and mend 'em too." Then the waiter, recollecting himself, turned pale and said: "For God's sake, sir, don't repeat one word of what Oi just now said, because if yow do they'll 'ave moy loife."

"Don't be silly. Where do they live?"

"Up on Hodd's Hill." The waiter was beginning to feel uneasy.

"Do they live well?"

"Oi don't know. Jezebel—Mrs. Narwall—feeds the servants off leavings, that's all Oi know."

"Yet I am told that he's very good to children."

"That's roight," said the waiter, with a short laugh. "Wrap

Willie up in red and yow couldn't tell the difference between Willie Narwall and Father Christmas. . . . The bloody little shrimp! When Oi was a boy at school with 'im, if Oi'd only known what 'e was going to turn out to be Oi'd've tanned 'is arse till 'e saw stars."

*   *   *   *   *

W. W. Narwall was, in fact, by no means unlike a shrimp before it is boiled pink. He was small, slippery, elusive and his colour was the colour of sand-and-water. Only his protuberant dark eyes took the light and threw it back—threw it back dead. His frock-coat and billycock hat were hanging on the door behind him. He was wearing an alpaca jacket. He did not look at Solly Schwartz—his shrimp-eyes were everywhere else, and he seemed to be taking note of every thud, rumble, rattle and buzz of the factory, in the centre of which his office was. Scraping his stiff, sandy whiskers, he said: "You wanted to see me urgently, Mr. . . ." and, looking at the card, pretended to have forgotten his visitor's name.

"Schwartz, 'r Mr. Narwall, S. Schwartz. Quite right. I wanted to see you."

Solly Schwartz was angry. He felt that he was face-to-face with an adversary.

Quick and cool as a shrimp W. W. Narwall said: "What about?"

Solly Schwartz had concocted a tremendous story, but, finding himself in the presence of Narwall and seeing the man he had to deal with, like a good general he changed his strategy in a split second; snapped the locks of his case, threw back the lid, pulled out a can of Narwall's peas, slammed it down on the table and said: "What's that?"

"That is a tin of my garden peas, of course."

Then Solly Schwartz took out one of the self-opening tins, wrapped in one of Abel Abelard's labels, and said: "And what's that?"

"Eh? What's that?" said W. W. Narwall, taken off his balance.

"There's your tin of Narwall's Garden Peas. And this is my tin of Narwall's Garden Peas. If you were going into a shop to buy peas, and you saw these two tins side by side on a shelf, for the same price, which one would you choose—give me an honest answer!"

W. W. Narwall blew his nose, which did not need blowing, while he considered the matter. Then he said: "Well?"

"Well!" said Solly Schwartz, "what's the good of the well without the water? You know what tin you'd buy as well as I do, specially if you could do *this* with it—look——" He turned the wheel and opened the tin; threw the jagged top of it on the table and thrust the empty can, neatly folded at the rim, under Narwall's nose. "What would you say to that, eh?" he shouted. "Would you say yes, or would you say no, eh?"

"That's clever," said W. W. Narwall.

Solly Schwartz, dripping with sweat, snatched five tin cans out of his suitcase and arranged them in a line on the edge of the table—one of the self-opening Pelly-Cans, labelled by Abelard, and four others, two on each side of it. Then he said: "You're a housewife out shopping. Quick—choose!" While Narwall blinked at him he pushed across the table one of the ordinary cans, with a tin-opener, saying: "Open it. Or perhaps you've opened a tin before, with a tin-opener, eh? All right. Take this. Take the little wheel with your finger and thumb and turn . . . that's right, right, left, any way you like, turn . . . that's what I've come to show you. Will you have it, or these people?" He pulled out of his bag another Pelly-Can of peas, packed by The Express Canning Company, and rolled it into W. W. Narwall's lap.

Narwall fingered the beautifully smooth folded edge of the can he had opened, at the same time looking at the neatly-cut lid, while Solly Schwartz, compelling himself to be calm, went on: "I could have gone to any of the bigger firms. I could have gone to America with this can. But I came to you first."

"Why did you come to me first?"

"Ask yourself why, Mr. Narwall. The big 'uns are all settled —they're all fat, lazy," said Solly Schwartz, "you're only a little man working your way up——" At this consummate impudence, Narwall's eyes grew more prominent and his cheeks became pink —"No, no, now wait, Mr. Narwall, let me finish. Compared with the big canners, you're . . . like a sprat to a whale. And you're trying to work your way up to being a Crosse & Blackwell. Now listen to me, just for a minute, and don't get excited."

"Don't you worry, young man, I won't get excited. Go on with what you've got to say, because I'm busy."

"I came to you first because you're not on top, do you follow?

Because you're *on the way* to the top," cried Solly Schwartz, striking the table with his open hand. "You're on the way to the top. So am I. This tin can will put you on the top. Put your stuff in it, advertise it, and everybody'll ask for it. Look at it —go on, open another one. Would you sweat your insides out and cut your fingers off with a rusty tin-opener if you could get a tin like that for the same price as an ordinary one? Answer me that question, Mr. Narwall."

"Did you invent this yourself?"

"That is neither here nor there, Mr. Narwall. Will you answer my question?"

"I don't see any patent number, Mr. Schwartz."

"I know you don't, for the simple reason that it isn't stamped on, because these are samples. But you needn't worry, Mr. Narwall. With all due respect, I wouldn't trust my own father. You don't think I'd show you this if it wasn't patented already, do you? Don't be silly. Now answer my question. Which would you buy: my tin, or that tin?"

"That would depend——"

"—Yes I know, that would depend. Give me a straight answer. Which?"

"Am I to understand, young man, that you want me to buy your tins? Are you trying to sell me the patent, or what?"

"Answer my question first, Mr. Narwall, and we'll talk about all that later on."

"It's not a bad idea, I'll go so far as to say that."

"Not a *bad* idea?" Solly Schwartz laughed. "It's a revolution. Mr. Narwall, just now I asked you a question: *which?*"

"Well . . . perhaps I might choose your can, if I was put to it, and had a fancy for novelties."

"If you would, wouldn't all the customers in your forty-eight shops? Wouldn't all the customers in everybody else's shops? Answer me that, Mr. Narwall."

"Mr. Schwartz, I am an honest man, and I tell you here and now, frankly and openly, face to face, that it's not a bad idea. But, as you said yourself, I'm only in a small way in business, so I couldn't go to much. I might consider putting this out as a novelty. How much were you thinking of asking for the patent of this little novelty?"

"Novelty? Don't make me laugh, Mr. Narwall. Patent? When hair grows in the palm of my hand I'll sell the patent.

Who said anything about selling patents? What are you talking about?"

Slowly turning the opened can between his flat, shiny palms, W. W. Narwall said: "I'll tell you what, Mr. Schwartz. I'm busy for half an hour, and then I go home to my tea. Come home and join us—we have a good meat tea—and bring them samples with you, and we'll talk the matter over. If you'd like to pass the time looking round the place, I'll meet you in the front in twenty minutes to half an hour."

"Right you are, Mr. Narwall, I'll be there on the dot." Solly Schwartz repacked his case and left the office with a high-beating heart. For twenty minutes he limped about the premises, hopping from floor to floor. He stood for ten minutes in the warehouse. Ten strong men hurried in and out carrying sides of bacon, huge cheeses, boxes of butter, and packing-cases of tinned food, without perceptibly diminishing the stock. Here was wealth indeed. But the jam-boilery was contemptible; the cannery was so small that two men, three boys, and six sickly-looking label-sticking girls could run it; and as for the pickle department, it made Solly Schwartz laugh. Three strapping young women, their sleeves rolled up to the shoulders, perspiring copiously, stooped over tubs vigorously mixing cucumber, cauliflower and onion in a mustard sauce. Four little girls were filling square-faced jars with the mixture before putting them along the bench to a middle-aged woman who closed them with a tin cap. Below her sat two girls who pasted on the labels, and pushed the jars within reach of a young man in a flannel shirt who picked them up four at a time and banged them down into boxes, two dozen jars to a box. After that a man with a grey moustache nailed the boxes down and put them on a little trolley. The pickle-mixers, in particular, fascinated Solly Schwartz; they were yellow with mustard sauce from head to foot. He attracted the attention of the foreman by poking him in the back with his stick. And, jerking his head at the mixers, said, for the sake of talking: "That's a dirty job."

"Somebody's got to do 't, or 'ow would yow get yowr pickles for your tea?"

"What do you put in that yellow stuff?"

"Mustard, vinegar, and one or two other things."

"Why don't you stir 'em up with some sort of big wooden spoon?"

"Too slow that way. Yow'd get tired in an hour mixing wi' a

193

spoon. Besoides they work better boi 'and. It keeps their skin whoite, and burns all the 'air off their arms."

Then Solly Schwartz went to meet W. W. Narwall at the front entrance. The little man was sitting in an old-fashioned barouche, which he must have impounded from some shabby-genteel bankrupt creditor. The coachman, in a dark grey brass-buttoned livery coat that was far too large for him, brooded over the reins and glowered at a bony old grey mare which appeared to rely for support upon the shafts.

"A nice turn-out," said Solly Schwartz, when he was seated.

Narwall looked at him suspiciously and said: "It's good enough for me. *I* like it. Them as don't can lump it. . . . Hoi there— what are you waiting for? Christmas?"

Notorious for their frugality, and proud of that notoriety, the Narwalls made a boast of the fact that they did not live in Woody Dell, but were content with an eight-roomed red-brick detached house in the quietest part of the dull and sullen town of Slupworth. They rejoiced in their parsimony. Hodd kept, fed, and paid wages to five servants; Dong had six, including a butler. The Narwalls employed only two, a man and his wife, Mr. and Mrs. Prince. Mr. Prince was coachman, odd-job-man, and gardener. Mrs. Prince did the cleaning and helped with the cooking. Also, she sewed and darned and mended. The Hodds and the Dongs looked down their noses at the Narwalls, but the Narwalls turned their noses up at the Dongs and the Hodds—but not in the open, because Charlotte Narwall, the Jezebel, was a dangerous woman to have for an enemy. She had a forked tongue and poisoned fangs. She was patient and malevolent. For years she could be still, coldly watchful like a snake on a rock, waiting for you to come within her range; and then she would strike. Then, God help you.

It was Jezebel who drove the Dongs out of Slupworth. The Dongs lived in style, with a butler, which was sensational, and a voluptuous Belgian cook—a plump woman of thirty-five with a china-white skin and bright red hair. Her name was Suzanne. She slept in a room on the third floor. Soon after she arrived Mr. Dong developed insomnia. His wife observed that, as soon as she breathed as if she were asleep, her husband would slide out of bed and creep away. He would be absent for half an hour, even an hour, and when she asked him where he had been he said: "Oh, I went to get a drink of water," or "Oh, I felt stuffy and went to get a breath of air." She said nothing, but noticed that he was always loitering about the kitchen. On one occasion she saw him pat Suzanne's buttocks. He said that he was killing a fly.

Suzanne was constantly complaining that she wanted certain rare herbs, the lack of which cramped her style and spoiled her best efforts. So one day, when Mr. Dong was at the Works, his wife gave Suzanne a little money and told her to go to London and buy what she wanted, adding that there was no need for her to return until the following day. She went gladly. Mr. and Mrs. Dong went to bed as usual at eleven o'clock. At one o'clock he whispered: "Are you awake, dear?" She snored, her eyes open in the dark. Then inch by inch Mr. Dong got out of bed and padded out of the room. Their bedroom had two doors. As soon as her husband was gone Mrs. Dong, who was light on her feet in spite of her size, opened the other door, ran upstairs to Suzanne's room, and leapt into bed. Soon, as she had anticipated, the door opened and closed silently, and a heavy man threw himself upon her. A little while later, when he had rolled away and was lying, relaxed, beside her, she struck a match and lit a candle, saying: "Aha, Mister *Dong*, I don't suppose you expected to find *me* here!"

"No, Mrs. Dong," said the butler.

Now this was almost certainly a product of Mrs. Narwall's malevolent imagination, but the story went around Slupworth. Dong discharged the butler, kicked out the cook, upbraided his wife, and even went so far as to beat the gardener. But in the end they had to go and live elsewhere. They were laughed out of Slupworth.

Mrs. Narwall, the Jezebel, would stop at nothing. She was bitterly hated, for her cold avarice, her indifference to the world, her remarkable height, and her beauty. She was the most beautiful woman in the town—even in the county. Strangers visiting Slupworth caught their breath when they saw her; one of them, a journalist, said that it was like finding "a marble masterpiece in a midden." That was well said. Marble was the word for Jezebel: you felt that if you took her in your arms she would take all the warmth out of you and leave you nothing but a chill; that nothing but a steel chisel could make an impression on her. She might break, but she could never bend. Everybody wondered how Willie Narwall had managed to get her with child: thinking of this, one imagined a demented shrimp dancing about on a Greek statue, for she was indeed statuesque and beautiful in the noblest and boldest Greek style. Beautiful, but hard, cold, and unyielding; beautiful in a stony, sinister way. Imagine Medusa, whose direct glance could petrify, with her snakes parted in the middle and brushed back and tied into an immense knot on her neck; skimpily dressed in sober worsted, with no ornament but a golden wedding ring that was priced at twenty-five shillings and bought after much haggling for twenty-three-and-six. That was Mrs. Narwall, the Jezebel. She was feared, not only because of what she could say, but because she could suck the strength out of people. Even in the old days when they had the little general shop in Paradise Lane, this vampirish quality of hers was remarked. A workman with a plausible and true story went to the shop to ask for five shillingsworth of goods on credit. He had been disabled for a month by a broken ankle, but now, being sound again and, as a skilled man, confident of getting back his old job or finding another, walked jauntily into Narwall's . . . and came out with a paper of salt which he had bought with his last penny. He said to his wife: "Oi don't know what it is, lass, but that Jezebel gives yow one look and then everything yow meant to say goes to jelly and won't come out."

She had two daughters. The elder, Sybil, about whose true parentage there had been so much whispering, resembled the Jezebel. She was nearly thirteen years old. The Baby, as they called her, although she was five years old, was called Ivy, and speaking of her to a friend the servant said: "She's a little loov. Quoiet as a blessed mouse, bless 'er 'eart, sucking 'er little dummy and playing wi' 'er little rattle the livelong day. She's such a little pretty she puts yow in moind o' one o' them dolls. You know, Mrs. 'Ood—when yow lay 'em down they close their oiyes and when yow pick 'em up they open 'em again. Oi can't believe she was muthered boi that black bitch, Mrs. 'Ood. But yow should know."

Mrs. Hood, who was the cheapest midwife in town, and had therefore been retained—not without haggling—for the Jezebel's lying-in, said: "It's 'ers all roight. Oh, it's 'ers. Oi didn't say 'is—Oi said 'ers. Never will Oi forget it to the longest day Oi live, Mary, moy dear. She loy there loike a dummy—not so much as a whisper—and when Oi asked 'er if she was bad all she said was: 'Git on wi' it, and 'old yowr tongue.' Eh, she's a hard 'un! She was in labour from seven in t'morning till two in t'afternoon, and never a word, not a croy. Eh, she's a proud one! Only when t'little darling's 'ead was coming out she bit 'er lip roight through, and yow can see t'marks to this day. And when Oi told 'er: 'Mrs. Narwall, mum, yow got a loovly little girl' she says: 'Wrap 'er oop, put 'er down, 'ave yowr tea, get yowr pay, and go away. And don't fuss me, Oi want to go to sleep.'

"Yow may well say that, Mary. As yow very well know," said Mrs. Hood, in a low voice, "Oi've 'elped certain parties out o' trooble once or twoice, to obloige friends, risking moy liberty, and Oi've known certain parties croy their oiyes out over unborn things that wasn't aloive or dead——

Mary wiped her eyes.

"—And all *she* does wi' that pretty little doll is shoov 'er breast into its mouth and say 'Go on, eat' and drop off to sleep. Oi stayed three hours. Oi was froightened she moight roll over, that great loomp, in 'er sleep, an' overlay t'little darling. But she slept loike nothing 'ad 'appened. That's *'er* sort. Unnatural." Grudgingly, but with something like admiration, the midwife added: " 'Er lip was swoled loike a sausage in a pan when yow've pronged it wi' a fork, where she bit it. But never a croy. Never so much as a moan. . . . And when Oi went to *'im* to draw what was due to me, 'e knocked off eighteenpence for meals eaten in t'ouse. Said arrangement didn't provoide for board. Eh well, that's the way to get rich, Mary."

"Oi druther be poor."

*   *   *   *   *

But Solly Schwartz, if uninspired by the Love that casts out Fear, was possessed by the Infatuation that casts out Doubt. He had faith in his gorgeously-labelled cylinders full of nothing. When Mr. Narwall introduced him to his wife, the Jezebel, Solly Schwartz gave her one quick sidelong glance and then, impervious to her Gorgon's eyes, began to talk. His eager earnestness, his urgent passion, and his unshakeable conviction must have been something like that of the bold apostle Paul when he came into the presence of Cæsar. He snapped open the clips of his suitcase, kicked back the lid with his iron foot, banged down tins, and declaimed. Standing close behind him, W. W. Narwall aimed enquiring gestures at his wife. Her beautiful face was like stone. At last, when Solly Schwartz had to pause for breath, she said: "Tea's brewed. Sit down."

"There's no law to force you to listen," said Solly Schwartz, throwing his tins back into his case and closing it, "so all right, let's have tea."

When all the ham and bread-and-butter was eaten, and all the tea was drunk, and Mr. and Mrs. Narwall had exchanged certain winks, nods, and little grimaces, the Jezebel toyed with a Pelly-Can and said: "It might suit. What do you want for it?"

Then Solly Schwartz looked straight into her terrifying eyes and said: "Listen, Mrs. Narwall. I told your husband why I came here to you instead of going to one of the big firms. Now listen. You've got shops. Most people would be glad of one of them, let alone forty-eight. And you've got a little tin-pot cannery, putting up a few stinking—excuse my language—peas. Now with a tin like mine, a label like mine, and advertising, my God——"

"—In this house we do not take the name of the Lord in vain," said W. W. Narwall.

"Never mind the Lord, never mind in vain! Do you want me to go on? If not, say so."

"Go on," said the Jezebel.

"With this can, this label, proper advertising, every shop in England, Ireland, Scotland and Wales will *have to* put what you turn out on their shelves—peas, tomatoes, soup—what I've got here is worth millions. Not thousands, but millions; and you're asking me what I want for it! I'll tell you here and I'll tell you now if you offered ten thousand pounds spot cash for this tin I'd laugh right in your face."

"Come to the point," said the Jezebel, coldly. "We asked you a simple question. Give us a simple answer. What do you want for it?" Her eyes would have frozen and her tone quelled another man.

But Solly Schwartz was throwing fire against her ice and, with the vehement *rat-at-at-at-at* of his impassioned talk, drilling the marble, said: "Let's not waste your time and mine, Mrs. Narwall. You're quite right, a simple question wants a simple answer. I'll tell you what I want for this can, straightforward without beating about the bush, and this is a case of take it or leave it, because I won't bate an inch. This tin is worth God knows how much. I'll invest it in your firm."

"And what do you expect to make out of it?" asked W. W. Narwall.

"That's up to you and me, Mr. Narwall—especially it's up

to me, see? Because you'll put up the cannery and I'll run it and manage all the advertising. And I want half the clear profit from the cannery, and a director's fee, and expenses. I want to be in charge of the travellers—I'll send travellers all over the country, and I swear by God that in twelve months I'll have this tin on every shelf in every grocer's shop in the country—and not only with peas in it, either. Beans, carrots, stew, a dozen different sorts of soup, pears, strawberries, raspberries, apricots, everything! I'll put in my tin and my work on the canning side. You put in the factory and the expenses. And as sure as I sit here, in three years' time we'll be making millions. Well, what do you say?"

"These tins of yours: won't they cost a terrible lot to manufacture?" asked the Jezebel.

"Certainly," snapped Solly Schwartz, "if you make them in dirty little thousands and piddling little tens of thousands. But I'm thinking in millions and millions, and you know very well that the more you make of a thing, the less it costs. But anyway, there's a way over that. Pack two ounces less in the tin. If you've been tinning fourteen ounces of peas, tin twelve ounces instead. Like that, on, say, ten thousand tins of peas you've got sixteen hundred and fifty extra tins, and you're already making up what you've put out. And on top of it all you've got the advantage over the other manufacturers—you've got the Pelly-Can, they haven't. And you've got Solly Schwartz. So there it is: my salary to be agreed upon, expenses at my discretion, and we go half-and-half in the profits. Think it over, but don't think too long, because I've got to go back to London to-morrow. I'll leave you now and come back at nine in the morning. Thanks for the tea. That was a very nice bit of ham—I'd like to buy one to take home with me. Well, I'll wish you good-evening now, and see you to-morrow."

When he was gone W. W. Narwall said: "If you ask me——"

"—If pigs had wings they'd fly. I don't ask you," said the Jezebel, and sat thinking until, ten minutes later, her husband found courage to ask how Solly Schwartz's proposition struck her. Then, looking at him with tired disdain, she said: "We'll do it, Willie."

"It'll run into thousands, Charlotte; it's a terrible risk."

"You always were a niddering little coward, Willie. We do it, and that's flat."

"But——"

"—Don't argue with me, Willie, you're wrong."

Her husband said: "Well, you're generally in the right, Charlotte," whereupon she nodded stiffly and hurried to the kitchen, for she had just remembered that she had forgotten to lock up the bread bin and the meat safe.

So it came to pass that W. W. Narwall threw capital into a cannery. The company was registered as Narwall & Schwartz Ltd. And so Solly Schwartz could tell I. Small in Appenrodt's that he was going to put the whole world in a tin can; and was able, later, to give that weak, bewildered man the two hundred pounds with which he paid his debts, saved his face, and withdrew from Noblett Street, Mayfair, in good order after having sold off the stock at a dead loss.

CHAPTER XVII

Dead loss, dead loss, dead loss! thinks Charles Small, gritting his teeth, wishing that the old fool had never been born both to beget and bedevil him. *Loss, and loss, and loss, and loss*—what was not loss? What had the old man to lose, what had he that was worth keeping? Furious, impotent little man! Pygmy!

Pygmy? Now Charles Small remembers the legend of Hercules who wrestled with and slew the giant Antæus in the Land of the Little People. The earthbound Antæus, that monstrous protector of the pygmy ones, having died in the terrible grip of the deified Greek, found a champion—a pygmy no bigger than Hercules' thumb, who challenged the conqueror to mortal combat with a sword no longer than a pin, which he dared to oppose to the Herculean brass-bound club that was cut from a whole oak tree. Hercules, amused, picked up his challenger and stood him on the palm of his hand, and looked with wonder at the tiny creature who stood there in an attitude of defiance urging him to come on and fight. At length he said: "You are a very little fellow, are you not? Tell me, how big is your soul?" And the pygmy replied, in a voice as high as the squeak of a bat: "My soul is as big as your own!" Whereupon Hercules, bowing respectfully, complimented the little hero on his valour, set him carefully down on the ground, and went on his way, marvelling.

Now there was a pygmy. He had no fear. There was a man. He went out to die for the dead giant, tiny sword in tiny fist. The old man was no pygmy—he was nothing, nobody. Now in such circumstances what would I. Small have done? Having retired to a safe distance he would have thundered in a voice like a knife scratching a plate that Antæus was dead, times were bad, he did not know which way to turn; all the time twirling his microscopic moustache. Then, slinking home to his little house no bigger than half a coconut shell—and a leaky coconut shell at that—he would have taken by the neck some baby pygmy as big as a cockroach, struck it repeatedly and ineffectually with a blade of grass, squeaking: "Bleddy well take a bleddy lesson, loafer! No fighting!"—while his wife wailed: "Not on the head! Chastise him but for God's sake not on the head!"

Meanwhile the valiant pygmy would be going about his business, challenging giants, challenging the mighty, challenging the gods, undefeatable; and Mr. and Mrs. Small would sit down glumly to their evening meal of birdseed, or whatever it was, and worry each other about where the next meal was coming from. Later, perhaps, I. Small would take the diminutive Charles for a walk to look at the stupendous corpse of Antæus, and moralise. "You see, boychik? He could have been a big man, only he's got to fight with every Tom Dick and Harry like a bleddy ruffian. Take a lesson!"

These idle reflections amuse Charles Small so that he laughs a little through his teeth. But then that sourness comes up from his stomach into the back of his throat, where it burns; and anger, impotent anger, returns. He wants to throw something again; takes hold of a feather pillow and dashes it to the floor, where it falls with scarcely a sound, and this again infuriates him. If he had had his way at that moment that feather pillow would have shaken the house. Chimneys would have fallen, walls would have cracked, screaming mothers would have clutched howling children to their bosoms. But there is nothing but a muffled *plop*. It is in keeping, and he laughs again, but bitterly. And now he has nothing on which to rest his spinning head, so he must reach for the pillow and put it back again—but not before he has tyrannically punched it into shape.

. . . *Dead loss, dead loss, dead loss.* Naturally, and Mrs. Small wept bitterly of course. So that was what he was; so that was what she was married to! They consulted estate agents and looked at advertisements and then, listening to the altercation, passers-by grew pale and hurried on, for it seemed that in Noblett Street at any moment blood must run like water. Suddenly I. Small put his foot down: he became pigheaded. He was determined, he was decided, once and for all, to take up his old trade. He was like rock. Nothing could move him. Words rebounded, as it were, like dried peas from his thick skull.

"You had your said——"

"—Had your say—had your say. Talk English!"

"Say, schmay! You said your . . . your . . . say, schmay, pay! A first-class boot shop she wanted, all right, in Mayfair! So she got it. What bleddy marvels did you do miv——"

"—With, not miv."

"Miv, schmiv—bleddy well listen to me!"

"Srul! No dirty language in front of the children!"

"Beggar the bleddy children, bless them!" roared I. Small, furiously beating the table with a newspaper. "Once and for all . . ."

"Well, go on."

Then, needless to say, he had to think for a minute or two before he remembered what he had intended to say, so that she had a chance to say to the children:

"Once a bootmaker, always a bootmaker. As long as I know. That's what he is. Oh, I'm so ashamed, so ashamed!"

"Repairs!" shouted I. Small. "High-class repairs! Sis my trade, my business! Mayfair they want! Mayfair, give them! Better I should took Solly's advice, with the Machine! Enough!"

"Solly. Solly. He's here again with his Solly, that humpty-dumpty."

"So what's the matter, what, miv a humpty-dumpty? Where would we be, where, without a humpty-dumpty?"

"More shame for you!"

"And now she's got a new madness—a drapery shop she wants!"

"Boots he wants to mend. That's all he's fit for."

Maddened with rage, I. Small tore the newspaper and screamed: "Fit for, fit for! All right, so that's what I'm fit for! So that's what I'll do. *Na!* Not another word! Do you bleddy well hear? Not another word when you talk to me! Enough is enough, so be quiet!"

She had prepared supper, some dish of fried fish, which she served at this point, putting down the plates with a great clatter, saying: "Go on, eat. I couldn't touch a thing."

"She couldn't touch a thing. All right then, so I can't touch a thing," said I. Small. Then he ate voraciously, looking furtively at his wife from time to time. She did not eat. Little Charles looked at them with trepidation until the old man, threatening to strike him with a soft roll, bellowed: "Bleddy well eat!"

Mrs. Small would not touch a thing. She said she was choked. I. Small affected indifference, but his eyes were full of worry. "Go on, eat, let him eat it all up while he's got it," said Mrs. Small, "the business man!"

"Millie, eat something," the old man said.

"I can't. I've got a lump here," said Mrs. Small, touching her chest.

"Lump?" cried I. Small, alarmed.

"A lump like a ball."

This took I. Small's appetite away. A lump like a ball! While he was drinking his tea Mrs. Small said nothing but: "Don't make so much noise—you're not in Cracow now."

The old man started to shout: "What's the bleddy matter with Cracow——" but stopped abruptly, so that he said: "What's the bled?"

"I haven't the heart."

Later, when Charles Small went to the kitchen for a glass of water, he saw his mother surreptitiously eating a large piece of fish. She said: "I'm just tasting."

Back in the living-room I. Small, who was gloomily perusing the advertisements in the torn evening paper, said: "Millie, for God's sake, eat. For strength!"

"I'm choked," she said.

"Choke! Choke!" cried I. Small, twisting the newspaper. "She's always choking! That's how she gets her living, is it? Choking? By her, choking is a full-time job!"—Goodness knows where the old idiot had picked up that phrase, full-time job.— He went on, very earnest now. He even lowered his voice a couple of decibels, and poked at the arm of his chair with a shapeless forefinger instead of thumping the table with his foolish fist. He even addressed his wife directly instead of talking to the sideboard or the ceiling: "Millie, not another word. This is final, do you hear? No draperies, no schmaperies. Final! No more Mayfairs, no more Noblett Streets. Final! I should sell boots to stray cats? Is that a full-time job? No more Noblett Streets, no more bleddy cats. I am the master here, did you heard?"

"—Did you *hear*, not *heard*," she said, "try to speak English. This isn't Cracow."

Then, it goes without saying, the old idiot, who had almost achieved an air of mastery, went up in the air again. He lost his temper, his silly little temper. His voice became thunder, thunder that frightens only children; his eyes flashed lightning, sheet-lightning that is powerless to strike, and merely flickers meaning-less threats over inaccessible horizons.

"Cracow! Schmakow! So by her Samovarna is a place? Cracow isn't good enough for her yet? Mayfair she wants better, eh? To tie herself up in a . . . a . . . a . . . bleddy sack miv *ferschtinkener* bleddy cats is by her a ... a ... a ... full-time job, all right! Bootmaker isn't good enough for her, the bleddy aristocrat! Shops, she wants! I swear by the children's life——"

"—Srul! Not by the children's life!"

"Beggar the bleddy children!" He raised his right hand in an awful gesture. "I swear by the children's life, I swear by my life and yours too, by my mother, by my father, by ... by ... your bleddy mother, by your bleddy father, by your health I swear and the children's health too! They should drop dead, I should be paralysed! *High-class gentlemen's boot repairs! Na!* I swore!" He brought down his clenched right hand. It hit the rim of his saucer and catapulted the dregs of his tea into his face, so that he sat there, ludicrous, with tea-leaves in his fierce moustache and the cup in his lap.

At this Charles Small, who had been listening with something like awe, burst out laughing. This, of course, was just what the old man needed. "He takes after his mother, the bleddy little murderer!" he said, in the voice of a hungry lion—and like a lion he sprang. A casual observer would have cried murder. Little Charles continued to giggle—he still remembers the curious pattern of tea-leaves on the old man's face, and the dribble of warm tea that turned down one end of his moustache, so that this masculine attribute was suddenly anti-clockwise. Slapping him sharply on the cheek ("Not on the head!" cried Mrs. Small) he cried, in a voice like no other voice on earth or in hell: "To bed! No supper! To bed! Final!"

Now where the devil had the old man picked up that word *final?* Probably from the Communist cobbler.

So little Charles went to bed, still giggling. He listened. From below came noises reminiscent of a fight between an enraged hippopotamus and a screech-owl. The words were indistinguishable. He caught only two, three phrases: *Nothing but my bleddy chains to lose. . . . And I swore by my mother's life. . . .*

"Your mother's dead," said the piercing voice of Mrs. Small: whereupon there was a thumping of tables and an incoherent bellow. A little later Mrs. Small came into his room with supper on a tray. She called him a bad boy; but obviously she could not bear to let him go to bed unfed. "Honour thy father and thy mother," she said. "Have respect for your father, or you'll get such a smacking!"

Charles Small remembers that he ate with extraordinary appetite, and read an instalment of "The Adventures of Jack, Sam, and Pete" in *The Boy's Friend*. He dozed, thinking of the gigantic negro. A stentorian voice jerked him, twitching like a hooked fish, out of the deep black waters of sleep. It said: "Mein mind is made up. Gents high-class repairs! I swore!" Then he slept deeply, as boys do.

But he knew, in the back of his mind, that the old man would not have his way—would never, never have his way. He was (Charles Small still harks back to his ancient, lost histrionic ambition) a tale told by an idiot, full of sound and fury, signifying nothing.

And as for his mother, she was nothing but a hysterical bitch.

Oh, when the maternal milk begins to curdle in his wretched stomach and the acid begins to bite, he is overcome by a most dreadful hatred for these two foolish people! But more hateful yet is an abominable nostalgia for these fools who thumbed him into the womb, dragged him out, and slapped his little bottom and sent him wailing into the world, into a life which they ruined; a life of which he is thoroughly sick and tired.

God bless my soul! thinks Charles Small, wondering. *Damn my eyes for a bloody fool—why I actually cried when they died!*

*   *   *   *   *

And now, sneering at himself as he remembers, Charles Small discovers that his curled lip is somewhat tremulous; a lump in his stomach has crept up towards his throat, and he needs to blink away a mist. Fool! Who but a slave weeps over the carcass of a tyrant? And these were tyrants, insidious tyrants, tyrants of a most detestable kind. For instance: Genghis Khan, he was a tyrant—when his hordes hit the road, you resisted and died, or stayed and died, or you fled and were free to hate him. Good, kind, merciful, murderous, emotionless Emperor of All Men! —with him you knew where you were, whether you were dead or alive. He took your body, but left you your soul. He never tried to make you love him, much less pity him. His was the straight thrust, the swift arrow, the clean slash . . . cool iron, hit or miss. But these vile wretches!—They went, not for the throat, but the heart; what they call the Soul.

So that now, with his belly full of sour milk, Charles Small lies, wrung like a wet rag—he feels like a wet rag—wrung between loathing and pity, disgustedly dropping a tear for all he ever had.

Had he the slightest desire to see the Old Tyrants alive? No. He wanted them to die, because he wanted to be free. They ate into him; they digested him . . . as he, through his stomach, is digesting himself. He hated them—oh, most bitterly!—for what they did to him, early and late. Their tyranny was from the very mouth of the womb, which is as the very mouth of hell.

He loathes the memory of this ridiculous father and despicable mother. Still, in his loneliness, there come back strange remembrances. . . . There was a dreadful November morning when the carriages drove to East Ham, and they went through the iron gates of the cemetery and walked through avenues of bitter cold monuments to an oblong hole in the ground, the cold ground, and into this hole two men with ropes let down a box; and in this box lay all that was corruptible of Millie Small. All the men of the family were assembled, darkly dressed, dressed (the bloody hypocrites!) in formal suits. And he, Charles Small—dirtiest hypocrite of all!—swathed in the blackest black, was almost overcome by a mad desire to giggle. And then he saw the old man, stricken, overwhelmed, crushed. The prayer was said—that resonant prayer:

Yisgadal Veyishkadash
Schme Rabbo!

—and the old ones plucked blades of grass, wizened frost-bitten grass, and threw them away, and let running water trickle over their fingers before they left the graveyard. The others seemed remarkably cheerful. Charles remembers that he was very annoyed at this. But on the other hand, you could not blame them. All said and done, what was his mother but a confounded nuisance to everyone with whom she came in contact—hysterical, cowardly, unstable, savage, weak, untruthful, malevolent. She blew hot and cold with the same breath. No doubt she loved her husband and her children; but her love was—sexlessly, of course—an impure love, curiously compounded of vanity, petty pride, hunger to possess, and fear of loss. It was a sort of jealousy—it was akin to hate. What were her virtues? Was she generous? She would give her last penny to a beggar in the street . . . but at home, if one asked her for a penny to buy chocolate, she would talk for half an hour about the value of a penny. You might say that after all it was only a penny, but then she would come back with: "If you wanted a piece of bread and was a penny short, would the baker say it's only a penny?" In the end, of course, you would get your penny. But it felt heavy in your hand, and the chocolate tasted bitter; you ate it guiltily, without appetite, joylessly, thinking all the time of hard shifts and close scrapes, of hands beaded with soapsuds out of the sink, hastily wiped on an apron and fumbling at the catch of a purse, while through the musty house echoed the thudding of the old man's hammer against the leather of dirty old boots. And while you so dolefully sucked your pitiful little bar of chocolate wishing you had bought marbles instead, some jolly beggar to whom she had graciously given sixpence without argument was cheerfully knocking back a pint of wallop in the nearest pub.

Charles Small wants to be sick. Once, for example, when the old man was hammering his guts out downstairs in Noblett Street, a flower-seller came to the door—a frightful figure of a man, more than six feet tall, with a red nose, a purple face, orange-coloured hair, yellow teeth, and a voice that sounded like a rasp upon leather. "Hoi!" he shouted, and the aspirate made the little shop smell like a beer house. He held out to Mrs. Small a horrible little pot of wilted chrysanthemums, and said: "'Ere y'are, lady, eighteenpence or one of your old man's old coats."

Charles Small was brooding solemnly in a corner, because she had just scolded him for asking for sixpence to buy fireworks, for it was early November, the day before Guy Fawkes Day, when the meanest wretch in town lit a cracker or fired a squib in memory of Guido who tried to blow up Parliament. Charles had had a great desire to burn Guy Fawkes in effigy, dancing round a bonfire and singing:

> *Guy, Guy, Guy*
> *Stick him up on high,*
> *Hang him on a lamp-post*
> *And there let him die!*

but his mother had reasoned with him severely, telling him that fireworks were a waste of money. You spent a halfpenny for a squib, and where did it get you? Nowhere. One—two—three

—it was all gone in smoke. And what was the use of wasting money on something for everyone else to see? For a halfpenny you could buy a roll of bread—seven rolls for threepence, fresh rolls. And to go and spend sixpence on squibs? Madness! In any case, they were dangerous. Charles pleaded that everybody let off fireworks over the Fifth of November:

> *Please to remember*
> *The fifth of November*
> *Gunpowder, treason and shot.*
> *I see no reason*
> *Why powder and treason*
> *Should ever be forgot.*

—it was History; and what was more, in the ashes of the bonfire the boys baked potatoes.

This, he now realises, was about the most injudicious thing he could possibly have said to Millie Small. What? Potatoes? He didn't have enough potatoes at home? He had to go out with little ruffians and cook potatoes like a tramp in the ashes and the dirt and come home with goodness knows what diseases? He could have baked potatoes to-morrow. No bonfires. No baked potatoes. No sixpence. No fireworks. They were dangerous.

It was useless to argue. Charles sulked in the shadows of the shop. Then in came the big coster with his musty little pot of dying chrysanthemums, and his beery breath, glaring at her with his great grey bloodshot eyes that looked like oysters caught in little nets of red thread.

"Lovely pot of 'zanths, lady—come on, lovely pot of 'zanths. Eighteenpence or an old coat. Come on!"

She screamed: "Srul!"

The old man came up, mumbling, his mouth full of nails, hammer in hand. He was in his shirt-sleeves, and his cuffs were turned back almost to the armpits. As he stood there, armed with a hammer, scowling over his military moustache, while his mouth bristled with bright iron brads, he might have passed as a terrifying figure. "What the bleddy——" he began.

"Lovely 'zanth. Eighteenpence or an old coat," said the coster.

Then Charles Small saw that his parents were afraid. The coster had an air of menace. I. Small, that shrewd man of affairs, said, "A couple of flowers in the house, eh, Millie. . . . I'll give you a shilling."

"Done for a bob!" said the coster, handing over the flower-pot and pocketing the shilling.

As soon as he was gone I. Small and his wife turned on each other, suddenly courageous.

"The rates to pay, and so flowers she wants!"

"He calls himself a man! Why didn't you throw the hooligan out?"

"By her, throwing out holligans is by me a full-time job."

"You should call a pleeceman."

"Pleeceman, schmeeseman! Flowers she wants! That's all she's short of."

I. Small went down noisily to his workshop. Soon they heard the noise of his hammer again. "A few flowers for the house," said Mrs. Small, wrapping the flower pot in red crêpe paper. But the chrysanthemums died that night. There was a terrible scene. Now she is dead, and serve her right. No one was really sorry; no one except I. Small, and he was heartbroken. Why? He never knew an unbroken hour of happiness with that woman. She crossed him at every path, she bedevilled and bewildered him. She humiliated him. She ruined him. Oh, if only Charles Small's father had hit Charles Small's mother a good swinging punch on the jaw! But he could only shout and flap about with a torn newspaper; a crushed man.

And so, perhaps, when she died, his heart was broken and his world had come to an end because there was no one at whom he could safely shout and flap; because, remembering all of him that was so ridiculous, everyone was sorry for him. Suddenly, they all became polite to I. Small, and went out of their way to be kind to him. So, by imperceptible degrees, the old man's world changed, and he was lost. Therefore he clung desperately to what he thought he knew: that is to say, he threw his hooks into his son, Charles Small.

* * * * *

To pity and to hate in retrospect: that way madness lies. But Charles Small's brain is spinning and whining and teetering like a humming-top . . . like the clockwork humming-top his mother bought him that grey day when she went to visit the Nameless Woman of Chelsea.

She, he had gathered, having long ears, this Nameless Woman, was an abomination of desolations. No decent woman would touch her with a broomstick, for fear of contracting an unmentionable disease that caused one to rot away, to fall into paralysis, and to go raving mad. Mrs. Small and her sisters talked of her only in whispers. I. Small, of course, did not whisper. He would break into the *psst-psst-psst* of the women with the buzz-saw cry of a hunting leopard—which was as close as he could get to a *sotto-voce*—saying: "Not in front of the children! That's what they are! All they can talk about is obstitutes. Not another word! In my house never should nobody mention that woman!"

To this, Lily, the wife of Nathan, the Photographer, said: "You mean prostitute, Srul."

"*Mnyeh!*" said I. Small, stamping out of the room, and dragging Charles after him. Charles, of course, was devoured by curiosity. "What's an obstitute?" he asked, when they were alone, for I. Small's male rage had gone in smoke, with a harmless *pop* like a Chinese cracker.

The old man said: "Don't use such language. It's . . . a Bad Woman."

"Daddy, what does she do?"

I. Small was embarrassed. He said: "Better you shouldn't know. But touch a Bad Woman, and your head falls off. Enough! Go; be a good boy."

For some time after that Charles Small wondered about Bad Women. In what way, exactly, was a woman Bad? He had, for example, been called a Bad Boy for playing with matches, for throwing stones, for getting his feet wet, and for losing a pocket handkerchief. Yet his mother and his father did all these things, and more. I. Small could not hang a picture without doing incalculable damage, or strike a match without setting light to the wrong thing. He could not boil a kettle of water without making an explosion, followed by an uproar. Mrs. Small never had a handkerchief—she was always losing them—and she always had a cold because her feet were always wet. They were Good. Then what was Bad? The boy pondered, and remembered one breakfast-time when he cracked an egg and an appalling stench came out. His mother snatched it away, pronouncing it Bad. He arrived at the conclusion that a Bad Woman was in some way comparable to a bad egg, and thereafter he went about sniffing at women. None of them smelled very good to him—only one, and she was the Bad Woman, the Nameless Woman.

She was a harmless young woman, he recollects, who had been a close friend of the Moss girls, and a frequent visitor at the Moss house, especially on Sundays. Then she fell in love with an Italian, a prosperous dried-fruit merchant, who could not marry her because his wife, a good Catholic, could not divorce him. So they went and lived in sin, in an elegant maisonette in Kensington, where he kept her in style. But thereafter the Moss girls shuddered, almost spat, when her name, or rather her namelessness, was mentioned in public. Secretly (trust them!) they went out of their way to meet her, the double-faced bitches, and, green with envy at her furs and her jewels, sighed over her fall; and went back to their husbands, full of embittered virtue and vague discontent, thanking God that they were not as she was; wishing to God that they were. Charles Small remembers . . .

Early one afternoon his mother took him to a shop in Oxford Street to buy him a hat. He wanted a virile tweed cap with a stiff peak. She would not hear of that—rough boys wore caps—and clapped on his head and paid for a hat which, even to this day, when he thinks of it, causes him to dig his nails into his palms, and knot his legs, and groan curses at the ceiling, the whey-coloured ceiling. It was a hat such as could never have been seen before or since—a furry pudding-basin with ear-flaps. On the crown, looking as if it might fall off at any moment, hung a fuzzy knob. Crowning humiliation! Charles Small was hauled out of the shop, crying at the top of his voice . . . and a pretty spectacle that must have been, with most of his teeth missing! Millie was embarrassed. She threatened him with grievous bodily harm, and in the same breath promised him rich rewards if only he would stop crying. He already knew the value of her threats and her promises, and cried on. Then, in the street, they almost collided with a most beautiful and elegant lady who exclaimed: "Why, Millie!" in an upper-class accent. Then Charles Small's mother and the lady kissed each other and conversed in undertones, while Charles, informed by some intuition that this was the Bad Woman, licked away some tears from his lip and cautiously sniffed. *If this is a Bad Woman*, he thought, *what does a Good Woman smell like?* Recollecting, he guesses that she must have used Opponax, that supposedly aphrodisiac perfume which was so popular in those days . . . those dead days unburied that walk, and walk, crying for a good deep grave. The Bad Woman, the Nameless One, took them to a quiet, elegant shop where they had tea and the most exquisite pastries, full of fresh cream and fruit. Charles Small regrets that he was too preoccupied with the confectionery to pay attention to the conversation. But at last, stuffed to the back teeth, he had a very urgent whisper of his own, tugging at his mother's skirt, so that Millie had to take him away for a minute or two. By the time they had returned the Nameless Woman had paid the bill and was ready to go. She and his mother embraced discreetly. The Nameless Woman (he has not forgotten the pressure of her hands, which were so slender and plump, and yet so strong) snatched him up and kissed him. He can still feel the pleasant roughness of some frill of lace at her bosom . . . and above all the good, the excellent, the inescapable smell of her. . . .

And now his mother looked left and right. She looked down at little Charles, and said: "You mustn't say anything," and led him to a toy shop where she bought him a mechanical spinning top made of painted tin. He forgets what it cost. It had a red, loose-looking wooden knob on top—not unlike the knob on the crown of the ridiculous hat—and when you twisted this knob you wound a spring, so that the top, placed on the floor, spun, while air rushed in through a little aperture and out of the over-blown empty darkness of this cheap toy monotonously whirling and whirling, inevitably staggering and falling and rolling away —out of this came what might have been a song. But it was only a whine, a windy whine. So spins and whines his unsteady ill-balanced head . . . his deceptively large head which encloses nothing but a little bit of imported clockwork and a ball of shadow. No, it did not fall off. Here it is, creaking and turning, turning and turning; and out of the hole in it, his mouth, comes nothing but a mean little noise of which he is ashamed.

*   *   *   *   *

Liars! Cheats! Charles Small asks himself once again what right they had to eat up his life and (even more bitterly) what right he had had to let them do it. Why, even as a child he recognised them as cowards and fools, liars and weaklings, cheats, creatures of the penumbra. Yes indeed, they lived in the half-shadow, and in that half-shadow they died and, presumably, were damned for their deceit, their wanton self-deceit. He pull

his hair until it stands upright and, staring incredulously at the
ceiling, laughs a little. It is fantastic. As a little child he knew.
As a grown man he knew them to the very soul. The more he
knew them, the more he despised them. Here, indeed, familiarity
bred contempt—the deeper the familiarity the deeper the
contempt. Yet—Charles Small cannot reconcile actuality with
common sense—the more he despised them the more he pitied
them, and the more he pitied them the more he despised himself.
So that when they were at their weakest and most abject and
he should have been at his strongest they had him in a death-
lock. Oh Lord, the misery of it, when Fear gives place to Compassion! And the double pity of it, when Pity muffles Loathing!

After his wife died I. Small was inconsolable, good for nothing.
Not that he had ever been good for anything much. Now he
could not eat, he could not sleep; when he stood up he wished
that he was sitting down, and having sat down it was necessary
for him to stand up. Standing up, he had to walk; walking, he
became weary and stood still. Standing still, he fidgeted. If he
saw a flight of stairs he felt compelled to walk up them, and,
having reached the top, walk down again to pick at something
—the flowers, his nails, anything. He opened drawers and shut
them. He fussed with tablecloths. It was as if the Great Curse
in the Book of Deuteronomy was upon him—at dawn he wished
it were even, and at even he wished that it were dawn. The old
man was shattered, like a pot. Charles Small, secretly wishing
that the old fool would drop dead, found himself worrying about
him. Forgetting vast tyrannies he remembered little secret
tendernesses—despising those tendernesses for the secretiveness
of them, while sighing sentimentally over them—and he decided
what the old man needed was something to do.

"I'm a burden. It would be better I should die."

Charles heartily agreed with him, but said: "Don't talk like
that, Father!" in a shocked voice.

"I don't like you should call me Father. When your poor
mother, God rest her soul, was alive, you used to call me Daddy.
So now it's Father. This is what we come to. I'm a burden, a
burden."

He had probably picked up that word *burden* out of the *News
of the World*, to which he had always subscribed because, as he
shrewdly observed, it had less advertisements. The paper was
always full of gruesome cases of old gentlemen who had swallowed

carbolic acid, cut their throats with bread-knives, thrown themselves under trains, hanged themselves with their braces, broken their ankles jumping out of first-storey windows, and put their heads in gas ovens, because they "felt they were a burden". The old man had been reading too many newspapers.

Charles Small went into conference with his wife, saying: "I mean, after all, he *is* my father."

She agreed. She always agreed, the insipid, unastonishable cow.

"We must give him something to do," said Charles Small. So they made conspiracies. They invented urgencies. They gave him nails to hammer into walls; they made pretexts for the whitewashing of ceilings (I. Small invariably upset a bucket); they exhausted themselves in their efforts to prove to this silly old burden that he was not a burden. Once they gave him a gross of pencils to sharpen very carefully at both ends. Still I. Small, disconsolate, said: "I'm a burden. A burden should go away." Nerves were on edge. The children kept asking: "What's a Burden? Grampa says he's a Burden. I thought he was Jewish." He took to hanging about in the kitchen, trying to help. At mealtimes they had to coax him to eat. Lustfully eyeing the chicken he would say: "Give it, better, to the children. What for waste chicken on a Burden?" Then, having taken away everyone's appetite, he would eat, saying between mouthfuls: "It chokes me." Charles Small knew where he had got that one. He remembered his mother, and the deceit of the fried fish, and pushed away his plate, nauseated—observing which, I. Small went on burdening and burdening and burdening.

At last, when they were all at their wits' end, some salesman of job lots waylaid Charles Small in his office and offered to sell him, dirt cheap, a million paper clips of various shapes and sizes. So he bought them, the whole million of them; had them shaken up, mixed, in bags, and brought them to the old man, saying: "Father, this is important. We want your help. These are vitally important paper-clips and fasteners. They've all got mixed up. They have all got to be sorted out and arranged according to size and quality. I need your help. Urgently! I want you to drop everything and sort out these fasteners. Look: see? The little brass ones, the little wire ones . . . the medium-sized, and the big ones . . . See? All in order. It's vitally important there should be no mistake. Is that clear?"

The old man was delighted. Now he had something to occupy his woolly old mind. It seemed, for a couple of days, that there might be peace in the house. But I. Small, becoming important again, again became even more intolerable. A case in point: one evening when Charles Small, after a hard day, put a Chopin Nocturne on the gramophone and sat down smoking a cigarette to listen quietly in the twilight, trying to soothe himself, I. Small came down raging in his shirt-sleeves, brandishing a paper-clip, roaring in something like his old voice: "Gramophones they want! No bleddy noise! How should a man concentrate in this bleddy house?"

Charles Small remembers that instead of telling the fool to go to the devil he said: "All right, Father" . . . and stopping the Nocturne, sat back disconsolately, thinking. His father was working like a demon on the paper-clips. Soon, they had all been arranged in order. Then what? He brooded. At last he remembered an engineer named Watt whom he had watched in an idle moment. Watt was swabbing some part of a machine with a wad of cotton-waste—an almost inextricable tangle of threads of different colours. When the old man was done with his paper-clips it would be a good idea to buy two, three hundred pounds of the cotton-waste, and say that he urgently needed the threads unravelled and grouped in their proper colours: that ought to keep him busy for a year at least.

So it did. But much good it did them all! I. Small became irritable, arrogant, unapproachable. He started work at dawn and continued until dusk, and then he wanted to rest; and then if you wanted to play a little Mozart he would come down like a thunderstorm. He worked his fingers to the bleddy bone, and all they knew was bleddy gramophones . . .

. . . Slice him which way you like, the old son of a bitch was a burden.

Now, thinks Charles Small, everything is a burden. Life is a burden. My wife is a burden. My children are a burden. And who is to blame? Mother? Agreed. Father? Agreed. Above all, who is to blame? I am to blame. *But for myself I might have been happy.*

Dead loss . . . dead loss . . .

CHAPTER XVIII

BUT between the Noblett Street fiasco and the death of Mrs. Small, many strange and terrible things had happened. Little men had grown great, great men had become small, lives had been spoiled and hearts broken.

Incredible things had come to pass.

The iron-footed hunchback Solly Schwartz, hopping and hobbling from strength to strength, had kicked down the mighty from their seats and exalted the humble.

When he left Slupworth, sales manager, advertising manager, and partner to Mr. Narwall—all signed and sealed—he sat in his first-class compartment, dreaming thunderous dreams of tremendous power, restlessly turning one of his cans in his sinewy right hand.

This was it! Use it and throw it away, and buy another; and so on and on eternally. Impermanent things—they were the only things that lasted—breakable things, things made to be broken or lost. He lit a cigarette and, looking at the smoke, thought, *Here again, another good thing—a smoker—what does he do? He burns money; he blows it away—pouf!—like that, the bloody fool.* . . . Then he thought of old Anselmi and his copper pots that lasted fifty years, and laughed a little. Who got rich on customers that came back once every fifty years? Smoke, ashes, tins for the midden—these were the things to sell—in general, waste-matter. Thinking deeply, he arrived at the conclusion that all the commodities worth selling were those that went down the drain or into the dust-bin. Consider coal: you burn it, and you're cold again, and must buy more. Would the mine-owner get rich on a shovelful of coal that burned for five years? It occurred to him that, tin cans aside, food itself was waste material. You went to work to dig a hole to buy the bread to get the strength to go to work and dig a hole. . . . Imagine a loaf of bread or a sausage that would keep you going for twelve months—or a potato that would stay your appetite for half a year! Everything would go to the dogs.

Now, people were people, human beings of a sort, and therefore everything that was most important to them, purchasable only with their blood, sweat and (same thing) money, was doomed to the ash-tray, the ash-can, the cesspool, or some dark hole in the ground. He lit another cigarette and considered the burned match. There you were again! Matches. People couldn't get along without them. The poorest of the poor had to spend his begged or borrowed or sweated-for penny on a few seconds of flickering flame. One puff, and they were in the dark once more, and all was to do again; another penny must be found. So it was with candles.

What was a candle? Half a farthing's worth of stearine and paraffin, bought for a halfpenny for the sake of an hour's freedom from the blackness of the night. Or ink—people had to write, and stroke by stroke the penny bottle of blue-black emptied itself.

Ink reminded him of paper, another highly destructible commodity. What happened to all the paper in the world? Pondering this, he decided that on the whole the best kind of paper to sell must be newspaper and toilet paper—the two kinds most in demand—but not wallpaper, which stuck for years . . . Solly Schwartz was enjoying this little meditation. He thought of pins and needles, and remembered Cohen's workshop. Cohen was a careful man with pins, yet every week or two he would have to buy another big box of these elusive, essential inches of pointed wire. . . . Pins, needles, thread, pencils, flowers, soap. Soap: however thoroughly you washed you got dirty again, and had to spend a little more of your sweat to purchase the wherewithal to lather it away. . . .

Somewhat tired, he rested his rugged chin on the ornate handle of his walking-stick and thought dreamily and happily of man's perpetual crying need for things that must day after day disappear into the air or be washed away back into the earth and must always be bought and paid for in hard cash.

He lit another cigarette and smiled at the smoke. Like everyone else he had lusted after smoke; had denied himself a pennyworth of fish and chips for the sake of five cigarettes for a penny . . . A pennyworth of smoke and ashes. True, fish and chips went the way of all replaceable things. But fish and chips gave a man strength. Fish and chips, especially on a cold night, lent a man the courage and the power to face another day, and achieve great things; whereas smoke begot nothing but a yearning for more smoke, and was productive of nothing. A bad habit, a bad

218

taste in the mouth, a stale smell, a cough. Now, Solly Schwartz looked angrily at his cigarette. He was smoking Dimitrinos, an expensive brand. In the sealed compartment the fragrant smoke went up in a diaphanous blue ribbon, gently weaving, until it spun itself away into the close air and disappeared. And all for Dimitrino! Solly Schwartz dashed the cigarette to the floor and ground it to dust under his iron foot. Then he took from his pocket the box with its Egyptian Government stamp, and threw it out of the window. It landed, he guessed, on a siding about ten miles out of Euston, where some delighted sucker would pick up the packet and suck smoke out of it, making ashes and dust to enrich Dimitrino; giving more power to his weakness; dribbling a few more pennies out of his pay envelope into the pockets of W.D. & H.O. Wills, John Player, Godfrey Phillips, and all the rest of them. He kept his cigarette-case filled, and his cigar-case too—for fools—but from that moment Solly Schwartz never smoked again.

As soon as the collector snatched away his ticket, he hobbled, respectably dressed as he was, to a fish shop in the Euston Road, and ate fish and fried potatoes voraciously and, between mouthfuls, thought of Goodridge, with his high sweet voice and his air of putrefaction—Goodridge, with his blackened nails and brain of crystal, Goodridge with his deft, delicate, filthy hands, making fine diagrams on a greasy marble table and expounding ever so gently the mysteries of strange machines.

The memory of Goodridge took away his appetite. All the same, Solly Schwartz finished his meal—he had eaten eight-pennyworth—threw down one-and-six, and went out in a bad temper. Here was what came of being over-eager, too generous. If he had kept Goodridge on beer, he might have had the Calculating Machine, as well as a lousy tin can. It was true that anyone who had an opponent by the belly had the death-grip; and Solly Schwartz had the world in a powerful grip, in the guts. Still, if he had not been so impetuously generous, he might have had this same world by the brain; he might have taken hold of Calculation by its . . . by its quadratic equations.

He went home, feeling, as he expressed it, flatter than a saucerful of cold piss, and slept like a dead man. But next morning he leaped up at seven o'clock; strapped on his iron foot; paced the floor, thinking, for half an hour; put on a con-spicuous suit with a red over-check and a pearl Trilby hat, took hold of a cane, the ivory handle of which was carved in the shape of a voluptuous mermaid, and went to see Abel Abelard.

* * * * *

He knew that people like Abel Abelard were not early risers. Still, such was his impatience, he reached Fitzroy Square at ten o'clock in the morning and poked impatiently with the ferrule of his stick at the scarred and blistered studio door. Which, to his astonishment, swung open. Abelard was awake, inspired, working at his great picture of The Destruction of the Library at Alexandria. The slatternly girl was posing stark naked, bending backwards in the grip of a lay-figure. Every muscle in her body expressed strain and anguish, and her tousled hair hung over her face and down her back in wild twists and strands. At the end of one stray wisp dangled a celluloid "slide" (now, Solly Schwartz reflected, they call them bobby pins . . . more costly detritus —more to be bought and lost, more to be paid for and thrown away). Her face was twisted with anguish, but her eyes were blankly happy, while, through her pouting lips, came a bubbling noise adjusted to the rhythm of "She's Only A Bird In A Gilded Cage". In her dangling left hand she held the smouldering half of a home-made cigarette.

Solly Schwartz, having made a mental note of the hair-clip, touched Abelard with his stick. The artist turned, palette in left hand and brush in right, his face full of menace. The tip of the brush was red. Solly Schwartz laughed, and struck it out of his hand with a flick of his stick, saying: "Come on, *trottel*, put a sock in it. Do you want a job, or don't you?"

Abelard said: "Oh, it's you, is it? I was working. I had an inspiration, Mr. . . . Mr. . . ."

"—Schwartz, Mr. Schwartz. To hell with your inspiration! *Schwartz!* . . . Tell her to go and get dressed. Put down that board of paints—you're dirty enough already—it's running down. I want to talk to you."

Turning his head, Abelard said to the girl: "Put something on, darling."

"Oh good!" she said, and, shamelessly stretching herself, strolled away, while the lay-figure, folding like a carpenter's ruler, fell into a kneeling position, hands outstretched as if in worship.

"I had an idea——" Abelard began.

"Idea be buggered," said Solly Schwartz. "*I've* got an idea. Put that bloody board down for a minute, do you mind? Put it away. I want a word." He looked with distaste at the only empty chair, and, although he was tired, said: "I'll stand. It won't take a minute. Listen. You want work?"

"I *am* working," said Abelard, pointing to the canvas.

"I mean *work*," said Solly Schwartz. "I mean *work*, regular hours, for money. *Work!*" he said leering at the canvas. "Is this work? What do you get out of such work? Work! . . . I mean seven pounds a week regular. That's what I call work. Well?"

Abelard could only say: "Well?"

"Listen," said Solly Schwartz.

"Do you mean seven pounds a week every week?" asked Abelard.

"Seven pounds a week every week to begin with. Later, if you do the job, ten, twelve, fifteen, twenty——"

"Would you like a glass of beer, Mr. Schwartz?"

"No. Listen. You remember those labels you done for me?"

Abel Abelard laughed and said: "Oh, those! That was nothing. . . ."

"Oh, those," said Solly Schwartz. "That was nothing, eh? And by you the pay was nothing? Give me an honest answer. No, don't waste your breath, save it. Sit down."

Abelard sat down, saying: "Yes, but what is all this about seven pounds a week?"—fumbling at his little beard with an irresolute hand.

Cumulatively, from petty deal to petty deal, there had grown in the hunchback's head a terrifying realisation of the brevity of life. There was so much to do, so little time. Now he felt as some fisherman might feel who, angling in a little boat on a wide sea lit by a sinking golden sun, feels the jerking of the hook in the jaw of a monstrous fish—and plays it and plays it, gritting his teeth and holding the slippery rod with all his might and main while the reel irresistibly rolls and the taut wet line slides away —the big fish is invisible; the line is unreliable; the light will not last; time is short, dreadfully short—but his will and his pride ordain that between the twilight and the dark, upon this fine thread, he must pull in a monster.

He struck his iron foot impatiently with his heavy cane. Abel Abelard drew a sketch of him from memory a little later—a

head, brilliantly expressive of courage, vanity, and blind pride—
a flattened head, curiously satanic with a crunched-up, irritable,
irascibly smiling mouth and deadly little watchful eyes.

Solly Schwartz said: "Be quiet. Listen." He looked for a
moment at the great canvas, shrugged his high shoulders and
went on, "That *scheiss* won't pay your rent. This *scheiss* will."
He took out of his pocket one of his tin cans, wrapped in one of
Abelard's labels. "I want more. I want more and more. I want
labels for everything—I want labels for cherries, strawberries,
plums, greengages, apples, pears, pineapple, anything you can
think of. I want labels for fish, sausages, ham, beef, stew. I
want labels for asparagus. I want labels, by God, I want labels
for everything! I want posters to stick on walls—big ones, little
ones, large ones, small ones! I want showcards for shops—you
know, cardboard showcards—so they can hang 'em up, stand 'em
up, stick 'em up. Like you did those labels, see? Delicious, works
of art, to make your mouth water. Do you understand? I want
big posters. . . ." Solly Schwartz tried to extend his arms beyond
the bounds of the studio.

"Forty-eight sheets," said Abelard.

"Forty-eight sheets, fifty-eight sheets; so long as they make
the *trottel's* mouth water! Little ones——"

"Double-crowns?"

"That's right, double-crowns. Double. That's the idea.
Colours. But I want them real, real, you understand, like a
photograph. Gooseberries, take gooseberries. I want gooseberries,
little green gooseberries and big red gooseberries—but I want to
see every bloody hair on every one of those bloody gooseberries—
every leaf!"

"Lea . . . leaf . . ." said Abel Abelard, thoughtfully. "If
you want realism, you know, mightn't it be a good idea to have,
say, a caterpillar on——"

"Talk sense!" said Solly Schwartz. "Caterpillars. Who buys
tinned caterpillars? Butterflies! Coloured butterflies."

"Same thing, in the long run," said Abelard. "A butterfly is
nothing but a caterpillar with a pair of wings."

"Same thing, eh? What would you rather have—a houseful of
caterpillars or a houseful of butterflies?"

"Butterflies, I suppose."

"Then if you like, butterflies. No caterpillars, understand?"
Solly Schwartz hesitated a moment and then said: "Just a minute.

Just a minute. It could be a good thing to have a trademark. A butterfly . . ."

Abelard handed him an album, saying: "Here are pretty nearly all the moths and butterflies in the world. Take your choice."

Solly Schwartz turned the pages and at last stopped, marking with his horny thumbnail a gaudy and magnificent insect with wonderful wings. "This one," he said.

Abel Abelard answered: "Hey, my dear sir, you can't put *that* on your tin! That's the Purple Emperor—he lives on rotten meat."

"So do lobsters. So do crabs. So do shrimps. So do eels. Didn't you ever stick your nose up against a shop-window in the Strand, with an empty belly? To look at the lobsters? They live on dead men. Well? What do you think you live on, eh? One of these days, big as you are, you're going to die," said Solly Schwartz, "and out of your guts what do you think is going to come? Diamonds? Grass? Who eats the grass? The lamb. Who eats the lamb? Eh? *I'll* eat you. Purple Emperors. . . . Now, listen. You work for me, five, five and a half, six days a week, and I pay you seven pounds a week. You draw. Later on, when things get better with me, you get more. Anything especially good you do, you get a bonus. In the meantime, seven pounds a week. What's the matter with that, eh?"

"Well, nothing," said Abelard. "Only I wonder if I might have something on account."

Solly Schwartz took out his wallet and put down two ten-pound notes, saying: "Here's twenty pounds."

"Oh, thank you! This is on account of salary, I take it?"

"Don't be such a bloody fool! Salary! This is a bonus in advance. Work with me, play straight with me, and I give you my word of honour—you'll want for nothing. Now, are you with me?"

Abelard said: "I am with you, Mr. Schwartz."

"That's settled then," said Solly Schwartz. "I'll get in touch with you. In the meantime, remember: seven pounds a week to begin with, and for the present, Good-bye!"

The girl, who had put on a dress and come out to hear the end of the conversation, ran to Solly Schwartz and, before he could recoil, kissed him wetly on the left cheek. He limped away. Looking down the stair-well she saw him scrubbing his cheek with the cuff of his conspicuous coat, rubbing her kiss away. This made her angry and sad: more sad than angry. But when Abel Abelard shⱼwed her the two ten-pound notes she squealed like a delighted child. They embraced, and went to a good restaurant, agreeing that God had sent them a fool.

Solly Schwartz went on his way, grinning.

Now this, if Charles Small only knew it, was the point at which Solly Schwartz began to be God—began unwittingly to involve himself in Charles Small's destiny and help to break his heart.

God: this is a strong word. Powerful though he was, alert though he was, the hunchback with the game leg was nothing but the unconscious agent of infinitely higher powers. Shrewd, keen, calculating as he was, how little Schwartz knew of the beautiful thing he had destroyed and in what manner he had been responsible for its destruction!

*   *   *   *   *

Now how had this happened? To Charles Small, when his life was torn asunder, when he was very young and wriggling like a cut worm in the dirt, it was a mystery. He clung to Solly Schwartz, for there was no one else strong enough to cling to. He became an atheist and, denying the existence of God, cursed Him. He denied God and the Devil, then, and considered himself as a marble between the fumbling forefinger and thumb of a blind man, or as one of a pair of dice in the clumsy hands of a myopic man . . . hopeless, helpless, lost.

Later he knew that Solly Schwartz, whom he loved then and always would love, was his evil genius. But now, thinking through the mud in which he feels that he is immersed, Charles Small knows that Solly Schwartz bore him nothing but goodwill— loved him—but was himself a bewildered wanderer in this world where men grow tired, in spite of the fact that he believed that he knew exactly where he was going and what he was doing. Now (the hunchback would break a walking-stick over his head if he said it) Charles Small, feeling sorry for himself, feels sorry for Solly Schwartz, the Superman. Schwartz was a better man than Charles, Charles's father, and twenty men put together . . . and yet he was, so to speak, in the grip of terrible forces. Even Schwartz, with all his spiritual might, never accomplished a design, or quite achieved an end. Even he, Schwartz, was a tool in an Invisible Hand. Yes, even Solly Schwartz, the Calculator, was nothing and nobody. He was sharp; but keenest of all is that part of the razor-edge which one cannot see. The part that cuts is invisible.

Charles Small knows, now; he understands that which was incomprehensible, and sees things to which in the old days he was blind.

> *O world invisible, we view thee!*
> *O world intangible, we touch thee!*
> *O world unknowable, we know thee!*
> *Inapprehensible, we clutch thee!*

Now it isn't necessary to recapitulate. It is essential to turn over in the mind the great passion of Solly Schwartz and its relation to the great love of Charles Small . . . how the one affected the other. . . how Passion locked horns with Love, and Passion, triumphant, went away wailing, empty, into the night.

Lara . . . Lara!

* * * * *

As soon as his contract was signed Solly Schwartz went to work with a sort of demoniac energy. He established the London office and, paying Abelard lavishly, drove him like a mule, beating him with the lash of his raw, contemptuous tongue. The forty-eight sheets were painted, printed, and pasted up; and so were the twenty-four sheets, the twelve sheets, and the double-crowns. The showcards were drawn and printed, and manufactured, each with its little red cord. Solly Schwartz went about like a madman from wholesale house to wholesale house, brandishing his tin can, talking through his lower teeth:

". . . Look, *trottel*. Look and see. There isn't any argument. Is it clear? The best product of its kind in the world. Taste these peas—wait a minute, no need for a tin-opener—here, look—they open like that, just as easy as that! Taste, and see! Judge, judge for yourself, mister! . . . Isn't that good enough for you? This other bloody rubbish you cut your fingers off with. With my can, so you turn a wheel, and there you are—peas, beans, tomatoes, anything . . . What? Not such a big can? I'm sorry. All right. For another pint of blood take another ounce of peas! Buy or don't buy—I'm not here to make sales."

But he was there to make sales, and they bought.

He would say, furthermore: "Here, look: here's a showcard for you! Did you ever in your life see a card like this? Look at it —it makes your mouth water. Well?"

The buyers bought. Then Solly Schwartz bought advertising space in the newspapers. Mr. Narwall protested, but Schwartz bought front-page space in the *Daily Special*. He took the whole front page, three months running, and Abel Abelard drew remarkable pictures. Money poured out; but money poured in. After two years with Narwall Solly Schwartz found that he had a hundred thousand pounds in the bank.

He was about to buy a house in the country, a walled house not far from Woking, quite near the river—a place to which anyone might invite guests—when Mr. Fourose came from America with bad news.

Now Mr. Fourose was a lonely, sinister character who procured information and sold it for ready money to whom it might concern. He was, in effect, a spy, a commercial spy. There are such people. While some men insinuate themselves into war departments and sell their finds to Governments, others insinuate and bribe and corrupt themselves into factories; their information is often more valuable.

Mr. Fourose was a man of medium height and indefinable colour. He had the air of a craftsman; but he had also a certain watchfulness such as one seldom sees in the eyes of a man who is accustomed to watching his tools rather than his men. He said to Solly Schwartz: "Mr. Schwartz, I have some information. Sound information. It will cost you a thousand pounds.

"Do me a favour, don't make me laugh—I've got a cracked lip. What do you mean, a thousand pounds?"

"A thousand pounds," said Mr. Fourose. "In advance."

"What for?"

"A few words. A thousand pounds. You know me, Mr. Schwartz. I don't swindle you. I'm an honest man. Put down a thousand pounds and I give you my word of honour that I'll put down something worth it. If you don't, I'll go elsewhere."

Solly Schwartz wrote a cheque for five hundred pounds and, putting it across the desk, said: "Don't touch it, it's wet. It's five hundred pounds. I'll give you the other five hundred pounds when you talk. What is it?"

Fourose, waving the cheque in the air, waited till it was dry before he put it in his pocket, when he said: "Mr. Schwartz, there's a firm called Paisley in Philadelphia. They've got a new can. It makes yours look silly."

"Show me."

"Look. See. Yours is too complicated. This works like . . . like *that!* Now do you see what I mean?"

Solly Schwartz wrote another cheque. "There's your thousand pounds," he said, "and no argument."

The men shook hands. Fourose hurried to the bank. Solly Schwartz said to his secretary: "Get me a ticket, quick, for Slupworth. Make me a telephone call to Mr. Narwall, tell him I want to see him quick! Above all, hurry; hurry up! I'm in a hurry!"

So, Mr. Fourose went his way and Solly Schwartz went his own, which was to Slupworth; where he changed, that day, the course of several lives.

He arrived early in the evening when Narwall was eating his tea—home-made bread and butter, ham and tongue—what they called a "meat tea". *Five bob a day and a good meat tea . . . and we're getting forrader and forrader.* Mrs. Narwall asked him to sit down, and served him lavishly, but Schwartz ate angrily, almost in silence until, his appetite satisfied, he pushed away his plate and said: "Mr. Narwall, now look!"

"Go to bed," said Mrs. Narwall to the children, and they left the room.

"Now look here," said Solly Schwartz, "I've had just about quite enough. I can't work like this. Every bloody damn thing I do you question——"

"No profanity, please!" said Mr. Narwall.

"Bugger your bloody profanity! Are you listening or are you not? Every damn bloody thing you query! You make me look like a tuppeny-ha'penny bloody bleeding bastard, do you hear?"

"Please, Mr. Schwartz, not in front of my wife."

Solly Schwartz told Mr. Narwall what he could go and do to his wife, expressing a doubt concerning his capacity to do it. Narwall's face became lead-coloured with rage. Mrs. Narwall, however, smiled a little secretive smile; whereupon Mr. Narwall asked her to leave the room, and she told him not to be silly.

"What have you to complain of, Mr. Schwartz?" she asked.

"I've got plenty of bloody God-damn blasted things to complain of!" shouted Schwartz.

"Let us discuss this without profanity," said Mr. Narwall. Solly Schwartz, telling him exactly what he could do with his

227

profanity, slipped into unprintable obscenity, at which the manufacturer stopped his ears. Mrs. Narwall remained calm, and said: "But what is in your mind, Mr. Schwartz?"

"I can't work like this!" said Solly Schwartz. "What the devil of a kind of way, God strike me dead, is this, to run a bloody business? Eh? Every bloody bleeding blasted penny I lay out, so you damn well query it. What sort of system is this, by Christ? What louse-bound stinking bloody rotten system, eh? . . . Oh, 'ladies present' you say. You can——your ladies! Or can you? I've had enough of you. Enough is enough. I can't work with you and I won't. Is that clear?"

Mr. Narwall said: "Wait a minute, Mr. Schwartz, please—do not be too impetuous."

Solly Schwartz said: "Impetuous. Impetuous be bloody well buggered for a lark!"

He saw Mrs. Narwall kick her husband under the table as she said, in a voice which she thought was deceptively sweet:

"But, dear! If Mr. Schwartz doesn't want to stay with us——"

"—You're bloody well right I don't!" cried Solly Schwartz. "I should work with stingy cows like you two!"

"Are you trying to insult me?" asked Mrs. Narwall.

Solly Schwartz replied: "Yes. Cows. Pigs, I should have said."

Rising, Mr. Narwall said: "Mr. Schwartz, get out!"

Solly Schwartz uttered a word which it is not customary to print, and added: "Let's break it up. How can I work with a stinkpot like you? You creeping bastard, you crawler! Break it, for God's sake, break it!"

"Thou shalt not take the name of the Lord thy God in vain," said Mr. Narwall.

"Never mind the name of the Lord your God in vain!" said Solly Schwartz.

Then Mrs. Narwall put her hand upon his pigeon-chest and pushed and he fell down.

He limped down the stairs, grinning like a little devil. As soon as the front door had closed behind him, Mr. Narwall said:

"My dear, are you crazy? Are you out of your mind? Schwartz is worth a million pounds."

"Don't be a fool. What is he? A salesman, a man handling advertising—a man. You employ him, you pay him, you give him a share of everything you earn. What for? A Can. Is that clear? It is clear, is it? How much have you made this last

couple of years? A hundred and fifty thousand? Well then . . .
consider it. You made him lose his temper, don't you see? He
has got the Can—don't you remember? Buy him out, buy him
out, buy him out!"

So it happened that on the following day Solly Schwartz,
who afterwards in Mr. Narwall's mind was to be symbolic of the
Evil One, sold his interest in the Narwall Cannery, and in the
patent can, for £100,000. They parted, reconciled, on good
terms. Mrs. Narwall, the schemer, smiled at him like a cat. Mr.
Narwall said: "It has been a profitable association, Mr. Schwartz,
and I am sorry that we have had to part company. God bless you."

Solly Schwartz said, with the air of a man who has done the
wrong thing: "Look here . . . It could be I was a bit hasty. . . ."

He appeared uneasy. Mrs. Narwall said, in her firm voice,
with her soft smile: "All signed and sealed now, Mr. Schwartz.
Good-bye!"

Solly Schwartz then went away, looking disconsolate—while
the Narwalls exchanged sly glances—and caught the express to
London, where he cashed the cheque.

Mrs. Narwall, meanwhile, said to her husband: "Come on now
—now is the time to go into production. Buy the cannery, buy
the plant—buy fruit, everything, and take with both hands!"

Her husband replied: "I think, my dear, that you are right."

"I know I'm right. Buy in, quick!"

So they did. They bought in the cannery, and everything else
their money could buy. Within fourteen days the Philadelphia
firm attacked the English market with a lower-priced product
packed in a better can, wrapped in a better label, and the firm
of Narwall crashed. It went down in sections, as one might say—
inevitably—like a mill-chimney. And there were the Narwalls
with two or three grocery shops in the south of England, and
nothing more. They had always lived frugally, but their morale
was eaten away. They had lost their accumulated capital. Their
hearts were broken—at least Mr. Narwall's heart was broken.
He was a common tradesman again. Mr. Lumpitt got drunk out
of sheer joy at the crash of this bloody tyrant. Solly Schwartz,
having £200,000 in the bank, executed a gleeful hop-skip-and-
jump, and went to Swaine and Adeney and bought a box-
wood walking-stick that weighed about three pounds, curiously
carved to represent clasped hands. The knob was a crude
turquoise.

So it came to pass that Narwall moved southward and that, in making this move necessary, Solly Schwartz made rack and ruin of Charles Small's life.

Try and tell him, go and try and explain! He did what he wanted to do. He spoiled my life. He spoiled my life! Good luck to him! cries Charles Small on his bed of pain—*Good luck to him for spoiling my life, because, by God, he had a great soul!*

* * * * *

Yes, he made and he broke people, that strange little man whom everyone considered as broken and improperly made. Shortly after the Narwall affair he went to Abel Abelard. Abelard was wrapped in a stained dressing-gown. The girl was wearing a camisole, as they used to call them. Solly Schwartz said to him: "Listen. The business is over and done with. But I'm going to tell you something. How much are you getting a week now?"

"Eh? How much? Nine pounds, I think."

"You had a job. You haven't got one. How do you like that?" asked Solly Schwartz.

Abel Abelard said: "Oh well, I don't know, I don't see that it makes such a great difference—do you?"

Nodding approvingly, Solly Schwartz said: "Quite right. Good attitude." Then he looked at this tousled young man in his filthy, paint-bespattered studio, pinching the bottom of his slatternly mistress, and a kind of wonder came upon him. Solly Schwartz, the man of iron, was awe-struck by this man of straw. He looked at them again. They were caressing each other affectionately; he with his left hand on her knee, while he applied strokes of white to his great panel of the Burning of the Library at Alexandria.

How, wondered Solly Schwartz—he who had always lived and always would live in hidden dumps and furnished places . . . in any case, in furnished places—how was it possible to live like this? It may be, at that moment, that he was bitten by a nostalgia, an envy. He had intended to say to Abel Abelard: *Look here. It's all over. I can't use you any more. Anyway, I can't pay you nine pounds a week any more because the business is, so to speak, liquidated, in a manner of speaking. If you want to stay on for a retainer of a fiver, all right.*

Instead, he said: "Look here, Abelard. I'm going to tell you something. How much are you getting now? About nine quid?

Well, I'm going to make it ten. We are going into a new business. Advertising. I'm going to start you off at ten pounds a week, do you hear? And if, by Christ, you've got sense enough to find your arse to wipe it—excuse me, Madam—you'll make thirty, forty, fifty! Do you hear?"

The girl said: "If he can find his arse to wipe it."

Solly Schwartz blushed; he did not like to hear such words from the lips of ladies.

Abel Abelard said: "I don't quite see what you mean, Mr. Schwartz. You have closed up your business, and raised my wages. Excuse me, but this doesn't make sense to me."

Solly Schwartz snapped: "*Schmerel!* You bloody fool—excuse me, Madam—what do you think I close a business for? Fun? I close one business, *schlemihl.* I close one business to open another business. What else for? Now, comes a new business. Stop messing about with your dirty paints and listen a minute, will you? Listen . . ." said Solly Schwartz, lowering his voice and balancing his great stick on his knees.

"Glass of beer, Mr. Schwartz?"

"No. Be quiet with your beer. Listen. You know what you've been doing with me the last year, two years? Making labels, posters?"

"I remember," said Abel Abelard.

"Keep on," said Solly Schwartz. "Keep on, Abel, as long as . . . able." It occurred to him that he had made a joke. Abelard smiled politely; the girl screamed with laughter. Solly Schwartz went on dreamily: "Listen. You know me. I can eat you and your father's father. Do you want to change grips with me? . . . No, no, no—I don't want to damage your hand. Listen to me. I'm making a new business. Do you know what? I'll tell you. Advertising. Do you know what that means?"

Abelard said: "Well, not exactly, but I should say that it was trying to induce people to buy things they didn't really want."

"Right!" said Solly Schwartz.

Teasing out his beard, and patting the girl's bottom, Abel Abelard said: "You know, it might be fun."

Solly Schwartz looked at him with fierce, astonished eyes, and said: "Fun? Fun? What do you mean, *fun?* What the bloody hell do you think I'm running—*Comic Cuts? Ally Sloper's Half-Holiday? Weary Willie and Tired Tim?* Fun? Listen, you bloody fool. Have your fun here. With me, no fun. With me, Abelard, work! You're an artist. Artist, fartist—have bloody fun. Have fun with your women, but with *me* you have no fun. You work like a dog and you get paid like a lord. Out of my office have fun. In my office, if you do your job, you get the money to have fun. Is it clear? Is it agreed?"

His vehemence frightened them as much as his offer of ten pounds a week had impressed them. The girl looked at Abelard, nudged him, and nodded; and Abelard said: "Very well."

When he was gone, Abel Abelard and his girl sighed, because the air felt lighter. Then, impelled by a sudden impulse, they made love together, before Solly Schwartz, resolutely limping, beating the paving stones with his heavy stick, disdaining cabs, reached the corner of the street. Giving the girl one of the ten-pound notes, Abelard said: "For God's sake, slut, go and buy a dress and some underclothes!"

"Well," she said, taking the money, "I could do with a dress, old thing, but underclothes . . . if you don't mind, I'm not used to them, and you know it. What's the matter with you? Just because you're going into business you want me to wear underclothes? All your fine-feathered friends aren't going to look up my skirts, I hope?"

"To the devil with your drawers, my darling! Amuse yourself, have fun."

"I wonder why he was so angry just now when you talked about Fun."

Abel Abelard said: "No idea, my dear, but . . . well, it might be that the little fellow is not having fun, or that his idea of fun isn't mine. We're rich. Wash your filthy face, and comb your hair, and I'll take you, by God, to eat lunch at the Café Royal!"

*   *   *   *   *

So there came into being the Schwartz Advertising Agency, and Solly Schwartz was happy, because now he dealt in what he believed to be the most impermanent commodities—words and visual impressions—print, paper, illusion. It is remarkable that, considering the success of John Bunny and Bill Hart, he did not turn his keen mind to the cinema, to the selling of images, perpetually replaceable shadows. Considering the fabulous perspicuity of the man, one wonders why he did not hook his strong hands into Marconi, and make trade in air and sound. No, considering the matter, Schwartz chose the most appropriate trade; here to-day, gone to-morrow, persuading the world to buy goods which other men had produced . . . employing artists to draw memorable pictures of lamps; hiring writers to put out prose descriptive of tables and chairs . . . lying cynically, and with a fistful of money persuading poor would-be-honest craftsmen to lie, and lie, and lie about toothpaste, cigarettes, soap, five-shilling watches, artificial silk stockings—all that was immediately consumable and, having been consumed, essentially replaceable.

Thus, Solly Schwartz, the cripple, a mighty man to help his friends, scratching his itch for power, became the father and begetter of liars and of lies.

*   *   *   *   *

So, through the years—not many years, only a few—Schwartz became a name, and Narwall became a mockery. The Narwalls came south partly because most of their shops were in the south of England, but mainly on account of the pride they had inspired in themselves, the hate they had inspired in everyone else, and the shame that came with the cracking of their pride. They dreaded the silent laughter and the unseen interchange of winks and nudges; they could not face the false smiles they knew so well—the smirking sympathy—the bland eyebrows which they had in their time so often opposed to ruined tradesmen in Slupworth.

It was not that they were ruined; only they had lost face and, knowing how much they were hated, hurried away out of earshot of the laughter, for they were Pride nicely fallen . . . especially Mrs. Narwall, the bitch, the beauty, the creature of ice. She would have stayed in Slupworth and braved it out if it had been murder. But Narwall, the mean weakling, the under-dog, found himself for the first time in his life in the right, and he made the most of it. He made it clear that she, his wife, was responsible for his crash. Confronted with what was, in fact, a bitter truth, she nodded—not bowed, but nodded—her proud head. So Mr. and Mrs. Narwall with their family, together with the faithful old servant, went to London.

To hear the lounging proletariat of Slupworth talk as they crossed and uncrossed their languid legs, leaning against the railings of the Library, you might have thought that the so-bitterly-hated Narwalls were tramping the roads of England with a barrel-organ, a monkey and a tin cup.

In point of fact, they owned four moderately prosperous shops in sound positions around Westminster. Occupying the upper part of a house over one of their shops—the very one which Mr. Lumpitt managed—they lived as well as, if not better than, they had lived before, although London was not Slupworth where they had been big fishes in a little pool.

Here was a great, roaring city. And even in this tremendous jungle of stone the Narwalls could not escape from Slupworth, because here, always, was Lumpitt, secretly smiling at their discomfiture.

Not long after it was necessary for Mrs. Narwall to demonstrate to Ivy certain facts and procedures that are generally communicable only between mothers and daughters, Mr. Narwall said: "No idle hands. To work. She must go to Business College. Yes, upon my word, Ivy must typewrite, she must short-hand, she must earn her bread!"

"Yes, Father," said Ivy. So she went to a Business College, that flimsy little fool, that weak drink of milk. . . .

Milk, milk, milk! *You humpy bastard, you, you ruined my life! Why in the name of God did you have to do what you did with the Narwalls?* Charles Small silently screams. Then, talking to a cloud in his mind, he says—still silently—*Ivy, Ivy, where are you now, Ivy, my one and only love?*

Where is she now? God knows. God knows? Idiot, idiot—she is in the telephone directory. She is living in state near Regent's Park, bloated with money, blonde with chemicals, slender with careful starvation, flashing with jewels, dressed by Schiaparelli and Hartnell, and—he hopes and believes—bitterly unhappy.

There is more hate in Charles Small's stomach than it can encompass. He is violently sick. The convulsion of his inside is such that he feels he is about to throw up something like a sack of potatoes. He retches, he strains, he bursts asunder . . . and out comes nothing but a mouthful of sour froth.

God is just. Froth. You cannot give more than you have . . . froth, froth . . . more loss, more dead loss!

CHAPTER XIX

. . . CHARLES SMALL sits up, looking for something to destroy, and all he can see is the eiderdown overlay, which he kicks as hard as he can. It curls up and coldly slaps him in the face. Then, pushing and kicking it away, he looks down into the china vessel that has received the contents of himself—bubbles, frothy bubbles, acrimonious acidulous water—sour emptiness. He knows perfectly well that downstairs his wife—oh, how he hates the shape of her nose, and how he has through the years yearned to change that shape with a quick blow!—his wife, who loves him and whom he hates, is exercising dictatorial influence on the children. *Daddy is ill.* And so, looking at the tablespoonful of pale froth which was all he had to offer to the chamber-pot, swallowing bile, Charles Small thinks of his wife and children and knows that even in his sickness and his silence he, the unhappy victim of a most dreadful tyranny, has himself become a dirty little tyrant . . . that his children will hate and despise him, pity him, avoid him, and ultimately be only too glad to bury him.

Swallowing the nausea that comes when he thinks of himself in relation to his wife and children—he who is all that he ever detested—he, the tyrant who abhors tyranny—Charles Small thinks with unutterable longing (that is to say, a longing he has never dared openly to utter) of Ivy Narwall, and he considers himself with such abhorrence that he wishes he had two faces so that he might spit in one.

He sees himself as the abject victim of sloppy wet pity, a sneaking Judas who sold true love for thirty easy tears . . . furtive Peter who denied the Christ at the moan of a dove—not even at the stern crow of a cock.

Oh, corruption upon corruption! Who is there in this world whom he does not hate? Above all, he hates Charles Small; and looking at himself, and spitting out some of the vile taste of himself—more froth, pities himself. Pitying himself now, he begins to be sorry for everyone. He does not exactly want to die. He wishes that he were young and of strong will.

Given strong will he might have been happy, and by virtue

235

of his strong will many other men and women might have found happiness. But he was weak, and out of his weakness has come interminable pain. Pain upon pain! Pain for himself, pain for his wife, and so for his children and his children's children, unless God sends them enlightenment . . . pain for Ivy, and her husband and her children, and their children's children . . . pain, pain! He sees himself now as the only begetter of woe and anguish, the poisoner of innumerable babes unborn. And he wishes that he was so constructed that he might kick himself in the arse for a fool.

* * * * *

Oh, how Charles Small reproaches himself, realising that by the pronunciation of one syllable—*NO!*—he might have altered the course of several lives in his generation and God knows how many beyond it. But he never learned how to say No, the little man—he never even learned how to say Yes. Here again come the misery and the hate. His mother and his father, whom he loves and detests, befuddled truth between them, blew hot and cold with the same breath. Liars and cowards, they brought into being this coward, this liar, this sour-gutted wretch on his well-deserved bed of pain, this frustrated fool, Charles Small, so angry with himself that he would destroy himself, if only he had the nerve, which he hasn't.

He thinks of Tristan and Isolde, of Heloise and Abelard, of Palamon and Arcite, who gave everything for love. They fell in love, by Heaven—they pursued their love—they fought with bare steel for love, and they died for love. Rightly so. What was love? Everything. And death? Nothing . . . Aie, aie, aie— for the days of the strong man with the strong sword! . . . And oh, woe, woe betide this despicable generation of grocers, canners, accountants, advertisers, and other liars that won greatness through lies and deception . . . bought themselves brides with lies and illusions . . . woe, woe, utter black woe to this generation of paid liars, of which Charles Small, to his sour shame, is one!

* * * * *

How much in love is he, now, with dreamful death, this nostalgic idiot, who touched happiness with the silly tips of his timid fingers, the dirty coward, and had not the strength to close his hand and pick it up! When he thinks how happy he might have been with Ivy Narwall, Charles Small curses himself as few men have cursed themselves before, from the crown of his head to the soles of his feet—he loathes himself with a bitter, terrible loathing. He sees himself blindfold and bound, strapped to a chair in a prison yard in a rainy dawn, while the firing squad falls into line to blast out of this world this wretch who has so abjectly betrayed himself, this utterly despicable recipient of 30 pieces of Nothing. And he wishes that he were of the firing squad . . . he derives a certain satisfaction from the fantasy of himself as he sees himself between the V of the back-sight and the bead of the fore-sight, taking aim at his own chicken-heart. No one in the world can be so repulsive to anyone in the world as Charles Small is to himself. Other men have given all for love, which, again, is everything; and he has given all for nothing, nothing. Now, since he lacks I. Small's knack of talking himself into great expectations, having more objectivity in his little finger than that old fool had in his body, he knows himself for what he is—a sort of bifurcated turd, a dropping cursed with consciousness, afflicted with sentience so that he can smell himself, worse luck; dropped with strain and pain out of one bloody hole to go in shame and pain into another, into the dirt, where lies his grubby little destiny.

Now, he has a wild longing for Ivy, and a mad impulse to rush out and find her. In fact, he puts one foot on the floor, but then, in despair, he remembers that downstairs, tremulously listening to his every movement, lurk his fat, fair, slushy, lachrymose poultice of a wife and, bribed into silence, his nasty little children . . . dictators, tyrants, jailers, enemies!

So he gets back on to the bed. And here, God damn him, he will lie, and here, God blast him, he will die—soon, oh God, soon! —and from here he will be tucked up, hauled away, screwed into an unnecessarily expensive bit of joinery, and given to the worms. Declaiming inwardly under the reverberating dome of his echoing skull, Charles Small tells himself that a coward dies a thousand times before his death; a brave man never tastes of death but once. How many times, God help him, has he died? How many thousands of times, miserable coward, has he hurled his soul into the hole in the ground while his puny, cringing body withheld itself from the good, clean, white maggots!

Take what you want, said God—*and pay for it.* Nonsense, utter nonsense! Charles Small is squirming in his little cell in hell because he did not take what he wanted, because he took what he did not want, because he took that which was thrust upon him . . . so that here he lies, remembering and remembering. . . .

So, you lose your reason. There is nothing like the critical contemplation of yourself to scatter your wits to the thirty-two points of the compass, God help your muddled little head! *Thus, conscience doth make cowards of us all*, says Charles Small to himself, glancing at his reflection in the pier-glass. He is revolted at the sight of himself—young yet old; handsome, but falsely so, for he appears haughty and proud, but is nothing of the sort. He scowls at himself and sees nothing but a ham actor's presentation of himself—and he throws something. It is a large cut-glass bottle of rose-water, which hits his reflection full in the face and, shattering itself, smashes the mirror into jagged shards. Now, at least, he has got rid of the need to look at himself. The noise, of course, is considerable. Charles Small found a certain satisfaction in chucking the cut-glass bottle at the plate-glass mirror . . . but then, with a certain trepidation, he hears the muffled clumping of stupid feet on the carpeted stairs. That idiot is trying to walk quietly again. He locks the door, and, when he hears her say: "Are you all right?" answers: "Leave me alone!"

Then, looking at the fragments of the broken mirror scattered on the floor, he sees all kinds of shifting, disconnected, fragmentary reflections of himself that he cannot put together to make one decent picture.

The dirty light dances on the splintered looking-glass, on the shadows of the room come to grips with the shadows of the encroaching night, against which the fading light fights to the death until the dark, at last, gets its thumbs in his eyes, and just before all goes black, he sees himself in the fragments of the broken mirror, like pieces of a child's puzzle . . . scattered, incomplete.

Now the darkness is encompassing him, and Charles Small, in his trivial misery, assuages his poor little pain and tries to still his uneasy conscience by the memory of truly dreadful, black, unforgivable, unforgettable cowardice and treachery.

If he lives a thousand years—and, knowing that he is hoping in vain, hoping that he will not live out the night—he will never forget the unspeakable business in the railway station.

*   *   *   *   *

. . . That was when he went crazy, and forgot that his mother had borne him. That was when he behaved like a wild beast, and like the dirtiest little coward in the world, who should have been dealt with as dung—shovelled away with other filth and tossed out to feed nice clean green grass to feed comparatively courageous sheep.

He is thinking, naturally, of his passionate love for Ivy Narwall, and how he lost it in circumstances so revolting that if his best-beloved child, the girl, slipped in the street and fell in front of an approaching steam-roller, and Charles Small saw Ivy crossing the road, he would feel an impulse to run the other way and bucket up a side turning. And it would not surprise him in the least if he obeyed that impulse.

*   *   *   *   *

Oh, how he aches, how he aches, with his fever in every one of the 365 bones of his body! How he throbs through every reticulation of his innumerable nerves! What pain, what maddening pain, crawls around and around the endless convolutions of his brain—the brain which, if he were a man and had a gun should be like porridge on the floor, with a bit of bone and a splash of lead behind it. . . . Guns, so now he needs guns—as if he'd have the nerve to thumb back a hammer and press a trigger, the cheap little liar to himself! *If you want to die, die, God damn you!* says Charles Small to himself. But he has no instantaneous poison, no prussic acid, no quick, clean pistol—if he had the knowledge to use a pistol and had the guts to press a trigger, neither of which he has.

All this comes out of the Great Romance, the Narwall-Small Idyll, the great mad passion of Charles for Ivy, the wild self-abnegatory passion of Ivy for Charles. He cannot for the moment be bothered with what led up to the unthinkable filthy end of the matter—he can only think around and about that filthy end, on the platform at Sealford, with the little train shuddering and gasping, and a porter wearing a red tie trundling a wobbling tropical trunk, while a goods train that seemed to have no end rolled and rolled, grumbling and muttering, away and away for ever on the other line. Would God never send that last flash of light, the last dazzling flash that, burning through the jammed shutter of his memory, might burn into decent darkness the clean-cut images of that moment?

239

There lies the station in the dying daylight. There rolls the trolley, trundled by the disconsolate porter with the red tie. There rolls away the goods train, interminable, laden largely with coal, to make black smoke God knows where . . . and the wheels of the porter's trolley go clickety-click while the porter's heels, which are downtrodden, thump behind, and the Sealford train seems to be swelling itself with steam as a deep-sea diver fills himself with air before plunging into unknown darkness. Darkness indeed! Soon, night must fall. Oh, if only to God it had already fallen—if only he, Charles Small, could have scuttled into his mouse-hole under the cover of the dark at the approach of the Cat or if only he had been born a mouse, and Mrs. Narwall had really been a cat with a licence to kill him! . . . If only he and Ivy had been the pair of mice that they were—but alone— how gleefully, whisker-to-whisker and paw-in-paw, would they have darted into the darkness of the tunnel, nimbly skipping the metals, fearfully yet triumphantly flattening themselves against the sooty sleepers while the rolling-stock went past, too big to hurt them, so that they could pipe their little triumph over Juggernaut!

*   *   *   *   *

Here, thinks Charles Small, must be the most abject end to the most pitiful love story in the history of fear-haunted passion . . . miserable, mousey passion. Of the preliminaries he cannot bring himself at present to think: there is bile enough in his blood and self-digesting acid enough in his guts without that. And over it all, of course, hangs the sickening tang of sour maternal milk, so that he has half a mind to go downstairs and hit his wife in the face for the simple reason that she is the mother of two children.

It is not difficult for him to shove the beginning and the middle of the love story out of his mind, but the end, the end—that hangs over.

With the love story and its permutations and combinations he will torment himself later. At present, he is stuffed with self-reproach, and haunted by the memory of the railway platform at Sealford.

He and Ivy Narwall fell in love. (They would have made a pretty pair.) They fell in love and, after all kinds of machinations, decided to run away together, to Sealford first of all, where they would get married. After that they intended to leave the country and go to South Africa, where they might make a new life, a brand-new life.

Why Sealford? Because it was, and is, the unlikeliest place in Sussex to which an eloping couple might flee—a silted fishing port, somnolescent, populated by old men in blue jerseys who had nothing to talk about but their memories of dead fish. Who the devil would go to Sealford? Who in the world could follow them there?

Who in the world but Mrs. Narwall, of whom he was afraid? The Cat had her cold green eyes on her mice and in her silent way she went after them.

Charles remembers how—after the preliminaries he is determined to forget but which, he knows, will come back to gnaw at his heart a little later on—he and Ivy made their secret, mad tryst one dirty day in Victoria Station. He had been most manly and business-like about it. They were to travel light, and therefore fast. One suitcase apiece, no more, and travelling expenses in paper money in the right-hand inside breast-pocket. One, two, three—go! It was to be as simple as all that.

Thus, Charles Small and Ivy Narwall met at Victoria under conditions of the utmost secrecy, to catch the train for Sealford. He went first, and found a first-class compartment in one of the carriages up in front near the engine. He remembers that he bought copies of *Tit Bits* and of the *Strand Magazine*, and some sweets—sugared almonds. Then, nervously smoking some fancy kind of aromatic cigarette, he looked out of the window. Time was ticking away. The engine was hissing. But where was Ivy? Oh God, where?

When all seemed lost, she came, carrying a Gladstone bag, and he leaped out and ran towards her, taking her bag from her, and whispering (as if that were necessary in the clamour of that station with its thunder of shunting, and its clash of buffers, and its screaming of whistles, and its leopard-like hoarse roaring of steam)—he whispered, timorous creature that he was: "Ivy, darling, hurry up, quick!

They almost ran to the compartment he had chosen, and there exchanged tears and kisses in an exhilaration begotten by Love upon the old hag, Fear. Now Charles Small was overcome by a dread. It seemed to him that somehow Mrs. Narwall was after them. The tumultuous, steamy station smelled of cats, and when the signal lights turned green his heart rattled in his breast like a flipped marble, for there were the cat's eyes. . . . And an incoming train from Brighton, braking to a standstill, gave out a caterwauling that scratched at his dry throat. Ivy and he exchanged a long look. He wished that the train would leave—but now the clock stood still. He gave Ivy the *Tit Bits*, the *Strand Magazine* and the sweets, and went out to try in his uncertain voice to call a porter to lock the carriage door so that he and Ivy might be alone. But even as he stepped out, an old gentleman in a billycock hat brushed past him and stepped in, and his agonised eyes, flickering up and down the platform, came to rest upon a hideously familiar figure at the barrier.

It was Mrs. Narwall. There was no mistaking her: the head of Tiberius upon the body of Juno, all draped in black, indomitability in every line of her, implacable purpose in every stride. In her left hand she grasped a black bag; in her right, an umbrella with an ivory handle, ponderous enough to crack a skull. She paused to argue with the ticket-collector, while the whistle hooted. *Oh God, let her miss the train*, prayed Charles Small. But the green cat's eyes grew brighter, and the smell of cats grew stronger, and just as the train jerked into motion Mrs. Narwall caught it. She leaped into a third-class compartment at the back, near the luggage van.

Then Charles Small knew that he was lost. He knew, then, that he was damned. As soon as the train started to move Ivy sighed with relief and grew cheerful. She had not seen what he had seen. She said: "Charley darling, you're white as a sheet. Aren't you well? . . . South Africa, only think! Isn't it going to be nice!"

Charles Small replied: "Yes, Ivy."

Hearing the words, *South Africa*, the old gentleman looked up from his *Morning Post* and said: "Are you young people off to South Africa?"

Charles Small said: "Yes."

"Oh yes," said Ivy.

"A land of opportunity," said the old gentleman. "Lived there most of my life, eighty years. Knew some of the old voortrekkers that were with Piet Retief, who went up against Dingaan. Met Cetewayo. Solly Joel, Beit, Rhodes, all the rest of them—I knew 'em like the back of my hand. I'm an old man now, young feller, but if I was your age I'd be off like you, God bless you. I think

I'd be off to Mashonaland—unbroken territory, almost. But I'm too old—eighty-six. Living like a cabbage with my grand-daughter in Sealford. Not a burden—made my whack—an old cabbage. Every time I cough their eyes light up. But there's life in the old dog yet, and they'll never see what I saw . . . and I'll never see what you're going to see, you lucky young feller! I was with Kitchener in the Sudan. Kruger, Delarey—I knew 'em all. Oh, you lucky people!"

Charles Small could think of nothing better to do than to offer the old gentleman a sweet, which he frowned at through his glasses, wrinkling the dry skin at the corners of his blinking eyes, and refused with a brusque shake of the head. Charles Small sat with a tight throat while the old gentleman rustled his newspaper back into position and Ivy sat, rapt, too full of emotion to talk.

The train ran slow and came to a stop. It was only some petty junction, but bitter fear took hold of the heart and soul of Charles Small, and he looked out of the window, half-expecting to see Mrs. Narwall coming at him with her umbrella and (which was worse) her cold and terrible face. But the engine seemed to cough and sneeze and hiccough, and the train jolted on again. Then, even while Ivy was holding his hand, he knew that he was going to desert and betray her, and knew himself for what he was

The old man said: "I used to be like you, once upon a time, young man—all hot sand and ginger, full of youth, full of courage. I regret nothing, but I envy you. Still, as the poet says: 'I paid the price for what I bought, nor never grutched the price I paid, But sat in clink without my boots, admirin' 'ow the world was made.' I don't lack the heart, mind you—only your health and strength, like I had when I fought the Zulus; and I was there with an assegai in my leg when that young French prince went down. Oh dear, oh dear, God bless you and your young wife, and if ever you pass through Bulawayo, ask for Van Dongen—the Christian name is Aloysius—and say you know Old Farrow. There will always be a knife and fork for you, and good advice too, because Aloysius knows the country as well as I know . . ."

The train was slowing to a standstill. The old man sighed, put his newspaper in his pocket, took hold of his stick, and said: "It isn't that I want the spirit—only your youth, my dear boy. Bless you, you go and find new worlds. And God bless you too, my dear"—he squeezed Ivy's hand—"if you pass through

243

Bulawayo tell Mrs. Van Dongen that I remember her, and I hope she remembers me. Here I am, and there's Mary on the platform. Thanks for your courage. Africa, eh? Here, this is from Africa. Take it. Good-bye, and good luck."

The old man pulled out of his tie a pin, the head of which was a little nugget of pure gold, and gave it to Charles Small before skipping nimbly out on to the platform. Charles stuck the pin in his coat, and, taking Ivy's bag and his own, quickly followed him, ceremoniously handing Ivy down.

The train was emptying itself and the platform was crowded. The old gentleman paused in mid-stride as a sly-looking woman forced a smile while she opened her arms to greet him; and, looking wistfully over his shoulder, he said: "Don't forget to mention Farrow in Bulawayo. Oh, and in the Kalahari Desert there's a city, a marvellous old city, all stone—nobody knows who built it—some say King Solomon. Only it's deserted, d'ye see, like Petra, except for the jackals and the vultures. Sometimes, baboons. I never saw the place, I never had the time; but it's there. You'll see it, you lucky boy. And see the Drakensberg! There's something marvellous for you! Wild, terrible—and on the veldt below, game, what game!"

The sly-looking woman tugged at his sleeve and said: "Grandpa . . ."

But the old man paused to say: "Blesbok, springbok, eland, klipspringer (but you'll never catch *him*) and lions too, and rhenosters, which is Afrikaans for rhinoceros, and buffalo. Get your guns at Purdey's, or Greener in St. James's if you can afford the price. Come and see me and I'll give you my old Express. It's knocked down a charging rhino more than once. You wait till he's within thirty yards, for he's a short-sighted fellow, when he lowers his head—and then you let him have it at the back of the neck. It's easy if you stand firm and feel no fear at all. For lion, aim at the chest, or behind the left shoulder."

"Grandpa, do hurry!" said the sly-looking woman.

The old gentleman nodded and, obedient to her tug, went on, but kept on talking over his shoulder: ". . . Never try to shoot a rhino in the head, or an elephant for that matter. Wait for a neck or a heart shot. I live at The Larches, Fir Tree Road. Farrow, remember, just ask for me. I'll give you my guns—I'm not likely to be using them again. Now, leopards——"

His granddaughter pulled him away. Charles Small remembers

that, somewhere between the squeal of wheels and the hissing of steam, the aged raucous voice insinuated itself, saying: "A lion leaps and strikes, but a leopard drops and rips—use this calibre——"

But then his granddaughter dragged him away. Ivy said: "What a nice old gentleman, and what a nice pin he gave you! Oh Charley, isn't it going to be wonderful?"

Charles Small said: "Yes"—but not more than half of his attention had been devoted to the old one: a good half, because his imagination was alight, and he saw himself, rifle-butt at shoulder, confronting the enraged rhenoster upon those brilliant, burnt-up plains of Africa. At the same time he was looking backwards at the butt-end of the third-class part of the train. Then, oh God, how he wished that this were the open veldt under the Drakensberg, and that he had a rifle in his hands and nothing but a maddened rhinoceros to confront! For he saw the powerful black figure of Mrs. Narwall shouldering the crowd aside and coming inexorably towards him.

Ivy's bag and his own squatted flank-to-flank. Charles Small looked at the bags, and at Ivy. He looked again at Mrs. Narwall. She was less than sixty feet away. Waxy-white and slippery with the sweat of pure fear, he said: "Excuse me just a minute, darling." Ivy had no knowledge of the Nemesis that was within thirty yards of her; she was in love, and full of dreams of rhinoceroses and lions, mysterious cities and the wild grandeur of the Drakensberg. She saw, through the smoke and the steam of the station, the clear, clean light of the veldt . . . and Charles drawing a bead upon something that was terrible even in a zoo. She smiled quietly. Now she was free. Then someone touched her shoulder, and she reached for her bag, saying: "Charley is me darling, me young chevalier!"

But it was the voice of her mother, Mrs. Narwall, that replied: "Come on home, Ivy." And then all was steam and smoke, metallic noises, thunderous transients. Africa evaporated in one whiff. The blesboks, springboks, klipspringers and lions went back behind bars to their zoological gardens, and the free plains receded and became what they always had been—dreams. Only the leopard remained, with her claws in Ivy's shrinking shoulder, for Charles was out of the barrier and away, slinking, hugging the walls, sobbing for shame.

Ivy cried: "Charley!" But he was two hundred yards away, in a tea shop. Mrs. Narwall said: "Pick up your bag." Ivy obeyed her, and, with her mother's powerful hand on her arm just above the elbow was half-dragged along the smoky, smutty platform towards the ticket-office. Once, she looked back, half hoping that Charles would come and save her. But all she saw on that grey platform, which was now deserted, was his abandoned suit-case—stark, alone. The train was drawing out. Now there was not even steam. The station was empty. Her mother's fingers were like iron pincers in her arm, but she was too unhappy to protest that they hurt.

In the tea shop Charles Small, having ordered the shilling tea, put down a florin before the waitress brought it, and walked madly up the road.

Where? He must squeeze his memory to remember where.

But why, why? Ah, that, that—that is another story.

CHAPTER XX

OH, the ignominy of it! That frightful flight was bad enough, but the preliminaries were really disgusting, and what came after . . . oh Lord . . . beyond words!

And now Charles Small, in agony and envy, remembers the first and the last love affair of Solly Schwartz.

It was about the time Charles Small involved himself in his great, shameful, cowardly love that Solly Schwartz became curious about Woman, and took a mistress.

By now, this humpbacked little limping abortion who appeared as if he had escaped from a jar of alcohol in a carnival side-show was fantastically prosperous—and, by the same token, quite soberly dressed, got up like the managing director of a great company, which he was, in a beautifully-cut black jacket and striped trousers that made his little legs look longer. It is true that he could not resist a fancy waistcoat, and that in his heavy black satin tie he wore a diamond as big as a button, but he carried with him an air of massive prosperity. Rightly so, for he was prosperous, solidly rich. Looking over his books, totting up figures, figuring, working everything out—not on paper, but with certain movements of his big knuckly fingers—Solly Schwartz decided to relax. How relax? How?

He put on an old check suit and wandered, without appetite, around the fried-fish shops and the pubs in Pimlico; but returned, greasy with nut oil and acidulous with beer, discontented. He went to vulgar music halls and joined in choruses. Now he had a flat of two rooms in Grosvenor Street, and did not like the place. After dark everything died. Mayfair, moribund, waited for the dawn. Suddenly it occurred to him that people were looking at him. So, one night, with a crisp curse, he picked up a ponderous Corfiote stick of olive-wood and limped out to look for a woman. Where did he go? To the Alhambra. He wanted no love, no passion, this devil of a Schwartz—only the company of a woman, out of curiosity; no desire beyond that. Apart from his loneliness, he wanted to find out what men saw in all this nonsense. So he went to the Alhambra in Leicester Square, where some quizzical, ginger-headed girl gave him the glad eye. She gave him the come-hither. He looked at her, in his keen way, and saw that her big grey eyes were focused upon the diamond in his tie. His eyes met hers with stealthy curiosity as she observed the quality of his clothes and the massiveness of the eighteen-carat gold ring set with a ruby on his middle finger. He knew that she was a whore, but he would not have had her otherwise. Something quickly replaceable—that was his cup of tea—to use, empty, toss to the dustman, and replace.

A whore, it was true, once used, was not as easily to be disposed of as an empty tin. She clung, she sucked, she cried, she made public scandal, she demanded money. All this Solly Schwartz could deal with. She might infect him with a dreadful disease. At this he sneered, for he knew himself for what he was: the very breath of life had been mephitic to him, and neither woman nor microbe could hurt him—therein lay his peculiar power.

It was apparent to him that he had excited the woman's professional interest, with his flash clothes and his ring. She lingered, looking at him. He was unacquainted with the technique of courtship, but he knew a trick twice as good as that: he took out of his breast pocket a wallet bulging with bank-notes and, showing it to the red-head, said: "Want a drink?"

"I don't mind if I do."

He put the wallet back in his pocket—observing that she was tipping the wink to a quiet, dapper-looking fellow dressed like King Edward VII, but beardless. This dapper man emptied his glass and, when they went out, followed them.

They went to a little flat near Wardour Street. The girl took off her clothes, and she was like a Gibson Girl. Solly Schwartz took off his hat and put down his stick, within reach, for he knew what was going to happen. The girl kissed him, and the taste of her was repulsive to him. She tasted of wine and tobacco, and she revolted him by pushing into his mouth a rough, coated tongue. Here was love.

Listening, he heard the stairs creak. Everything, in his mind, was anticipated. The girl, shaking her red hair loose, embraced him, and unbuttoned his jacket. Solly Schwartz had heard of this trick before. He sneered as the light went down— memorising the resting-place of his Corfiote stick of olive-wood— and waited. The red-headed girl wanted him to take off his clothes, but he did not do so because he was ashamed of the

248

malformation of himself. He did not like even to look at himself when he was alone.

She said: "Are you going to give me a little present? My last friend gave me two pounds."

Solly Schwartz gave her a five-pound note, which she tucked into a Dorothy-bag. An awful coldness came down upon him as he watched her moving from her bag to her bed, with a calculating eye on his breast pocket, cocking an ear at the door. She threw her arms around him, and he inhaled the peppery smell of the red-head—still listening.

Outside, on the landing, a floorboard creaked, and a cautious hand slipped an oiled key into the lock of the door. Solly Schwartz waited for it with something like glee. Exactly as he had foreseen, the door flew open, the light went up, and the dapper man burst in, crying: "My wife! My wife!" Behind him slouched a heavy man.

Solly Schwartz laughed—it was the old badger game. He went for the big man first, with the olive-wood stick; struck him on the side of the head and knocked him downstairs. Then he took hold of the dapper one by the face and a shoulder and shook him, and nudged him with a knee almost into the well of the staircase. There was a clamour from below, but soon the voices faded.

"Stay with me," said the red-head.

Solly Schwartz stayed, but he kept on all his clothes. She said: "Aren't you strong? Aren't you brave? Somebody told me humpbacks were . . ." Then she fell asleep quietly, like a child. But he lay awake for a long while, thinking not without pleasure of the crack of the Corfiote stick upon the thick skull of the unknown thug, and the thunder of his tumble down the stairs.

He hoped they would come back. He was in just the right mood to receive them—them and a dozen like them, by God! A full moon shone in the fine clean sky that was wonderful with stars beyond the smeared window, and in this cold blue moonlight Solly Schwartz looked at the naked body of the girl, with its large, firm breasts, its slender waist—not so slender now that it was unlaced—and at that part of her which was, when all was said and done, the target, the ultimate objective. He observed with distaste the corset-marks, exaggerated by the shadows, between her breasts and her belly, and sneered at the cast-off corset on the floor.

249

So women squeezed and laced themselves into living lies.

He picked it up and weighed it in his powerful hands, noting that the ribs were not of whale-bone, but of metal, with rounded ends not unlike the heads of safety pins. He sniffed at it and caught a tang of gingerish sweat and stale cheap perfume; dropped it in disgust and turned his attention again to the sleeping girl. Usable, essentially-replaceable goods. . . .

He placed a chair by the door in such a position that, if anyone opened it ever so cautiously, it would fall with a clatter. He was not a man to be taken unawares. Then, still fully dressed and clutching his heavy stick, laughing at himself out of one side of his mouth, he lay down beside the naked whore, and dozed.

If this was love, he knew a trick worth two of that.

Solly Schwartz fell asleep.

*　　　*　　　*　　　*　　　*

He awoke at daybreak, no longer angry or nauseated, but calm. The girl slept peacefully on her polluted bed, smiling in her sleep, her legs spread at an angle of about forty-five degrees—an angle for which, presumably, God had designed them. In the daylight she appeared pasty and wan (even though she was smiling in her sleep) and emanated a stale stink of unhealthy sweat, bad breath, left-over perfume at sixpence a bottle, and goodness knows what else besides. Love! Solly Schwartz opened and closed his right hand to ease it, for he had not until then relaxed his grip on the heavy stick, and tentatively touched her shoulder. She was sweaty. Gingerly he sniffed at his finger, and there again was the repulsive smell of a woman. He sat and thought. Below, in the street, a milkman's barrow clattered to a standstill while the man's voice yodelled: "Milk o-hoo, milk o-hoo"—and then there came the clang of cans, and dogs barked, and not far away a cock crowed. The girl awoke and looked at Solly Schwartz with surprise. He was fully dressed except for his hat, and even had his stick in his hand.

She said: "What . . . what . . ."

Solly Schwartz replied: "Yes, what, what. You know what, what. I laid out your two Charlies and I gave you a fiver, for nothing, that's what, what! Now get up, and get washed and dressed. I want to watch you."

"Oh, I couldn't do that!" said the girl.

"Why not?"

She said: "It wouldn't be——"

Solly Schwartz took out another five-pound note and said: "All right, no?"

"All right," said the girl, reaching for the money.

"After," said Solly Schwartz, leaning on his stick.

"All right," said the girl, "but I can tell you, I'm not accustomed to this kind of thing."

She proceeded, however, to dress. Solly Schwartz watched with intense interest, abstractedly waving the five-pound note, fanning away some of the filthy air with the wind of it. Pausing at the sink, she said, with a certain delicacy: "Look the other way." Solly Schwartz waved the five-pound note and touched his breast, where his pocket was, and kept his keen eyes fixed upon her. So, from this attitude, cold and hard and ugly as a gargoyle, he kept his eyes stonily upon the girl as she made her toilet. At one point she began to ask: "Did you——?"

"Yes, I did," lied Solly Schwartz, "go on." And he rustled the five-pound note. She went on, shame-faced, not letting that bit of white paper out of her sight. Emptying a basin into a slop-pail, she said, hopefully: "Well, now are you satisfied?"

Solly Schwartz answered: "Certainly not. Go on dressing just like you dress to go out. I'm not here. Only this fiver's here. Get on with the job."

She was afraid of this intense little man who had smashed down Mick the Ox and half-killed her protector—who gave her five pounds for nothing at all and, fresh and alert, fully dressed in elegant style in the dimmest hours of the morning, dangled another five-pound note between two formidable fingers, and ordered her to dress. Forget that he was there! She could not keep her mind or her gaze from him. But—the five-pound note apart—she felt that she had to obey him, to do exactly as he wished, irrespective of the dangling bank-note.

So she dressed, and in the manner of whores of her class in those days, made up her face, while the hunchback watched, missing nothing.

Now, when her pasty cheeks were rosy, her pink eyelashes were black, and her pallid lips were pink—when her waist was laced and her prominent breasts and big buttocks consequently conspicuous—she made a pirouette before her strange visitor, and said: "Well, m'lord?"—holding out her hand.

"Right you are, m'lady," said Solly Schwartz, and he dropped the five-pound note into the slop-pail, clapped on his hat, and limped down the stairs without so much as a Good-day, brandishing his olive-wood stick.

The girl, bewildered, looked at the two five-pound notes. She held them to the light, saw that they were genuine, and began to wonder what she had done to earn ten pounds of this terrible little man's money—he who had calmly held his own against two bad men—she who had done unmentionable things for a pound note. A kind of wonder came over her while she undressed again (for it was only nine o'clock in the morning) and she felt an admiration, a yearning born of curiosity, for that odd little fellow, while she shook her own slops out of the Bank of England note and read the words, *I promise*.

Solly Schwartz, in high humour, limped to Lanzi's Café in Dean Street and, rubbing his hands over a pot of coffee and a dish of ham and eggs, congratulated himself on having not wasted a night and upon the sound investment of a ten-pound note. An observer from the outside might have wondered why Solly Schwartz was so gay.

But he knew why he was happy that morning. It was because of Love.

*   *   *   *   *

He gloated over love, gulping down his ham and eggs. The waitress, a Sardinian girl who had a superstitious terror of hunchbacks, watched him with awe: she had never seen a man eat quite so fast—let alone a hunchback with a game leg, dressed loud, and audibly chuckling while he shoved the food into his frog-mouth.

Having finished his ham and eggs, he ordered another pot of coffee and a ham omelette, still grinning and rubbing his hands. She was perturbed; she wondered quite fearfully what it was that amused him so. Her name was Giglio, and she had seen hunchbacks before, one in particular in Sardinia, who was considered as a man possessed of the devil. Calling "Amb omblet!" down the hatch, Mrs. Giglio wondered about that deformed little man. He was laughing to himself. That was unhealthy. Laughter was healthy only in company.

The fact of the matter is, that he had achieved a sort of divinity, because God is Love, and, having discovered a means of mastery over love, Solly Schwartz had become God. That is to say, God of what he thought was Love.

Love. Gulping eggs and at the same time chewing bread and swallowing coffee, he opened his mouth in a smile full of champed-up food. A sporting sort of lady at the next table, catching a glimpse of him, turned her head aside and asked her escort to get the bill, for Solly Schwartz made her think of Dr. Jekyll and Mr. Hyde. She whispered: "Norman, that little man is *looking* at me!"

The man called Norman, who was, as the saying went, "in drink", scowled at Solly Schwartz and asked: "Were you looking at this lady?"

Solly Schwartz said: "Yes, I was. What's the matter? What does she get herself up for, if not to be looked at? Answer me that! Are you trying to pick a fight with me? Start, Charley, and I'll finish!"

"Who are you calling Charley?" asked the man, drawing back his cuffs.

"You, Charley," said Solly Schwartz, ghoulishly gulping the last of his ham. Then he became contemptuously eloquent. He continued: "I've warned you in advance—you start, and by Christ I'll finish! Try it and see."

"Hit him, hit him!" said the sporting young lady, but the gentleman held back, for he did not like the look of this peculiar man who, in spite of his stunted and deformed figure, appeared so calm, confident, and desperate; leaning, like something out of a Punch and Judy show, upon the handle of that ponderous yellow stick with its carved inscription: *Corfu*.

Schwartz went on: "Looking at, looking at! What am I looking at? I'm looking at something that has been stuck under my nose to be looked at, *trottel!* I'm looking out of curiosity, *schlemihl!* What is she looking like that for, if it isn't to be looked at?"

The gentleman called Mrs. Giglio, the waitress, and, pointing towards Solly Schwartz, said: "This man is being offensive. Please ask him to leave." But the waitress had just brought his new order, and pretended not to understand.

Between forkfuls of food, Solly Schwartz mocked at the gentleman and his lady, saying: "Mug! Do you know what you're making eyes at? What d'you think you've got there? You idiot! Love, eh? I'll tell you—powder, paint, perfume, and on her belly corset-marks. Wash her face and look at her without her stays, *trottel!* What d'you think she colours herself up for, except to be looked at, eh?"

The gentleman rose and said: "If you will step outside, I'll knock you down."

Solly Schwartz replied: "Why wait? Try it now, *trottel*," and swallowed another great mouthful.

The lady whispered: "Do come away, dear!" and stood up; whereupon the gentleman threw down a two-shilling piece and, without a look at Solly Schwartz, conducted her to the door.

She, however, before the door slammed to, looked back. Solly Schwartz grinned at her. She smiled at him. Then the door closed, and they disappeared into the pale morning.

Now, Solly Schwartz, taking a great handful of Cioccalato Baci—the sweetmeats that contained amorous messages—sat back to consider the state of the universe.

Munching, confidently smiling, remembering every detail of the night, he knew that his money had not been thrown away. He turned over every idea with which the harlot had inspired him; every detail of her whorish maquillage, and every aspect of her saleable body—the used-up perfume dabbed on to overlay the exhausted odour of sweaty arm-pits, clumsily scraped, and of other body smells . . . the growths of incongruously coloured hair . . . and the aroma of Woman, at which his wide nostrils twitched.

When the waitress came with his bill, Solly Schwartz contrived to manœuvre his nose close to her shoulder, without giving offence; and recoiled in disgust because she was redolent of the sweat of the night, just like the strange woman out of the Alhambra.

This delighted him. He was beginning to understand Sex as Commerce. Women, on the whole, were physically unpleasant to mankind and to themselves. They were ashamed of themselves. They were ashamed of their axillary and pubic tufts, of the straightness of the hair on the head, the flaccid hang of their breasts, the stink of their breath—and other exhalations of themselves—and the pallor of their bloodless lips and pasty faces. The time was to come when every woman should put on a new face every morning, just as every month . . .

. . . This was another possibility. It could wait.

He thought again of the dyeings and cosmeticisings, the

perfumings and deodorizings and depilatings of the woman of the Alhambra, and of every detail of her dressing, while he drank yet another cup of coffee. After that, when he called the girl, Giglio, over to change a pound note, he said to her: "My dear, I don't like to tell you, but you smell horrible."

"What, me?" she said.

"Sorry," said Solly Schwartz, and went out.

Before the door closed, he saw her sniffing at herself, suspiciously. Walking along Dean Street, chuckling, he exclaimed: "Wow!"—and gave half a crown to a beggar woman in a doorway, who, having incredulously examined the coin, tucked it into a secret pocket, assuming that the hunchback was drunk.

But he was very far from drunk that morning—few men have ever been more sober than Solly Schwartz on that occasion.

*　　*　　*　　*　　*

He, who had developed something like a fanatical yearning for the transient, had found the consummation of it—love and beauty, pruritus and vanity. His iron foot and the steel ferrule of his heavy stick made something like music as he almost danced into Shaftesbury Avenue. He had his powerful hands locked upon the most evanescent and profitable things in the world. He had several of the Deadly Sins in his grasp—Envy, Hatred, Malice, Vanity, Pride. . . . He had dreamed of a commodity that should be impermanent as smoke. Now, by the Lord, he had found something even less tangible and more saleable than smoke—Maya—Illusion.

Solly Schwartz had discovered himself as an advertising man, and a pioneer in the marvellously replaceable business of painted, powdered, scented, shaved, plucked, curled, varnished bodily pride. Overnight, this exhilarated little man had become an expert in the exterior aspects of love, and a connoisseur of female vanity. He was too excited to ride, so he walked—hopped, rather—to his little flat, thinking of all the things that might be bought and sold, and come and go . . . of the desire of the male for the female; the need of the woman for the man, and how she had to deceive him always, living in disguise. Once she had represented herself as a woman wearing a certain mask, or disguise, she dared not drop it until she had him hooked. Later on, of course, wise to the false face, the laced tits, the drop-dilated eyes that pouched in the dawn when the lips grew pallid and the breath began to stink—later, he would seek a new illusion . . . another mask, another lie, another hole, another emptiness.

Between Leicester Square and Haymarket, Solly Schwartz conceived the idea of a great Beauty Trade.

CHAPTER XXI

CHARLES SMALL remembers another festive occasion when his
mother went, on an emergency call, to visit goodness-knows-
who—one of her detested sisters who had to be operated on for
what was called a Carneous Mole. What Mrs. Small proposed to
do about it, barring weeping, God knew. She had, however,
heard that this Carneous Mole had something to do with the
womb, and therefore it was necessary for her to assist in the
matter, if only to the extent of whispering and biting at her forefinger, and saying: "Men! Selfishness!" So she went to join her
foregathered sisters—who were no better than she—always
excepting the detested wife of Nathan, the abhorred Photographer.
Before she left, Millie Small laid out a cold roast fowl and a salad
containing hard-boiled eggs, and left strict instructions concerning
the making of a cup of tea. Then, carrying a big bunch of flowers,
she departed. And again the atmosphere of the house grew
lighter.

It was a Bank Holiday. I. Small (give the devil his due, he was
not a bad old stick) slapped his son on the shoulder in a comradely
fashion, and said: "Not a word, boychik—what about Hempstead
Heat?"

"Hampstead Heath?" said Charles Small.

"What did I said? Hempstead Heat! Get your cap, boychik—
come on!"

So they went to Hampstead Heath on the Bank Holiday, the
furtive, festive, liberated I. Small and his bewildered but delighted
son, Charles.

A quarter of a mile away they could hear the screaming of
calliopes, and a sort of mutter which resolved itself into the
joyous babble of a multitude of proletarian nobodies who, for
once, had decided to throw away their savings to get away from
the memory of the means whereby they had scraped them
together. They whirled around and around on the merry-go-
rounds, and swung desperately on the swing-boats . . . always
grating or rocking to a standstill and getting off at the very
spot where they had climbed on. They blew little striped strident

paper trumpets, and wore curious hats. They blew away their
hard-earned money in the rifle ranges. They were out of their
minds. I. Small, again, went mad with the rest. He had a go at
skittles, hurling the balls with all his might, hitting nothing. He
even attempted, gingerly, to fire a tiny rifle at a clay figure. He
missed every time. He spent eighteenpence on any number of
goes at smashing up The Happy Home—throwing wooden balls
at a dresser full of plates, cups and saucers. (He broke one saucer.)
So, exhausted, he conducted his son to the gambling games. The
most conspicuous of these was a round table covered with soup-
plates. On the face of each plate was clearly marked a sum of
money, ranging from twopence to two shillings. The two-shilling
plates were most remote, in the middle of this little arena, right
next to the hole into which the balls dropped after they had
missed their objectives. The balls were celluloid ping-pong balls,
penny a ball. It was almost impossible to get one to come to rest
in a plate. Still, the old man bought a shilling's-worth of balls
and gave six of them to Charles. Then they started to throw.
Charles aimed for the two-shilling plates. He missed, of course
—the balls bounced away into the black hole, and so these penny-
worths of ambition were lost. I. Small went cautiously for the
smaller numbers. Needless to say, he missed. But just as his
fifth ball bounced out of a sixpenny plate and he growled: "Bleddy
beggary!"—somebody, by some mad freak of chance, flipped a
ping-pong ball into a two-shilling plate, and roared bloody murder,
so that the side-show man turned to attend to him. Taking
advantage of this moment, I. Small leaned forward and dropped
a ball into the nearest threepenny plate.

Charles Small was terrified—perhaps one of those black
gypsies was watching. But the side-show man, having settled
his accounts, gave I. Small threepence, and a dark look. Now
I. Small was in high spirits. He took Charles to Jack Straw's
Castle. Edging his way through the throng, he said: "Ginger-
beer? A smoked selmon sendwich?" But he produced one ginger-
beer, one pint of bitter, and two ham sandwiches.

Winking, the old man said: "Nice smoked selmon? Eat—
what's the matter, what?"

Charles Small ate, without much appetite.

He was somehow humiliated by his father's laying out of a
shilling, cursing at the loss of elevenpence, and rejoicing at the
return of threepence.

Cheat!

Yet who is he to talk? He does not like to think of the old man dropping his ball into the threepenny plate; but it enrages him to think of his own penny balls, aimed at the highest and most dangerous prizes and always falling down into the dark hole.

Tap, tap, tap go the ping-pong balls from dish to dish. Once launched, you could scarcely follow them with a normal naked eye. So, between the daylight and the inevitable black hole bounces his uncontrollable light mind—will-less, empty, inflammable and, after two or three half-hearted bounces, rolling, dispirited, into the Pit.

*   *   *   *   *

. . . Balls! It was all balls. Charles Small clenches his hands at the thought of the loss of his balls. (Aie, aie, aie—the image of the old man hurling his balls at The Happy Home and knocking over nothing but a saucer!)

When he was a schoolboy, he was made one of the cricket team, and stood high in the opinion of the captain, because he had a quick eye and a supple wrist with a bat. As a bowler—a thrower of balls, he was wild and inaccurate, just like the old man—but when it came to fending them off and sending them elsewhere, he was not bad.

The time came when he was invited to make one of a team that was to play an important match in public against another little school. It was necessary for him to wear white flannel trousers, a cricket-shirt, and a cricket-cap. He spoke of the matter to his father. The old man said sententiously: "Well, sis already not a bad thing. Everybody looks at you, you're a Something, a Somebody. You can make touch miv people after your critic match— get a good job." Now unexpectedly I. Small began to roar: "Job! Schmob! Beggar the bleddy job! So long as you're not a dirty bleddy boot-maker, beggar the bleddy job! Critic, schmitic— play, play! . . . White shoes? Not worth while to knock you up a pair—can get a pair rubber-soled plimsolls, for one-and-six. White trousers? Take the few shillings and play, *Khatzkele!*"

Charles did not thank his father. He only said: "Charles, not *Khatzkele*." And then he went skipping to his mother with the news.

Now Mrs. Small had been talking, over tea, with one Mrs. Fitch, a woman who was a bladder of lurid reminiscence. If you pricked her with a word, gassy lies squirted out of her until she collapsed into the shrivelled membrane that she was, and dragged herself away vampirishly to bloat herself with more tales. This woman had told Mrs. Small terrible stories about small boys. Many years previous her son had burned himself in some boyish prank. It was a dangerous game, but all the boys played it. One tied a string to a punctured tin can, stuffed the can with inflammable material, set light to it, and whirled it round and round until it burst into flames and became red-hot. Her son had had an accident. The blazing can had hit him in the right arm-pit. "The blisters were like a bunch of grapes," she said. She was an ambulant chapter of accidents. She exercised a profound influence upon Mrs. Small. Now, when Charles arrived breathless with his news of the cricket match, Mrs. Fitch shook her head solemnly and said: "Mrs. Small, if they're going to play with hard balls, put a stop to it. Do you know Mrs. Shade? Her husband was a cricketer, and he was hit in the privates by a hard cricket ball and . . . well, it's not for me to tell you what to do, but if I were you, I'd put a stop to it."

Mrs. Small said: "No cricket!"

"But Father promised! I'm in the team!" shouted Charles Small.

"No more cricket," said Mrs. Small, "not with hard balls. No more hard balls."

So, as Charles Small remembers, he played the game alone in his little room. He had a bat. In fantasy he knocked a shadowy ball to boundary, blocked the slow bowler, subtly deflected the fast bowler for a bye.

The old man, to do him justice, stood up for young Charles, but not for long, against Mrs. Small. As in the Mongolian proverb: *When the egg contended with the stone, the yolk came out.*

Later when Charles Small, humiliated, told the old man that he had let down his team, I. Small wearily said: "You must do like your mother says," and, patting Charles's shoulder, gave him sixpence.

But the boy did not want the sixpence. He went back to his little room and played with his bat—a most vigorous game, if there had been a ball. Only there were no balls except those that were thrown away—there are only balls of shadow.

* * * * *

Balls, balls, balls! How deep was Charles Small's yearning for balls such as all the other boys normally played with! He asked his mother if he might have, at least, a rubber ball—for what was the use of a bat without a ball? But Millie Small said, firmly: "No cricket!" And there he was with a cricket bat, a toy cricket bat at that, cut out of one miserable end of pine wood and perfunctorily shaped by some fly-by-night novelty vendor. The other boys, the real boys, the ones that played cricket, had proper bats made of willow, with spliced cane handles.

Charles Small bites his lips when he remembers how he took his bat, which he had begun to detest, to a fellow with an irregular hair-line—a little brute named Whiteside—and said: "1 say, Whiteside—what'll you give me for this?"

Whiteside looked at the bat and said: "I'll give you a magic lantern and twelve slides. What say?"

Now Charles Small was excited. What say? What was to be said? One word: Done! So Whiteside took the bat and gave him one of the most tawdry contraptions of tin that ever sickened the heart of a small boy. It was about the size of a grapefruit—a deformed grapefruit. From the front of it protruded something like a snout with a glass eye at the end of it. At the back there was a nasty little door, as in an old-fashioned burglar's dark lantern, into which one pushed a tiny paraffin lamp by the light of which it was possible to project meaningless images at short range upon a screen.

Charles was jubilant. I. Small, looking stern, could scarcely restrain his excitement at this new toy, which he turned over and over, and examined with a critical eye. Mrs. Small asked: "Is it dangerous? Will it go off?"

"Don't be bleddy silly—I'll fill it up myself," said 1. Small, taking the little lamp away. Charles Small hopped with impatience until the old man came back with the lamp filled and trimmed. A linen table-cloth was pinned to the wall. The magic lantern was set on the table. The slides were laid in order. At this point, Charles Small felt that perhaps this might be better than cricket. His hands were upon the controls; his audience tense.

"Now watch," he said, and put a match to the wick of the little lamp—whereupon the whole thing blew up with an ear-splitting bang, and blue flames crawled over the table. I. Small (he had filled the lamp with benzene) went flapping about like a

261

demented walrus, bleddying and bleddying, puffing and snorting, while Mrs. Small did all that she was capable of doing: she screamed; as poor little Charles fingered the hot tin ruin that represented all that he had to show for his bat, for his ambition in the cricket field, and his aspiration to showmanship.

When the piddling little flame flickered out, I. Small, panting as if he had rescued a family from a five-storey fire, struck Charles a shrewd blow with the *Evening News* and shouted: "Murderer!"

"For God's sake, not in the head!" screamed Mrs. Small.

I. Small put the poor little magic lantern carefully into a fire-shovel and carried it to the dust-bin. For hours Mrs. Small roamed about the place sniffing for fire. Twice she had a nervous diarrhœa.

No more pretty pictures in the dark for Charles Small.

But there must have been a stubbornness in him, he thinks bitterly, for he did not quite abandon his position. In October he was invited to make one of the football team. Bursting with pride, he told his mother—not without trepidation. Could he have a pair of footballs boots, he asked. Mrs. Small, preoccupied at the moment with Priscilla, who had turned out to be a problem child, said: "Yes, if you're a good boy. . . ."

And then, oh good God, how good he was! Butter wouldn't melt in his mouth. He sat dreaming of the field, the wet field under the threatening sky, and the wary contact of the twenty-two men . . . Charles Small was to the fore . . . he dribbled the ball—passed it to Jones. But Jones was charged by Smith—yet before Smith had time to take advantage of his opportunity, Charles Small's shoulder had crashed into him, and the ball was at his feet, and the goal in easy reach. The goal-keeper stood, bobbing and weaving. The men of the opposing side were thundering up behind him . . . Charles Small kicked, quick and hard, and the heavy, soggy, leather ball left the mud and flew, straight and true, between the hands of the goal-keeper and into the net, while the crowd roared: "Goal!"

But Mrs. Fitch came to tea, and when she heard that young Charles wanted football boots, having been nominated for a team, she drew a deep breath and raised her hands. Football, she said, was a ruffian's game. Mrs. Foley's little Edward played football and was kicked in the privates, so that he was ruptured, crippled for life, and might never marry. Mrs. Small was her own mistress, of course; but for her part, Mrs. Fitch would as soon give her son a vial of prussic acid as a football. It was a very dangerous game. Now tennis, Mrs. Fitch said, was a gentlemanly game, played with a soft ball. Even ladies played it. But football? She would as soon, the heavens forbid, see her son underground, as being ruptured on a football field. . . .

So Charles Small was dreaming his dreams when his mother came to him and said, not without commiseration: "Charley, no football. No football boots, Charley."

The boy was appalled. He cried: "You promised! You promised!"

Mrs. Small knew that she had promised, but her fear was stronger than her conscience, so she grew angry and shouted: "Be quiet when you speak to your mother!"

After that, knowing that she was at fault, she stroked Charles's head and said: "I'll get you a big box of plasticine."

He shook himself away, put his face to the wall, and—when his mother was gone—wept, wept most bitterly.

A little later she came up with some dish of eggs and potatoes that he especially favoured.

He ate the food because he was young and hungry—although he detested his mother, who had cooked it. Millie watched him while he ate, shedding tears as usual. He was inclined to say, like his mother when she wanted to make his father miserable, that he could not touch a thing or swallow a bite, but appetite prevailed over grief, and he ate everything that was put before him—and plenty was put before him, because Mrs. Small was sorry for him, and feeling guilty, ashamed of herself.

I. Small sat gloomily, smoking, fumbling at the *Star*. For once, Mrs. Small was quiet and complaisant, while the old man was gruff and indifferent. In spite of the lump in his throat, Charles swallowed a great deal of food, curiously calm.

He achieved, just then, what might be described as a subjective objectivity—he pitied himself, hated them, seeing them for what they were; pitied them for being so pitiable; and hated himself for pitying them.

Later, when he went to bed, his mother came into his little room to see that he was tucked up. He had been crying a little. At the sight of the tear-marks on his cheeks, her eyes gave out salt water. She said: "Don't fret, Charley—to-morrow I'll buy you a big box of plasticine."

Charles turned his face to the wall, weeping for the broken

promise of the lost football. His mother went away, closing the door quietly (this was something to be remembered) because somewhere in her muddled head there was an impression . . . somewhere in her heart there was a feeling . . . that she had deceived a child as she in her time had been deceived. . . .

As she went downstairs she remembered an uncle, exhausted by goodness knows what excesses, who had come from South Africa with a belt full of gold. He was a well-dressed, distinguished-looking old man with a fine white moustache and a little imperial. But he had a growth in his throat, spoke in a growl, and had to be fed through his anus with some kind of a tube. . . . She remembered how she and her sisters used to giggle over this, making fantasies of the old man walking to the dinner table on his hands, taking a leg of chicken between his toes, and sticking it into his bottom. She was his favourite. He used to take her for little walks, treating her to ice-cream, sweets, or fruits; nothing that cost more than a halfpenny. The old man was dying, riding the white horse. He was not expected to last more than a month or two. His growl had turned to a sort of fierce whisper, a malodorous whisper. The family was breathless. It was expected that Millie was to inherit the thousands in bank-notes and gold that the old uncle kept in his belt.

At last there came a day when he called her to him, saying that he had something important to give her, something to set her up for the rest of her life. Then there was a commotion. The youthful Millie was scoured and scrubbed from head to foot. Her hair was almost torn out of its roots with a fine comb, and she was put into a fancy dress. All this was not done without some smacking and weeping. At last, with a big butterfly-bow of pink ribbon in her hair, she was led into the presence of the rich old dying man. She expected a shower of gold.

He gave her an old tin can with a slot crudely poked through the lid, dropped in a halfpenny, said: "Save!"—and died.

She never forgot that disillusion, or the disgusting rattle of the little coin in the can.

And now she was sorry. Still, Charley might have been kicked in the privates. As far as she was concerned, the privates were unnecessary. Nevertheless, remembering childish disappointment, she felt badly.

Before he fell asleep, Charles Small heard the great voice of little Mr. Small in the bedroom below, saying: "Beggar the bleddy bats! Balls, schmalls! What's the matter, what, with balls already? Yes and no, she says, in the same mouth. No son of hers, by her, should have balls. Let me alone. I want you should be quiet when you make these ructions. Balls, schmalls!"

Then Charles Small heard no more, because he fell asleep.

*　　*　　*　　*　　*

Similarly, there was the affair of the skeleton. Charles Small had a kind of morbid interest in skeletons; dried, artificially-articulated bones. His mother, who disapproved of this, because to be interested in skeletons meant to be aware of the fact of death, forbade him to go to the Natural History Museum, which was full of the most tremendous skeletons—of Brontosauri, for example, fifty feet long. This was something like a skeleton: here was Death with a vengeance!

"No more museums!" she said, dragging him away, and shuddering past the mounted remains of the Triceratops.

On the ground floor there were wax models of lice, fleas, and bedbugs, none less than eighteen inches long. Charles wanted to stop and examine these interesting things, but there was a contretemps. I. Small paused, with his son, and looked with awe at the waxen model of a louse, saying: "What for a vermin! Look, *Khatzkele*—see what comes from not combing your head." He became pale—probably he thought that this was a special kind of louse, stuffed; and visualised hundreds of them walking over him, biting like bulldogs. Charles was fascinated. Millie tried to drag him away, but his eyes were riveted on the effigy of the bedbug, which, weighing several pounds, looked horrible. It was red, it had six legs, it was nauseating: Charles Small could have looked at it for hours, and so, for that matter, could his old man. But Mrs. Small was embarrassed. Again, there was a monumental waxen reproduction of a flea. It stood about sixteen inches high. "You see, that's what you get, not washing between your toes," said I. Small.

Mrs. Small said: "So that's what he is. That's all he can think of, fleas! Come out!"

I. Small was helpless. Charles said that he wanted to have another look at the bedbug, but the old man said: "Beggar the bleddy bug!" in a voice that reverberated and echoed through the museum and stimulated into action a blue-uniformed attendant, who started out of a coma and sternly, in the voice of an old

Sergeant of Guards, said: "None of that, now, d'yer 'ear?"

Startled, I. Small said: "What did I said? Bugger the bleddy beg. What's the matter, what?"

"I want to look at the bug!" yelled Charles Small.

The attendant said: "We can't 'ave this sort of thing 'ere. Better be orf."

"No bugs!" said Mrs. Small, drawing her son to her with a firm hand. To the attendant, apologetically, she said: "They take fits into their heads."

"Yes, ma'am."

They dragged Charles to an A. B. C. tea shop off the Cromwell Road, where they ordered tea, crumpets, and pastries—fat cream buns and chocolate éclairs crammed with custard. Charles lusted after these delicacies, especially the crumpets, but he had a nostalgia for the great bedbug. So, apparently, had the old man, because before poking at his first crumpet Charles heard him mutter: "Beggar the bloody bug-begs!"

Then he and Charles ate with gloomy voracity, while Mrs. Small, trying to eat a buttered crumpet with her gloves on, said: "So that's what he is. Bugs they want. I haven't got enough trouble. Bugs he wants. He takes after his father. As long as I know."

"Bugs, schmugs—beggar the bleddy buggers!" cried I. Small, overturning the teapot and crying out in pain as the hot liquid poured over his knees. He, too, was deeply interested in that bedbug. In his time he had killed things like that, no more than an eighth of an inch long, with his thumb, and seen his own blood squirt out of them. He wanted to look one square in the face; and this last simple pleasure was denied him.

"Bugs, schmugs!" he said again.

"Be quiet. You're in the A. B C., not in Cracow," whispered Mrs. Small. "If you want bugs, go to Cracow."

Charles Small was snivelling over his third buttered crumpet. "Blow your nose—I mean use your handkerchief—this minute!" cried Mrs. Small.

Charles did so, with a frightful bubbling noise, while the manageress of the tea shop anxiously stood off and on, because there was suddenly the air of an impending massacre.

All that happened was this: the old man patted the boy's cheek and said: "Don't worry, boychik, you'll have bugs."

Then Charles Small, comforted, devoured a cream bun.

But after that he found that he had a secret predilection for parasitic insects and for skeletons.

So came the Affair of the Articulated Rabbit.

There was a boy named Noggin—a dirty, furtive, self-seeking boy who, hearing that Charles Small was willing to pay good money for skeletons, offered skeletons. Charles Small wanted to start a museum; he wanted skeletons. Noggin said that he had the articulated skeleton of a rabbit, which he would sell for six-pence. Now Charles Small's pocket money was carefully assigned: he bought the *Magnet*, and chocolate marshmallows. But for one week he deprived himself of the adventures of Billy Bunter and the delectable liquidation of a chocolate-covered oblong, and went hungry because he wanted to look at bones. For a whole week he wondered what had happened to Billy Bunter, Harry Wharton, and all the rest of the boys at Greyfriars' School, yearning for his sixpenny skeleton.

Noggin never came across. He was a dirty liar. He never had a skeleton, even of a wretched rabbit.

Charles Small has not forgotten how, at long last, he went for Noggin with both hands. Noggin knocked him down. Charles got up, flinging ineffectual fists. Noggin, with a carefree laugh, knocked him down again. After a little while Charles Small, a little muddy, bloody, tearful, and bruised, said: "Why? Why?"

"Because I wanted to," said Noggin.

Then Charles went to the lavatory and cried as if his silly little heart would break—not because he had been punched in the mouth by Noggin, but because Noggin had punched him in the mouth because he wanted to, because he was triumphant, because he had swindled Charles Small and had an easy victim. This filled little Charles Small with a great sorrow.

* * * * *

Every mother's son travails with a skeleton. The son of Millie Small, the bedevilled, bewildered Charles, had—as his mother might have said—bones on the brain. It seemed to him, somehow, that there was wisdom in the naked framework of the body, clean of flesh and guts, nice and dry, liberated from liver and lights. At that time he wanted to run a museum full of skeletons. But after the Noggin affair, looking at his collection, he knew that this was only a dream. Charles Small had the shells of a sparrow's egg, a swallow's egg, a chicken's egg, a seagull's egg; six assorted

267

butterflies; a stag beetle pinned to a cork; and a number of stones of significant shapes which he had chosen to categorise as Stone Age.

Now, all this was repulsive to him. Empty eggshells, cold stones! He swapped the whole collection for a broken Waterbury watch from the works of which it was possible to make spinning tops, and a pocket compass—for he had an idea that his destiny lay in the Congo, where such an article might come in handy. Later, he traded the watch and the compass for a white rat. He will never forget that incident. He came home at tea-time, jubilant for the nonce. He was late, having spent half an hour in passionate negotiation. I. Small and Millie were already sitting down to tea. There were muffins, jam, and some relish of tinned fish.

"What have you been up to? Have you been kept in?" asked Mrs. Small.

I. Small said: "Let him give a bleddy account from himself!" (Where he picked up that word, "account", Charles was never able to discover.) "An account, a bleddy account," shouted I. Small, picking up an immense steel poker with a brass knob. "Bleddy well account, or over goes this poker on the wrong side of your head!"

"Not on the head! Srul, for God's sake, not on the head!" cried Mrs. Small.

It was a formidable poker, one of a set of brass-and-steel fire-irons—another of the old man's acquisitions. Poker, tongs, shovel, brush, and brass fender—it would have been hard to give that rubbish away. I. Small, however, had come home sweating under the weight of them, triumphantly proclaiming that he had got the lot for fifteen shillings. The poker alone was massive enough to knock down a cow, and this he brandished over the boy's head, repeating: "Or over goes this poker on the wrong side of your head, beggar it!" He was muddled, of course, as usual: by "wrong side" he meant the other end, the great brass butt. It was all hot air, naturally. A rolled-up newspaper, preferably the *Westminster Gazette*, was more like I. Small's weapon—and even armed with this he had run, screaming bloody murder, from a bumble bee.

At last they sat at table in uneasy peace, and Charles devoured buttered muffins, while his mother—with her usual air of anxiety, as if this might be the end of the world—asked where had he been? What had he done? Had he offended the teachers?

Comforted with muffins, smeared with butter, Charles took out of his jacket pocket the little pink-eyed white rat, and, putting it on the table, said: "Look at what I've got."

Ah, Lord God in Heaven, then there was a to-do! Mrs. Small opened her mouth and let out such a screech that (as it was later falsely alleged) the workmen in a factory several streets away knocked off the shift, thinking that it was the whistle. I. Small was petrified with terror. He sat rigid, looking at the white rat on the white table-cloth. The white rat, almost equally terrified, crouched on the white table-cloth, stealthily watching I. Small—who later said that it had "eyes like a bleddy murderer."

Mrs. Small screamed: "Srul, be careful! They fly at your throat!"

"They fly?" whispered I. Small, too frightened to move. One could see that he was gathering himself for direct action. Suddenly he leaped away, bounded backwards, took hold of the mighty poker in order to annihilate the rat; but dropped the poker with a yell of agony because, having thrown it down too near the fire, the end was hot. So he got the tongs, immense brass tongs that weighed about ten pounds. With these tongs he proposed to catch the little white rat before it flew (he probably thought that it had wings) at his throat, and . . . he was not quite sure of what might happen after that.

Crying: "Stand back, beggar it!" he snapped at the rat with the tongs, and broke the sugar bowl. The white rat, having regained something like composure, leaped off the table and into a partly-opened cupboard. Now I. Small became terrible. He hurled a full teapot at the rat, following it up with a saucer, a muffin, and a pot of jam. But the rat got into the cupboard. "Lock the bleddy door!" bellowed I. Small. "Bleddy-well lock the bleddy door! Don't worry! From me the bleddy beggar bleddy-well doesn't get away! Sis an order! Boil a kettle water!"

Pale as the paper upon which this is written, Millie Small put on a kettle, while I. Small stood on guard at a reasonable distance with the poker. Charles was appalled by all this. Tea was disorganised, ruined. In a few minutes Mrs. Small came out of the kitchen with a kettle full of boiling water. "Funny!" shouted I. Small, the strategian.

Even in this crisis, Mrs. Small instinctively said: "You mean a funnel—you're not in Cracow now."

"Funnel, schmunnel—quick!"

So Mrs. Small brought a tin funnel, which I. Small applied to the keyhole of the cupboard, whispering: "Stand back." Then, with a trembling hand, he poured in boiling water; some of it splashed his hand, and he moaned like an Aeolian harp. Mrs. Small crouched, half-admiring him, by the fireplace. (She had a dread of rats and mice. They might fly at her throat, or run up her skirts into her private parts . . . as if any self-respecting rat . . .) Then from the cupboard came a plantive howl.

I. Small, putting down the kettle, and gasping like a horse, nodded heavily, and said: "See? I got the bleddy little beggar."

The noise continued in the cupboard. Mrs. Small said: "Better call a policeman."

I. Small, arming himself again with the poker, said: "Policeman? What should I do with a policeman, what? Stand back! I am going to open the bleddy door!"

Mrs. Small covered Charles with her body in a corner of the room, while I. Small with the ponderous poker unlocked the cupboard and, with a magnificent gesture, threw the door open. Then he appalled the neighbourhood with a noise such as had never been heard before. An immense white thing came out. It was the cat, slightly scalded.

The white rat got away, found a hole, dived into it, but a pair of brown rats tore it to pieces and devoured it. So wags the world. I. Small beat Charles severely with the middle page of the *Globe*, shouting: "Rets he should bring into the house, bleddy murderer! Thank God he doesn't take after me!"

"He doesn't get it from my side!" said Millie.

"He's a born murderer!" said I. Small, belabouring Charles with the front and back pages of the *Globe*, rolled into a hollow truncheon. "To bed! To bed!"

The indignant white cat, licking herself, curled up before the dying fire and, out of her yellow eyes, looked complacently and contemptuously upon the scene.

CHAPTER XXII

Now, in his agony and shame, Charles Small wonders why he was born. But in those days he was beginning to wonder how. One day when his mother was in the kitchen making (of all things!) *kreplach*, the boy, having brooded fruitlessly over the mystery of his coming into being, approached her and asked: "Mummy, how was I born?"

Millie's face grew red, then pale, and she put her hand to her heart. The hand was thick with flour, and Charles Small remembers the ghostly imprint on her bosom. To this day, he cannot see a hand in a white glove without an uncomfortable sensation of embarrassment and the fear of birth and death. Mrs. Small had been dreading this moment. She had lain awake at night worrying about it, when she had explored all the other avenues of anxiety and could find nothing more with which to harass herself. What was she to say? How was it possible to tell a child the truth?

Finally, she said: "You were found under a cabbage."

Charles Small was unconvinced. He went to his father and asked: "Daddy, how was I born?"

I. Small stood aghast. Muddle-headed at the best of times, this completely stumped him. He said: "Bleddy beggary—wait a minute!" and went to the kitchen, where little Charles heard him demanding, in his penetrating whisper: "Millie, for God's sake —the bleddy little beggar wants to know how he was born! Quick! You've got the education. How was he bleddy-well born?"

"Under a cabbage," said Mrs. Small.

At this the old man, in relief, drew a deep breath and came back jauntily saying: "Under a cebbage."

"Where? Did you grow cabbages?"

Now I. Small was in a quandary. Explanations were exhausted. He flapped at his son with a handkerchief, shouting: "Murderer, if your father says cebbages, it's cebbages!"

He hoped that he had put an end to this zoological research. It was embarrassing, it brought blood to the cheeks. Born, schmorn—what for did they want to know, the bleddy little beggars? As a matter of fact I. Small himself was not quite sure. He knew that it was a frightful business, a necessary evil, an unmentionable process in the course of which a woman who was superficially like any other woman became a martyr, and a plain decent man became a ravening beast. He shied away from the whole business. You did something bloodily culpable under the blanket of the dark, and after many months of sighing, sewing, knitting, vomiting, languishing, and secret conferences with dirty old women, there came a dreadful dawn or midnight when the wife of your bosom burst asunder with great outcries, and had dragged out of her an inhuman-looking thing with a bottom that was smacked, so that from the other end there proceeded a wail of misery. So. That was how you were born. A smack on the arse, a doleful cry, and off you went into the world, always feeling a little guilty for having been born out of your mother; and—he shed a couple of tears—a man had only one mother. Of love and birth, these filthy things, how was it possible to talk to a child? He had an inspiration. He would tell little Charles that his mother had laid an egg.

Meanwhile, Charles, making his way into some near-by fields, was caught by a small-holder crouching on his hams by a big cabbage. The small-holder, who also kept pigs, took Charles by the ear and said: "After my cabbages, are you?"

Charles Small whispered: "I was looking for babies, sir."

"What d'you mean, babies, you young imp?"

"Please, sir, babies are found under cabbages."

The small-holder, a huge man named Scrip, threw his head back and laughed thunderously into the crisp air. Then Charles Small heard him say: "Bloody lot of fools. Come with me, son," —and led him to a pen where there stood a great white sow, steadily chewing at something—a muddy, dirty-looking animal. "Here's how you were born," said Scrip. Out of a pen came a black boar. He coupled with the sow in a few seconds and then trotted off to bury his dirty muzzle in a mess of mash. Mr. Scrip took Charles to another pen and showed him eight little pink pigs, saying: "That's how it is, my son. That's how it goes, see? One thing leads to another, get the idea? Get away with your cabbages!"

Charles Small walked home thoughtfully. It was somehow unimaginable. He could not for the life of him see I. Small trotting out and mounting his mother, who stood, cloven-hoofed, in the filth, and behaving in so improper a fashion. As for the little pink pigs, he could not imagine from which body orifice they might have come. His first guess was, the mouth. (He remembered that when his mother was big with Priscilla, she was occasionally sick, and there were always, somehow, tomatoes. He still associates tomatoes with gestation.)

Well, away he went, enlightened, visualising the old man prancing or waddling with amorous snorts after a Millie Small who, wide-legged in the mud, received the seed that was to germinate into the wretchedness that was himself.

He got home in time for tea. Seated, he looked from I. Small to Millie, thought of the pigs, and shuddered. In spite of his nausea he ate heartily, and then sat by the fire with a paper-backed book about Sexton Blake, the detective. And then there were more ructions.

I. Small, that confounded idiot, had made a bosom friend of the radical cobbler who had told him that he had nothing but his chains to lose. One day the cobbler saw I. Small poring over a copy of the *Boy's Friend*. At this the journeyman-cobbler became indignant, and said that such rubbish was the working-man's drug. He had nothing but his chains to lose, and all the world to gain. Such literature was devised by the bourgeosie to keep the toiler in subjection. Into the fire with it! "Make him read Robert Blatchford—knock that rubbish out of him!" cried the demented cobbler.

Now, seeing young Charles crouching over the adventures of Sexton Blake, I. Small became a crusader, an intellectual. Snatching the little book out of the boy's hands he roared: "My bleddy chains you want to lose? Into the bleddy fire, bourgeois!"

Mrs. Small said: "Charley, how much did you pay for it?"

"Threepence."

"Let him finish it first," she said.

So Charles Small read the last ten pages of Sexton Blake, and then I. Small snatched the little book out of his hands and hurled it into the fire, crying: "Bleddy bourgeois!"

*   *   *   *   *

Yet Charles Small remembers that he was not quite satisfied with the explanation of the pigs. Such carryings on were, some-how, beyond this world, out of imagination. He brooded over the pigs and his parents for a while, and then saw a pair of dogs coupling in a graveyard. The bitch was some kind of mongrel terrier. The male was a bumbling kind of crossbred Airedale with huge feet. They were ill-matched. The little white bitch, in heat, presented herself; whereupon, with a masculine growl, the big dog took her by the shoulders and made ardent love to the empty air four inches above her tail. It was all over in a minute. The big dog, having shot his seed into empty air, stood back lashing about with his silly great tail, panting, full of dark male ecstasy. The little white bitch, still randy, but hopelessly frustrated, turned and bit him viciously in the face. Then she went to look for something like herself; but strong and resolute. The dog, perplexed, put out a long pink tongue to lick away the blood the bitch had shed, pissed upon the headstone of a grave of a gentleman named Kessler, and wandered away.

This was rather more like it. This touched a button. Yet it was not quite as it should be. Charles Small asked—he had a passion for confirmation of fact—how he was born, addressing himself to a school-mistress. He will always remember the dreadful embarrassment of this old maid, when she said: "You mustn't ask questions . . . you were brought by a stork. Now run away and play."

So now it was a stork. He went home, deep in thought, and said to the old man: "Daddy, it wasn't a cabbage, it was a stork."

I. Small became maroon-coloured with shame, but then he had an inspiration. He shouted: "Cebbeges! Storks! So for this you go to school? Haven't cebbages got stalks?"—and aimed a terrible blow at the boy with the *Observer*.

Pigs, cabbages, storks—Charles was confused. He looked up Storks in some children's encylopædia of natural history, decided that the stork was nothing but a bird; inquired where birds got babies—did they lay them in eggs? "Eggs, schmeggs!" howled I. Small, hitting him with *The Times*.

At last Charles Small spoke to his aunt, the wife of Nathan, the Photographer, and asked: "Auntie, how was I born?"

She replied: "Out of your mother's body."

Charles Small went away, overwhelmed. This was more than he had bargained for. At supper, having eaten enough to sustain a strong man for a week, and feeling chipper, as the saying goes, he said: "I know how I was born."

Then, indeed, there was the Affair to end all Affairs. Mrs. Small swallowed a peach-stone. I. Small came near to swallowing a teaspoon. There were upheavals such as had never been heard before in that house. Catching his spoon in the nick of time between finger and thumb—it came out with a glutinous noise—beating his wife on the back with one hand and his son on the head with the other—I. Small shouted: "Murderer, bourgeois, what d'you mean?"

Charles Small said: "Out of my mother's body."

Once again I. Small became dreadful. He took up a dish, and he put it down. He picked up a heavy copper casserole, brandished it, and shouted: "Bodies? Bodies? Where the bleddy hell do they bleddy-well pick up such talk? Apologise, or over goes this saucepan on the wrong side of your head! Bodies! Your own mother? Bodies, yet?"

Millie said: "Srul, for my sake, not on the head! He's a child —he didn't know what he was saying. Chastise him, yes; but not on the head!"

"Bodies!" roared I. Small, striking his son a deadly blow with the *News of the World*, "bodies! What d'you mean, bodies? Have respect, him and his bodies!"

"Not on the head!" cried Millie Small.

The meal ended in silence. Charles saw his parents exchanging looks full of guilty meaning. His mother looked at the ceiling. His father looked at his boots. At last, furtively, Millie wormed out of him the name of the miscreant who had corrupted him with talk of bodies. Then, with a pretty little quarrel in hand, she went to bed. I. Small ordered the boy to follow her, shouting. He was a dignified figure, with his red moustache—awe-inspiring. With his upraised hand he looked like a Statue of Liberty. All he needed was a torch, a toga, tits, and lights in his hair, as he said: "No buddy bleddies!"

Then an exhausted peace came down on the house.

Charles Small took up this business of bodies later on, and, learning the ins and outs of it, was incredulous. A pig, yes. But . . .

*   *   *   *   *

. . . But, how, and why . . . After all these years Charles Small cannot get to the bottom of it all. He recognises himself as one of the most despicable cowards that ever infested the face of the earth, but, compared with I. Small, he was by way of being an Ajax, a Ulysses, a Jason.

There was, he remembers, the dreadful business of the Stick Insects. At that time, in his school, some broad-beamed head-mistress got a progressive idea. She took it into her head that, by observing stick insects, children might in some mysterious way become nobler, wiser, better citizens. Stick insects, Charles Small recalls, are narrow, green things something like grasshoppers. They eat leaves, and remain safe because of their extraordinary ability to keep still and become indistinguishable from the stem of the common privet. (This, of course, was perfectly in keeping. The stick insect, as an example. Dissolve, melt into your sur-roudings, nibble when no one is looking; be furtive, disguise yourself, hide—that was how it had been, was, and should be!)

This head-mistress informed the school that every child might have, free of charge, a couple of stick insects, on condition that he brought a quantity of privet leaves in a cardboard box. All the boys went raving mad—there was scarcely a privet hedge left intact in the neighbourhood, and the tradesmen were driven almost to desperation by requests for cardboard boxes. Stick insects. They made a bit of a change.

Charles Small, naturally, hadn't the nerve to go to a hosier and ask for an empty box. He went to a tobacconist across the street, with whom the old man was on friendly terms, and was given a great box that had contained threepenny cigars, and a well-intentioned pinch into the bargain. Under the cover of twilight he picked a few sprigs of privet from a neighbouring hedge, put them in the box, and so received two live stick insects, which attached themselves at once to the stalks and became invisible. Informed, at this point, that now he could not see them, Charles Small was profoundly impressed. He carried the box home after school, put it on the dining-room table, opened it and watched. It seemed to be full of leaves. Nothing stirred. He blew, he waggled his fingers: the stick insects were not having any of it. They lay doggo, played possum. Then there was the echo of a "bleddy" and the old man tripped over the door-mat, and Charles hurriedly closed the cigar-box. I. Small came in, genially disposed, and saw the cigar-box on the table. His eyes twinkled, and he smiled, for he loved a good cigar—to him, any cigar was a good cigar—opened the box, and saw nothing but leaves. He was disappointed—there had flashed into his foggy mind an idea that Millie might have bought him a box of cigars for a surprise, just as she used to buy his ties, which were the most ornate that could be bought for the money.

"So what's this? Leaves? A Kensington Gardens he wants to make of the bleddy place?"

"They're stick insects," said Charles Small. "You can't see them."

I. Small had been in conference with the atheistic cobbler. He raised his voice: "Bleddy superstition! What is, you can see. What isn't, you can't. Take a lesson—what is, is. What isn't, isn't. What new bleddy rubbish are they knocking into his head now?"

Charles Small said: "Well, you can't see the wind, can you?"

This was a new one. I. Small shouted: "Sis a difference!" Then, to demonstrate to the boy his superstitious folly, he stirred up the privet leaves with a finger, saying: "See? What isn't there isn't. Education give them! Superstition!" At that moment a stick insect, presumably perturbed, leaped out of the privet leaves on to I. Small's hand. The old man looked from the box to his hand, and from his hand to the box. The very leaves of the forest were reaching out to bite him. He made an ululation, aimed a blow at Charles—with an empty glove—and rushed away calling out for policemen, detectives, zoologists, etymologists, biologists, while the unhappy insect, foredoomed to death on the pavement, clung to the back of his hand. At the corner of the street he encountered a big policeman, under whose nose he extended his hand, with the terrified stick insect on the back of it, and said one word: "Quick!"

The policeman picked the insect off, crushed it between two fingers and said: "Yes?"

"Nothing," said I. Small. After that he went home. He was ashamed. A common bleddy bobby had come to the rescue. Little Charles was to blame for his humiliation. All the same, the animal might have bitten him, poisonously. He composed himself before he reached the door of his house and, taking the cigar-box and holding it at arm's length, burst into the kitchen, urged his wife to stand back, and thrust the box deep into the heart of the fire.

What's that for?" asked Millie Small.

I. Small, fumbling in the inside pocket of his mind for a coherent answer, replied: "Shush—they create mice!"

Later that evening Charles saw his old man, in heavy boots,

277

tightly wrapped up—he feared that the stick insects would run up his legs—prowling on tiptoe with a heavy rolling pin.

"Defeat," he said at last; and, exhausted, fell into a heavy sleep.

*   *   *   *   *

"The many men so beautiful and they all dead did lie,
And a thousand thousand slimy things lived on, and so did I ..."

So thinks Charles Small, because now he remembers the outbreak of the Great War in 1914. Charles Small, who was a boy at that time, was enthusiastic about the business. He was stirred when, after the Declaration, trolley-loads of able-bodied men rolled past, while the hot August air quivered to the shouting of: "Berlin in a month!" Everybody believed that the British troops and the French and the Belgians would be occupying Berlin in a month. This was not the case. Numerically superior, better-organised German forces drove the Old Contemptibles back out of Mons. After that the Englishmen, in their indignation, became terrible.

Into action rushed the flower of the flock—the many men so beautiful—out and out, to gasp themselves away in the gas; perish, ripped into rags under the box barrages; or go under in the mud.

Charles Small remembers that he wished he had been of military age. He was fired by the example of a pair of very distant relations—cousins three times removed—twins, nineteen years old, who had died like men on the Western Front.

Men so beautiful, indeed! The twins were big, light-coloured boys. They enlisted in some infantry regiment, because they were inseparable. Not long after the shambles at Vimy Ridge, in some bayonet engagement over the top, they both went down, but like men. Charles Small can visualise the scene: the dirty dawn, the icy mud; the issue of rum; the men shivering in the damp, while the young officers (we were always running short of them), with synchronised watches, counted the seconds . . . *Five Seconds to go, Men—Four Seconds—Are you ready?—Three Seconds — Two — One! — Over the Top!* — while the Company Sergeant-Major roared: "Over, you buggers—do you want to live for ever?"

He can see it as clearly as he can see the tastefully papered

278

bedroom wall, and hear it as clearly as he hears the hushing and shushing downstairs.

. . . In this dreary, hopeless dawn, the men advance, led by this little subaltern, who goes down under the first machine-gun burst before he has had time to raise a moustache—picked off, conspicuous, because he was carrying a revolver instead of a rifle. Oh for that mud, oh for that bitter dawn, and oh, oh, oh for the clean and beautiful end of those fine twins in the bloody mud of the trench!

They were first over, first in, happy warriors, confronting the enemy man-to-man with the naked steel. One of them, with a hand-grenade, silenced a machine-gun—for which he received a D.C.M. (posthumous). His brother was at his shoulder, fighting with bayonet and butt. The rest of the platoon leaped down, howling like devils, but a German reinforcement had come rushing up, and the German grenades began to burst, and the machine-guns started to stutter, so that the English were driven back thirty yards—good God!—to their front-line trench, with the sergeant-major, hitherto hated but now mourned, lying disembowelled, his hands locked in the throat of a junior German officer with an Iron Cross. The twins stayed. One of them was down—the one who had thrown the grenade, the first one in—and the other, who could not leave him, picked him up and tried to carry him in his arms to the home lines. Carrying exactly his own weight, more—because his brother was already dead, and the dead are heavy—he managed to wallow ten yards through the mud, before the German machine-gunner of the reinforcements squeezed his trigger, and the brothers went down, shot through and through, and lay in a comradely attitude, arm about neck, black with the bloody mud, but clean, sublime . . .

. . . While Millie Small was making a fuss about smuts of soot on Charles's nose, and spitting on her handkerchief to scrub them off, and I. Small, pinning up a poster saying *Your King and Country Need You,* "bleddied" away, leaping like a grasshopper, because he had wounded himself with a thumb-tack. . . .

At the same time, others were beginning their military careers. There was indescribable consternation in the family. Casualties were terrible. Man-power was short, and in urgent demand. I. Small (and if he was Man-Power, gallstones were jewellery) received a paper requiring him to turn up for a medical examination.

Millie Small had hysterics and wet herself. I. Small, deathly pale, shaking, as he afterwards said, like "an aspirin leaf", threw out his chest and bellowed: "What the bleddy beggary! All is fair in love and—what's-'er-name?—war! You can only die once, twice, schmice! Give me a bleddy rifle!"

Nathan, the Photographer, who also was called up, had a trick worth two of anyone else's. He sat up for three days and three nights, drinking highly concentrated black coffee, so that when he arrived, haggard and wan, at the office of the medical officer, he had palpitations, and was rejected, because of a weak heart—after which, having slept twenty-four hours, he began to make a small fortune photographing men in uniform.

The estate agent, Ruth's husband, lost his nerve and did something drastic. He had learned that if you swallowed the cordite contents of a cartridge you temporarily developed all the symptoms of chronic heart disease. So he got hold of a Short Lee-Enfield bullet and devoured the contents of it, which worked to such effect that he died in agony.

Pearl's husband went to Ireland, where he incarcerated himself in a kosher boarding-house in Dublin, and returned when all was safe, talking of the "throubles".

I. Small—trust him to louse everything up—consulted the atheistic cobbler, who told him that glycerine was dangerous, because it was an ingredient of nitro-glycerine. So he went to a chemist and, speaking behind his hand, ordered a shilling's-worth of glycerine. This was another Occasion. It was on a Friday night, after Mrs. Small had set light to the Sabbath candles. I. Small could not eat his supper. He sat with a little bottle of glycerine in front of him, brooding. Charles Small remembers that he and his sister were packed off to bed. But he crept downstairs and peered through a crack in the door.

I. Small uncorked the little bottle.

"Not near the candles!" hissed Mrs. Small, "it can go off."

"Bleddy beggary!" cried I. Small, knocking over his chair. He retired to a neutral corner of the room, and drained the little bottle of glycerine, retching and groaning. He felt, now, the need for a smoke; but after he had put a cigarette in his mouth, Millie knocked the match-box out of his hand, crying: "So that's what he is! He wants to blow the place up!" In her trepidation she even blew out the Sabbath candles.

Later, I. Small, with a noise that roused the neighbourhood, regurgitated a shilling's-worth of glycerine. Millie Small followed him into the lavatory. His convulsions were terrible—not unlike those of a dying sperm whale. *Erhook!—Erhook!*—One might have expected ambergris. There came out nothing but a thin stream of colourless liquid. When it was all over he struck a match to see what monstrosity he had thrown out. Mrs. Small again knocked the match-box out of his hand, crying: "So that's what he is! Does he want to blow us up?"

Under stress of emotion, I. Small broke wind with the noise of a bugle.

"You see?" said Mrs. Small in an ominous voice.

The old man fell into a heavy, exhausted sleep.

Next day, although he complained of bad eyes, bad nerves, bad stomach, constipation, diarrhœa, deafness, a weak heart, a snotty nose, and peculiar feet, he was passed as A-1, and put into the Army. The fact of the matter is that the old man was as strong as a horse.

Mrs. Small, after having made such noises as cause men to throw boots at bereaved cats in the dead of night, was on the whole proud of her husband's conscription. She baked cakes, cooked chickens, made pies, bottled fruits, sent huge parcels to some barracks in the south of England.

One day, a few weeks later, the old man turned up in uniform. He had always been a fastidious man with his clothes. Now he was terrific. His puttees were just so. His tunic fitted him like a glove. He had got someone to set up his cap, his boots shone like black diamonds, and his fierce moustache tickled his cheek-bones. Over all, there was an air of indefinable bleddy command.

"Srul, are you an officer?" asked Mrs. Small.

I. Small replied, in a sergeant-major's voice: "Officer, schmofficer! Not if you paid me!"

"Srul, what are they doing to you? What are you doing? Do you get enough to eat?"

"Hm! A cup tea, Millie?"

Tea was ready. I. Small ate and drank with a military air. After tea Millie Small asked again: "What are you doing?"— for she had a new respect for this martial figure.

Brushing crumbs from his moustache, I. Small said, with some pride: "I am bleddy-well boot-maker for the bleddy battalion! . . . What does she mean—'Hmm?' . . . What does she mean —'So that's what I am!' . . . What's the matter, what, miv a

281

boot-maker? What does she think a bleddy army marches on? Its stomach?"

So I. Small, in a state of outraged dignity, retired into his shell, his little brittle shell. Mrs. Small, who had made all sorts of noises and messes when she heard the news of his conscription, and was already preparing to have her clothes dyed black, was indefinably disappointed, because he had a safe job, and humiliated because this job was a cobbler's job; and not the West-End trade at that.

It happened that during I. Small's seven-day furlough, something occurred in London that was unprecedented in that century. Enraged mobs arose with intent to destroy—not to pillage or plunder, simply to destroy. The casualty lists had been coming in. Everyone over military age wanted to do something about it. Middle-aged men saw the boys gassed, gutted by howitzer shells, or, as the soldiers sang, hanging on the old barbed wire . .

> *"If you want to find the old battalion,*
> *I know where they are, I know where they are,*
> *They're 'anging on the old barbed wire,*
> *They're 'anging on the old barbed wire . . ."*

Everybody wanted to do something to a German. There was a movement afoot to forbid the playing of Beethoven's symphonies. The proletariat took direct action; they went for anyone with a German name. Bewildered bandsmen, veterans of the Franco-Prussian War, were beaten over the head with their own bombardons.

One aged Uhlan, who had had his brains blown out at Sedan, and never missed them—a skilful carpenter who was employed by the Moss family—an aged man with a white beard more than a foot long, was denounced as a Spy. Spy! He could not have espied his hand in front of his eyes. He was manually dexterous, but practically witless; absent-minded. Sometimes, planing a plank, he would forget when to stop, and end up bewildered in a heap of shavings, with no plank. Every year, up to 1914, he attended a Meeting of Veterans: they drank seidels of Muenchner Loewenbrau, guzzled pig's feet and sour kraut, sang *"Ach, du lieber Augustin"* and the *"Lorelei"*, and got drunk more with sentiment than alcohol. This old man, Betsendorfer, accused of espionage and pro-German sympathies, touched his heaving bosom with a gnarled finger, said: "Who? Me?"—and dropped dead.

Charles Small remembers the leader of a German band. In a shabby, frogged uniform, he used to lead a handful of seedy Teutons in even shabbier, frogless uniforms up and down the street, all of them blowing trumpets, tubas, and trombones, until people gave them money on condition that they went elsewhere. Charles remembers this man with a certain nostalgia. On very hot days he and his friends would walk in front of the band, backwards, ostentatiously sucking lemons. The bandsmen's mouths would water, and there followed a bubbly confusion. This band leader finally bribed them to lay off. He was an ox-headed Swabian named Krauss. They clapped him and his crew into an internment camp, where, for several years, they mournfully blew abominable travesties of Schubert until their compatriots practically lynched them. Krauss took to carving beef bones into flower vases, but even at this he failed. He languished, and emerged, a broken man, an artist who had discovered his limitations.

All this was funny enough, but the temper of the mob was ugly, because of those casualty lists, and they took hold of bricks and stones and set out to smash up any shop upon the fascia of which was painted a foreign-sounding name—Lefcovitch, Rosenberg, Eisenstein, Shapiro, Prager—anything. They were all Germans.

There was a German baker across the street from I. Small's shop, a pop-eyed Bavarian named Schleicher, who was later hanged for popping his wife into the oven. (The horrible smell of the smoke, and certain charred bones, buttons, and corset stiffeners gave him away. These, with the evidence of two fellow countrymen, proved his undoing, and he got the rope and took the drop in Holloway Gaol.) But this one they overlooked.

They picked on I. Small—naturally; that was what he was born for. Some lout who had heard him speak with a foreign accent, and didn't like it, led the mob to the shop. Millie screamed and had diarrhœa. Little Priscilla jumped for joy. Charles was afraid. The old man would have run for his life, but he was frozen with terror, so that he stood in the doorway, like a statue in his uniform. Seeing him, someone said: "Hold hard, boys—he's a Tommy!" Then the crowd was all for him. Men offered him packets of cigarettes, banged him on the back, squeezed his hands. A woman gave him a bunch of violets. After the crowd had passed, I. Small became radiant. He swaggered like a drum-major, to the lavatory, where his wife was wiping herself; handed

283

her the bunch of violets, before she slammed the door in his face; and walked around the house strutting like a peacock, muttering: "A Tommy! Oi, a Tommy yet!"

It was not so with Solly Schwartz. By this time he had impressive business premises in the City with the name SCHWARTZ in lurid letters of red outlined with white on a black background. Red, white, and black—the German colours. Schwartz! An infuriated mob of elderly ladies, idle gentlemen, and assorted loafers started hooting under the windows, and one of them threw a stone.

Then Solly Schwartz was in his glory. He took from a drawer a loaded revolver, a big black ugly one of the largest calibre; grasped in the other hand a walking-stick of some wood so heavy that it would not float in water; hopped downstairs, and, panting with delight, confronted the mob, shouting: "Piss-pots! What bugger threw that stone? Come forward, and by Christ I'll shoot you down! . . . What, frightened, eh? The whole lousy hundred of you? Of one pistol? Lucky for you, you're not in France, stinkers!"

Then he put the revolver in his pocket, hobbled forward swinging his stick, and knocked the foremost man stone cold.

"What are you waiting for, eh? Cavalry? Artillery? *Trottels, scheisspots*, eh?" Then he fell into the jargon of the Fun Fair which he loved: "Any more for any more? Step right up, step right up! Have a go—your mother won't know!" and poked a vociferous man in the stomach with his stick. "Drop those bloody stones, or by God I'll batter the piss out of the whole bleeding lot of you!"

And such was the power of the man that there was a rattling noise as eighty or ninety bricks and stones fell to the ground. Solly Schwartz's keen eye picked out one young man at the back of the crowd who, poising half a brick, appeared to be taking aim at him. Clattering with his iron foot, Solly Schwartz went into the crowd like a diver into deep water, took the young man by the hair, and belaboured his back with that terrible stick. Just then the mounted police arrived. The mob dispersed.

The sergeant asked: "All right, sir? No damage?"

Resting his iron foot on a dropped rock, Solly Schwartz laughed as he replied: "What d'you think? Do you think two or three hundred of those little shit-bags can frighten *me*? Go and ride your horses."

Then he went back to his office, much stimulated. These people were his cattle. As for the War; for Solly Schwartz all life was perpetual war, permanent crisis. He enjoyed this kind of thing. At the door of his office he encountered a laughing office-boy who had been relishing the whole affair, and glared at him.

"What's your name, boy?"

"Ibbertson, sir," said the office-boy.

"What are you grinning at, eh?"

"You, sir. Sorry, sir."

"What are you doing with my paper-weight?"

"I was coming down the stairs to join in the fun—I mean, stand by, like, sir."

"How much are you getting?"

"Ten shillings a week, Mr. Schwartz, sir."

"You're a liar. You're getting a pound a week. Put back that paper-weight and go about your business."

And in good times and bad, for the rest of Solly Schwartz's life, Ibbertson loved him and followed him like a dog.

*   *   *   *   *

A few days later, Solly Schwartz was bitten by a nostalgia —he wanted to see I. Small, and take him out for a beer and a ham sandwich. Solly Schwartz arrived at the shop in the side street, in a Napier car of immense power. Charles Small remembers that, an hour or two before, the old man had gone back, more military than Marshal Ney, twirling his bleddy moustachios, carrying a paper bag full of pies. Mrs. Small, by this time, had got over her loathing for the hunchback. She wanted to offer him a cup of tea.

But, learning that I. Small was not there, Solly Schwartz picked on the children. He said: "Come for a ride in my car and I'll buy you toys."

"But——" said Millie Small.

"Shush!" hissed Schwartz, taking the children by the hands. He sat with them on the back seat of the limousine, and told the chauffeur to drive to Hamley's. When they arrived at this most magnificent of toy shops, Solly Schwartz took them inside. Now here was richness! "Point out what you want," said Solly Schwartz.

The children were stupefied. Charles Small was embarrassed.

He suggested a penny bar of plasticine. Priscilla poked her finger boldly towards the most expensive thing she could think of—a rocking-horse, magnificently piebald. Then Solly Schwartz, looking—Charles remembers—like something out of a Punch and Judy show, said: "A pennyworth of plasticine, that's all you want?"

Charles Small's eyes were fixed upon a miniature theatre, complete with puppets.

Solly Schwartz, whose keen eyes had followed the desirous glance of the boy, said: "You want that? Eh?"

"But it costs two pounds, Mr. Schwartz," said Charles Small.

"Ask for it. Say 'I want it!'"

"I want it," faltered Charles Small.

"Pack that up!" said Solly Schwartz to the sales-lady, looking with contempt at the boy. Then he said to the girl: "Tell me, is there anything else you fancy?"

Without hesitation Priscilla pointed to an expensive doll's-house and, looking him between the eyes, said: "That." That was one of the most costly articles in the toy shop.

"Wrap it up," said Solly Schwartz, taking out his wallet. All these playthings were loaded in the big car. They went back to the house. Millie Small was shaken by such generosity, and offered Solly Schwartz a wedge of cheese-cake, which he devoured in four gulps. Then (paper money was just coming in) he gave Priscilla five pound-notes—which she accepted with the air of a gracious creditor.

"Say thank you," said Mrs. Small.

The little girl put the money in her pocket, shrugged, and turned away. She wanted to play with her rocking-horse. Her mother was mortified, but Solly Schwartz laughed heartily and banged his iron foot with his heavy cane.

"I'm so ashamed——" Millie Small began to say.

"Ashamed? Be proud!" cried the hunchback, and offered a pound-note to the boy. Charles Small remembers that he looked from Schwartz to his mother and back again, indeterminate. At last, timorously, he took the money. By then, the whole house was rattling while Priscilla was rocking her wooden horse.

"*Nebbisch!*" said Solly Schwartz, curling his lip; and after a brief farewell, he hopped into the Napier, and went away.

CHAPTER XXIII

So, while Priscilla went up and down, wielding a piece of string as a whip, see-sawing on her rocking-horse and (in defiance of her mother) shouting defiant battle-cries and brandishing a tin sword, the Cossacks went down before the Germans over the Russian border; while Charles played with his toy theatre. And in another theatre, a theatre of war, the Germans were attacking Verdun. And there went some more of the flower of the flock, the many men so beautiful. It seemed that all was lost; that every man wanted to commit suicide, to die with his generation. That was when well-grown boys of sixteen perjured themselves and swore that they were eighteen, and men of forty-eight swore by the Almighty God that they were thirty-eight years old, and men with one arm and men with wooden legs tried to insinuate themselves into the Army to have a crack at the Jerry.

German Intelligence gleefully reported defeatism in the British Army because Cockney companies, lugubriously singing:

> *"I don't wanna die,*
> *I wanno go 'ome*
> *And live on the earnings*
> *Of a lady typist—*
> *Far over the sea I wanna be*
> *Where the alleyman can't get at me . . ."*

—while they went into action like demons, out for blood.

Solly Schwartz, interested in advertising, made a note of the fact that the German High Command had given it out that British man-power was so depleted that the Allies had to send out women to fight. The Germans went into action light-heartedly. It was alleged that some of them carried pillows to put under the hips of the foe. And over came a mad-doggery of Highland Scots in kilts, bent on murder, to the great discomfiture —as long as they lived to be discomfited—of the attacking forces. The kilted men of Scotland rushed in. They were no ladies. Thousands of bull-necked Germans died, somewhat

287

bewildered, in the ditches, and the Highlanders danced on their graves, and went through the dug-outs for chocolate and such-like stuff.

So much for the public, thought Solly Schwartz; tell 'em a lie and they swallow it, hook, line and sinker. But where does it lead to? Is there any future in it? No. In advertising, better tell the truth. . . . At least, tell a lie not so easily exposed. The rumour was flying that the Germans were leaving behind them cakes of poisoned chocolate. Few men, in captured trenches, ate the enemy's chocolate cakes. Here, again, was good Public Relations: sow doubt in a mind, thereby dividing and conquering it. Solly Schwartz was learning fast. On the other hand—considering the example of the chocolate—there were always sceptics who cheerfully crammed that chocolate into their mouths, and gulped it down, and were the better for it. Then, before it had had time to take, bang went the lie. One sceptic makes many. One reasoning human being, like a speckled apple, can corrupt a bushel. Now . . . now . . . this was not the right way. This was the Compromising Way, the Wrong Way. . . . There were only two ways from which a man might choose: the Truth, the Whole Truth, and Nothing but the Truth, or the Lie, the Whole Lie, and Nothing but the Lie, so help him God! He realised then that a man defeats his own ends if he tells a Lie that he cannot back up with facts—even if he has to invent the facts—and that a Truth is quite useless naked, but very powerful draped in the shimmering gauze of an alluring Lie.

Advertising! The fine young men with straight legs and straight backs who had seen the posters that said *Do Your Bit!* and *Your King and Country Need You!* . . . the *trottels* who had allowed themselves to be impressed by this stuff had paid through the nose. They had paid through the head, the heart, the belly —paid with their lives. *Schlemihls!* . . . No, there was no doubt about it: a straight lie was impermanent; a common truth was unpalatable. The only thing to do was create a State of War and impose a new sense of duty.

Here was Advertising.

* * * * *

Considering all this, Solly Schwartz remembered an old story about Truth. Once upon a time there was a young Prince who, having been told of Truth by his philosophical tutors, wanted to know the nature of Truth. (*"Quid est veritas?"*—*"Est vir qui adest!"*) The Prince saw a purple butterfly upon a rose. "Are these True?" he asked. His tutor said, certainly they were True. He pointed to a wonderfully rosy-golden sunrise. Was that True? Then he indicated a sky that came down like frowning eyebrows, shooting out forks of lightning that split the trees. This too was True. A beggar covered with ulcers, blind and toothless, whimpering for alms at the palace gate—he was also Truth. And so was a beautiful little girl, light as gossamer, who danced on the grass, picking flowers to put in her hair. The great proud horses were Truth. So was their dung. Shining horses, smoking dung—flowery girls and ulcerated beggars—everything was Truth, nothing was Truth.

So at last the Prince decided to go and seek Pure Truth, for he was bewildered. He gathered a dozen of his comrades about him, and they left the comfort of their mansions and their palaces, and went out into the world in search of the Truth. They wandered—oh, how they wandered! They went from the Black Sea to the Sea of Japan, from the Sea of Japan to the White Sea, down again to the Sea of Azov, out to the Danube, up to the Baltic, down again to the Mediterranean—never finding Truth —until they found themselves in some awful wilderness, a desert, through which they made their way and came to the fringe of a frightful jungle of plants like saw-toothed swords, where they found an old hermit squatting on his hams and eating a root.

"What do you seek, gentlemen?" asked the hermit.

"We seek Truth," said the Prince.

Jerking his thumb over his shoulder in the direction of the sword-leafed jungle, the hermit smiled and said: "That way, gentlemen."

The Prince and his friends slashed their way through the murderous, spiny vegetable things that pricked and pricked at them, and at last, exhausted, found themselves on the outer edge of the forest upon the rim of a smiling valley bathed in golden sunlight. Below them, in this valley, stood a palace of crystal—all light, pure, blinding.

By this time, the Prince and his companions were old and haggard, bearded, filthy, weary. Yet, from the palace of crystal twelve or thirteen naked maidens, most exquisitely formed, came running with cries of delight.

"Who are you?" asked the Prince.

"We are the Hand-Maidens of Truth," said one of the girls, throwing her arms around his neck.

The Prince asked: "Where is Truth? Where is your mistress?"

"In the palace . . . Stay with me . . ."

The Prince pushed her away and strode down the valley to the palace of crystal. There, he roamed room after room, until at last, in a little room, he saw the figure of a woman draped in gauze of the finest silk, impenetrable to the human eye, which emphasised the contours of the most superb form that ever Man beheld.

The Prince asked: "Who are you?"

In a low sweet voice the woman replied: "I am Truth."

"Unveil!"

"No, better not," said Truth.

The Prince stepped forward, took hold of the gauze veil and ripped it down. Truth stood naked.

The Prince uttered a loud cry. Her body was beautiful, but her face was loathsomely ugly—like the pimplous, fly-blown face of a beggar-woman.

"Are you indeed Truth?" asked the Prince, weeping.

The hag with the beautiful body said, in her melodious voice: "I am Truth, and you have found me."

"But you are horrible, you are hideous!" sobbed the Prince. "You are Truth! I have found you! You are repulsive! What am I to tell my friends who are companying with your Hand-Maidens? What can I say of you? For twenty years we have hacked our way through all the jungles of the world to find you. And now—what can I tell them?"

Very gently: "You must lie," said Truth.

This hit Solly Schwartz right where he lived.

* * * * *

Solly Schwartz was one of the loneliest of men. All that he had, he poured into that which was yet to be. He was a speculator in life, time and energy—he invested To-day in To-morrow, leaving only a narrow margin of emotion, mild emotion concerned with fine motor-cars, fine clothes, extraordinary walking-sticks, and delicatessen and fish and chips. The fire of him shot beyond him, like the *flammenwerfers* that were being used on the Western Front—which spat their terrible flames forward, and advanced, cool and insulated behind the flames.

All the same—to shift the analogy—while he lifted his leg against the lamp-post and aimed, as high as he could to make one with the bright light, his nose was perpetually twitching at little present scents, at the dust of the earth. There was something of Lucifer in this little man who, with his eyes yearning towards Heaven, hooked his fingers into the World, and tried to subdue it in the teeth of The God. Women were not for him. His pride and his shame surpassed the love of women. He amused himself alone and was, in a way, happy in his loneliness, because of his fearlessness, his faith in himself and in the power of his money. Richard Crookback! He would take the country and fit his hump into the soft purple velvet of a little crooked throne.

This strange, solitary man, elegantly dressed, with a diamond in his tie as big as your fourth finger-nail, and his ruby ring, went to the music halls, and the boxing and the wrestling matches. He enjoyed the music halls, but not alone: somehow, in these places, he felt that he needed someone to prod, nudge, exchange laughter with, and stand treat to drinks and spiced snacks. Once, for example, at the ringside, fascinated, he watched two perfect specimens—Gunboat Groth and Bombardier Layton—fighting it out toe-to-toe. They were heavy-weights. The Bombardier won on a knock-out. The referee raised the Bombardier's right hand, and there, battered and bloody, but magnificently triumphant, stood a Man. His opponent, knocked out with a straight right to the jaw, delivered in the English style, was still unconscious. While the crowd roared, the winner picked Gunboat up in his arms very tenderly, and carried him to his corner before running to his dressing-room, where his handlers and a doctor were waiting to patch his wounds, which were not inconsiderable, for it had been a terrible fight through twenty rounds.

Solly Schwartz had the idea of taking over this fighter. Between the first round and the nineteenth he had conceived a great respect for this mighty man with long straight legs, long straight back, and long flat muscles, who went down nine times under punches that might have knocked over a buffalo—but always came back fighting, and won the fight in the last ditch.

He went to see the winner in his dressing-room, and there he lay, bleeding and bruised, while a man in a white sweater massaged his ribs, which were strawberry-coloured with bruises and would soon be mulberry-coloured. How much did he get out of it? A few pounds.

"*Trottel!*" muttered Solly Schwartz, limping out.

He was the stronger man. He wished that he might encounter a heavy-weight boxer in anger. With the hammer of his stick and the tongs of his hands, he would show the boxer who was who. . . .

The clanking of his iron foot reminded him that he was still, in spite of himself, obedient to the ineluctable Law of Gravity that bound better bodies than his to the earth, the dust, the gutters, the pavements, and the blood-spattered canvas. Yet no muddy gravitation had a drag upon his imagination, which soared beyond the stars . . .

. . . Things to be used, things to be used and thrown away like empty cans—men, women, strength, blood, beauty. There was money without doubt in a champion like the Bombardier. There was big money in boxing . . . yes, again, ephemera. And here again was Maya, illusion. Once upon a time, in the proud days of the Fancy, in the time of Tom Spring, the game was clean, and it was possible to have faith in a man; to stake your life and your fortune on his cleanliness and integrity. But now, there was no cleanliness and little integrity—only the main chance, the money in it . . . Solly Schwartz didn't mind money, but something in his heart made him shy away from boxers. He, the lame hunchback, felt a great, magnanimous pity for these superbly-constructed fellows, who gave their youth and the springtime of their beauty to the perfection of a punch—who, training themselves to smash one another, destroyed themselves, yet loved one another—who admired the enemies that broke their defences, and nodded red-dripping approval of punches in the face—who, bashed to pulp, smiled through black eyes and cracked lips, and thanked their butchers for a good fight. Without doubt, there was money in it; yes, without doubt, but Solly Schwartz did not want that kind of money. He was sorry for these beautiful men, these excellent athletes, who cut each other up, while the mob howled, to put money in the pockets of Ginzberg, Riley and the rest—soon to go away, worn out at thirty, impoverished, broken in health, and forgotten, to cadge sandwiches from little men who chose to remember them. No, no, no—these poor fellows were not Solly Schwartz's meat. Apart from the fact that, being a fighter himself, he liked them while he pitied and despised them, they were too little for him.

He remembered the roar of the multitude when the Bombardier

landed that last clean right-hand punch, and the other man went down, struggling against the inexorable seconds of time. The hall, stinking of humanity and of smoke, seemed to seethe like a pot. A man in a pink shirt, on his left, screamed: "Good old Bombardier—kill 'im!" A man behind him cried: "Get up, Gunboat, get up!"—in an injured tone. When the referee declared the Bombardier winner, a few of the spectators groaned, but most of them clapped their hands and cried "Hooray!" The man behind cried "Boo—boo!"—lowing like a steer. But when the Bombardier picked up his fallen opponent and carried him to his corner, the whole great mass of spectators rose spontaneously and sent up a roar of delighted approval that shook the roof.

Now, even his enemies—those who had lost money because of his victory—were in love with the Bombardier. Only a few loyal *trottels* were concerned with the dragged-out body of Gunboat. . . . No, no; why waste time and energy on one fool when there were ten thousand fools ready and willing to be turned inside out? . . . Ten thousand? Ten thousand million, blowing hot and cold with the same mouth—suckers—puppets! Pull the proper string, and up goes the right hand or the left; press the appropriate lever, sitting these dummies on your knee, and snap go the jaws of these ventriloquist's dummies and out of their grinning mouths come the words that you put into them.

He would deal with the whole damned lot in one handful. The mob, with its childish cruelty, its womanish tenderness, its easily-squeezed tears, and shillings—the mob was the thing. Who would waste his life handling one fool—a sympathetic fool, at that—when he could sit on his back-side and handle ten million?

Puppets, puppets!

* * * * *

Touching the matter of puppets, Charles Small thinks, it was curious that the little girl, Priscilla, should be enthusiastic over the horse and the sword, while he was preoccupied with the little dancing dolls on the toy stage. With the strings on his fingers, he made the dolls gesticulate and dance. At the flick of a finger a painted Parisienne showed black stockings, an area of pink thigh, and frilly lace drawers in the high kick of a Can-can. At the twitch of a thumb Harlequin made a pirouette and fell upon his knees. He had only to beckon, and some ogreish Punchinello (not unlike Solly Schwartz) lived or died. There was also a fairy, with the wings of a butterfly, helplessly obedient to every movement of the third finger of his left hand; and a comical horse that performed fantastic antics when he tickled a bit of string with his index finger.

In a way, it was something like being God. After much practice, Charles Small made a display of his puppets for the benefit of his parents and Uncle Nathan and Aunti Lily. I. Small bellowed and bleddied with delight. Mrs. Small was pleased because her sister and brother-in-law were amused. Priscilla was unimpressed. But Nathan, the Photographer, in his slow, considered tones, said: "The boy has a talent for the theatre."

At this, Charles Small's heart bounded into his throat; because although it gave him great pleasure to play with puppets and win applause, he felt that, in point of fact, it was the puppet that caught the eye and got the laughter and jerked the tears. He wanted to be a puppet—an actor.

When his little show was over, his mother said: "Charley, recite for Uncle Nathan—with actions!"

Charles Small made a corkscrew of his right foot on the floor and another of his left forefinger in one of his nostrils, and blushed burning red from head to foot. The old man whispered —it sounded like an escape of steam from a boiler at bursting point—"Bleddy-well do what you're told! Honour thy bleddy father and thy bleddy mother! Recite, with bleddy actions, beggar it!"

So young Charles composed himself, stood in front of the toy theatre by the fallen puppets, struck all kinds of dramatic attitudes, and quoted Macbeth:

> ". . . *To-morrow, and to-morrow, and to-morrow,*
> *Creeps in this petty pace from day to day,*
> *To the last syllable of recorded time;*
> *And all our yesterdays have lighted fools*
> *The way to dusty death. . . .*"

—but at this point Millie Small said: "Shush! You mustn't talk about such things!"

I. Small, taking his cue, bellowed: "Break his neck! Death, schmeth—where do they pick up such dirty-rotten words, the bleddy hooligans? Education, give them! Apologise, at once, or over goes this bleddy teapot on the wrong side of your head!"

He brandished the big brown teapot, the contents of which poured through his sleeve into his arm-pit; whereupon he cried out like a hare in the teeth of a greyhound, and danced a wild *Lezgouinka*, knocking a jar of cherry jam into Nathan's lap. He, with characteristic coolness, scraped jam off his fly with a knife and—with characteristic presence of mind—smeared it on a slice of bread and butter, cleaning his trousers with a corner of the table-cloth moistened in one of the little puddles of spilled tea, saying meanwhile: "Let the boy go on."

Millie Small said to Charles: "Charley—recite; but no death! There's no such word."

With the air of a philologist, a Dr. Johnson, a Roget, a Webster, I. Small growled: "No such bleddy word!"

Then Charles Small, who really yearned for an audience, began again:

> ". . . *Friends, Romans, countrymen, lend me your ears;*
> *I come to bury Cæsar, not to praise him.*
> *The evil that men do lives after them;*
> *The good is oft interred with their bones . . .*"

I. Small shouted: "Here he is again with his bones! What kind of respectable talk is bones? To bed! Bury, schmury—bones, schmones! God forbid! Death, God forbid, is all they can think of! A goy he's turning out to be! Any more death and I'll break his bleddy neck!"

But Nathan, the Photographer, said soothingly: "Quiet, Srul. It's poetry. Let the boy recite."

Although they all hated him, everyone had respect for Nathan. Millie looked at I. Small, who looked back, shrugging his shoulders.

"Let him recite," said Nathan. "What's the matter? It's Shakespeare."

"Oi, Shakespeare," muttered I. Small.

So Charles Small began again:

> ". . . *To be, or not to be: that is the question:*
> *Whether 'tis nobler in the mind to suffer*
> *The slings and arrows of outrageous fortune,*

Or to take arms against a sea of troubles,
And by opposing end them. To die: to sleep;
No more; . . ."

"Here he is again with his death! To bed! To sleep! No more!"
cried I. Small.

So Charles Small was sent to bed, while Priscilla laughed
heartily at the whole affair.

Twenty minutes later as he lay, strengthening his determination
to become an actor, the old man came upstairs with an orange,
which he pressed into Charles's hand while he patted his shoulder
and said: *"Na!* A liddle orange. Eat it . . . Be a good boy . . .
It serves you right . . . I don't want you should use such talk—
death! No more!"

More than an hour later, when the Nathans were gone, I. Small
shook Charles out of a deep sleep to offer him a liver-sausage
sandwich, a banana, and a piece of stewed mackerel. Charles
Small remembers turning away with a grunt. He would have
dropped back into oblivion if the old man, tip-toeing downstairs
with the tray, had not tripped over a loose stair-rod and tumbled
headlong with a noise that aroused not only his son, but half the
dogs in the neighbourhood, so that the night became hideous.

Charles Small got out of bed and went downstairs, followed by
Priscilla, who, seeing her father with mackerel in his moustache
and liver sausage all over his chin, clambered over him, shrieking
with glee, to lick it off, especially the liver sausage—at which
the old man muttered "Bleddy murderer," or something of the
sort, but submitted. The sensation, in fact, was not unpleasant.
Then there was a roaring of water and the slam of a door, and
Mrs. Small ran screaming out of the lavatory with a newspaper
folded back at the account of an exceptionally atrocious mass
murder with which she had hoped to curl up. Soon, the children
were slapped, I. Small was told off, Mrs. Small, indignant at the
thought of death, went back to her mass murder, and Charles
went back to sleep and dreamed that he was an actor.

As for Priscilla, she never dreamed, except when she was
conscious—and only then with calculation.

* * * * *

. . . *Oh, dear Lord God!* Charles Small moans to himself,
helplessly snatching at the ping-pong ball of his memory, which

296

will not go where he wants it to go, but bounces inevitably to the place where the Showman has arranged for it—the black hole in the centre of things, the dark deep, the nothingness.

Can Charles Small ever forget his awful grief when they would not let him go on the stage and be a great actor?

By some incredible fluke he won a County Scholarship, which entitled him to free entrance to a Secondary School, and a few pounds a year for books, etc. . . . Oh, woe is Charles Small when he goes over in his mind the last dreadful days of that examination! He had succeeded in all the written tests; but there was a last, terrible one to pass—the Oral Examination.

The boy was almost out of his mind with anxiety. The day before he had to face the black-gowned examiners at the Middlesex Grammar School, he developed a sore throat. His uvula suddenly made its existence felt—it waggled like the pendulum of a clock out of order; heavy, erratic, but burning hot, while his head seemed to glow like a gas-fire, stifling his nostrils with its mephitic fumes. Charles Small knew that if he said one word the old man would pirouette like Nijinsky, bleddying and beggaring until the pigeons on the roof flew away in fright, while his mother had convulsions and nervous diarrhœa. Then there would be called in the swag-bellied Dr. Fleming, who would poke a spatula into his palate and tell him to say *Arh-h-h* and give him a frightful gargle compounded of alum and vinegar. After that, by main force, they would keep him in bed if they had to trice him up or hobble him like a horse, and there he'd lie, while the old man, hands clasped under coat-tails, rushed up and down doing nothing but bleddying, and Mrs. Small administered her specific. This was an indescribably vile mixture of Ipecacuhana, Squills, and Tolu. It made one vomit. It was worse than an ulcerated throat. His mother was a wonderful one for homely remedies. She was especially good at purgatives. Even on the palmiest days she dosed him with California Syrup of Figs—until Nathan, the Photographer, told her that this stuff was nothing but figs boiled with senna pods—whereupon she bought a lot of dried figs and senna pods, and boiled them with sugar in a saucepan until all the goodness was out of them, and forced this explosive mixture down his throat. Priscilla, naturally, simply spat it out; but Charles Small—despicable creature—gulped it down just to keep the peace. Priscilla said that she didn't want it, she didn't need it, it made her make unnecessary Noises, and they could kill her if they liked but she just wasn't going to have it. He took it, and—Wow!—what Noises he made!

On the whole, it was better to be quietly sick than painfully and noisily cured. Millie Small had a great predilection for excrement. Like an American, she regarded the egestion of a great heap of dung as a sign of health and vitality. To her, an apple was not something to eat and enjoy: it was a means to an end, a lower end—it kept the bowels open. In any case, the family was on tip-toe. The old man was bleddying and beggaring up and down the neighbourhood, bragging about Charles Small's "Ural Examinations", while Millie Small, hopping like a sparrow from sister to sister, was boasting about little Charley's Scholarship.

If he flopped now, no one would ever hear the end of it. So he covered up. At breakfast he said nothing, because he was quite dumb. He did not eat, because it was impossible for him to eat. It was assumed that he was too preoccupied with scholastic affairs. I. Small, with egg on his moustache, looked grave, and wagged an admonitory finger. Mrs. Small said: "I'll make you a chicken for when you come back." Charles did not reply because, quite simply, he could not. He took the tram to the grammar school, and was confronted by someone like Boris Karloff in a black cotton gown, who demanded of him where Havelock fought, and in what war.

Charles Small had some idea that Havelock had fought in the Indian Mutiny, but all he could say was: "*Ook.*" Then the examiner asked him to recite the names of the British kings from Henry II to Elizabeth. Charles Small said: "*Oo-ook . . . Eek . . . Gook . . . Heek . . .*"—until the Oral Examiner took him on in Mental Arithmetic.

"Twice two?"

"*Ooo!*"

"Divide five-hundred-and-thirty-six by two."

"*Boop!*"

Now the examiner, who might have been designed by Charles Addams, was a good fellow. He saw the feverish, incoherent little boy, and was sorry for him. Still, he had to finish the examination with the Geography Test. He made it easy. "What is the capital of France?" he asked.

"*Moop,*" said Charles Small.

"Correct," said the examiner, patting Charles Small on the

cheek—and then, having passed him, took him in his arms and carried him out, and put him in a taxi, and gave the driver half a crown, saying: "Take this young fellow to wherever he lives . . . Where do you live, m'boy?"

"*Bloop!*"

"Wait a minute." The examiner, fluttering in his black gown like a vampire bat, ran back into the building, and came back with a piece of paper, which he handed to the taxi-driver, saying: "Take him there. Take him away. Please go away."

So, Charles Small was dragged, unconscious, out of a taxi, while Millie Small knocked over a pot of coffee, which (of course) poured over I. Small's ankles, and some visiting sister nodded wisely and said: "I knew it all along. Education. That's how they kill themselves."

I. Small, furious, cried: "Education—schmeducation! Before I let the bleddy beggar kill himself, I'll break his bleddy neck!"

Charles Small passed out, but he had won the Junior County Scholarship—and so, in due course, became an important man in the Dramatic Society.

*   *   *   *   *

It was said, later on, that the Higher Education had been the ruin of the boy. He won the Reading Prize, uproariously repeating Pitt's speech concerning the employment of German mercenary troops by George III in the War of Independence—with actions. When he got to the peroration: ". . . If I were an American as I am an Englishman . . . I nevah would lay down my arms, nevah, *nevah*, *NEVAH!*" his vehemence was such that, at the last word, his nose began to bleed. It was impossible, in these circumstances, not to award the boy the Reading Prize—a somewhat shoddy-looking copy of Boswell's *Life of Johnson*, printed microscopically in a type called Pearl, so that it was illegible, and bound in some frightful imitation leather called Rexine. Never will Charles Small forget the last *NEVAH!*—he bled for hours afterwards. His mother, weeping with delight, and his father, growling so terribly that the crowd made a passage for him, dragged Charles Small—who was dripping blood from his nose all over Boswell's *Life of Johnson*—into a taxi, where he bled all over the old man's trousers. "Bleddy education!" shouted I. Small.

Then Charles Small was put to bed. The old man came back

with a pound of rump steak, bellowing: "Quick, Millie! Underdo it for the little beggar, the butcher told me—it makes up for the loss from bloody bled—bleddy blood—blood, schmud, mud!— Underdo it, don't overdo it!"

While the pots and pans were clattering in the kitchen downstairs, the old man sat on the edge of his son's bed, and, being proud of the boy, gave him a dusty peppermint tablet out of his waistcoat pocket. Charles Small remembers that, on the whole, he enjoyed this affair. The old man gingerly picked up the Boswell, opened it at random, and read a few words. He grumbled a little under his breath, and muttered: " 'Yes sir' . . . 'no sir' . . . sir, schmir! That's what they teach them already! Take a lesson. Sis the bourgeoisie. No sirs, schmirs! If I was an American as I am a bleddy Englishman . . . goodness knows what!" Stroking his sleeves contemplatively, he concluded: "Boychik, take it from me: never will I lay down these arms— to the bones I'd work them for you!"

Then Millie Small came up with a pound of fried steak on a platter, which the boy Charles attacked with something like ecstasy, while the old man, nodding and smiling, brushing up his moustache, his eyes moist with pride, stammered: "Eat it all up! . . . It, it, it makes blood . . . I mean bled . . . I mean . . ." Confused, he shouted: "I haven't had your bleddy education."

Millie took Boswell's *Life of Johnson* downstairs, and, dressing herself in her best, rushed out to show it to Lily, the wife of Nathan, the Photographer.

Thus, Charles Small became acquainted with the Drama.

* * * * *

After this there was no stopping him. The old man nearly jumped out of his skin one afternoon when he came into the sitting-room and found Charles Small horribly hunch-backed, with a cushion stuffed under his jacket, his face distorted, clawing at his reflection in a mirror, and declaiming lines by Shakespeare out of the mouth of Richard Crookback. I. Small was frightened. It seemed to him that the boy had gone mad.

> ". . . *I am determined to prove a villain,*
> *And hate the idle pleasures of these days.*
> *Plots have I laid, inductions dangerous,*
> *By drunken prophecies, libels and dreams . . .*"

He groped for something heavy, because it seemed to him that the child might bite him. But when Charles turned and confronted him, still scratching the air with curved fingers and leering disgustingly—carried away by his rôle—all the old man could say was: "Shhh!"

"Shakespeare!" cried Charles Small. "King Richard!"

Charles dragged the cushion from under his jacket and resumed his natural form, while his features composed themselves.

Poking at the cushion with his left hand, while, feeling his son's spine with his right, I. Small sighed and said: "Ah, ah, Shakespeare. Sis different." Then, stroking the boy's shoulder, he said: "Khatzkele, I want you should always make with Shakespeare, do you hear? A Yiddisher boy should stick miv his own people—no bourgeois! . . . *Na!*—take already the cushion. Sis Shakespeare. But put it back. And don't twist your face like that—liddle boys what twist up their faces, they stay like that."

Charles Small stuffed the cushion back under his coat and made such faces at himself that he could not sleep for several nights for dreaming of himself; while the old man went downstairs to the kitchen and said to Mrs. Small: "He'll turn out to be an actor, yet!"—grinning like an imbecile

Millie Small (trust her to spoil everything) said: "An actor. That's all we are short of, an actor!"

*   *   *   *   *

Yet Charles Small really did turn out to be an actor *manqué*. He knows that he still is a player who has missed the bus as he lies there putting on the devil of an act with his belly-ache, which is not acute, and his nerves, which are no more snarled and tangled than the line on a fisherman's carelessly-cast reel that an hour of patient concentration will disentangle and make slick and smooth again. Actor *manqué*—actor *râté!* Monkey, rat!

A year after he won the Reading Prize with his "nevah, *nevah*, *NEVAH*" (The old man, loaded with bloody towels, his moustache anti-clockwise, warned him at the top of his voice never to shout again, brandishing a chamber-pot: "—or over goes this bleddy chamber on the wrong side of your head." Of course, the contents of the china vessel into which Charles Small had bled from the nose, and micturated, poured over I. Small's head and also up his sleeve, so that there were ructions in the house. Flapping about with his sodden collar and trying to wring out his soaking sleeve at the same time, the old man howled: "No more never! There's no such bleddy word! Never no more never! If I were a bleddy American as I am a bleddy Englishman, over would go this pot on the wrong side of your head! I never would lay down my bleddy arms! . . . No more never, or you'll get something, bleddy little beggar!")—a year later, there was a Speech Day and School Concert. Suddenly, prematurely, Charles Small's voice broke, so that he spoke with grotesque intonations. He sounded like a fantasia for the wood-winds and strings: now, he was a bassoon; half a second later, he was a flute; and then, blushing like a letter-box, took over the oboe and got in a few pure notes before something went pizzicato in his larynx and precipitated him into the tuneless depths of the double-bass . . . out of which he struggled, making a noise like a tin whistle. This was very embarrassing to Charles Small. To make matters worse, hair began to grow on his legs, so that, since he wore short knickers, he was ashamed. He begged abjectly for trousers—at which Millie Small was so overcome that she got to the lavatory in what might be described as a photo-finish and the old man struck him on the wrist with a buttered muffin, and punished him by taking away his silver watch and chain, saying: 'You have nothing but your chains to bleddy-well lose! No trousers, *schnip!*" (He returned the watch and chain three minutes later, thunderously scowling and growling: "Let it be a lesson! Trousers, schmousers!")

So the boy became shyly silent. At one gathering of the family he was coaxed into a recitation. "No bleddy death!" I. Small warned him, letting off steam in a terrible blast through the safety valve under his moustache, so that drops of tea flew all over the place. "No death, or I'll kill you!"

Now the last poem Charles Small had been compelled to learn in school was Grey's *Elegy in a Country Churchyard*. He recited it with actions again, in a voice something like that of Feodor Chaliapin, but raucous. It set everyone's nerves on edge—it vibrated in the ears. He thought that he was going pretty well, until he came to the verse:

> "Can storied urn or animated bust
> Back to its mansion call the fleeting breath?
> Can honour's voice invoke the silent dust,
> Or flattery soothe the dull cold ear of death? . . ."

Then one of the sisters, who was pregnant, folded her arms over bloated mammary glands, and said: "Bust! Bust! That's the language they pick up in school!"

I. Small, purple with humiliation, threatened him with a thin slice of bread and butter, snorting like a grampus: "He's here again, with his bleddy death, the hooligan!" Charles Small was not put out by this: but one thing seriously perturbed him—he had begun beautifully in a fine bass-baritone, slipped by easy stages up and down the range of a cello, and ended on the shrill note of a fife.

He had disgraced himself again. After that he became sardonic, taciturn—he was afraid to open his mouth. But—here was one of the cock-eyed idiosyncracies of his larynx—when it came to singing he could keep his voice stable. When he sang it sounded like some fantastic cross between a kettle-drum and a horn. Consequently he was chosen for a leading part in an act out of *The Pirates of Penzance* in the Prize Day Concert. He led the policemen, singing:

> *"When the enterprising burglar's not a-burgling,*
> *When the cut-throat isn't occupied in crime*
> *He loves to hear the little brook a-gurgling,*
> *And listen to the merry village chime.*
> *When the coster's finished jumping on his mother,*
> *He loves to lie a-basking in the sun;*
> *Ah—take one consideration with another,*
> *A policeman's life is not a happy one. . . ."*

The applause was deafening. I. Small bounced on his seat, pounding the floor with his stick, his face wet with joy and pride. Millie, who was as happy as he, looked sour—she would never give him the satisfaction of sharing his delights—and said, ominously: "Hm! So that's what they are. Jumping on his mother, eh? As long as we know!"

"So what you want I should bleddy do?" asked I. Small in his piercing whisper. "Split his bleddy head open? Sis Shakespeare! Listen to the bleddy clapping."

Indeed, Charles Small took a curtain call, and a visiting Lord, who had been prevailed upon to preside over the prize-giving, shook him warmly by the hand. He also shook the hands of Mr. and Mrs. Small and told them that they had "a promising young fellow." Mrs. Small got to the lavatory one jump ahead of another proud mother—her son had been Chief of the Pirates—who could not contain her urine.

Millie Small scuttled back just in time to see the Lord and his Lady pausing by Charles Small and the old man. Millie could have sunk into the ground with embarrassment; for her husband, bent on doing the right thing, dragged out of his breast pocket a silver cigar-case not much smaller than a two-pound biscuit tin and said: "A cigar, Your Majesty?" This immense case contained one twopenny cigar, somewhat frayed. The Lord took it with a gracious expression of gratitude, and said to his Lady: "Give the child a sweet, my dear."

The Lady rummaged in her silver-mesh bag and found a black-currant throat pastille, brushed some loose rice powder from the surface of it, and popped it into Charles's mouth. He was so overwhelmed, and the pastille so nauseating, that he swallowed it whole. Then the Lord and the Lady passed on. I. Small had some crack-brained idea of rushing after them and inviting them to Appenrodt's, but his wife stopped him by pinching him in the arm so savagely that he squeaked, and started to say: "Bled——". But then he remembered where he was, and whispered: "—dy beggary!" Charles Small stood, still dressed like a policeman, gulping and gulping back what threatened to be a regurgitation of expensive perfume. He looked to the left and to the right: he was hemmed in. He feared that he might not be able to make the dash for the place in time, and started to edge his way into the crowded aisle, but the old man, wet-eyed, grabbed him by the collar, saying, almost insanely incoherent: "Khatzkele! Boychik! . . . You see what is! Is Shakespeare! . . . Honour thy bleddy mother! . . . Shakespeare! . . . His proper name was Shocket. I was told! Stand by your own people, boychik, and you get education under the English flag!"

Charles Small's collar was an Eton collar, and the old man's affectionate grip and emphatic jolting constricted the boy's throat. He managed to say: "His name wasn't Shocket—it was Bacon."

He heard his mother say, vigorously nodding: "Hm! So that's what he is. Bacon. Nice language for a Jewish person!"

Then, overcome by emotion and poisoned by the pastille— *Erhook!—Bouah!*—Charles Small threw up a little glutinous lump of medicated confectionery, which bounced off the Headmaster's waistcoat. He had nothing more inside him to regurgitate, having been too preoccupied with his art to eat since suppertime the night before. Surreptitiously, Millie Small picked up the pastille and wrapped it in a handkerchief, to show her sisters that her son was by way of becoming a pet of the Nobility and Gentry. The Headmaster shook I. Small warmly by the hand, saying: "The Theatre is your son's bench."

The old man, for this occasion, had gone to a barber and had his moustache drastically trimmed and fixed in the Guardee style —rolled upwards with fine curling-tongs into two neat cylinders. His emotion, now, was such that the cylinders of hair uncurled and, moistened with perspiration, hung down so that he looked like an excitable baby walrus. But he did not care. The Smalls were the last out of the hall. In the vestibule the old man stopped, frozen in his tracks, staring at something on the floor. It was the cigar he had given to the Lord. Now this hurt his feelings and tied his tongue so that he said: "Begging bleddary! Chains I should have to lose!" But at that moment a crowd of boys made a circle around Charles Small, singing "For he's a jolly good fellow! . . ."—and everybody was happy.

This, as they said later, was the "ruination" of Charles Small.

CHAPTER XXIV

YES, after this, Charles Small remembers his lust for self-exhibition became unbridled. Wherever there was a mirror, there was Charles Small, mowing and gibbering at himself, almost biting himself. Once, playing Hotspur, and shouting:

> ". . . *This is no time*
> *To play with mammets or to tilt with lips:*
> *We must have bloody noses and cracked crowns,*
> *And pass them current too . . ."*

—he knocked over a vase and cracked the overmantel mirror, incurring the wrath of I. Small, who had been spellbound up to that point. The old man didn't mind the loss of the vase—it was a present from Lily, the wife of Nathan, the Photographer, inscribed *A Present from Margate*—but he took exception to "bloody noses".

He shouted: "What kind of bleddy talk is this, 'bloody noses'? Already he's starting to bleddy-well bloody, the hooligan!"

"But it's in the book, Dad—look—that's the way Shakespeare wrote it. See?"

I. Small scrutinised the passage and, somewhat mollified, said: "Shakespeare, yes. But no bleddy-well bloodying by you. You're not Shakespeare . . . and what's a Mammet?"

Charles Small had not been informed that mammets were the lactatory appendages vulgarly known as Tits. But the old man, somehow, was intrigued by the word. Possibly it reminded him—that mother-haunted slob—of "mama". Mammet! The very sound was like a bell. The word worked its way into his system, like Bleddy—he could not get rid of it. It hooked itself to his vocabulary like a burr when, after a quarrel with the milk-man, he called the man a bleddy mammet—when he was out of ear-shot. After that it was Mammet this, and Mammet that. . . .

"What do they take me for, what? A bleddy mammet?" . . .

"Don't worry me, Charley—go play with mammets" . . . and so forth.

Meanwhile Mr. and Mrs. Small encouraged their boy to recite in public. On one occasion, when the family gathered to shed crocodile tears over the corpse of a cousin three times removed —a poor relation; he could not be removed too many times or too far—Charles was called upon to recite a piece of solemn poetry. He did so with gusto. A relation, even more distant (she wore a wig; they wished her beyond the horizon; she was not elegant enough for them) came and kissed him and said, with tears in her eyes: "Bless him! All my life I should have such a funeral, God forbid!"

The boy became stage-struck. He entertained the family in the evenings with masterful Shakespearean characterisations. He stuffed a cushion between his shoulders, playing King Richard; he put on one of Millie's petticoats, glued to his chin a handful of horsehair torn from the sofa, and played Macbeth. (There was the devil to pay about that—the stuff wouldn't come off.) He smeared his face with a paste of flour and water, smothered it with cotton wool, shoved a great pillow under his jersey and did a Falstaff which, as Nathan, the Photographer, said was as good as Beerbohm Tree. But in this rôle he offended Millie Small, in the soliloquy on the battlefield, when Falstaff speaks of Honour:

"Honour pricks me on. Yea, but how if honour prick me off when I do come on? How then? . . ."

Mrs. Small blushed. She was not used to such language, and shut him up pretty quick. I. Small, in his hurricane-whisper, said: "Millie, for goodness sake, don't be a mammet—sis Shakespeare!"

"I don't like that kind of talk. You're not in Cracow now," said Millie Small.

So Charles Small blackened himself with soot, wrapped himself in a coconut doormat with *Welcome* stamped on it and played Caliban:

". . . Be not afeared, the isle is full of noises,
Sounds and sweet airs that give delight and hurt not.
Sometimes a thousand twangling instruments
Will hum about mine ears; and sometimes voices,
That, if I then had waked after long sleep,
Will make me sleep again; and then, in dreaming,

The clouds methought would open and show riches
Ready to drop upon me, that, when I waked,
I cried to dream again . . ."

With this, I. Small was content. "Riches to drop upon me,"
he said, "but what for the bleddy doormat? What for the dirty
face?"

Charles Small was developing an artistic temperament. He
shrugged his way out of the room, replaced the doormat, and
went to his bedroom, a misunderstood genius. Then he realised
that he was hungry. But his artist's pride held him in thrall. He
consoled himself with the plays of Richard Brinsley Sheridan,
rehearsing the rôle of Sir Lucius O'Trigger. Carried away, making
war-like gestures, he boomed: *"Od's balls and barrels!"*—just as
the old man crept into the room with some fish on a plate.

For once, I. Small did not drop the plate. He stepped backwards in alarm and nearly fell over the banisters; but came back
with the fish, saying: "Eat it up, boychik."

He left the fish and fried potatoes, and rolls and butter, and a
glass of milk, on the chest-of-drawers, with a parting benediction:
"Sleep well, boychik; so long you shouldn't grow up to be a
mammet."

Charles Small, the histrionic prodigy with soot in his ears,
scornfully ate his supper to the last crumb, always misunderstood.

He knows now that his mother sent up the food; that the old
man insisted on carrying it; and—this at the back of his mind—
poor I. Small was tremendously moved by the line about "crying
to dream again".

Charles Small wriggles. The isle is full of noises—it is a
pandemonium. He has not the least relish for what the heavens
are going to drop upon him. The sounds give no delight, and hurt
like the devil. He doesn't want any more dreams—he will settle
for plain black sleep.

Sleep. He may whistle for it. It won't come. Memory bounces
back like the ping-pong ball. Why, oh why for the love of God
won't it take the last cool dive into the deep dark hole and be
over and done?

*   *   *   *   *

Weak as a rat, weak as a rat, weak as a rat! thinks Charles
Small, ineffectually snapping his teeth at the empty air in the

308

jaws of the terrier, Time—Time, that is shaking him as a terrier shakes a rat, before throwing his limp corpse over the right shoulder into the dust behind.

He would die before he admitted the fact to anyone but a sympathetic stranger, but they were right—in the Drama lay his ruin; or at least, the seeds of his ruin.

Few men had ever been cursed as Charles Small curses himself now, while he rolls and writhes in one of his "Moods", biting the pillow in self-torment. Trust him! He achieves, in the anguish of his impotence, something which he could never accomplish by considered endeavour—he bites right through the pillow, and, coughing, blows out into the room a quantity of chicken feathers, some of which fly into his nostrils and make him sneeze. Thereupon—I. Small to the life!—he takes it out on the pillow, gives it a thorough beating with a feeble fist—and is suffocated with feathers again. The air is full of the pluckings from the hindquarters of clucking fowl. Charles Small cannot get away from them. The feathers are in his eyes, his ears, his hair, his nostrils. He pokes his head out of the window into the open air, but there he finds no relief. He is being tickled all over; sneezing, hawking, scratching, weeping. Fluff and snot, tears and feathers, self-imposed irritation . . . *c'est la vie, c'est la bleddy vie.*

The front door slams. Hettie has sent the brats (he nearly called them "bleddy beggars") to see Humphrey-Bleddy-Bogart —he means Humphrey-Bloody-Bogart—and much good it may do them!

He knows that that sloppy, tear-soaked poultice of a wife is loitering about downstairs, probably preparing a milk-pudding; waiting and hoping. The thought fills him with rage. She is quieter than a mouse, but, on the spur of the moment Charles Small tears open the bedroom door and yells: "Can't a man rest? Hold that bloody noise, will you?"

(As God is his judge, he said "bleddy".)

Hettie comes running, whimpering: "Charley, what's the matter? What did I do?"

"Matter!" (He nearly said *Matter, schmatter.*) "Why didn't you go to the pictures with the kids?"

Hettie says: "But, Charley darling, I can't leave you like this."

Now Charles Small, coughing up feathers, screams: "Go, for God's sake!"

"Yes, Charley," says Hettie, and goes. Then Charles Small's heart is so full of grief and guilt that unshed tears flush out his acidulous stomach and, for a few minutes, he feels like a human being again.

He opens the bedroom door, crying: "Hey, Hettie! Wait a minute, we'll go together!" He would quite like to see Humphrey Bogart; only, somehow, he could not give Hettie the satisfaction. "Oh Hettie!" he calls, shambling in stockinged feet into the dining-room. Only an echo answers. Upon the expensive mahogany dining-room table stands a covered dish of delicious chicken, all ready for him, with trimmings. But no Hettie. He picks the chicken up by one leg and makes as if to dash it into the Tudor fireplace; thinks better of it; puts it back on the dish and re-covers it. (Now why does this strike so strangely familiar a note in his mind?)

Just out of spite he will not eat a thing, although all of a sudden he is hungry. He will die of starvation before he eats that woman's chicken—her and her Humphrey Bogart! Well, perhaps one wing . . . No! His will is iron! He goes to the refrigerator in the kitchen and makes himself an inch-thick sandwich of cold beef (cunningly disguising the cut) and pads back to the bedroom, gulping like a wolf. When Hettie comes home and sees the chicken untouched, she will be worried. "Just give me a glass of water," he will say in a feeble voice. That will teach her. Let her have her Humphrey Bogart. . . .

He wants his Ivy.

*   *   *   *   *

Now, Charles Small has such a paroxysm of rage that he bounces upon the bed until the springs groan and the woodwork makes a noise like the trapped mouse that he knows himself to be. Gulping back a mouthful of liquid that feels like the stuff they use to clean stained water-closets, and sitting up to facilitate its passage back to where it belongs—in his unhygienic crap-house of a heart—he is burned up with a great sour hate. This hate is different from the hates that have come and gone before. It is a slow, itchy, smouldering hate that oozes out of him in horrid yellow drops, and pollutes that which is most sacred and secret.

Now he starts to hate Solly Schwartz, whom, in his self-pity, he begins to think of as his evil genius. Flash little hunchback! In his mind's eye Charles Small sees Schwartz over the sights of a

310

shotgun. He has never handled a shotgun, but remembers having seen one in the window of a shop near Charing Cross Hospital—a tremendous thing designed to be screwed with a swivel to a punt, for the butchery of ducks. He dreamed, then, of beautiful bitter mornings in the Norfolk marshes . . . dawn rises, day breaks, and over come the big grey wild ducks in V-formation. *Bang!* goes the duck-gun, and—ploppety-plop— down comes the whole bloody lot. (The old man was looking with yearning at a brass blunderbuss: then a taxicab back-fired, and the two dreamers jumped out of their skins.) That was when, having slipped on a banana skin, Charles Small was taken to Charing Cross with a sprained wrist.

A sprain—oi!—a *sprain!* On the whole, he enjoyed it. The bandages made him feel important. He exaggerated the pain, which, when his wrist was tied up, was inconsiderable. But he made the most of it, of course; he cashed in on it. He had already developed quite a histrionic knack. The old man and the old woman were almost out of their minds with worry—they were always almost out of their minds with worry—and, to comfort him, took him to Mme. Tussaud's Waxworks Show in the Marylebone Road, where I. Small, having made a laughing-stock of himself, asking questions of a wax policeman, and saying "Hoxcuse me" when he passed a wax doorman, became erudite. In Mme. Tussaud's I. Small positively spouted information. He pointed out the image of Henry VIII, saying: "Khatzkele, Charley, boychik, take a lesson! He married nine hundred wives, so they chopped his head off." Looking up at the model of the Russian Giant, he said: "See? He ate up all his cebbage!" Mrs. Small, who—God knows why—was gazing fondly at a waxen image of Mr. Gladstone, rejoined them at a moment when I. Small became silent, gazing at a representation of Alexander Pope. The hunchbacked poet, his head wrapped in a kind of turban, glared angrily into space.

"He's here again with his humps," said Millie Small.

Coming out of a reverie, I. Small said: "Humpbacks, schmump-backs! A Yid is a Yid!"

Millie Small said: "Shhh! You're not in Cracow now. No more humpy angels—let's go to the Chamber of Horrors."

And so they went downstairs into the depths.

Charles Small remembers that he was fascinated by the Coiners' Den, and had to be dragged away, while his mother

muttered: "That's all I'm short of—a coiner he wants to be!"
I. Small, also fascinated, said: "Bled——" and then shut up,
because Mrs. Small was standing, open-mouthed, looking at Dr.
Crippen, who murdered, chopped up, and concealed under a stone
the body of his wife whom he had poisoned with hyoscin—this
drug being anaphrodisiac—so that he could enjoy his mistress
with an easy conscience. She decided that Dr. Crippen was a
harmless-looking man. If he had turned up his moustaches and
had a little more chin there might even have been some resem-
blance between him and . . . *brrr!* . . . she didn't like to think
of it. I. Small and Charles were looking at the loathsome coun-
tenances of Burke and Hare, the body-snatchers. I. Small (he
had developed a mania for cabbage) said: "So you see? Sis what
comes of not eating up your cebbage. It should be a lesson."
He might have gone on in this vein but he saw Mrs. Dyer, the
Baby Farmer, who had been hanged for several atrocious murders,
and said: "Beggary!"—and turned his attention to the Original
Electric Chair. Having keenly scrutinised this hideous apparatus
I. Small said: "See? Electricity! Sis good for rheumatism!"
After that his attention was caught by some extraordinarily
horrid prints of Turkish tortures. In one of them a man with a
moustache was portrayed, hanging by the chin on a hook. This
was a little more than he could stomach. He said: "See? He
didn't eat his bleddy cebbage!" So they left the Chamber of
Horrors—but not before I. Small, pretending that he had lost
his handkerchief, slipped back for a last lingering look at the
Coiners' Den, to which he had taken a fancy.

On the way out he made a detour so that they passed Alexander
Pope. Millie had to drag him away. Muttering something about
"Yiddisher boys should eat their cebbage," and . . . "be a good
boy and please God you'll end up in the Chamber of Horror"—
he probably meant the Chamber of Commerce—the old man
conducted them to a tea shop in Baker Street, where they ate
pastries. For a change there were no scenes—except once, when
Millie told him not to make such a noise drinking tea.

After that (one does not sprain one's wrist every day) they
took Charles to the Zoo. I. Small laid out twopence for monkey-
nuts, or peanuts as they are called now, and they went to look
at the unhappy beasts in captivity. Now, Charles Small wonders
who was on which side of the bars. They went to the Lion House.
Charles tried to give the tiger a monkey-nut. The beast uttered

a low growl—at which I. Small leaped into the air and, dragging his wife and child out into the open air, growled—much more fiercely than the tiger—"Bleddy ruffian." After that they went to the Monkey House. Now this was charming. Charles Small and the old man were enchanted. A Rhesus monkey took monkey-nuts, shelled them, and ate them. I. Small rumbled: "Take a lesson, Charley—sis . . . sis . . . economics, boozology. We are all equal, see?" He was remembering the pronunciamentoes of Lizzard, the atheistic cobbler. "Monkeys, people—you got nothing but your chains to lose. Liberty, equality, eternity, or (God forbid) death!"

The monkey masturbated.

On the way home I. Small was pensive. Charles was quite happy. He had had a good day. Looking at the old man, one might have imagined that he was a philosopher—at least, a military theoretician like von Clausewitz, or Falkenhayn. His brows came down to meet his moustache, which he twirled with one hand while he plucked at his hair with the other. After some cogitation he twisted a bus ticket into the form of a propeller, impaled it on a pin, and held it over the rail of the bus-top, so that it spun round and round. He had intended this for the diversion of Charles Small; but somehow he could not part with it. After thirty seconds the pin broke loose and, flying backwards, stuck in Mrs. Small's left breast. After a few whispered bleddy beggaries the affair was hushed up, and the old man became pensive again. What could he be thinking of? Charles Small found out when they got home, when I. Small, in an undertone that sounded like the flushing of a lavatory, said: "Boychik, you saw? Take a lesson. Do like monkeys, they put you in a zoo. But the other one, eh? A hump, bandages on the head, eh? You saw? A humpback, a Yiddisher boy, and he worked his way up to be Pope!"

All this is very fine and large, excruciatingly funny, a perfect scream—yet all the same, Charles Small would give a good deal for one crack at the hunchback, Solly Schwartz, with that cannon of a duck-gun. Much as he loves and admires that awe-inspiring, iron-footed creature, it would please him no end to see him disappear in a red shower. He owes Solly Schwartz more than he can ever repay . . . both good and evil. . . .

*　　*　　*　　*　　*

While he appreciates the great benefits that have come to him through Solly Schwartz—his nice house in Highgate, his car, his clothes at ten pounds a suit, his well-filled refrigerator and American kitchen unit—something rankles, so that now his stomach feels like a flytrap full of angry wasps.

This dates back to the time when he, Charles Small, went into open revolt against the old man and Mrs. Small. It was a dramatic passage. Having won his little Scholarship, he was entitled to several years free education, with a grant of money, at a Secondary School. Now there was some thumb-biting as to the advisability of this. Millie—her voice was like Pibroch of Donuil Dhu, the Gathering Song of Donald the Black—filled her bag and skirled to summon the Clan. There was no gainsaying her, no ignoring that Call. They left the sheep unattended, the bride at the altar . . . left the deer, left the steer, left nets and barges; came in their fighting gear, broadswords and targes. They foregathered at the Mosses' house, where, until after dinner, the men talked of trade, politics, and war, while the women, sagely nodding, discussed the private affairs of the Royal Family —whereupon Lily asked when Millie was last in Buckingham Palace. The Pibroch of Millie Small knelled for the onset, and all the women cried out at once, while the men with one voice roared for silence. Out of this brouhaha came the slow, deliberate voice of Nathan, the Photographer, saying: "Let us be reasonable."

It was understood that the meeting had been called to decide whether Charles Small should go to school until he was sixteen, or be apprenticed forthwith to a tradesman.

I. Small—it was inevitable—made a perfect ass of himself. He drew himself up in his chair, shook out a handkerchief, and made such a noise with his nose that Old Man Moss choked on a glass of tea and had to be banged on the back. Then he lit a little cheroot, blew out the match with an air, shot his cuffs, pushed up his military moustachios, and, remembering that confounded atheistic cobbler again, said: "Education, education is the opium of the pipple! Through religion you lose your chains! A trade! *But!* . . ." Then he looked silly again, and said in a much smaller voice: "Eh, Nathan?"—and paused for a reply.

Millie Small looked daggers and kicked I. Small in the ankle. The old man started to bleddy, but said: "Bl—*arhem*"—pretending to cough, for which no one blamed him, considering the quality of his cheroots.

"Education——" began Nathan, the Photographer, portentously.

I. Small's rosy face was glowing. He said: "I made a mistake. Not religion, education, sis the opium of the pipple!" It was observed, at this point, that his face was set in a fierce expression, and that he pinched Charles's cheek and gave him a puff of his little stinking cheroot. Charles Small remembers the odour of the smoke to this day. It is almost comical. Where did the old man find such things? People shied away from him on all sides. He was blowing out fumes compounded of ammonia and dung.

"Education," said Nathan, the Photographer, "is a good thing, but you must afford it—you must afford it. Only people of, of, of *brilliance* want education. So, the boy is brilliant. Bear all this in mind. He goes to school till sixteen. Then, what? A clerk in a city office? It's an honest living, let us not argue about that. But . . . education, proper education, takes money. Where is it to come from? What comes after? What are you going to do when the boy leaves school? Eh, Millie? Make a doctor of him? Make a dentist of him? A lawyer of him? No, put him into business, let him learn a trade."

He spoke. Millie, through snot and tears, said: "You see? . . . You see what I told you?"

I. Small's cheroot had burned down, and there was a smell of burnt hair. Nevertheless, he inflated his chest, and in that moment became magnificent. He had conducted young Charles to the grammar school where the Preliminary Examinations were to be held and there he had seen scholastic-looking men sweeping through the cold corridors in black gowns; and this had made a deep impression on him. Brushing the charcoal out of his moustache he shouted:

"Nathan, beggar your bleddy trade! Give me opium or give me death! School! Not another word!"

There were many more words. Catching something like a sardonic smile on Lily's face, Millie—on one of the few recorded occasions in family history—took sides with her husband, and so with much emotion the sisters and brothers-in-law parted not without sidelong looks.

Thus, Charles Small went to Secondary School.

Recapitulating, those years in school were the most wretched of his life because, as a Parthian shot, kissing Millie on the cheek and patting her comfortingly on the shoulder, Lily said: "Cheer up, Millie. He'll do the best he can. Our Stanley's going to go in for the Dentistry."

After this, it was education or bust.

May dogs lift their legs against the chaste gravestones of I. and Millie Small, tastefully inscribed with *GOD TOOK YOU FROM US ONLY BECAUSE THE ANGELS GREW LONELY* and *DEEPLY MOURNED BY THEIR HEARTBROKEN SON, CHARLES, DAUGHTER, PRISCILLA, RELATIVES AND FRIENDS*—a list as long as your arm!

Now it was expected of Charles Small that he should grow up to be a Scholar and a Dentist, a Gentleman, fighting duels with stinking breath at two feet while he foully poked nicotine-stained fingers into the mouths of hapless opponents, for which (glad to be rid of him) they would throw him ten shillings before scuttling downstairs moaning in unendurable agony, never to return.

From now on at all hours, I. Small brought up the subject of Teeth. "Charley, boychik, you see?" he would say at tea-time when the boy was biting into a buttered crumpet, "without teet, where are you? Cruffins, mumpets you got to suck like grand-father at his mother's chest. Everybody's got to have teet. Sis the Facts of Life. Teet *you got to have!*"

Charles Small, who was breaking out in pimples and found it impossible to look anyone in the face—but was nevertheless getting cocky—muttered: "What about boots?"

I. Small was tolerant on this occasion. He merely said: "Boots —boots—boots—boots——" in the manner of Kipling, managing somehow to flip a teaspoon over his shoulder. But he said at last: "Charley, I'm older than you; take it from me—boots don't ache."

And for once Millie Small did not put her oar in.

She asked him: "What did you learn to-day, Charley?"

Now how, Charles Small wonders, how is it possible for a boy to give an honest answer to such a question? Is he to say that he has learned almost nothing at all? That he has learned a couple of naughty stories which will stick to his memory like pitch as long as memory exists? That he was called a congenital idiot because he could not grasp the inwardness of the Present Indicative of the Verb, To Be, in the recitation of which he did not get beyond *Je*? (Later he remembered *suis*, but that was *l'esprit d'escalier*.) That he had successfully recited Wordsworth's "Daffodils"? That the history master had called him a beast and said that he had better be in a pigsty because, overwhelmed by the Saxon kings, he had made a disgusting smell in class? That arithmetically he was already foredoomed to the bottom of the Form?

He looked for no understanding here, and buried his lip in another crumpet, smearing his acneous face with the best fresh butter, while I. Small whispered: "Shhh! He's t'inking."

Those years were nightmarish. They were full of lies and deceit—and terror. At the end of the school year he received a Report which had to be returned with his parents' signatures at the foot. Charles Small forged them, and was kept down in class in his second year. Much they knew about it! And all the time I. Small went on about teeth, teeth, teeth. The old man had excellent teeth and was conscious of the fact that few other men had—let alone women. Charles Small remembers, with distaste, a Dissertation on Teeth, which was as follows: "Teet. Who goes about widout teet? Charley, you're a good-looking boychik. A good-looking boy should concentrate miv teet! *Because*? Listen, an old man, so he can go *fsss—fsss—fsss*—and who cares? But a young woman mivout teet, she's a dud. Take my advice, Khatzkele. Who to does a woman go? To a nice-looking feller. *Keep you bleddy mind on teet!*"

Young Charles Small struggled like a rabbit in a bag, but, for the life of him, he could not even matriculate. Before he left in the morning to sit for the first examinations Millie filled him with eggs, standing over him and saying: "Remember! The most important thing is Mathematics!"

It was hopeless. He concealed half Euclid up his sleeve, and still he got only six per cent of marks under the very nose of a blind examiner.

When the results of the examination came out, I. Small shouted: "Matriculation, schmatriculation! Let the bleddy beggar learn a trade!"

Now Millie Small had read in the Sunday papers of boys who, having failed their examinations, hanged themselves; and she was afraid.

"A trade, a trade!" screamed I. Small.

Giving Charles gooseberry pie, to which he was exceptionally partial, his mother said, with one of her rare caresses: "You've got to have a trade, Charley. What trade? Tell us?"

Charles Small, tearful and humiliated, brought the house

317

down. Drawing himself up proudly, he said: "I am going to be an actor!"

*　　*　　*　　*　　*

Then (to paraphrase the humpbacked Mr. Pope in the manner of Silas Wegg), then flashed the living lightning from I. Small's eyes, while screams of terror rent the affrighted skies. As for Mrs. Small: no louder shrieks to pitying Heaven are cast when husbands—God forbid—or lap-dogs breathe their last.

Thinking of hunchbacks and mock-heroics, it is inevitable that Charles Small should hark back to that earth-shaking moment when Belinda lost her lock of hair. "No louder shrieks . . ."

Mrs. Small was a perfect treat, and she tore out with her own hand a small lock of her own hair, and threw it at her husband, crying: "You see? What did I tell you?"

The lock—twelve or fifteen hairs—clung to I. Small's moustache, so that all of a sudden he had two moustaches, one going up and the other going down. He had to pick it away before he could speak and then, his nostrils having been tickled, he sneezed one of his famous sneezes: "*Ah, Russia!—Ah, Tooshka!—Ah, Rash-Ho!*"—and made a noise like a bull seal as he used his handkerchief—which later he opened, as was his habit, and carefully consulted. What with the honking, barking, and bellowing of the old man, and the screaming of the good lady, the Smalls' house must have sounded like Pribilov Island in the mating season, when men go out armed with clubs to knock frustrated holluschickies on the head. (Charles Small, who is well read in the romantic literature of daring endeavour, and has a sneaking nostalgia for the Great White Silences, wishes to God that some hairy-arsed sealer had knocked the pair of them on the head before he was born or thought of.)

It was Charles Small, however, who was knocked on the head, with the fourth edition of the *Star*—the one that had the racing results; for I. Small, influenced by Lizzard, the atheistic cobbler, had taken to playing the horses—sixpence each way, a shilling to win, even sixpenny Doubles, Cross-Doubles, Up-and-Down: God knows what, for I. Small did not. The silly old sod pinned his faith in Lizzard—his belief was in the Unbeliever. He always lost, poor fool, as much as three-and-sixpence a week; but to see him poring over the fourth *Star*, a visitor from a foreign country might have said: "I saw the Distinguished Professor Small. His

318

great brow was wrinkled as his keen but weary eyes scrutinised a closely printed sheet. Between the forefinger and thumb of his right hand he held a pin. As I watched, he closed his eyes, described a circle with a pin, and drove it down, puncturing the paper, exclaiming: 'Bleddy beggary! Mayflower, Newmarket, 130!' Obviously this man is a genius, and should be invited to make a lecture tour."

This is a digression. The old man struck Charles Small with such violence that he bent the evening newspaper over the boy's head, trumpeting: "Actor, schmactor! I'll actor you! *Na!*—Take that!" The leading article broke on Charles Small's skull. "I'll knock it out of him!" he said, as an aside, belabouring the boy with an advertisement for Coal Tar Soap. "I'll break every bleddy bone in his bleddy body, the beggar!"

He stopped, at last, breathless, brandishing the stump of the little newspaper, his moustache anti-clockwise, as it generally was in such circumstances. Catching his breath, he said: "*Now* do you want to be an actor?"

Calm and pale, covered with bits of news-print, Charles Small said: "Yes!" He felt something like Coriolanus

This was the last straw. Dashing down his little bit of news-paper, I. Small went into the hall (as they called the passage) and came back with an immense oaken cudgel, which he grasped by the ferrule and held high, baring his teeth—the primeval I. Small, red-eyed, murderous—saying: "An actor, yes or no, or over goes this stick on the wrong side of your bleddy head!"

Millie Small, terrified, shrieked: "Srul, Srul, not on the head! On the bottom, not on the head!"

"Bottom, schmottom—yes or no—quick!"

Charles Small remembers that, thinking of Coriolanus, he drew himself up proudly, and said: "I want to be an actor"—and waited for the club to fall, knowing perfectly well that it never would fall. It didn't. The old man lowered the great stick which, properly wielded, might have knocked down a bullock (Charles remembers seeing him run like a maniac when a heifer mooed in a meadow, leaving his wife and children behind him) and said, portentously: "So! All right! You wait! You'll see!"

Then he grounded his stick imperiously, but—as if you didn't know!—imperiously drove the ferrule into his own instep. Then, by the Lord, there was the devil to pay. Blinding and beggaring blasting and bleddying, making like Job covered with boils and

God out of the Whirlwind all in one—with a certain flavour of Jeremiah and Habakkuk—violent and incomprehensible as the Book of Revelations—I. Small went off the deep end. He cast his shoe over Edom; at least he kicked himself. He smote the Amalekites; he beat his breast and smacked himself in the face. He wiped out the Amorites, and slew Og, king of Bashan. He punched himself on the nose. If he had been a contortionist he would have kicked himself in the stomach. And all the time he hopped, caressing his injured foot. He hurled the great oak stick away; and even that did no harm: it rebounded from a stuffed sofa and fell to the carpeted floor.

Charles Small, with the scornful smile he had so often rehearsed —when he was not busy picking at his pimples—stood like a rock . . . well, if not exactly a rock, a well-set jelly . . . until the old man, quite exhausted, sat down on the first available piece of furniture. This happened to be a coal scuttle, an aristocratic coal scuttle of oak with plenty of brass on it. On top of this coal scuttle there was a brass knob shaped like an acorn. As luck would have it—trust the old man!—when he threw himself down with all his weight, something untoward happened. If you paid him for it, he could never have managed it in a hundred years. But on this night of all nights, by some trick of chance, the brass acorn went through his trousers and into his anus.

Little Priscilla, who had witnessed the entire scene, danced happily around the room, crying: "More again, Daddy! More again!"

"Go to bed," said Mrs. Small. "Srul, don't make a fool of yourself, get up!"

In a whisper that sounded like a buzz-saw going through knotty wood, I. Small said: "Send the bleddy beggars to bed. A nice thing!" Then he bellowed: "To bed! To bleddy bed! Quick! By my life and yours too, Millie!"

Coriolanus, with folded arms, scornfully looking down his nose at the rabble, said:

> ". . . *You common cry of curs! whose breath I hate*
> *As reek o' the rotten fens, whose loves I prize*
> *As the dead carcasses of unburied men*
> *That do corrupt my air, I banish you . . .*"

At this, despite his agony, I. Small started to get up, but the lid of the coal scuttle came with him so that he sat down again with a shrill cry of pain. Charles (the noblest Roman of them all) strode out, draped in his imaginary toga. The ludicrous I. Small sat helplessly gesticulating while Millie Small got Priscilla out of the room. Priscilla was a difficult child, and a perspicacious one. (Most of the difficultness of children has its roots in precocious perspicacity.) Priscilla wanted to see the show right through to the Curtain. Millie Small got her to bed at last. When she was neatly tucked in she said, clearly and with resolution: "I am going to be an actress too, Mummy."

"Don't be a naughty girl, or I'll give you such a smacking! Only wicked women are actresses."

"I don't care," said Priscilla.

"You dare say that again!"

"I don't care. I'm going to be an actress."

Mrs. Small slapped her, slapped her with all her might. When she was exhausted, and had to pause for breath, Priscilla, who had swallowed her tears, said with tremendous vigour—as if punishment had strengthened her determination: "I don't care, don't care, don't care! Going to be an actress! So there!"

"I'll kill you," said Millie Small.

"Don't care!"

Millie Small was defeated. What was there to do? Take a hatchet and kill the child? She raised a threatening finger and said: "You wait!"—turned out the light, slammed the door, and went downstairs. Her right hand tingled. The child was hard as iron.

In the sitting-room, I. Small, making noises like a stuck pig, was anointing himself with Vaseline. For the nonce Millie was sorry for him. "Risk your life for them, kill yourself for them, and that's what you get for it," she said, and gave the old man a powerful infusion of senna pods; carefully polished the knob on top of the coal scuttle, and went to bed. It had been a heavy day.

* * * * *

Now, indeed, I. Small was in trouble. He could not sit down, he could not stand up, he could not lie down—the only comfortable posture was kneeling, especially after Millie anointed his fundament with a burning ointment which (as it later transpired) had been given to her by some tea-drinking crony whose husband ran a livery stable. It was all a mistake—I. Small was smeared with some stuff used by horse-chaunters to patch up scabs on the insensitive hides of old cab-horses.

The state of affairs became intolerable. He had to eat his meals on his knees, leaning over two chairs. At last, discomfort proving stronger than shame, he went to a local doctor—some cantankerous old failure who regarded the stethoscope as a new-fangled doodah—a doctor highly regarded in the locality because he had an evil temper and bad manners. I. Small consulted this doctor upon the advice of Lizzard, the atheistic cobbler, who said: "You go to Dr. Ribbon. That man's no hypocrite. A few years ago, cutting a bit of leather, I gashed my thigh to the bone. Quick as lightning I get a wax-end and needle, and stitch it up. Then I go to Dr. Ribbon and I say: 'Dr. Ribbon, what'll I do now?' and Dr. Ribbon says: 'Go to hell, that will be three-and-six.' There's a man what's lost his chains. You go to Dr. Ribbon!"

So I. Small, walking at an odd angle, went to Dr. Ribbon. He could not sit on the grubby sofa in the dingy green waiting-room, so he stood, leaning on his stick, looking so sad and so noble that a woman whose womb had fallen out but who patronised Dr. Ribbon because he insulted her, whispered to a neighbour with scabies: "There's a proper gentleman."

The womb and the scabies having been more or less kicked out of the surgery, a frightful voice cried: "Next!" and I. Small limped into the presence of a disappointed-looking man with bloodshot eyes and a purple face reticulated with burst capillaries and studded with warts. He was about seventy-five years old. His black morning coat was glossy with grease and grey with ashes. He wore an artificial shirt-front of celluloid, which had broken loose from its mooring, so that I. Small could see some square inches of grey flannel shirt. The surgery stank of chloroform and alcohol. I. Small was profoundly impressed. This was the way to live—do what you like, treat people like dogs.

"Well? What's the matter with you?" asked Dr. Ribbon.

I. Small did not know quite how to speak to such a man. He said: "My—hoxcuse me—bottom."

This caused the doctor to fly into a rage. "Bottom? Bottom? I asked you what's the matter with you! Your bottom's not the matter with you. What's the matter with your bottom? Drop your trousers and look sharp about it!"

I. Small did so, and a fine figure he must have cut, lifting the skirts of his coat and the tail of his shirt with his left hand while he covered his puny nakedness with his right, with his trousers about his ankles. Dr. Ribbon poked at him with a grimy forefinger and then, rolling a cigarette, said: "Apply Vaseline. You have a simple abrasion of the anus. Button up your trousers. Three-and-sixpence. Good day to you."

Pale as ashes, I. Small put down a half-crown and a shilling, and said, in a tremulous voice: "*Gevalt!*"

On the way home he had to fortify himself with sixpennyworth of brandy, because this diagnosis had shaken him. When he reached home Millie, who had been worrying herself sick, greeted him with wild cries. "Srul! What did the doctor say?"

Smiling bravely in his pain I. Small patted her shoulder and said: "I don't want I should have the pleasure of bringing bad news, Millie, but you got to grin and bear it. I got Anus."

Four days later he went back to Dr. Ribbon, because this affair was preying on his mind. "Well, what is it now?" asked the Doctor.

"Please. This, this, disease, this Anus—sis catching?"

"Your anus is your arse-hole, you fool. Three-and-sixpence. Go away."

I. Small went home, dejected. When Millie asked him what the doctor had said, he waved her away and replied: "Don't ask!"

He was thoroughly wretched. Maya, Illusion! He had been led to believe that he had an Anus, and it had turned out to be an arse-hole, such as one might find in any Tom Dick or Harry.

About this time Priscilla developed an interest in tadpoles. Goodness knows how she caught them, but she came home one afternoon with a jam-jar full of water in which swam five little black things shaped like commas. (Charles Small believes that she wheedled those tadpoles out of a bewildered boy.) The old man looked at these creatures with horror. "What new madness is this, already?" he asked.

Clear-eyed and indignant, Priscilla replied: "They are tadpoles, Daddy!"

"Hm—tedpoles!" said I. Small, and went away. Later he came back to look at these strange creatures, lashing about with their diaphanous tails. He spent hours before the jam-jar. Once, he offered them a little bit of liver sausage, which sank to the bottom of the jar, where it remained ignored, while the disconsolate tadpoles swam around and seemed to look at him with disdain. He was interested to observe their growth. He was an early riser. One morning, about six-thirty, the Small ménage—and half the street, for that matter—was awakened by something that sounded like Roland's Horn. Millie Small hurried down in her night-dress, saying that she had "just dozed off"—she pretended, the liar, that she never slept—she was always too full of care to do anything but doze off. Charles came running, buttoning his trousers, followed by Priscilla, half-naked, scratching her bottom.

"For God's sake! What's the matter with him now?"

Pointing a trembling forefinger at the jam-jar, I. Small stammered: "What next will they bring into the house? The bleddy beggars have got *hands!* Chuck 'em in the dust-bin! . . . Hands, already!"

Despite Priscilla's shrill protests, the old man forced Charles to throw the tadpoles into the dust-bin. He was afraid to touch the jar himself—no doubt he had some creepy idea that they might leap out and grab him by the throat. But he could not get away with that kind of thing with Priscilla. On the afternoon of that same day, at tea-time, she placed before her father a large plate covered with a bowl. I. Small pinched her cheek playfully, smiled in anticipation, called her a good girl, and lifted the bowl. Then he cried to God like a damned soul because, with a *"Brekekekex—koax—koax——!"* two large frogs jumped into his lap. He held them at bay with a bread-knife, shouting: "Stand back!" Millie Small went out to call a policeman, while Priscilla laughed herself into convulsions and Charles sucked his thumb, not daring to laugh. When the policeman arrived he saw the old man slicing empty air with a bread-knife, and said: "Come on now, this won't do. Stick that knife in me, and you'll be the sufferer."

"Bleddy liddle green beggars jumping all over me! Where's your cruncheon?"

"You put that knife down, or you'll soon find out," said the policeman. "Does he drink, Missus?"

"Oh no!"

"Ever threaten before?"

"No, no."

"Want to make a charge?"

"Certainly not!"

The policeman was disappointed. He pocketed his notebook, gave I. Small a long, hard stare, and said in a cold clear voice: "Lucky for you. We've got our eye on you. You'd better be careful. I know your sort. Better watch out!"

"The bleddy things jumped all over me off of the bleddy plate!" I. Small shouted.

"That's all right now. We've heard that tale before. Now you've been warned. Remember. We've got our eye on you. . . . Are you quite sure you don't want to make a charge, Ma'am?"

The policeman sounded so wistful that Millie Small was half-inclined to oblige him. But she said: "No, thanks. Would you like a nice cup of tea?"

The policeman said that he had to be on his beat. Some other time, perhaps. In the meantime Mrs. Small might rest assured that her dangerous husband would be under constant supervision.

This was why, thereafter, I. Small, when he went out, scuttled like a rat to the corner of the street before turning up his moustache and walking on his way, whistling "*Lily of Laguna*".

On the following day Priscilla brought home six newts. I. Small hated the sight of them, but he dared not say a word. They, too, had horrid little hands. She kept them in a bedpan. For fear of what she might do next, the old man did not say a word. For all he knew she might bring home a bleddy crocodile. But one night he crept into the room Priscilla shared with her brother, and poured carbolic into the water, so that by dawn the newts were liquidated.

* * * * *

If I. Small thought that Priscilla would be discouraged by the death of her newts, he was to learn that, as the saying goes, he was talking out of his hat. Two days later she came in from school at tea-time with a hop, a skip and a jump, and put on the table an animal at the sight of which Millie Small went off like a factory whistle and the old man bayed like a bloodhound. It was, in fact, a dangerous-looking creature. It was deathly white, with an arched spine, a pink nose and ruby-red eyes. From nose to tail it must have measured about twelve inches. Charles, also, as he remembers, was afraid of this beast because, looking first at him and then at the old man, it bared two rows of teeth like needles. I. Small was petrified, frozen with dread. He tried to say "Bleddy——" through a mouthful of muffin, but made a noise like *Blubby*—while the animal watched him closely.

325

"It's a ferret," said Priscilla. "His name is Dicky."

I. Small gulped his mouthful, washed it down with tea, wiped his moustache, filled his lungs for a nice loud outcry and raised the *Westminster Gazette* for a deadly stroke; while Millie Small said, in an hysterical voice: "This is all I'm short of!"

"Better be nice to him—Dicky bites," said Priscilla. "Ferrets bite. They kill rats and rabbits. When they bite, they don't let go until their teeth meet. They suck blood. Old Gonger told me."

Cautiously drawing back his chair—knocking over his cup in the process—the old man, moist with hot tea and cold sweat, stared fearfully at the ferret. All he could say was: "Who's Gonger?" in a feeble voice.

Old Gonger, it appeared, was one of Priscilla's gentleman friends. He was a professional rat-catcher: a horrid old man. Looking at him, sensitive observers felt that his business was fratricidal. He looked like a rodent; he was rat-coloured, he smelled like a rat, he was verminous, and thoroughly detestable. He was generally seen lurking in the twilight with a sack full of sewer rats, great ferocious ones, which he sold at the back door to a sporting publican who kept a bull terrier that could kill twenty-eight of the fiercest rats in two minutes. For a quart of ale, Gonger would bite a live rat's head off. He was a species of Geek. Yet, by some mysterious means, Priscilla had touched some tender spot in the heart of this malodorous man. He let her accompany him to a rat-infested warehouse, where he delighted her by pulling out of his pockets (his trousers pockets, at that) a pair of deadly little red-eyed animals that went, silent as smoke, after their grey enemies . . . and then there was much agonised squeaking followed by a sickening silence. Also, he laid down poison and set traps, big wire traps of the Catch-'Em-Alive-O type. Suddenly he started, thrust his right hand into his left armpit and, with an impatient exclamation, dragged out another ferret which—recognising him for what he was perhaps—had buried its teeth in his arm. Gonger cuffed the ferret's head, saying: "Dicky! Haven't I told you a thousand times? Spiteful bugger!"

Priscilla was entranced. She said: "Mr. Gonger, please, can I have him?"

"What, Dicky? I wouldn't part with Dicky for a thousand pound."

"You give me Dicky, and I'll give you a kiss," said Priscilla.

Old Gonger was deeply moved. Something stirred within him. He picked the ferret up, holding it under the belly, and gave it to the child, saying: "All right then, it's a go. Lift him like this—so—see? He's a good-natured feller but he hasn't been fed for two days, and he's sort of irritable. Feed him a bit o' raw meat. Now then, where's m' kiss?"

Holding the ferret by the belly, Priscilla laughed and said: "No. You smell." Then she was gone with Dicky before old Gonger could catch her.

. . . So, Dicky crouched on the tea table. I. Small approached the ferret cautiously, offering it a lump of sugar. (He would have offered it a cigar, if he had had a cigar.) Dicky, the ferret, took a small circular piece out of his thumb. I. Small roared like a hurricane: tea and muffins flew in all directions. Looking for the wherewithal to annihilate this bleddy little murderer, he found a pot of black-currant jam which, brandished on high, emptied itself on his head; so that he stood there, waggling a bloody thumb, dripping with black-currant jam, bleddying and beggaring to shake the house. Priscilla, of course, was overjoyed. She clasped Dicky to her bosom. He didn't bite her. Probably he hadn't the nerve. Mrs. Small threatened to call a policeman. The old man, who felt that he had been dangerously wounded and was in a critical condition rushed bareheaded to Dr. Ribbon; burst into the consulting-room, gasping like a donkey-engine: "Quick! Look!"

Having looked, the doctor said: "All right. Suck it. That will be three-and-six."

As an afterthought he grudgingly applied a bit of cotton-wool soaked in iodine, adding: "Four shillings."

"Sis not poisonous, Doctor?"

"How many consultations do you expect for your dirty four shillings? Go home, go away, get out of here!"

So I. Small returned to the house, full of anger, determined to thrash his parricidal daughter until she was red, white and blue. He weighed in his hands his heaviest stick, but, taking into consideration her youth and weakness, rolled up last week's *Jewish Chronicle*, and went to her room—for Millie Small had sent her to bed. There she lay, serene and beautiful, smiling in her sleep, with the ferret warm and comfortable, draped like ermine about her throat. It opened its bright red eyes and gave the old man a look that seemed to be fraught with menace. He dropped the *Jewish Chronicle* and ran for his life.

Downstairs he said to Millie: "You see what she is?"

"Thank goodness she doesn't take after me," said Mrs. Small, "she's bad to the backbone—she's got bad blood."

"Who then does she bleddy-well take after, with her bleddy blad blood? The bleddy little rotter! Stinkpot! Who does she take after? Me, if I said one word to my father, over went the wrong side of his strap on my *tukhess* till it was like a rainbow! And this one, your bleddy Priscilla, she lets bleddy wild beasts tear, already, her own father to pieces—and she goes to sleep laughing! That's what she is!"

He was right for once in his life. That was what she was, thinks Charles Small; and wishes that there were a few more like her.

It pleases him to remember such little incidents: the memory of them tickles him, even if, in strengthening his admiration for Priscilla, they exacerbate his self-contempt.

At the recollection of the old man, dishevelled, balancing a blob of ruddy-brown cotton-wool on the tip of a tremulous thumb, Charles Small laughs, for a change—and with the laugh comes a kind of hiccough with a nauseating eructation, as if that brief *pop* of mirth has uncorked a carboy of fuming acid, concentrated, destructive, sour stuff—that which is eating his life away and utterly destroying him.

*　　*　　*　　*　　*

The poor old man, I. Small, opened his heart to Lizzard, the atheistic cobbler. This was after the Drapery Business came to its inevitable, ignominious end, and I. Small stubbornly insisted on going into High Class Ladies' and Gents' Repairs—at which, at last, he made a respectable living; for whatever one might say of the old man, it could not be denied that he was a tireless worker, for whom no job was too large or too small. Millie hated the business. She preferred something clean and quiet. But the drapery business had come to grief. Having laid in a large stock of preposterous and unsaleable haberdashery—Edwardian drawers that split in the middle and had lace at the knees, job-lots of perished elastic, millions of pearl buttons, rolls of wide satin ribbon to tie up little girls' hair, thick lisle stockings—in short, everything the wholesalers were delighted to sell and

nobody wanted to buy, Millie Small became businesslike. She
went to a stationer and bought a whole lot of tickets, red-and-
white, inscribed:

NORMAL PRICE . . .
SALE PRICE . . !

Then (this was her idea of salesmanship) she wrote 2/- under
NORMAL PRICE . . ., crossed it out with a blue pencil, and
wrote 1/11¾d. under *SALE PRICE* . . .! By these subtle
machinations she hoped that the world would beat a path to the
dingy shop in Lewisham. What the devil made them think of
Lewisham, Charles Small wonders, remembering the dreadful
desolation of that boring suburb.

Nathan, the Photographer, suggested a nice position in the Old
Kent Road, but Millie would not hear of that. What, was he
trying to humiliate her? The Old Kent Road! Among the costers,
the drunkards? She could just see herself selling tape, hygienic
diapers, perished elastic, and so forth, to a hulking Pearly Queen
of a coster-woman who came in, reeking of beer, running at the
nose and saying: "Quick, ducks—gimme a bleedin' snot-rag."
Nathan, the Photographer, should live so sure. They went
further afield, to Lewisham, which was neither alive nor dead, but
respectable. Nathan, the Photographer, took over the premises
in the Old Kent Road, and there established a Studio, out of
which he made a lot of money. He employed some miserable
wretch to take photographs of the local Pearly Kings and Pearly
Queens, and grew fat on the fat of the land. Bawdy, ribald
Cockneys in bell-bottomed trousers and ostrich feathers reeled
past, drunk as lords, singing *"Down the Road Away Went Polly"*,
and:

> ". . . *Who're you going to meet, Bill?*
> *'Ave you bought the street, Bill?*
> *Laugh! I thought I should've died!*
> *Knocked 'em in the Old Kent Road, Gorblimey* . . ."

Much Nathan cared! He drew his dividends from the Old
Kent Road and Bond Street, while Millie Small, inspired, fluttered
from stationery shop to stationery shop buying tickets and little
signs. Her last gesture was the purchase of a sort of streamer,
about six square feet of paper, upon which was printed in lurid
colours the ominous words: *CLEARANCE SALE!* She crossed

out previous prices and slashed what remained of the prices until they bled, bleddy-well bled. No one paid any attention. If women wanted drawers, garters, hosiery, buttons, etcetera, they could get them across the street from Messrs. Tom Dick and Harry at half the price.

It could not be denied that I. Small had done his bit. He dressed, up, and showed at least three inches of stiff cuff—pink cuff, brilliantly starched. The ladies of Lewisham went for him in a big way. Here, between good laundering and the careful barbering of a ginger moustache, here was Dark Male Ecstasy. If it had not been for the old man, the establishment would not have lasted three months. He talked, and hawked, and snorted like the oaf that he was; but looking at him you would have put him down as a visiting diplomat, a Minister Plenipotentiary.

The ladies of the locality preferred him to Millie Small. The old man strutted like a peacock, while the Missus screamed like a pea-hen; until at last, when she had hysterics, I. Small took her by the shoulders and shook her, shouting: "Enough! No more bleddy drawers, no more bleddy elastic! Ribbon, schmibbon! Back to the bleddy boots, or to bleddy beggary!"

It sounded like King Richard III before the Battle: "Back to the bleddy boots, or to bleddy beggary!"

So, they went back—Millie was so ashamed—to cobblery. The old man's working dress consisted in an old pair of evening-dress trousers, carpet slippers, and a flannel shirt. He kept up his trousers with a belt, clasped by a buckle with which he might have knocked down a cow—only he would have run away from a cow. Then he was quite happy. He was doing what he knew, and he had company, the atheistic cobbler, Lizzard, from whose conversation he derived much pleasure, if not profit.

One day, in a slack period in August, when everyone was at the seaside, a big man dressed in khaki stamped in, twirled a pair of light moustaches at I. Small, and said in a rasping voice: "Our snob's dead. Want to stud some boots?"

I. Small attempted feebly to twirl his own moustache right back at the Quartermaster Sergeant, saying: "So?"

The Quartermaster said: "Put the business your way, if you make it worth my while. Be worth your while, you make it worth my while."

"Certainly!" said I. Small.

"Right you are then."

After the door had slammed behind the soldier, the old man said: "A bit of luck, thenk God, thenk God!"

Lizzard, who was whetting his knives on a well-worn stone, looked up sharply and snapped: "Thank *God?* What d'you mean, *God?*"

"What does he mean, what do I mean? God!"

"May I harst, Mr. Small, exactly what d'you mean by God?"

Charles Small was present at the time, and he saw that the old man was stumped. But he came up fighting with: "Mean, schmean! God! I said God! *Na!*"

Lizzard purred: "You believe in God, Mr. Small."

"Bleddy-well yes!"

"All right, sir. Is God good?"

"What the bleddy hell does he think, with his 'Is God good?' Certainly! A bird lives from the *scheiss* from a horse—God is good!"

"Very well," said Lizzard. "God is good. God is all-good. Is He all-powerful?"

"Certainly. What then should he be?"

"But—par'm me—are there bad things in this world of ours, Comrade Small? Is there . . . indigestion, corns, cancer, tooth-ache, hunger, thirst, eh? Are these good?"

"No bleddy good," said I. Small.

"Evil, then, eh?"

"No bleddy good."

"Now you say that your God is all-good and all-powerful. If your God is all-good and all-powerful, I harst you how you reconcile an all-good and all-powerful God with the existence of Evil! Eh?"

I. Small made a noise like coals sliding off a rusty shovel; then lost his temper and shouted: "No argument! There must be Something, and God is good!"

"Prove it," said Lizzard. "D'you believe in a life after death?"

"What the bleddy rubbishing hell is this?" cried I. Small. "When you're dead, you're done for, gefinished! What new madness is this? Life after death, beggar it! Schmife after death, the bleddy fool!"

Lizzard began to say: "Then how do you reconcile——"

I. Small, very angry, fumbled in a pocket, took out some money, and slammed it down on the bench, saying: "No arguments! Nothing but your chains to lose, all right. But God is good, d'you hear? *Na!* A week's wages! Wrap up your bleddy knives and go to beggary!"

The old man had given Lizzard the sack every week for years. Now the atheistic cobbler took it in silence. He put his few tools into a little linen bag, picked up his money, and went out without another word. I. Small was first disconcerted, then enraged. He cried: "What did I said, idiot? God is good! By you is a crime?"

Lizzard slammed the door, and shambled away. I. Small turned to Charles. "What did I say wrong, Charley?"

"Nothing, Dad."

"I didn't said nothing wrong. He's a good man, Lizzard. It's all right. I kicked him out of the bleddy place a thousand times. Did I said something? 'God is good'—sis a crime? All right, never mind, to-morrow he'll come back, the drunkard."

The old man went back to work, disconsolate, for he had a fondness for the courageous Lizzard, who denied God and spat upon the State. I. Small could visualise Lizzard, somehow, as one of the desperate men in the breathless Battle of Sidney Street, when the Anarchists, as they were called, opened fire on the police, and a bright young Home Secretary named Winston Churchill called out the Guards.

I. Small shook his head and said: "Sis a heathen, a—a—a Atheist, a Intellectual."

Charles Small remembers that, next morning, munching buttered toast, the old man, obedient to an imperious knock, went to open the side door. There stood a big blue policeman. Startled out of his wits, the old man choked on a crust, spraying the policeman with moist fragments. Charles went to tell his mother, but when they came down the policeman was gone and I. Small was crying at his bench. Lizzard, the atheistic cobbler, had killed himself—cut his throat. Before doing so he had addressed a little package to I. Small. This package, screwed up in a brown paper bag, contained two paper-backed books: *The Age of Reason* by Tom Paine, and *Free Will and Determinism* by Goodness-Knows-Who. These were his treasures. He had nothing else; only a few razor-edged leather-knives, a spare pair of trousers, two flannel shirts, a broken watch, and a bloody blanket. There were also his boots. He had soled and heeled them only a week before, sewing on thick leather of the finest quality, hammering iron tips into heel and toe, and saying: "These will last me a good seven years."

CHAPTER XXV

BUT Charles Small's passion for the theatre had become a monomania. Opening a boiled egg, for instance, he would rant and roar like Othello: ". . . I took by the throat the circumcised dog and smote him—thus! . . ." Stabbing a piece of pudding with his fork he muttered: ". . . Cæsar, now be still! I killed not thee with half so good a will! . . ."

At first the old man said: "*Sha!* Shakespeare!" But when, at a family gathering, Charles was invited to recite, and let fly with:

> ". . . *Thou shalt not die: die for adultery! No:*
> *The wren goes to't and the small gilded fly*
> *Does lecher in my sight . . .*"

And so on to:

> ". . . *But to the girdle do the Gods inherit,*
> *Beneath is all the fiends';*
> *There's hell, there's darkness, there's the sulphurous pit*
> *Burning, scalding stench, consumption; fie, fie, fie! Pah!*
> *Pah! . . .*"

—then all the sisters, who were very particular about their feminine hygiene, looked aghast. (Later, Becky went to the Library and took out a copy of *The Tragedy of King Lear* and went through it carefully, in search of the spicy bits.) Millie did not know where to look. Nathan, the Photographer, looked grave and shook his heavy head. His son, Stanley, the handsome one, had decided to go in for Diseases of Women instead of Dentistry; he was such a nice-looking fellow that it was generally agreed that few women could resist the temptation to be professionally fumbled by him. And here was this *nebbisch*, Charley, with his stenches and his sulphurous pits!

It was generally agreed that the idea of acting had to be knocked out of the boy's head. I. Small looked stern, and took a firm hold of a rolled-up copy of the Sunday *Referee*.

Later, Millie went to Nathan and tearfully asked what on earth she could do. It was more than she could bear. The little girl, Priscilla, was picking up Charley's dirty talk; she, too, had caught the infection and wanted to go on the stage. Srul, she said, was as good as gold but . . . he was a foreign fellow—he could not understand. "Nathan, do me a favour—talk to Charley," she said.

So, one evening, the Jesuitical Nathan dropped in as it were *en passant*, for a casual visit. The old man poured a glass of whisky. Millie buzzed about like a blue-arsed fly, preparing a monumental tea—nobody was going to say that there was a lack of food in the house. Nathan ate and drank everything that was put before him; he was one of those slow, deliberate, insatiable eaters. And he talked in the same way that he ate—ponderously, chewing every word thirty-two times before spitting it out. (A Cockney charwoman, whom he dismissed on the spot, irritated to the verge of madness by his long drawn-out periods, had said: "Come to the bleedin' point, Mister—either piss or get off the pot!") Charles Small sensed funny business. It was in the air. It was not like Uncle Nathan to go out of his way to pay visits to poor relations, and when at last the man said to him: "Let's go for a walk, Charley. Come on, I'll take you to the theatre"— why, then, Charles Small smelled a rat. However, he was not going to let suspicion come between him and a little free entertainment, so he went with Nathan, who, to his astonishment and delight, carried him off to a music hall. They rode in a cab. All the way, Nathan made sly allusions to the precariousness of the Stage as a profession. The life of an actor was a hard one, a squalid, wretched, anxious life . . . your theatrical people lived from hand to mouth, never knowing where the next meal was coming from; begging, borrowing, stealing, lying, writing stumer cheques, and ending in the gutter. . . . Actors lived miserably in bug-infested furnished rooms, for which landladies, justly suspicious, demanded rent in advance. . . . They had no roots, no homes, no lives of their own. . . . Who ever heard of an actor coming home to a nice little house after an honest day's work, with a regular Friday pay envelope in his pocket, and sitting down in a familiar arm-chair by a nice fire while his respectable wife took off his shoes and helped him put on his slippers, and the Little Ones called him Daddy, and the kettle began to sing, and a clean housemaid made music with cups and saucers and spoons,

while, like incense, there came the aroma of muffins, and all that?
. . . No, the actor was outside in the raw night, coughing in the
fog, threadbare, shivering in the rain. . . .

So Nathan ran on until the chicken-heart of Charles Small
grew cold in his pitiful little breast. But at last they reached a
famous music hall, and there was richness! Everybody was on
the bill. He wept when Albert Chevalier sang:

> *". . . We've lived together now for forty years*
> *An' it don't seem a day too much—*
> *There ain't a lady livin' in the land*
> *As I'd swap for my dear old Dutch! . . ."*

And he screamed with laughter at the grotesqueries of T. E. Dunville. A trick cyclist got up to look like a tramp, who rode on
only one wheel, sent him into convulsions. So did an intoxicated-
looking lady who sang a song called *"I'm One of the Ruins That
Cromwell Knocked About a Bit"*. Charles Small may be getting
things a little mixed up, but he thinks he remembers seeing the
mighty Cinquevalli supporting on his broad back a platform
upon which a little man sat at a piano, while he juggled three
cannon-balls. . . . Or was it the great Rastelli, who balanced
a screw of tissue-paper on his nose, simultaneously juggling a
match-box and a match so that at a certain moment the match
caught fire, when he set light to the tissue-paper and, when it
burned down to the tip of his nose, miraculously balanced the
ash? It was an enchanted evening. The memory of it is somewhat
blurred, so that he cannot quite remember whether it was on that
occasion or another that he heard Leo Dryden singing *"Don't
Go Down the Mine, Daddy,"* or Harry Champion going off like
a machine-gun with *"Any Old Iron"* . . . or was it Maidie Scott
singing *"The Naughty Little Bird on Mary's Hat"*? . . . or
J. Laurier, coming out with *"I Do Like a Nice Mince Pie"*? . . .

Whatever it was, he was enchanted. Then Nathan, the Photographer, proceeded to disenchant him. (Nathan, by the way,
had been having the time of his life.) But after the show was
over he became solemn, ominous. "These are successful theatrical
people," he said. "And how many of them are there? Ten?
Twenty? Thirty? And how many unsuccessful ones do you think
there are? I'll tell you: Hundreds of Thousands. How many
T. E. Dunvilles are there, making a hundred pounds a week?

And how many comedians who are lucky enough to earn a hundred pounds a year? How many Harry Champions are there? How many Albert Chevaliers? How many names do you see printed in big letters on top of the bill, in the West End, worth a hundred pounds a week? And how many do you see in little tiny letters, lucky to be engaged at all in the West End for a dirty fiver, and only for a week at that? Work out the chances, Charley, work it out. The Stage is like—painting pictures, like book writing—you have to be one in a million. One in a million gets his name in big letters. The other nine hundred ninety-nine thousand, nine hundred and ninety-nine don't know where their next bit of bread is coming from. And then again, Charley, these big pots —how long do they last? You saw them. They're middle-aged men. For twenty, thirty years they lived like dogs in dog kennels to get where they are now. And now they've got where they are, they're old. Three, four, five, six more years, and they'll be in the gutter again. And they," said Nathan, tapping Charles's shoulder, "they are the cream of the Profession, geniuses! See where they end—look!"

It happened that at this moment a horribly dilapidated old man shuffled on broken boots up to a queue that was lining up for the next show and, filling his lungs, wheezed: "Ladies and Gentlemen—impersonations of characters out of Charles Dickens!"

"There, do you see?" said Nathan, the Photographer.

The old busker was a deplorable spectacle. He was stamped indelibly with the marks of the doss-house, where you could get a lousy bed for fourpence a night, the ante-rooms of the Abyss. What remained of his overcoat was fastened with safety-pins, one of which had come loose, so that it was obvious that this was his only garment, apart from his trousers and his ruined boots. He wore a cracked old billycock hat which he must have begged at somebody's back door because it was so much too large for him that it pressed down his ears. He looked like a starved, sickly spaniel that has made its way out of a pond into which some compassionate man had thrown it to put it out of its misery. He had been clean-shaven, once upon a time.

Having attracted the attention of the queue, he said: "Ladies and Gentlemen, Uriah Heep!"—and proceeded to wring his hands, and leer, and cringe, and whine: ". . . My 'umble abode, Master Copperfield . . ." until at last he went up and down the line holding out his hat. He collected about sixpence-halfpenny.

Charles Small gave him twopence. Nathan gave him nothing, but, leading the boy away, went on talking.

"You see, Charley? The people you saw to-night, they are one in a million. They are geniuses. Even so, they've got to have influence, luck, something special. The average, the ordinary ones, they end up like that—and him an educated man; you could tell by the way he talked. . . . Now, Charley, there's nothing in it. A good steady job, a good steady job. If you want acting, there's plenty of Dramatic Societies. Then, with a good steady job, and a home of your own, and a pound in your pocket, you can act to your heart's content. Do you follow me?"

Loathing himself, Charles Small remembers that he followed Nathan, the Photographer. That poor old tramp with his well-trained husky voice, shivering in the cold of the night and cringing for pennies, impressed him profoundly.

He gulped, and nodded at Nathan, the Photographer: oh yes, he followed him all right.

*   *   *   *   *

Lord, Lord, Lord—how sour these memories can get! Charles Small remembers one summer when, Millie Small being pregnant, and hysterical, he was taken with Priscilla into the country. There was, as usual, quite a to-do about it. Millie Small knew only one place out of London and that was Brighton. There was a conference. The family was divided against itself. Nathan, the Photographer, suggested Scotland, the farther away the better, he thought, no doubt. But Pearl's husband knew a man who had a friend who owned a farm in Essex, near a place named St. Osyth, where Millie and the two children could stay for next to nothing, and where the air was healthy.

Charles Small remembers it as one of the greyest places on God's green earth. It was surrounded by grey mud-flats and muddy grey water, over which grey gulls flapped perpetually, squawking. Sometimes a gaggle of grey wild geese passed in V-formation, disconsolately honking. The farm-house was grey, the farmer was grey—and incidentally his name was Gray. But old Gray was not a bad fellow, and Charles took to him. He knew little, but what he knew he knew that he knew. I. Small, who visited his family every week-end, felt superior to old Gray, with his outlandish accent and unkempt moustache; he patronised him, and gave him a fivepenny cigar, which the farmer crammed into an old pipe. The old man and Millie did not like the smell of Gray's farm—the scents of wood-smoke and horse dung were distasteful to them. Good enough for *goyim*—they preferred petrol, and the cones of incense you burned in a bedroom after the invalid has used a bedpan!

I. Small, prompted by his wife, made the children look in the opposite direction while a cow defæcated, calling it a "bleddy, uncivilised beast"—presumably because it did not wipe itself and pull a chain. He and Millie observed the mating of a boar and a sow—thank God the children were not there to have ideas put into their bleddy heads—and the old man snorted: "*Khazza!* Pig! You see, Millie? A *khazza* isn't called a *khazza* for nothing." Also—trust I. Small—he achieved what few men have achieved in a ridiculous way: he was bitten by a lamb. He was captivated by the little bounding bundle of wool, and tried to play with it. Farmer Gray was weaning it from its mother. He dragged the lamb up to a pan of milk, dipped his finger into the milk, and poked it into the lamb's mouth, the idea being that the lamb should learn to lap, and hence to eat rather than suck. I. Small had a go. And the lamb bit his finger. The farmer was vastly amused. He said: "Never ye mind, Mister, you come and look at this"—and led him to a dark, odoriferous place with a half-door.

I. Small, already unnerved by the thought of lamb-poisoning, could see nothing but pitch darkness. "So what is?" he asked.

"Come in," said the farmer.

He drew I. Small after him, and prodded the darkness with his stick, whereupon with an angry bellow there appeared a huge black bull with blood-shot eyes, petulantly chewing his cud and showing two neat rows of white teeth. I. Small tripped over his feet and fell backwards into the muck, bellowing: "Take him away, bleddy beggary!"—so that the bull was frightened. He also fought a losing battle with a gander. He thought, no doubt, that geese were merely birds, and offered the great white gander a piece of chewing-gum. The bird rushed at him, hissing like a snake, and pecked him in the knee. I. Small called it a murderer and ran away, but not before the angry gander had got in a shrewd blow on the right cheek of his bottom. After that he was suspicious of domestic animals. When Priscilla dropped into his lap a newly-hatched chick, he fell into the fire and singed his hair.

Mrs. Small, although she was afraid of cows, sheep, pigs, sea-gulls, live chickens, and practically everything else, had the

338

courage to confront an egg, from a respectable distance. She watched the incubator. The children watched too. One day a brown egg gave out a tapping noise; the shell broke outwards, and a ridiculously bedraggled little head appeared, followed by a bundle of stuck-down yellow fluff. She was inspired to say: "See? That's how they're born. No more questions."

Priscilla said nothing. If that was how she was born, why was Mama not thrown away like an empty shell? But she nosed her way about the farm; saw the bull serving the cows, and was soon in a position to tell her mother the Facts of Life.

Brooding over his cowardice, the old man screwed up his courage for his third week-end and tried to caress a fowl. Trust the old man again—he picked on a fighting cock, which flew at him and wounded him in the hand. Only a man with no heart could restrain his tears at the discomfiture of this poor silly fellow chased by a chicken, plaintively protesting that he meant it no harm —and only a man with no soul could help laughing until he cried.

Recollecting the incident, Charles Small decides that on the whole he had better cry.

But this is beside the point. He remembers, most vividly, the Muck Heap.

He and Priscilla used to follow Farmer Gray around, while Mrs. Small was having morning sickness. (No matter what she had eaten, she seemed invariably to bring up tomatoes.) It seemed to Charles Small that this old farmer was morbidly preoccupied with stuff that, by rights, should have been flushed away in lavatories or carted away by dustmen—dung, garbage, and the urine of cattle. I. Small muttered something about Farmer Gray being a "bleddy uncivilised beast", and forbade the children, on pain of chastisement with the *Essex Advertiser*, ever to go near the stalls, the pens, and the stables. Charles obeyed, at first. Priscilla did not, and her brother followed her. Fascinated, they watched the farmer and a labourer shovelling up barrow-loads of straw, sodden with cow-shit—dealing with the stuff quite reverently. The sanitation of the farm-house was primitive. Every day a labourer carried from a little out-house a brimming, malodorous bucket. One day Priscilla asked the farmer what was the idea, the purpose in all that. Sucking at a foul pipe and smiling under his ungentlemanly moustache, the old farmer said: "Come here, then," and beckoned them towards a place where one of the labourers was making a kind of layer-cake or *mille feuilles* of polluted straw, the excrement of pigs, men, horses, women, and cows, that stank to high Heaven. Rotten vegetables went into it, and spoiled fruits. It was something like the Borbonessa Tart, immortalised by Rabelais. Old Gray and the labourer covered it carefully with straw. "She isn't pretty, is she? She don't smell sweet, eh?" said Gray. "But now come here."

He took them to another heap, the straw crust of which was discoloured, dried up. While the children watched, aghast, he thrust his hand into the heart of this heap and withdrew it full of something light and flaky, which he held under their noses, saying: "Smell it."

Its odour was pleasant, reminiscent of ripe walnuts; it had a wonderfully clean and healthy smell.

"This," said Farmer Gray, jerking a thumb in the direction of the new heap, "this is *that*, d'ye see? After three years, don't ye see? This is compost. Ye give it time, my chicks, and it'll get sweet. Ye give it time, and it'll give ye time. Don't you see? What ye take out of the ground ye've got to put back, one way or another. This good stuff lightens my soil, and grows the crops. The roses don't stink, do they now? So now ye know: that's the way to get rich—puttin' back into the ground, one way or another, what ye take out of it. To grass we will return—it says so in the Bible. Flesh is grass, grass is flesh . . . look at they Jersey cows, for instance. There's flesh and blood and cream! All out of grass, m'dears, all out of grass; and back to grass they'll go in God's good time."

As the children went away Priscilla heard him mutter—they were not supposed to hear—"Shit is money, money is shit, flesh is grass." Then he bellowed: "You there, Harlow, spread that straw even!"

Remembering this, and he remembers it most vividly, Charles Small wishes to God that he had a compost heap in place of a brain—something that Time might purify and make sweet and life-giving, instead of this stinking, sour, stagnant untransmuted mass of human, animal, mineral, and vegetable detritus that is himself. It occurs to him that a man, properly considered in the light of a higher wisdom, patiently cherished, might in time achieve sweetness and the dignity of . . . dung.

* * * * *

Oh well, thinks Charles Small, *such was not my destiny*. No clean compost, he; but something foul, a filthy sodden chaos of blurred words—a kind of old-fashioned water-closet, out of order, stuffed with used newsprint. No, no, he has not the dignity of dung—the self-purifying power of that which makes the roses sweet and the wheat grow tall. He is by way of being a constipated cow, doomed to carry in his congested belly the weight of his own muck.

He despises himself. He let them defeat him. *I gave in to them*, he says to himself—as an embittered mouse, frozen with terror, might talk to a trap. Wee, timorous, cow'ring beastie! He could not, he dared not gnaw his way through the dark tunnels of the night to the light—he was afraid of the dark. He wanted the little bit of cheese dangling, tantalising, on a little hook; and he nibbled at it, and—*snap!* There he was, caught in a little cage. And it was a fair cop, and there was no one but himself whom Charles Small could honestly blame.

He remembers, belching acidulous laughter, his last miserable protest to the old man, when, after an appalling scene in the course of which I. Small smashed a fly with a rolled-up copy of a circular advertising the Jewish Encyclopædia, Millie Small, who had internal trouble, begged him to go into business. "For *my* sake, Charley—for *MY* sake!"

She really had been far from well, since the miscarriage of the child she had been carrying in Essex. (The child was still-born at seven months. The old man, confident that it would be a boy, had already decided to name it after his grandfather, Nehemiah. Millie insisted that Nehemiah was all right for Cracow. Neil was the name. Naturally, it came out a girl, and stone dead at that. They couldn't do anything right.)

After that, Millie Small became a chronic invalid, and in her misery she became irresistibly pitiable. She could not eat, she could not sleep, she could not walk, sit, bend, stretch, stand, or lie down without suffering; and her occasional outcries were of such a nature that the old man, tearing his moustache, galloped out of earshot, bleddying to frighten the very cockroaches. Priscilla was unimpressed. Charles, the softie, was twisted like a wet dish-rag. *For MY sake!* Who, having read his Shakespeare, could resist? But Charles Small shed a few tears after his mother had gone to bed, and the old man tried to comfort him, clumsily caressing him with an uncertain hand, which Charles nudged away while he toyed with his untasted supper.

"Charley, boychik, what is it? What do you want I should do? What do you *want?* What do you want from my life?"

Charles said, in the manner of Brutus: "I want to be free, free!"

"What do you mean, free? From what do you want to be free?"

"From you, from everything," said Charles.

The old man—now he was a nice old man—tried to push a strawberry into his son's mouth, and spoke gently, saying: "So, boychik, so you want to be free from me, yes?"

Charles Small nodded, spitting out the strawberry. I. Small sighed and said: "Me, also, I wanted to be free. Free, schmee—sis a lot of eyewash, freedom! No such thing. From mine father, God rest his soul, I wanted I should be free. From Cracow I wanted I should be free. And from . . . well, free . . . From what free? Free for what? Why should you want you should be free from your Mama what you owe your life to? Why should you want to be free from your Dad what works his fingers to the bone for you? Believe me, Khatzkele, I mean Charley, boychik, when I was young and foolish I wanted to be Free. I couldn't rest. I wanted to go away. I knew where from I wanted to go away. But where *to?* Still I don't know. Still I'm a *schusterkopf.* I might have stayed at home." The old man was unaccountably moved by what he was saying. ". . . Only here is schooling, education. You can shake hands miv the King of England . . . miv Society. I know from what I wanted to be free. For what I know—for you, boychik! . . . And your mother, bless her, is not a well woman. . . ."

I. Small shed tears. Charles Small said heavily: "All right, Dad, I'll do what you say."

Making a noise like a gannet between his nose and a pocket handkerchief, I. Small snuffled: "Good boy. Come with me to Mr. Solly Schwartz. He'll make a man of you." He lighted a twopenny cheroot with a flourish, adding in an awful whisper: "I made him what he is to-day."

Charles Small, curiously purged of anger, went to bed with a secreted orange. But before he had time to peel it he was asleep, and before twenty-four hours had passed he was in the hands of the terrible Solly Schwartz.

*   *   *   *   *

I. Small, although he knew that Solly Schwartz had made his way up in the world, had an idea that he had simply to rap a door

342

with the head of his stick, and Solly would come out, hobbling and clanking with his iron foot. He dressed himself in his best. By this time he had given up cut-away coats, and, reluctantly obedient to the general trend, wore a jacket-suit of blue-grey; but no persuasion could induce him to put off his two-inch single collar with little wings and the necktie with a knot half as big as his fist, riveted with an imitation pearl tiepin not much smaller than a grape. Say what you like about the old man, he knew how to turn himself out like a gentleman. Even at the bench, he frequently wore starched cuffs, and his shoes were immaculate. For the occasion he laid in a couple of Havana cigars at ninepence apiece. A few days before, an impecunious Swiss had come into the shop, offering for sale a contraption about the size of a very large match-box. He pressed a knob, and, with a loud click a lid sprang back and a flame leaped up. I. Small, captivated, bought it for ten shillings. All you had to do was, fill it with benzene, and there you were—in forty years it would save its cost in matches. He put this, also, in a waistcoat pocket. Charles, too, was dressed to kill in a black coat, dark trousers, and a stiff collar. The old man made him wear a bowler hat—a Boiler, he called it —and a red rose in his buttonhole. I. Small, for this occasion, wore kid gloves and cuffs of the first magnitude, and carried the stick Solly Schwartz had given him in the old days. They went to Oxford Circus by bus, but rode the last half-mile in a taxi. The old man had an idea that if he turned up in a taxi it would make a favourable impression.

They stopped at a big building in the front of which hung a great painted sign that said: *SCHWARTZ, LTD.* A doorman held open the outer door of the building while the old man, bothered by his gloves and embarrassed by his walking-stick, overtipped the taxi driver. "Yes, sir?" asked the doorman.

"I want to see Mr. Schwartz, sir," said I. Small.

"Your name, please, sir?"

"I. Small, sir."

"One moment, please," said the doorman.

"Much obliged to you, sir," said I. Small, trying to pick his nose with a gloved finger, complacently leaning on his stick, confident in his belief that he was doing the right thing

The doorman led him to an ante-room, where a tall lady who might have been moulded of gold and ice asked: "Have you an appointment with Mr. Schwartz, Mr. Small?"

"Tell 'im sis Small, sir."

"I'm sorry, Mr. Small, Mr. Schwartz is engaged; he is in a conference."

Conference!—that shook I. Small. So now it was conferences, already! He felt the expectant eyes of his son upon him, and became desperate. He started to say "Bleddy——" but managed to turn it into a brouhaha of coughing. "Say Mr. Small is here," he said.

"Have you an appointment, Mr. Small? I'm afraid——"

"Bled——"

Then there was a stomping, a clanking, and a thudding of the ferrule of a heavy stick, and Solly Schwartz came out in a hurry, dressed for the street in an overcoat by Simpson and London in Grosvenor Street, shoes by Lobb of St. James's, a hat by Lock, a shirt by Sulka, a tie by Budd; with such an air of importance and of elegance that I. Small broke wind so forcibly that he stirred the tails of his coat.

"Shloimele!" cried I. Small.

The hunchback looked up angrily, and then said: "What's that? . . . What, is it you, *trottel?* How are you? Good to see you again."

"Like a weiss!" said I. Small, after they had shaken hands, "always a grip like a weiss. Solly, a minute, please?"

Solly Schwartz said to the lady: "Miss Persimmon, tell Halfacre to wait five minutes." The beautiful lady of ice and gold became slush and tinsel. "Come upstairs, *trottel.* Not much time, but nice to see you again."

It was like something out of a dream. They walked behind Solly Schwartz through an office that ticked and clicked and vibrated with twenty typewriters (the noise grew louder when Solly Schwartz appeared) and were led into a room furnished in morocco leather and luxuriously carpeted. I. Small fumbled for his ninepenny cigars. They came out in small pieces—he had broken them in his emotional convulsion—and fell to the floor in flakes. Schwartz, meanwhile, had opened an elaborate box, which he pushed across the desk. It was full of great fat Corona-Coronas. "Help yourself," he said, "have a cigar, old *trottel*—grab a handful, put 'em in your pocket. God almighty, you're getting fat as a pig!"

"It's the cooking, God bless her," said I. Small. "You don't change, Shloimele . . . Oi! How times change, no? . . . Typewriters—offices—my little Solly!" I. Small was stirred; he had to wipe his eyes.

Solly Schwartz was not unchanged. His face, now, was no longer mobile. It was fixed between the jutting chin and the great hooked nose; the wide mouth was sucked inwards until it was nothing but a dry slit in his sallow face, while his eyes, which had been restlessly busy as black ants, were steady now. His hands, however, were never still; they fidgeted with an ivory paper-knife, ran like spiders to lift and let fall the silver lids of a pair of crystal ink-pots, riffled a Whitaker's Almanack, and measured a ruler inch by inch.

"Well, what d'you want?" he asked.

I. Small saw him reaching for a pen and a cheque-book. "No, no, for God's sake!" he said, "for God's sake, Solly, what do you take me for, what for?"

He was confused; he did not know what to say. But he managed to stammer: "Solly . . . the boy . . . Charley, this one . . . a little something to do, a job . . . steady with prospects, could be?"

Solly Schwartz looked at Charles Small and shrugged his misshapen shoulders. Charles Small will never forget how, looking from the old man to him, the hunchback's expression changed from warm pity to cold contempt. He put down the cheque-book and the pen and said: "All right, I'll give him a job. He's a *nebbisch*—I remember when I took him to the toy shop—I'd rather have his sister. But all right, Srul, I'll give him a job. . . . Come in to-morrow at nine o'clock in the morning—but not in those trousers. Don't come dressed up like a pox-doctor's clerk. Come dressed like a human being. Time enough to get yourself up like a poppy-show. Anything you want, Srul?"

"Solly, I'm more than grateful," said the old man, using his handkerchief.

"Small," said Solly Schwartz to Charles, "nine o'clock to-morrow morning. No flowers in your buttonhole." Then he scooped up the contents of the cigar box in one of his disproportionately large hands, stuffed twenty Corona-Coronas into I. Small's pocket, and genially beat him towards the door, slapping him on the back as one slaps a cherished old dog.

In the street the old man lit a cigar. He could not bring himself to throw away a wide red-and-gold band; let people see that he was smoking a Corona-Corona! He was happy. "What did I told

345

you, Charley?" he said. "D'you see? You're a made man. You
heard what Mr. Schwartz said? Nine to-morrow morning, and
no flowers in no bleddy buttonholes. Now, what about a
smoked selmon sandwich and a cup coffee?" He remembered
one of Lizzard's expressions when, at noon, the old cobbler went
out for bread-and-cheese and beer. It was always on the first
stroke of twelve—Lizzard would leave a nail half driven, because
he knew his Rights: "An army marches on its bleddy stomach."

They went to Appenrodt's and ate ham and potato salad, and
drank lager beer. "Smoked selmon," said the old man signifi-
cantly. The bill paid, they hurried home to break the good news.
Poor I. Small knew that the boy was unhappy. On the way out
he put an arm about Charles's shoulders and said: "Sis Life,
Charley. You got to make your living. Cheer up. Make a living.
Sis Life."

Charles Small looked like Hamlet in the graveyard scene, but
he remembers that he was not as unhappy as he looked, because
there was something about Solly Schwartz that excited him.

* * * * *

Solly Schwartz's nervous energy wore everyone else's nerves to
shreds and tatters. He was the Schwartz Advertising Company;
he was—the irony of ironies!—Schwartz for Beauty. Now,
bursting with money and bloated with credit, universally acclaimed
and deferred to as a sound young prodigy, he was throwing himself into the fulfilment of an old desire. There was a little itch
in him which he was determined to scratch out, if he tore himself
to pieces in the process—the memory of Monopol, who, by this
time, had shops all over London, selling high-class gentlemen's
clothing at 45 shillings a suit, and not a bad suit of clothes at
that. He was out to compete with Monopol, to put him out of
business, to smash Monopol into jelly, and melt him, and pour
him into the gutter. At the same time, he wanted—that the
Prophecy might be fulfilled—to do something for old Cohen,
and for the other old man (he had already forgotten his name)
who had been kind to him in the sweat-shop; but they were
certainly dead. Old Monopol was alive, and Solly Schwartz was
resolved to break him and have the last laugh.

He went about the business feverishly. He was in and out
of earnest conferences with dry-cleaned American salesmen of
ingenious machinery, and with estate agents from the thirty-two

points of the compass, and with Abel Abelard, who was now earning thirty pounds a week, and, his mighty canvas abandoned, his cheerful mistress dismissed, and his belly somewhat round, was respectably married, and head of Schwartz's Art Department. Wool salesmen came with samples from Yorkshire. Urgently-pushing cotton salesmen from Lancashire barged in, rubbing elbows with designers of Gents' Styles, and builders and decorators waving estimates concerning fascias, counters, windows, fitting-rooms, show-cases. The office seethed, bubbled, and sputtered like a pan of fish—a pan of small-fry in deep boiling oil. Staff came and went. Solly Schwartz, that devourer of little fried fishes, scooped out the cooked ones, chucked in the fresh ones, and scoured the markets for more. He was going to crush Monopol. The time had come. The time having come, Schwartz would not waste one second of it.

In spite of himself, Charles Small was fascinated. He was, in the Schwartz organisation, a sort of office-boy—he rushed from department to department, carrying papers. One day—it was at Easter—eating a hot-cross bun and drinking a cup of tea in an Express Dairy near the office during a fifteen-minute interval at four o'clock, it occurred to him that in the past week he must have made the journey from the Counting House to the Head Office several hundred times. That was why his legs ached. Nevertheless, he was exhilarated, because these mad oscillations seemed to be waggling to a certain point. He felt like a needle in an electrometer.

Then, dreamily drinking the dregs of his tea, he had his first great idea. It was an inspiration. He swallowed, with difficulty, his last mouthful of bun, and ran back to the office. Ibbertson, who was now Office Manager—stern and sedate—gave him some papers, saying: "Small, take these to Mr. Schwartz's office, at the double."

Charles Small desired nothing better. He walked—oh, his beating heart!—right into Solly Schwartz's presence, put the papers on the great desk, and waited, scratching his ear.

"What d'you want?" asked Solly Schwartz.

Charles Small dug into his tiny reservoir of courage, and managed to say: "I have an idea, sir."

"An idea? What, *you?*"

"Yes sir."

"Spit it out, and look sharp about it."

Mysteriously confident, bold with inspiration, Charles Small said: "I was thinking, Mr. Schwartz——"

"Think quick or get about your business."

"Yes sir. I was thinking: I run up and down from the Counting House to here a hundred times a day."

"That's what you're paid for. Well?"

"You see, Mr. Schwartz, it gave me a sort of idea."

"Out with it."

"It's about these new shops you're starting," said Charles Small. Now, the idea was carrying him away; his face glowed. "An advertising idea, Mr. Schwartz."

"Oh, yes?"

Charles Small continued: "You see, sir, I bring papers from the Counting House to you ever so many times a day, and it makes my legs ache, you see? Well, say instead of a paper it was a pound-note. Just say, Mr. Schwartz, that I had a thousand pound-notes to bring you, one at a time, in such-and-such a time . . . a sort of race, you see, and the winner gets the thousand pounds. You see? Isn't that a good idea for advertising?"

Solly Schwartz blinked, smiled, thought a while, and said: "Not bad. Get to work now. I'll talk to you later."

Before the office closed, the hunchback sent for Charles Small and said: "Charley, that was not a bad idea of yours, about the race for the pound notes. But I've got a better one. All the same, you gave me the idea, and I give you credit for it. Here's twenty-five pounds for you. To-morrow morning report to Mr. Tillip on the Advertising side. Start there again, at two-pounds-ten a week. All right, go. Give my regards to the *trottel*, your old man. Think of a few more ideas like that, and you won't go hungry."

Charles Small strutted, intolerably jubilant. When he brought home the twenty-five pounds and the good news, the old man cried: "My boychik!" and kissed him on the cheek. Before he had time to rub the kiss away, his mother burst into tears and kissed him on the other cheek. One of her tears ran into his mouth. He had licked away many of his own tears in his time, but this tear, on top of his emotion, tasted so horrible that he felt sick at the stomach and almost vomited. He went to the lavatory and spat several times into the pan, and gargled with a disinfectant solution. Even then his stomach was delicate, and easily upset by maternal tears. It was bad enough to look at this eye-water, let alone drink the filthy stuff.

But while, on the following day, Millie Small rushed from member to member of the family bragging of her son's promotion, Solly Schwartz went intently to work. Charles's was a good idea but, as he had said, Solly Schwartz had an idea worth two of that—an idea at once audacious, revolutionary, and dead safe. The Main Branch of his clothing enterprise was about to open in the Strand—a large shop, vividly decorated with a thirty-foot plate-glass window. Solly Schwartz put all of Abelard's available staff on to the job of drafting an advertisement that was destined to shake the country, and, when it was drafted to his satisfaction, he spent thousands of pounds buying space in the newspapers. His idea was intrepid, cruel, and irresistible. It was as follows:

Before the opening of the Strand Branch, the great window was to be a transparent screen between the public and an extraordinary spectacle—perhaps the most breath-taking contest the world had ever seen, free of charge. At one end of the shop window he placed an immense trough, specially constructed, into which bank-messengers poured 1,000,000 silver sixpences— £25,000. At the other end he put a similar trough, empty. The terms, or rules, of the competition he devised were simple. If any man, of any age, transferred the contents of the full trough to the empty one, seven paces away, carrying one sixpence at a time, in seven days—that man should carry away the £25,000 unconditionally, and be rich for life.

The country went mad. It was like an outbreak of war. From north, south, east and west, athletes entrained for London. They all believed that they could do it. Statisticians, mathematicians, physicists, and doctors wrote to the Press proving, unquestionably, that it was absurd, impossible. A man would have to walk 112,000,000 paces in a week. This could not be. It was crazy. But the prospect of £25,000 to be got simply by picking the money up and carrying it drove everyone crazy. Besides, as Solly Schwartz shrewdly guessed, very few people appreciated the magnitude of a million: it was an abstract term; it meant nothing.

Thus he launched the publicity drive that started the remarkable upheavals in the Strand. Crowds blocked the road in front of Schwartz's window, while a famous athlete named Walker, the Walker, of Yorkshire—a long, wiry man whose legs were so long that they seemed to be a little tight under the arms—paced back and forth, seemingly inexhaustible. Hundreds of pounds

349

changed hands in bets. He lasted four days, nine hours, fifteen minutes, and forty-five seconds. Then he dropped like a pole-axed ox, still clutching a thin sixpence, which was gently taken from between his fingers and put back into the trough. It began to occur to some of the punters that a million was the devil of a lot. The newspapers were full of the affair, so that Schwartz Suits got at least £50,000 worth of publicity—free of charge, photographs included. A lithe matron, who had twice won the pram-race from London to Brighton, was the next to attempt the impossible. She lasted five days, one hour, and one minute, ending in raging hysterics. *One More Week To Go!* Mounted police were called out to disperse the mob. Solly Schwartz was in luck: the next contestant, a professional footballer, fell dead on the second day, and the newspapers brimmed over with the subject. Clergymen protested. The statisticians reiterated their protests. Old ladies tried to picket the Schwartz shop, carrying banners. Nobody won the £25,000, because no human being could. Then Solly Schwartz made a great show of presenting two hundred pounds in sixpences to each of the disconsolate contestants—the footballer's widow drew the money and was gypped out of it in due course by a Cockney gigolo named Hix.

Then the shop opened. The crowds were reluctant to clear off. They loitered about for weeks, watching the window, expecting something to happen. Rumour had it that the wax dummies were not dummies at all, but walkers asleep in their tracks. Idiots came from beyond the Border, just to look. They came to look, and they stayed to buy. Schwartz did a roaring trade in the Strand Branch. And then he went after Monopol with a vengeance. Money was no object. Wherever there was a Monopol shop, a Schwartz shop opened a few doors away, cutting prices, giving away free shirts, socks, shoes, hats, and loud ties for bonuses; selling at cost price and even under cost. Monopol's tried to fight, but the hunchback was on their neck like a wildcat. Before eighteen months passed, Monopol's went into voluntary liquidation. When the news of this broke, Charles Small hoped to see Solly Schwartz dancing with glee. Instead, he saw him biting his lips and growling over the ruin of an ebony cigar-box which he had smashed with his fists in an outburst of anger.

Old Monopol had dropped dead two days before. Schwartz had merely ruined his widow.

"The little I ask of life!" cried Solly Schwartz.

CHAPTER XXVI

Honour thy father and thy mother, says the Commandment, *that thy days may be long in the land*, etcetera, etcetera . . . "Tripe! Bilge! Crap! Eyewash!" Charles Small cries aloud, remembering things. Honour thy father and thy mother, forsooth! All right, honour them. But have they no obligation to conduct themselves so that they are honourably worthy of honour? Does a little respectable, shame-faced, half-disgusted fumbling in the marriage bed, and the forced feedings and washings and dressings and beatings of the protesting wretches they have brought into the world—does this entitle them to Honour? Oh, that he had been born a beast in the wilds, a lion cub, protected until he was weaned, and then free to hunt and to mate for himself!

The lion analogy pleases him. He can imagine the old man as a kind of *nebbisch* among lions, roaring to wake the dead, shaking his mane, baring terrible teeth, bounding out purposefully—and coming home to the den with a mouse, while the lioness (more dangerous than the male) snarled and snapped and clawed at him, saying that if only she didn't have a pain in her Inside, she would show him what was what, and demanding: "Do you call yourself a lion?"—while the cubs mewed, and were consequently knocked about and roared at until they became sullenly and secretively silent. It is an engaging thought . . . Srul the lion, making a thunderous noise like *Grrbleddyargh!* goes out again with an injured air, and is lucky enough to find the remains of an eland which a bolder lion has killed. His whiskers bristling, he roars so that the hyenas, the jackals, and the vultures slink and flap away. Then he swaggers back to the cave with a gnawed haunch and some guts; throws them down, says *Gneeargh!*—and purrs. A good provider. The cubs, of course, grow up, and want to leave the cave. Then the whole veldt resounds to the uproar. The old lion, worn out by catching mice and—when he has had a good day—rabbits, complains of feebleness. The old lioness has a Pain. Did she not drop them when they were pups? Was she not therefore entitled to Respect? So the little tyrannised lions stay close to the cave. They dream of mighty night attacks upon the great beasts—the ponderous eland, the mighty buffalo, the blesbok. But no, it is too *brghleddy* dangerous. The male cub goes out and kills a tiny klipspringer, and dutifully brings it home. His mother licks him all over! He is working his way up. Maybe one day, when he is a full-grown lion, he will bring home a springbok. Meanwhile she whines: four of her tits, the tits from which he sucked life, are sore . . . and somewhere near her tail she has a nagging pain. The old lion, replete, makes reminiscence, lying horribly about the time when he drove seven vultures away from the half-eaten carcass of a badger, and pulled down a six-month-old buck with a broken leg. . . . He thunders dramatically of bad old times when they lived on grasshoppers, and shows the scars of the wounds he got when he sat down on a porcupine, and repeats what he said to the porcupine, which was so terrified that it curled itself into a ball, and serve it bleddy-well right. . . .

No, no, no! It is funny, but it flies in the face of Nature. The fledgelings must leave the nest, the cubs must leave the den and the lair. The merest kitten must become an independent individual, fending for itself, as soon as it has got the taste of maternal milk out of its mouth and feels its claws. Charles Small has a respect for dogs and cats. With them it is: "I bore you because I wanted to; I fed and protected you because that was the least I could do; you are old enough to look after yourself—get the hell out, for I am no longer interested in you." —and: "That suits me, Mama. I sucked your milk. That's what it was for. What else would you have done with it? Had it framed? You don't need me to relieve you of your milk (incidentally, I have come to prefer fish) and so, *prrooey* and *tchah* to you! Before departing for the ringing battlefields on the tiles, where tomcat fights tom-cat for the warm embraces of the slim tabbies of the back alleys until the fur flies, and the garbage cans offer me their open mouths—I spit at you."

Now Priscilla, she was the cat that walked by herself. Like a cat, she was self-sufficient, and almost indestructible. When angry, she went straight for the eyes, just like a cat, in attack; but in defence she was quick and yielding—a galvanised mass of lithe muscle, bristling with sharp claws, became, suddenly, a cuddly ball of fur, gently purring, rubbing itself against you, licking your hands, not out of affection but because the cat needed salt. You could not keep Priscilla where she did not choose to stay: bolts and bars could not hold her then. Some mysterious instinct guided her, wherever she was, to where she wanted to go—the most comfortable place available. She was patient and impenetrable, sensuous and selfish, quick and lazy, hypersensitive yet insensitive. There was a fold of loose skin behind her head by which one might pick her up without hurting her, and she could in a split second turn the velvet of a little paw into something like a handful of fish-hooks. If she fell out of a third-storey window she would have landed on her feet. Man had been created to serve her. As a cat watches and catches a mouse, so was Priscilla with a man: your sleek cat has no desire to eat the mouse—she torments it and kills it for sport, letting it think it has escaped, hooking it back with one quick paw, destroying it at last out of boredom, leaving the limp body, stretching herself and going back to the saucer of fish—fish excellently prepared by Millie Small—salmon, soles, and plaice, and herrings ("lives of men", as they used to call them) hauled in by the North Sea drifters, and highly palatable in the form of kippers.

Priscilla loved food. She would eat anything, with anyone, anywhere. Charles Small remembers an occasion when, commissioned by his mother to buy a pound of butter beans, some dried peas, four pickled cucumbers, and two salt herrings from a grocer called Ashkenazi, young Priscilla so vamped and captivated the shopkeeper that he gave her the run of the place. She ate broad beans and butter beans raw, unwashed salt anchovies out of the barrel, a roll, a fruit pie, seven pickled onions, a piece of cheese-cake, a bar of chocolate, and Heaven knows what besides—enough to feed two full-grown men, and give them indigestion into the bargain. Then she went home, and, half an hour later, sat down to dinner, complaining that she was starving. Yet she remained slender—which worried Millie, as everything else worried Millie. Priscilla was outgrowing her strength, not eating enough, eating too much. A crony suggested that she might have Worms, so Priscilla was wormed; they fed her some kind of rending and blasting medicine disguised as a confection, which she ate with relish. There were no worms: only the usual thing. Priscilla's lungs were examined, because she had a good complexion. The doctor said that he would give five years of his life for such a pair of lungs. There was not enough the matter with the girl; that was the trouble. It was a cause for worry. All children must be ill. When Charles had

353

measles the uninfected Priscilla was put into bed with him so that she might catch measles at the same time, and two birds killed with one stone, this being one of the ideas Millie had picked up from her cronies; it being believed that a child may have measles only once. Charles came out in spots until he looked like a strawberry; Priscilla remained uninfected. It was the same with whooping-cough and chicken-pox and mumps. Charles caught them all: Priscilla caught nothing; only she devoured most of the dainties at the sickbed. Her failure to contract infantile diseases was a source of great anxiety to her parents.

At last Millie Small said: "Thank goodness she doesn't take after me. She's unnatural."

At this, I. Small went up in the air. He swelled, he inflated like a balloon, and became red as a sunset. He shouted so loud that (it may have been a coincidence) all the electric lights went out in the house; and since the old man could not touch even an insulated wire without collapsing in a shower of bleddies in a blinding flash, the Company had to be called to put in two inches of fuse-wire. For the rest of the evening I. Small talked in a whisper, not audible beyond fifteen yards. "Who *then* does she take after? Bleddy-well knock it out of her!" he hissed

Millie consulted her sisters. Nathan, the Photographer, shook his head. Even he could not talk the child into having measles. Priscilla was quietly obstinate, the cat! Her parents didn't know what to do with her. There was, in fact, nothing to be done. Millie Small, moaning with a real or imaginary pain and rocking herself to and fro, might say: "You'll be sorry when I'm gone!" Priscilla would reply in a tone of polite interest: "Will I? Why?"

One day she referred to her mother as "she". Priscilla meant no disrespect; she did not care one way or another. I. Small, that formidable figure of a man, plastered with cobblers' wax, with a bit of bootlace hanging on his moustache as if he had been eating the stuff, rushed into the sitting-room and, whispering like a foghorn with laryngitis, asked: "Prissie, where is your Mummy?"

"Oh, her? She's asleep," said Priscilla.

Now in the society in which Millie Small moved, one never referred to a respectable female as "she"; only as Mother or Auntie. "She" and "her" were disrespectful, even opprobrious. I. Small let off steam like a farting rhinoceros. The poor old man was worried, because Millie was really sick, and in pain. He cried "Her, *her*? She, *she*? Her own bleddy mother she calls *She!*"

He picked up a pair of heavy fire-tongs of massive brass, and shouted: "Eat them words! Say 'Mummy' or over goes this shovel on the wrong side of your bleddy head!"

"It isn't a shovel, it's tongs," said Priscilla.

Disconcerted, as usual, I. Small bellowed: "Then bleddy-well be quiet, let your Mummy rest!"—and put the tongs back in the fireplace, knocking over about fifty pounds' weight of sounding brass. Then, putting a finger to his lips, he said: "*Sha!*" and, tiptoeing back to the workshop, fell downstairs with a crash and a howl that froze the blood in the veins of everyone who heard it —of everyone but Priscilla. She danced on the landing, shamelessly kicking empty air, showing her legs, and laughing at the top of her voice.

The old man slunk away. He was afraid of that girl. Over everyone else, too, she exercised a sort of fascination. She was nonchalant, she was fearless, she did not give a good God damn whether you lived or died. When, after old Mr. Moss, her grandfather, breathed his last, her aged grandmother cried: "Take me with him, take me with!" Priscilla smiled.

And she was beautiful. Even when she was very young, men liked to cuddle her. Even Nathan, the Photographer, dandled her on his knee and bought her boxes of chocolates costing half a crown. She was not so popular with women. Lily summed up the reason why:

"She gets her own way."

Yes, thinks Charles Small, swallowing bitter green bile and feeling as if Gene Krupa is beating a masterly trap-drum roll on his tight-stretched diaphragm and shaking a maraca where his heart ought to be and clashing dazzling, shuddering brass cymbals behind his eyes while he thumps the big drum at the back of his head with an impatient, insistent foot—yes, Priscilla got her own way. How and why? Simply: she had a calm, dispassionate, amoral disregard for everyone but herself, and everything but her own convenience. A cat, a nihilistic cat; warm on the outside, cold on the inside . . . a prize cat, a dangerous cat. She would go, unerringly, wherever the carpet was softest and the cream was thickest. Stroke her, and she rewarded you with a purr. Aim a blow at her, and you slapped empty air. Corner her, and she ran up a wall to sit, impregnable and immaculate, delicately licking herself clean, sixty feet out of reach, serene and triumphant in the leaden gutter at the edge of the roof. You loved and cherished her because she was so beautiful. But to her, you (poor fool) were just like anyone else, a provider of the creature comforts—fish and milk—caviare and cream—fun and games. Threats could not move her, tears could not melt her. She was a law unto herself; exasperating in her imperturbability, appealing in her superficial warmth, maddening in her capacity to withdraw strategically and unemotionally into herself. You feared to lose her, because she was so pretty; but she knew that, whoever lost her, some other infatuated cat-lover would find her . . . and there would always be milk, fish, a warm fire, caresses, and a soft bed.

No doubt about it: to Priscilla, the strange, tortuous gorges and caverns of this weary world were so many mouse-holes out of which, under the cover of the dark, timorous little scuttling grey creatures emerged for her amusement, if not her nourishment.

Good luck to her, thinks Charles Small.

*   *   *   *   *

Swollen-headed as he was, on account of his promotion and subsequent rapid and lucky rise in the House of Schwartz, Charles Small could not get the Theatre out of his system. He joined the local Dramatic Society, of which he became a leading light. He always played the leads. He made a smash hit as Macbeth—brought the house down in laughter—because his beard fell off at a critical moment. As Othello (he squirms at the recollection) he threw himself into such a sweat over the death scene that his make-up ran, and he looked like a zebra; whereupon, flustered, he really smote himself in the midriff with the dummy dagger and had a fit of coughing. As Romeo he fell down the ladder and sprained his ankle, but courageously went up again, hopping—the show had to go on. The Dramatic Society put on *King Lear*, and Charles was in his glory, and everything would have been perfect if a rival amateur, who wanted to play Lear but was relegated to the part of Edgar, had not played a dirty trick on him. Edgar's rôle is by no means to be sneezed at, said Charles, patronisingly. Still Edgar (his name was Moggs) wanted to be the King. "Sneezed at" gave him an idea. He went to one of those novelty shops where they sell stink-bombs, little farting concertinas to put under cushions, itching powder, etcetera, and bought a sixpenny packet of an irritant dust called *Sneezo*. A

356

little of this powder, blown through a keyhole, was guaranteed to set the whole company sneezing and weeping—presumably to the amusement and instruction of all bystanders. So, just when Charles was getting his stride as the demented monarch on the blasted heath, Moggs let loose a shower of the stuff, and Charles Small convulsed his audience by shouting:

> ". . . *Die for ATISHOO? She shall not RASH-HO . . .*
> *The ASHOO goes ATISHOO . . .*
> *And the little gilded fly does ISHAH in my ATISHOO*
> *Let AHOOSH-HO thrive, for I lack ATISHOO . . .*"

—and had to blow his nose into his white beard.

He was so outraged on that occasion that he challenged Moggs to a fight; but when Moggs said: "All right, come on then," he backed out. But he was always addicted to false beards, false man that he was. In *The Tempest* he insisted on the part of Prospero, mainly because the Magician had to wear a beard eighteen inches llong.

Here, Priscilla came in. She had insinuated herself into the good graces of everyone in the Dramatic Society and, when she asked if she could have a go at Ariel, she was received with enthusiasm by everyone but Charles Small. He knew in his heart that she would steal the show. And so she did. When she sang the song that ends:

> ". . . *Merrily, merrily shall I live now*
> *Under the blossom that hangs on the bough . . .*"

her voice was so silvery, and she had such an air of having put on the incorruptible, and drifted so like gossamer, that there was a burst of applause. And when Charles, stroking his beard in the region of his navel, said:

> ". . . *Why, that's my dainty Ariel! I shall miss thee;*
> *But yet thou shalt have freedom: so, so, so . . .*"

he sounded just like the old man. All he needed was the *Jewish Chronicle*, rolled-up, to swat this fairy. When he called her his "*tricky spirit*", he made a noise like I. Small after a bad bargain: he nearly called her a bleddy tricky spirit. And when he said:

357

"*Now my charms are all o'erthrown,*" he meant it. It was the only decent line he delivered in the play. Moggs played Caliban, walking on all fours and dressed in coconut matting. An aged man (he was not a day under thirty) played the drunken Stephano. He was, in fact, blind drunk, and was loudly applauded. His name was Gooch, and he was the stage-struck son of a notoriously wealthy ironmonger of the district. He had a car, a Renault; a pocketful of pound-notes, and a dissipated air: Priscilla took to him like a duck to water. And water he was. She paddled delicately upon the rippling surface of him, dived to the depths of him to spoon up his basic content, and left him disconsolate and disturbed with nothing but the memory of a waggling wet tail that sprinkled him with rejected drops of himself, making more ripples—ripples that did not soon leave the surface of him.

Charles Small remembers that it was Priscilla, the little bitch (would to God he had had only a few feet of her guts!), who brought Ivy Narwall into his miserably frustrated life.

Here, again, was where Solly Schwartz came in. Love and admiration aside, how deeply Charles Small wishes that the hunchback had never been born! For Solly Schwartz smashed Narwall, who came to London with his family. His wife could not face the sneers of Slupworth—the sneers of the people she despised, who had good cause to hate her. She went south with her head high, giving the porter sixpence for carrying six heavy trunks. The Narwalls travelled first class—she took it out of the housekeeping later on—and established themselves in London. They were still well-to-do, but they were now mere retailers; they manufactured nothing. They held no tradesmen by the short hair. Public demand compelled them, indeed, to lay in considerable stocks of American canned products through Schwartz, who had the agency. Mrs. Narwall had nothing to do, no one to intrigue against, only Ivy to dominate, because the elder daughter, Sybil, got married.

And there again, *God have mercy on the old cow*, there again was dust and ashes! Sybil took after her mother. She had a hard head and a hard face. She had been engaged to be married to a decent young fellow from the Midlands, an engineer with prospects. His name was Dunkerton. One day Dunkerton got his left leg caught in some machinery. They stopped the machine when the teeth of the cogs had chewed him up to the thigh, so that his leg had to come off, and he was a sad-looking creature with his skinny white face and his crutches. Sybil, beautiful and proud, told Dunkerton that she could never marry a cripple. (In Slupworth, old jokes were resuscitated; e.g., *She heard he had a wooden leg and so she broke it off.*) Then Sybil married a motor-car salesman who turned out to be a rotter, and led her the devil of a life. His name was Glass; he gave her a black eye; but she stayed by him, out of vanity rather than affection, until he took her to South Africa with their child, who, curiously enough, had one leg shorter than the other, or longer than the other.

Old Narwall ran about from shop to shop, making everyone's life a burden. Lumpitt was so delighted at Narwall's discomfiture that he got drunk, and was sacked. He called on Solly Schwartz in a contrite mood and asked for a job, and was given a five-pound note and told to go and take a flying leap at himself and never to show his face again. Mrs. Narwall, having nothing else to do, took to drink. She decanted her gin into medicine bottles and took it out of a tablespoon. Old Narwall, although he sometimes raised his eyebrows at the grocery bills, had not the courage to protest. He took it out on Ivy. So did the old woman. Between them, they bewildered and bedevilled the girl until, one night, she swallowed five aspirin tablets, hoping that she might die. She had heard that aspirin was bad for the heart. It didn't work—in fact she felt somewhat better afterwards.

Mrs. Narwall and her husband took to following each other up and down the house, spying, peeping, turning off the gas, counting match-sticks and sheets of toilet-paper Mrs. Narwall was mad with pride—she dressed opulently always—and Narwall was mad with fear, fear of poverty. Both of them were eaten up with avarice, although, at that time, they must have been making more than three thousand pounds a year—which was a great deal of money in those days.

One day old Narwall said to Ivy: "Ivy, there is no room in this world for idle hands. You must go to Harrison's Business College, and learn short-hand and typewriting. You must put your nose to the grindstone."

"Yes, Father," said Ivy.

A week later I. Small suggested—poor fool—that Priscilla ought to go into the millinery business; he had a customer who was a milliner. Then it was Millie Small's turn to speak, and by Christ she spoke! . . . Oh, so that's what he was, was it? Milliners, already! He was only waiting for her to die, so that

359

he could fiddle about with milliners. It was quite all right. As long as she knew. Milliners! But while she lived, the girl should be a florist. What were milliners? Nothing!

In the end there was a conference with Nathan, the Photographer. He, putting fingertip to fingertip, said: "Millinery is millinery."

No one denied this.

He continued: "What is millinery? Hats. There are milliners in Paris who make hats for eight, ten pounds a time. But is this Paris? No. You've got to be a person of . . . of reputation to make money out of millinery. You must have talent. You must have . . . *khine*—taste!"

I. Small said: "Milliner, schmilliner—you see, Millie?"

Nathan, the Photographer, continued: "Then again, florists . . ."

". . . Schmorists," said I. Small.

"Florists. Now the florists' business is, is—precarious. How long does a flower last? I ask you. Ask yourself."

"Like a bleddy firework," said I. Small.

"Exactly," said Nathan, the Photographer. "Flowers, they come up, they pass away. It takes push, it takes drive, above all it takes capital to be a florist. You buy tulips. Tulips, all right. So-much a dozen to-day. To-morrow? Where are your tulips? Or say roses. A bud to-day and gone to-morrow. So much money down the drain. Let her learn short-hand—that'll do her more good."

I. Small nodded. Priscilla said: "I'm going to be a dancer."

"Bleddy-well short-hand," said I. Small.

So Priscilla went to Harrison's Business College, saying over her shoulder: "All the same, I'm going to be a dancer."

As a pupil she did not amount to much, but at Harrison's she met Ivy Narwall, who adored her, and whom she dragged to the Dramatic Society, where Charles Small fell in love with her.

*   *   *   *   *

Pondering these matters, Charles Small, whose empty stomach is trying to digest itself, undergoes such convulsions of disgust at the sour taste of himself that he vomits into the chamber-pot; but out of his empty self nothing emerges but pale green foam. He can't even vomit properly—even in this he is frustrated, poor sod. It is not merely the memory of his disgraceful behaviour at the railway station, when he ran away and left Ivy at the mercy of her terrible mother. There are other things with which he must reproach himself; other cowardices, unforgivable weaknesses galore.

He remembers, with agony, what Ivy told him when they met again many years later. Mrs. Narwall had dragged her home ignominiously through the smoky streets, so impatient to get her hands on the girl that she actually spent sixpence for tram-fare instead of walking to her suburb as she would normally have done. Having pushed Ivy into her bedroom and shut the door, she threw her face-down on the bed, pulled down her drawers (durable, respectable blue serge drawers with a detachable cotton lining) and beat her on the bottom with a heavy clothes brush until her arm was tired. And Mrs. Narwall had an arm like a stevedore, a good fourteen inches round the biceps. Having got her breath, she let loose a torrent of vituperation such as Ivy had never heard before. Probably Mrs. Narwall had picked it up from her grandfather, a drunken tackler, a murderous brute from whom she had inherited her mighty arms. Slut, street-walker, fly-by-night, common prostitute, whore, and Jezebel were among the milder of her epithets. Then, her arm being rested, she went to work again with the clothes brush, until Ivy's tender bottom was purple with bruises, and bleeding in two places. Even then she would not have desisted, only the girl's shrieks grew so loud and vibrated with such pain that neighbours called a policeman. Ivy fainted. Mrs. Narwall locked her in her room, where she was incarcerated for a week. She was beaten every day, she told Charles, with the clothes brush, a hair brush, and a cane, and fed on bread and water, until even Mr. Narwall was moved to say: "For goodness' sake, woman, enough!"

Then Ivy tossed for a week in a high fever, so that a doctor had to be called in—another five shillings down the drain. He was a drunken old failure with a frayed collar, dirty cuffs and grubby hands, reeking of whisky and shag tobacco. He prescribed what he called a Cooling Medicine. Then—this was worst of all—Mrs. Narwall made him examine Ivy to ascertain that she was still a virgin. She was, of course: Charles Small, that milky little man, was far too timorous for that kind of thing. When Ivy was healed and, red-eyed with weeping, began to creep about the house again, her spirit—such as it was—forever broken, Mrs. Narwall said: "Let that be a lesson to you, you bad girl! Running off like a prostitute with a dirty Jew!" She could not forget Solly Schwartz, who had been the ruin of the Narwalls in Slupworth. "A nasty little Jew-boy. Thank your lucky stars, my girl, that you've a mother that knows what's good for you. He jewed you all right—ran like a rabbit and left you standing. Now, my girl, you'll do as you're bid. You shall marry Jack Squire."

"Yes, Mother," said Ivy.

"And until you do, you don't set foot out of this house if I have to kill you, you little prostitute, and thank your lucky stars for your mother who takes care of you, because if it wasn't for her you'd be ruined by now. Say 'Thank you, Mother.' "

"Thank you, Mother," said Ivy.

"You'll marry Jack Squire then."

Ivy fished up one last chewed-out fibre of courage, and, bursting into tears, said: "But please, please, Mother—I don't like him!"

"You will marry Jack Squire, my girl, if I have to kill you first. I'll make a respectable woman of you, whether you like it or lump it. There!" She picked up a rolling-pin.

Ivy cringed and said: "Yes, Mother, yes, I'll marry Jack Squire; I'll do anything you tell me to do, only please don't beat me any more because I can't bear it."

"Right!" said Mrs. Narwall, and went back to her task of rolling pastry. She was making a steak-and-kidney pie, with precious little steak in it.

This Jack Squire was *persona grata* with the Narwall family. Ivy loathed him; he set her teeth on edge. She did not like the way he looked at her; she shuddered at the lustfulness of his eyes and the looseness of his constantly-licked lips that belied the unctuous piety of his conversation. He was well known and highly respected among the Congregationalists; dressed in black; was inclined, at forty, to a certain rotundity, a chubbiness which Ivy found revolting. He made an excellent living as agent for a great Lancashire cotton manufacturer and, having worked his way up from the position of junior salesman, had acquired a habit of jocularity—very proper jocularity—what he called "rational enjoyment". He neither drank nor smoked. He contended that if God had intended him to smoke He would have put a chimney-pot on top of his head. This was his idea of a joke. There was that about him which made Ivy's blood run cold. Whenever he came to the house he shook hands with her, and his hand-clasp lingered—it seemed to last for hours—it was like taking hold of a squid. He lost no opportunity of brushing against her or touching her, for he was, as the saying goes, "sweet" on her. Ivy told Charles, when they met again, that the very sight of him made her physically sick. But her detestation of Jack Squire, deep-rooted as it was, was not so powerful as her deadly, ineradicable fear of her mother and her father. So, pliable little thing that she was, she married Jack Squire. She cried at the wedding, thinking (the irony of it!) of the lean, lively, passionate Romeo that was Charles Small; of the noble Othello that was Charles Small; of the powerful and sinister Macbeth that was Charles Small. On her wedding night she locked herself in a cupboard, but had to come out for lack of air. Jack Squire was waiting. . . .

The memory of all this is about as much as Charles can bear. His mind grows confused. Suddenly he finds himself laughing quietly and singing:

> "*. . . A boy's best friend is his mother.*
> *Then cherish her with care*
> *And smooth her silvery hair;*
> *When gone you will never get another,*
> *And wherever we may turn*
> *A lesson we will learn:*
> *A boy's best friend is his mother . . ."*

At this he laughs outright. It is too damned funny for words. A boy's worst enemy is his mother. First of all, impelled by an uncontrollable compulsion to couple with her ally, his father, she squeezes him out into the world, and, blast her, makes a virtue of necessity. It is possible to forgive a woman for having borne you, but not for having ruined you. *Best Friend, my arse*, thinks Charles Small; *My worst enemies should have such Best Friends!* The child is the victim of its begetters, trained with blows, bamboozled with threats, cajoled with promises, bitched and bewildered with lies, poisoned with pity. Oh, parents, parents, parents—how he hates them, fools that they are, saboteurs! That which they produce, they smash, the wreckers! . . . *In this head,* he thinks, *were all the glories that were Greece, the grandeurs that were Rome, the nobility that was England, and all the capacity to marvel, to dream, and to act that drove fine men to charm magic casements opening upon the foam of perilous seas. . . .* It is

363

madness, nothing but madness, this craze of Man to make Man in his own image—this God-intoxication—this desire of hairy babies to coax, gouge, and pound flesh and blood into fanciful shapes as a child plays with plasticine! Mothers and Fathers be buggered! Oh, filthy, mother-dominated Earth! A Boy's Best Friend is His Mother, indeed. Having had the boy dragged out of her belly, with loud outcries and a hell of a to-do, she devotes the rest of her life to a campaign calculated to stuff him back into stifling darkness . . . Mothers! What is a mother? Millie Small. And what is a father? The old man. And what is he, Charles Small? Their droppings, involuntarily egested like dung.

Now, again, Charles Small questions himself. Who is he, silly little man, to make recrimination? Solly Schwartz, born twisted, crooked, and deformed, found his own strength and made his own life. Schwartz's parents were sick at the sight of him, and got rid of him as soon as possible, and that, perhaps, was the making of Solly Schwartz . . . Or was it? Charles Small cannot make up his mind. He is angry and confused. Was every repulsively deformed hunchback ironfoot, kicked out into the street or left on the steps of a Foundling Hospital, a Solly Schwartz? No. Why not?

This brings him back to contemplation of the immortal soul, the unconquerable soul, the soul a man carries with him from God—the Pure, the Intangible, the Incorruptible, that makes a man a man, and takes him out of that stinking, blood-and-watery darkness into the daylight and up to the stars.

Yes, just as there are bodies and bodies, so there are souls and souls. An object of derision, cruelly abused, out on the streets, utterly alone in the world, Solly Schwartz might have been selling matches, whining on a street corner. Instead, he was a master of men and of money . . . Priscilla, who had been born in the same bed as Charles, was as calm and unconquerable as her brother was tremulous and abject. She was brass. He was mud. How come? They had both come out of the same uncertain loins and the same frightened womb. . . . It occurs to Charles Small, as it has often occurred to him at one time or another, that he alone is to blame. If he had stood up to these hysterical bullies . . . if, if, if! But it wasn't in him to do so, coward slave that he was. . . . Coward slave—there he was, the actor *manqué*, on Shakespeare again.

If he were half a man he should have punched the old cow Narwall right on the nose, gone off with Ivy, chucked up his job

with Solly Schwartz, and followed his destiny as he saw it—
"dree'd his weird"—and to hell with everyone.

But it was to hell with Charles Small—to the Last Circle of
Ice, where the traitors go—for he betrayed both Ivy and himself.

"Damme!" he shouts, and, half-falling out of bed, puts his
foot in the piss-pot, where it jams, to his further discomfiture;
so that for a quarter of a minute, shaking himself loose, he hobbles,
clanking, just like the hunchback. Only Solly Schwartz's ham-
pered foot is firmly planted on ringing steel, while his slithers in
his own vomit.

*   *   *   *   *

Solly Schwartz kept his eye on Charles, because that idea of
his involving the race for the million sixpences had brought in
vast revenues. It became apparent that it pays to advertise.
Huge accounts came in. Solly Schwartz proved that go-getters
to whom minutes were precious and a spruce appearance essential
could get a quicker, cleaner shave by using a messy preparation
of lanolin which he called *Suave*. It was pronounced "Swave",
and the slogan cried *"SHAVE WITH SUAVE!"* He could
prove that a perfectly ordinary kind of liquid glue, attractively
packed, somehow stuck faster than any other glue, and sent out
plaster figurines of Hercules straining every muscle to tear the
leg off a chair and saying: *"IT MUST HAVE STUCK WITH
STICKO!"* . . . that kind of thing. He was especially strong
on cigarettes that could not make you cough, coffee that could
not keep you awake, and patent medicines in general. He made
a small fortune advertising a Universal Remedy which he called
Panacea. It was supposed to be good for everything from catarrh
to cancer. He paid a disbarred doctor to write an impressive
book about it, which he gave away at cost price. Gullible hypo-
chondriacs all over the world kept this book next to their Bibles
at their bed-heads—it was translated into six languages. *Panacea*
was popular because of its almost intolerably vile taste. A
medicine that tasted as bad as all that *had* to do you good, or
what was the purpose of a bad taste? Unsolicited testimonials
came in by the thousands. Bed-ridden women who had lain on
their backs for fifteen years wrote saying that after three doses
they got up and did everything but dance the Irish jig. *Bona
fide* doctors confirmed their patients' accounts of miraculous
cures. An old man with cancer of the stomach took only one

bottle, arose, and ate a beefsteak; it was not mentioned in the advertisement that he dropped dead half an hour later, screaming like a stuck pig. *Panacea* was a sensation.

Then it crashed overnight. Solly Schwartz had decided to take full front pages in twelve consecutive issues of a famous daily paper, at fifteen hundred pounds a page. When the contract arrived, he saw that the *Daily Special* had put their rates up to two thousand pounds a page and so he had a row with the advertising manager of the newspaper. This unscrupulous fellow went away in a huff. Two days later, on Page Two, the *Daily Special* printed a sensational exposure of *Panacea*. A public analyst had examined it carefully and certified that the half-crown bottle contained nothing but a pennyworth of paraldehyde diluted with tap-water, and a trace of blue aniline dye. The stuff was, in fact, likely to prove harmful if taken regularly, and certainly could do no good. It was coloured water made to taste awful, quite simply. Invalids all over the world relapsed and perished miserably. A few people like Millie Small insisted that it did them the world of good, and kept on buying it. But in general, there was a howl of execration from London to the Antipodes and from Norway to the Black Sea, and the manufacturer of *Panacea* went into liquidation, and there was no more advertising account for Solly Schwartz.

Then Schwartz became mad with rage. The Press, the Press, the dirty, stinking, corrupt, mercenary Press! He would show the Press what was what. No more advertising in the *Daily Special*, he swore. But this was a decision which might have had grave consequences, for the *Daily Special* was at that time the most widely circulated daily newspaper in the country, and the big advertisers liked to see their products advertised in its pages. So Solly Schwartz made one of his Napoleonic resolutions, a formidably dramatic one.

The *Daily Special* was the biggest of all the English daily papers, and its sister paper, the *Sunday Special*, was also powerful. The smallest, dullest newspaper in England was the *London Inquirer*—a most unpalatable, gloomy sheet, that circulated among clergymen, maiden ladies, church-goers, and retired officers of the Indian Army, and was stumbling and mumbling on its way to Carey Street. Solly Schwartz went to the proprietor and bought the *London Inquirer* lock, stock and barrel, for £200,000. He went about it with his old frenetic energy. He hurt the feelings of the seventy-year-old editor and the rest of the staff by giving them the sack at a minute's notice, and then turned his predatory nose towards Fleet Street. There, satanically persuasive, he got hold of the keenest reporters, the most sensational feature writers, the best cartoonists, the most outrageously vituperative leader writers; and seduced them. He offered them double wages, three-year contracts, and their names in large type on the by-lines. He swore he would make them great. He offered them bonuses, unheard-of rewards. He chose for editor a young man named Tom Paradise, features editor of the *Daily Special* —a daring little fellow, restless, impatient, itching with ambition as with prickly-heat, desirous of new and startling things, and straining at the leash.

At vast expense he had made a new type-face, something to catch the eye. He poured all that he had into the *Inquirer*, and more, for his credit was good all over England. He plastered the hoardings with glaring posters, ominously worded:

LOOK OUT! IT'S COMING! . . .
. . . HOLD YOUR BREATH! ANY MINUTE NOW! . . .
. . . NEXT SUNDAY! WAIT FOR IT! . . .
And then, *"THE NEW INQUIRER!" FEARLESS, SENSATIONAL!*

People wondered what the hell it was all about, for this kind of advertising inspired public interest then. He addressed the editor and the staff saying: ". . . If you've got to be serious, make it rough. I want love, marriage and divorce. I want crime. There's a man under sentence in Pentonville Gaol who killed three wives for the insurance money—get his story, write it for him, pay him what he asks. Blood and thunder, offences against small boys, rape, robbery, that's what the public wants, the *trottels*—excitement! . . . Politics? We haven't got no politics —we're independent of politics—we go for everybody. We cater to the common *trottel*, the man in the street, the grumbler, see? And specially, *specially*, for the woman in the street. Once you've got the woman, you've got the man by the balls. Pictures, ructions—d'you follow me?" . . . and so on in this vein.

They followed him all right. He had chosen his men well. They were men after his own heart.

The *New Inquirer* shook the country. Mothers forbade their

367

daughters to read it. But they read it themselves. It was so scandalous, so sexy, so eminently suitable for reading on a Sabbath afternoon, when you were relaxed, after you and the old man had taken advantage of the kids' absence at Sunday school to have a bit of a cuddle. Then, again, Solly Schwartz stopped at nothing in his efforts to inflate the circulation. A flock of seedy salesmen went bleating from door to door all over London with Free Gift Offers. If you took out a subscription to the *New Enquirer* for one year, you received something valuable, such as a tea set, a camera, or an illustrated dictionary. It looked like sheer benevolence; Schwartz was giving away more than he was receiving. But the circulation soared phenomenally and so, therefore, did the advertising rates. Soon, most of the other newspapers tried the same trick, but Schwartz was one jump ahead of them. He put out an unprecedented offer—Free Insurance. He got the idea from an actuary named Rappoport. It was sublime in its simplicity: you had simply to register yourself as a permanent subscriber to the *New Inquirer* and you were automatically insured against accidents. The *New Inquirer* paid quite a considerable sum for the loss of both arms and/or legs, and something worth having if you put out both your eyes. If you were lucky enough to die under the wheels of a truck, your compensation ran into thousands. So the circulation swelled and swelled, and the *Inquirer* grew so fat with advertising that eager readers had to look twice for the news, although the scabrous stuff remained conspicuous enough.

Charles Small, who was now earning a good salary, played his part, too. Still secretly stage-struck, he went to Solly Schwartz and said: "Look, Mr. Schwartz, I've got an idea."

"Out with it, quick, *trottel*. I haven't got all day."

"Well . . . say the *Inquirer* organised Dramatic Societies all over the country, amateur Dramatic Societies, and rented theatres for special performances and . . . and gave cash prizes. I could look after that side of it, you know."

"Hm, yes, it's not a bad idea. But listen, I've got a better one. Never mind Dramatic Societies. Who wants to go and see some little pimple-face rushing about like a fart in a colander playing King Henry, or whatever it is? No, for that you want a whole rigmarole with rehearsals and all that. Waste of time. What you mean is this—an *Inquirer* Local Talent Competition, with cash prizes. You know these *trottels*—they all think they can sing, and dance, and do conjuring tricks, and make comedy acts. The thing to do is, get a few big names from the music-halls to go here, there, everywhere—all sorts of big names—and act as judges and award cash prizes. And a chance, maybe, for every prize-winner to get a little employment somewhere. That can be done through old Jolly Isaacs. It's not a bad idea. Work out details along those lines, and I'll put you in charge of the scheme."

Then Solly Schwartz raised his wages and gave him a bonus, and Charles Small found some little comfort in organising the *Inquirer* Local Talent Competitions. He made contact with famous figures in Variety. Still he was unhappy, because he was in love with Ivy Narwall, passionately in love, and Ivy Narwall was not a Jewish girl.

CHAPTER XXVII

CHARLES SMALL throws himself back on the bed with a hissing sigh of exhaustion. He has a slow puncture; he is nearly empty. He tries to refresh himself by biting his nails—a habit which soothes him because it occupies all his attention and leaves no room for thought—like nose-picking. But here again he is frustrated. He generally saved one finger-nail—the little one on his left hand—for a week-end treat, but he remembers that he extravagantly ate it all up on Friday. And there he lies, poor man, picking and gnawing and worrying the ragged edges of himself until the blood comes and there is nothing left to bite— no comfort left, not even the consolation of the feel of himself under his own teeth.

(Once he tried to cure himself of the habit by biting quill tooth-picks, but it didn't work; he had to eat himself.)

. . . Yes, Ivy was a *schiksa*, a woman of the Gentiles, and he was one of God's Chosen People. What drivel! He had been circumcised in the flesh of his silly little foreskin; so he was one of the Chosen People. He had been taught to gabble prayers in a language neither he, nor his father, nor his friends understood —"Let him know he's a Yid," I. Small had said. He had a hooked nose and kinky hair, and was fed on meat that had been soaked and salted to tastelessness; so he was one of the Chosen People. Why, the confounded kosher butchers who bled their bleddy beef did not even know why they bled it. He was not allowed to smoke between sunset on Friday and sunset on Saturday. The Law of Moses ordains that the Chosen People must rest on the Sabbath; and to kindle fire, to strike a match, was to work. (The old man had an idea that it was because Moses was prejudiced against tobacco. He used to smoke in the lavatory, reading a newspaper. But they cooked and warmed themselves all right.) The Chosen People were forbidden to do business, or even talk of money, on Saturday. Yet they kept their shops open and lit their fires. The Lord rested on the Seventh Day: Charles Small remembers one snotty old man who, on Saturday, would not even carry a handkerchief, because the transportation of that square of linen from his house to the synagogue might be classified as Labour. He tied his handkerchief about his waist, so that it might be argued that it was a garment; putting one over on Jehovah. The whole damned Law, as Charles sees it, is nothing but a mass of absurd prohibitions, productive of nothing but evasions, deceits, dirty secrets, and nauseous hypocrisy. *How odd of God to choose the Jews . . .* what was that reply? *It isn't odd, the Jews chose God. . . .* The whole thing is too absurd. They beat their breasts in the synagogues on the Day of Atonement and lived strictly kosher between the four comfortable Wailing Walls of their homes . . . but ate in unclean, fashionable restaurants, with *goys*—ate forbidden food, and enjoyed it—the flesh of animals that have cloven hoofs but do not chew the cud, preparations of fishes that have no scales, birds that have been shot, not ritually butchered. They shaved their beards. They howled their heads off over Zion and the Land of Israel to which—if the Prophecy is to be fulfilled, which it must—they must return. Wild horses couldn't drag the meanest old-clothes man to the Levantine Coast—let alone Nathan, the Photographer, who is a great man in the Movement, and induces silly fools of humble artisans to drop their sweaty pennies into blue tin boxes. According to the Law, the wives of the Chosen People were supposed to segregate themselves to be purified for ten days after menstruation. He can just see them doing it. . . . And as for that miraculous flight of quails in the Wilderness—were quails kosher? Did they cut the quails' throats with a gabbled ritual and hang them up to bleed? Just try it and see. A quail, after having flown a thousand miles from Africa to Italy, and almost exhausted, poor bird, is hard enough to hit with a shot-gun. . . . He could go on for hours about who was Cain's Wife; and why, having chanted an appalling list of slayings, the Chosen, at the Passover feast, cried: "For His Mercy endureth forever!" And it does not seem reasonable to him that these secretive circumcised pig-eaters, these kosher whore-mongers should raise their hands in protest at his love, his deep pure love, for gentle Ivy Narwall.

But so they did. When, at last, Charles Small scraped up enough pluck to say: "I'm going to marry Ivy," one supper-time, the old man cut himself in the corner of the mouth with a knife —he was eating peas—and Millie Small had to go and lie down. This was all they were short of. This was the crowning disgrace.

Charles Small, one of the Chosen People, handpicked by the Lord God Almighty, wanted to marry—to *marry*, mind you—a *goyah*, a Christer, a Jew-hater, an eater of pigs! So that was what he was, was it?

Charles Small lost his puny temper and shouted: "You ought to talk about eating pigs! Haven't I seen you with my own eyes eating ham—pig's arse—in Appenrodt's? Don't talk to me about eating pigs! Pig-eater yourself!"

At this, I. Small called him a bleddy dirty liar, and made as if to impale him upon a fork. Charles Small caught up a dessert spoon, and so they stood, with crossed cutlery, until the old man knuckled under, whimpering: "*Sha!* Be quiet with your Appenrodt's . . . smoked selmon . . . I made a mistake. Didn't we all make mistakes, isn't it? Ham, schmam, we all make mistakes. But a *schiksa* to marry? Sooner or later she calls you a dirty Jew. Then comes bleddy murder, and you break your poor mother's bleddy heart. On the gellows you end like Crappen——"

"—Crippen!"

"Crippen, schmippen! Your mother, she's not a well woman, and she bore you. Charley, Charley, think of your mother, all she went through. . . . You should have heard. . . . It was something terrible. And now she's not well in her inside, and you want to take her life away! What do you want from our lives? We are not youngsters any more. A year, two years, have pity, Khatzkele, have pity on thy father and thy bleddy mother. For your sake she tore her insides out like a chicken! Marry Hettie, a respectable Yiddisher girl. You got nothing but your chains to lose. Don't break your poor mother's heart, Charley."

"I hate Hettie. I love Ivy," said Charles Small, "I want to marry Ivy. I'm not going to marry Hettie. That's final."

"Then out of this bleddy house you go this minute!" howled I. Small, picking up a plate of stewed apples and custard. Charles Small, proud and pale, said: "I desire nothing better. I am earning my own living. I do not propose to stay."

He strode to the door. Before he turned the door-knob, there was a terrible outcry of women. Millie Small had had a hæmorrhage.

All the same, Charles Small walked steadfastly to his room and packed a suitcase. I. Small stopped him at the foot of the stairs. All the bluster and bluff were knocked out of him, and he

372

looked terribly old. He had been crying; one tear still trembled
on his woe-begone moustache, and that martial moustache had
retreated from his wet eyes towards his chin. "Charley . . .
my darling . . ." he stammered, ". . . to please me, for your
mother's sake. If you must go, God forbid, if you *must* go—why
now, just this minute? Your mother's taken bad, Charley.
Please!"

It was this *please* that brought Charles Small to a halt, and
that was his undoing. Three or four more of the old man's
tears so watered his already diluted resolution that he put down
the suitcase.

"At least, Charley, go in, say good-bye. She's been a good
mother to you, Charley. Is it too much to ask? Bled——"
I. Small wept, and even that he did clumsily, making a noise like
an unskilled motorist changing gears. He had gone from third
into reverse and stripped himself; and, skidding on the slippery
contents of his handkerchief, sounded the wavering horn of his
poor red nose until even the power to make a noise went out of
him. His lights went out. He was still and silent.

Then Charles, who had at first been inclined to laugh hysteri-
cally, remembered little things, such as the cold chicken carved
with the curved cobbler's knife and the drop of blood on the plate;
and the surreptitious outings, and the little bursts of tenderness.
Not far from tears himself, he put an arm about the old man's
shaking shoulders, and led him back to the sitting-room. The
doctor, with his black bag, was putting on his overcoat. "Well,
Doctor, what is?" asked I. Small. "Please!"

Charles Small almost weeps, remembering that word, popping
and hissing from under that tear-bedraggled moustache.

The doctor said: "I'm afraid I'll have to call in a specialist.
There is Mr. Ellery of Harley Street, if you can afford——"

"—Ellery, schmellery, afford, call, call!" cried I. Small, pluck-
ing at his moustache. "A . . . a . . . a mother . . . she bore
you . . . sis . . . Afford? Everything, anything—take, take!
A boy's best friend!"

Charles Small asked: "Is it serious?"

The doctor said: "I think so, but I'd rather consult Mr. Ellery."

"*Mister* did you say, Doctor?" Charles asked.

"Mr. Ellery," said the doctor.

Something like a wet feather seemed to run from Charles
Small's neck down to his coccyx, because he knew that in the

medical profession *Mister* meant F.R.C.S., Fellow of the Royal College of Surgeons, the smiler with the knife under his cloak.

Leaving his packed suitcase where he had put it down, by the umbrella stand, Charles Small went back to his room and thought of Ivy Narwall, envying the old man for his power to weep. For Charles, that night, there was no relief in tears. He lay awake, twisting and turning between the sheets, and yearning, always yearning, for a little calm, a little peace in the gentle arms of soft-eyed Ivy Narwall.

*   *   *   *   *

Soft-eyed Ivy Narwall! *Soft* Ivy Narwall! As quickly as you can snap your fingers, Charles Small flies from sentimental reminiscence into retrospective rage. A nice pair they would have made. Shit and sugar! She was as abject as he, and there was not much to choose between her people and his. Hers also were Chosen People, smiters of the Amalekites and the Amorites; casters of their shoes over their Edoms, the ranting, canting, hip-and-thigh Nonconformists. He could see Jack Squire, who moved that the Dramatic Society use the Bowdlerised Shakespeare—who blushed at pleasure's name—who saw lustful thighs in the fork of a tree and phallic symbols in every toadstool and acorn—who tittered, shaking a deprecating head at the sound of the word "naked". . . . Oh, how clearly could he see the pious Squire leaping out of the Chapel and into the bridal chamber, to slake his dirty lust, demanding his marital rights! Legitimatised, respectable rapist! Purified pervert! He, too, was Chosen, like the Narwalls, and would gladly have burned at the stake his equivalent of *goyim*—Baptists, Methodists, Peculiar Methodists, Primitive Methodists, Jews, Greek-Orthodoxes, and above all Roman Catholics. Charles Small wrings his hands when he thinks of his Ivy lying, sick and shuddering, under that unctuous bulk, crying in the dark, no doubt, and wishing that he would stop his insistent fumbling and go to sleep, and leave her to mourn over the perfidy of Charles Small. He can see this podgy Congregationalist devil, first with unacceptable caresses and later with sanctified violence, exacting his due. Charles Small can see the whole business as clearly as if he had his eye to the keyhole of the bedroom . . . the complacent ferocity of Squire, licensed at last by the Church to make three-dimensional his furtive fantasies, worrying and probing at his lawfully wedded wife who

374

wishes that Charles were there to save her. *Oh, dear God, if you are all-powerful, how can you be all-good? And if you are all-good, how can you be all-powerful? . . .*

He is lost in a labyrinth; a dark, nightmarish maze, in which Man stalks himself, with malice aforethought, wet-mouthed and bare-toothed, fearfully biting at his own shadow, ignorant of the ambient light.

For the sake of sanity, Charles Small—having no nails left to bite—is forced back into a state of subjective objectivity.

Charles Small, in his theatrical fantasies, has insinuated himself into the shapes of many men who were great of heart and soul. He has swung his sword at the right hand of Gideon. He has burned at the stake with Ridley and Latimer, saying, while the flames licked at his belly: "Be of good cheer, Brother Ridley. We have this day in England lit such a candle as by God's grace shall never be put out." He was Job. It was he, Charles Small, who had taken the wings of the morning and dwelled in the uttermost parts of the sea. He was Saint Thomas More, who, jesting at the gallow's foot, and being somewhat enfeebled, said to the executioner: "Help me up, and for my going down let me fend for myself." He was brave Grindecobbe of St. Albans, who put his neck into the noose in the name of common liberty and the rights of the common man. He was Jack Straw, at the head of the men of Kent, and he was Wat Tyler, out of Surrey. He was, in a Chassidic way, the mad priest, John Ball, the wild rhymester of the hopeless revolt, singing. He was Richard, he was Raymond, he was Bohemund, Belisarius, Beethoven . . . a dreamer of great dreams and a fighter of mighty fights in the name of the Dream—a man of great faith . . .

So says Charles Small's dream . . .

> ". . . So says my dream, but what am I?
> A child crying in the night,
> A child crying for the light
> And with no language but a cry . . ."

No language but a cry. The poet hit the nail on the head, thinks Charles Small, bang on the head as far as he is concerned. He knows how to cry, but is inarticulate, impotent, newly-born in middle life, mewling and puking in his ghostly mother's arms, powerless to bite, powerless to grip, incoherent; strong only in his

375

power to inspire pity and the fear and the hate that pity begets
—just as he was when the midwife washed his eyes—just as his
father and his mother were when they saw that he might be a
man and humbly became children again.

Where does it begin, where does it end? Charles Small asks of the
ceiling. *And where?* he shouts into the chamber-pot, which does
not even throw back an echo. It seems to him that everything
is a beginning, and there is no middle, only a lonely road leading
into a receding mist which veils an unknown end. It may be that
there is a God, and it may be that there is a Devil. It may be
that there is no God; nothing but a rolling ball whirling at
twenty-five thousand miles an hour on its orbit around the sun,
which, huge and bright as it is, is nothing but a dust-mote
borrowing a little light from God-knows-where. . . .

And if there is no God? It is possible that there is no God.
But if not, what? Your atheist is as cruel a sectarian as your
Jew, Catholic, Churchman, Nonconformist, Mohammedan, or
what-have-you. All belief begets fanaticism. . . . One might
make an equation: Father, Son, and Holy Mother *equal* persecu-
tion and pain. They are interdependent. The young sucks the
old for milk; the old sucks the young for blood; and so spins the
Wheel.

Then where can one fly? Into Nothingness? No, no, no—
Man's mind balks at that. But he has the right to choose his own
company, by God!

—Ah, ah—there he goes with God again! Well, and why not?
Charles Small, petty, petulant, sickly little creature that he is,
rendered calm by exhaustion, considers that there must be, in his
unsavoury self, something more than snot, guts, blood, salt,
phosphorus, iodine, keratin, carbon, iron, nitrogen, and so forth
to the value of five shillings. If this were the case, Charles Small
would be the equal of Shakespeare, and the old man would
exchange peroration for peroration with Demosthenes and
Cicero. . . .

No, there must be the soul, the struggling soul, wriggling like
a bubble out of the stinking soft mud of the stagnant pool of the
flesh, striving to burst and be free. As for God . . . who knows?
All this universe may be one little part of God, the all-encompass-
ing God—good and evil—as ecstasy and bellyache may be contained in the same skin.

It is too high, too deep.

Charles Small knows one thing, and that is, he is no good—and with this, with a sour eructation, he falls asleep, worn out.

*   *   *   *   *

But there is no rest for the wicked, no peace for Judas Iscariot —except that questionable respite suggested by that silly Saint who said that for one little day in every year Judas was allowed to crawl out of the boiling sulphur, out of the torments of the everlasting fire, and cool himself on the ice floes. And if that was God's mercy, by God, God could keep it! Charles Small can see Judas wriggling out of the fires that die not, into the bitter eternal cold, and lying there on a drifting Arctic berg, with chattering teeth, trying to acclimatise himself; knowing that he has one short day; tortured by hope, tortured by fear, tortured by the anticipation of to-morrow's dawn; cursing God for His mercy, which is a refinement of cruelty, His day of grace which is —if God is really omniscient—a subtle supplement to his eternal torment . . . There could be no peace for Judas cooling on the ice floe; only chattering of teeth in the sudden cold . . . poor Judas (Narwall's all-knowing God must have foredamned him to burn in hell). He wants to get back to hell; he is used to it; he has had a couple of thousand years of home-cooking in the blue sulphurous flames, and the cold burns. He misses the barbed tridents of the barbed-tailed torturers. He wants to go home to his quiet room in hell . . . God, as the sectarians see Him, must be either a blithering idiot, like Narwall and I. Small and the rest, or the Devil in disguise.

There is no such God. If, by any chance, such a Narwall, such an I. Small, of a God exists, Charles Small wants none of Him; for he sees through the peep-hole of that God's narrow mind, has learned to laugh at His thunder, shrug at His curses, sneer at His exercise of superior force over His children. Narwall's God, God damn Him, is a very powerful Narwall; I. Small's God is a universal I. Small, a continuous portentous rumble of thunder and a flashing of summer lightning, powerless to reward or to punish—something in which Charles Small could never have believed if the old man had not created Him in his own image. . . .

He drops into that heavy sleep (that blessed respite) as Judas flops, red-hot out of the Pit, to sizzle and steam on the ice.

Sleep, sleep . . . an interlude, a recess. . . . Hell has adjourned to refresh itself, to strengthen itself for another go at him. Hell

can wait. Narwall's God has given it all Eternity, and Hell's
fires need no stokers; and the Pit is always wide open. But in
sleep Charles Small finds no rest. Out of the darkness come little
hooks, like claws out of the black pads of a great cat, hooking
him, while a remote throaty voice says: "Wait a bit!" and now he
is dragged down and down through nightmarish corridors, backward and forward—back to what he remembers and hates, and
forward to what he dreads but recognises as inevitable. And in
the inevitability of it lies the horror of it. . . . Down the nights
and down the days and through the arches of the years he flees
himself, trying to elude himself. He may leap into the air, but
the shadow is waiting to catch him by the heels in the staring
moonlight. If the light is behind him, the shadow of himself
is in front of him, and when he turns and tries to run back, his
feet are lead, his blood is water, and out of the corner of his eye
he sees that long shadow waiting for him on the moonlit road, and
knows that he must follow it. When he stops, it stops. It can
wait. But he must go on. As he moves, the shadow of himself
obligingly leads the way, along that empty road without perspective, that endless road, that haunted road of moonlight and mist,
down which a creature that might have been a man is dragged in
silence at the heels of his shadow. . . .

If sleep is a little death, in the name of God how can one face
the terrors and the dangers of the Coming Night—the Big Sleep?
Oh, fools! What has the God of Retribution to do with ice and
fire, when all He needs to do is chain you to yourself, never letting
you escape from yourself? Who would not gladly exchange
Remorse for burning sulphur, or Shame for the Absolute Cold?
It is better to be gnawed by the hounds of hell, than to bite one's
own finger-nails in self-contempt. One may defy the black dogs;
but who can defy or outface his secret self? . . . Judas does not
boil in a pit—Judas is not worried by fanged monsters; that would
be too easy. No, Judas lights his own fires and provides his own
pitch-forks, and nauseates himself not with silly little satyrs and
serpents, but with the eternal contemplation of himself as he
made himself; by the inescapable secret knowledge of himself;
he hounds himself, finds himself and bites his nails . . . *Forgive
us our trespasses* wails Charles Small, *God, give me dreamless sleep!*
For when his exhausted flesh goes limp in the mysterious little
death of Sleep, all that is Charles Small—all that he knows to be
himself—comes doubly awake. From the back of his head comes

a beam of light that beats against the inner walls of his lowered eyelids and shows himself to himself, laying bare all the agonising secrets that he never dared to confess to himself. . . . But horrible, horrible . . . for now the dirt that is himself is sucked clean of the sugar of self-justification, and there it is in three, four, five dimensions—Nightmare!

No rest for the wicked—it isn't so. Whoever said that should have said: *No rest for the man who knows he is guilty;* for the amoral sleep sound. Only the transgressors have nightmares—only those who know the difference between right and wrong, and, looking over their shoulders at the Good, slide with delicious terror to the Evil, just for the fun of the run. . . . The good man, the man of God—the Unknown God—can make do with nothing. The ravens will feed him, and even if they do not he can go unfed forty days and forty nights in his wilderness. How? By wrapping himself up in himself, but there are selves and selves. The pure man is a piece of the Eternal; indestructible, an infinity beyond the bone and the meat of the perishable self.

But Charles Small is vulnerable. He is a man *moyen sensuel,* and as soon as he switches off the light and closes his eyes there rises that ghostly moon that throws the distorted shadow that drags him, whichever way he turns, into the mist . . . the impenetrable mist. . . .

The world whirls away, but not into God's quiet darkness—into a horrible, howling, dizzy vortex spinning so that it is neither black nor white, neither light nor dark . . . like the gramophone record again. . . . And Charles's sleep is not a sleep, but a sort of dark exercise in gymnastics. He takes flying leaps over the vaulting-horse of himself into a bowl of fog; he does Swedish Exercises—meaningless bendings and stretchings and pawings and gropings, all alone in the cold, obedient to a great Voice. Right hand over left hand, gripping with knees and feet, he climbs a rope, up, up, and up, until he is hanging between heaven and earth on a thread, clouds above and mist below; holding fast with hands and knees that are losing their power to hold. . . . And then—oh, woe!—he is falling and falling until he hits the soft mattress of his springy modern bed and, crying to sleep again like Caliban, closes his feverish eyes. . . . But what happens when he closes his eyes again? He is standing on a window-ledge a thousand feet above the ground—he cannot keep his balance —he falls, sickeningly, into a brief spell of consciousness, wakefulness from which he prays the good Lord to deliver him . . . and drifts back to sleep to dream of a railway station. He has arrived in the nick of time; the train is whistling. Somewhere on a platform, to the left of parallel rails that have no perspective, stands one forlorn woman; he must get to her, but his feet are nailed to the ground. . . . And then with an *ah-cha, ah-cha!* the train goes away in thunder, snorting out its nightmarish steam, steam through which he can see nothing but himself, abject, fumbling from pocket to pocket for a lost ticket and finding nothing but the memory of things forgotten. In his hands, emptiness. The train gasps and whistles away towards the wide sea . . . and as the train goes away the little figure of the woman recedes . . . only he can see her eyes. Then he runs blindly out of the station and is horrified to find himself on the lip of a precipice that goes down a sheer mile into a black fog, into which he knows he must fall. And fall he does, dying a thousand deaths, to hit the mattress of his soft bed.

And from this mattress he bounces, his heart ticking like a metronome with the weight in its belly, back into the pocket of confusion that is Charles Small. Yes, the Curse is upon him— he cannot stay awake and he dares not sleep for fear of the dreams that may come. Like a guilty creditor, he sees himself coming round the corner, and tries to cross the street to avoid himself, pretending not to see himself . . . dances like Nijinsky in and out of thunderous traffic; slides like a ghost between clashing bumpers while colours change from red to green—bilious green—runs, runs until he breaks through the throng of men and women who are baring their teeth in laughter, and finds a lonely alley, into which he jumps. . . . Under the white moon the muddy cobblestones look like the back of a crocodile that must take him by the legs and drag him down through the rotting drift-wood into the mud. But this is only the way it appears. He is free, for the moment; he has shaken off the Thing that pursues him.

So he turns—and finds himself standing toe-to-toe with that black shadow, frightfully elongated, mimicking his every gesture and exaggerating every movement of his muscles in the ghastly light of the mottled moon that stares down at the stones and the naked mud. He is deep-frozen. His shadow peels itself away from the stones and takes hold of him, and a great cold rushes into him—the cold, the sweaty cold, that is born of pure horror. . . .

And now his shadow is the substance and he is the shadow—
they have changed places, and are flying . . . where? Up, and
up, and up. The moon looms large. The earth is a green luminous
ball. Suddenly the shadow slips away and Charles Small hangs
for a moment in interplanetary space, cold and lonely before he
falls, twisting and turning, begging himself to wake up—which
he does forthwith, between his clean linen sheets. He has been
asleep for about twelve seconds . . . and there is Space, Time
and Eternity for you! In those few seconds he has had a Season
in Hell. He has known the horror of the great heights and felt
the dread of the great depths, and the numb chill of the Absolute
Cold in the Outer Dark. . . .

He forces himself out of his sick sleep, for even wakefulness,
with all its menace, is better than such sleep.

As the old man used to say: "Better the devil you know than
the devil you don't know."

Charles Small sits on the edge of the bed and tries to be
reasonable.

*   *   *   *   *

But he has not the wherewithal. He cannot be reasonable in
his own right. His ratiocination, like his passions and his philo-
sophisings and his contemplations, are metrical; he has them on
loan. Take away the Poets, and what is left of Charles Small?
Pump out Shakespeare, Tennyson, and all the rest, and what is
left of his deflated self? A few kosher fibres bled white with salt
—the salt of tears—tears of self-pity and shame, which are all
he has to give to the world. But what is he to do, and where is
he to turn for comfort? He must go back . . . he must fall back
upon the articulated thoughts of better men, without which he is
nothing but a bladder of sour milk and tears, swelling; saved
before bursting point by a squirt of bitter bile through the safety-
valve of his nasty temper . . . but stretched, strained—a
bursting bladder, a congested bowel, a gut full of wind. All that
Charles has which is good, true and beautiful belongs to someone
else—to someone who took his inspiration from God and the
rightful Sons of God, and scraped the slime from his eyes and saw
stars. Charles Small's stars are second-hand stars, borrowed
stars, for the loan of which he has pledged himself.

With whose reason can he be reasonable, for God's sake?

His brain rattles inside his skull like a stale monkey-nut in its shell. *Nuts!* An American expression, Charles Small remembers, signifying *Shucks*, peelings, membranes to be thrown away . . . the bearded shucks, the withering bearded shucks of tall corn. . . .

Rattling his little dried-up brain in the flimsy shell of his silly skull, Charles Small tries to moisten himself with other men's juices, muttering:

> ". . . *I am a part of all that I have met:*
> *Yet all experience is but an arch*
> *Where through gleams the untravelled world*
> *Whose margin fades forever and forever*
> *As I move . . ."*

. . . Arches, arches . . . Charles Small remembers a picture that haunts his dreams—as if he has not enough pictures to haunt his dreams—a picture painted by Chirico, depicting a little girl bowling a hoop down a desolate arcade, inevitably skipping to a certain corner where there lurks a horrid masculine shadow. . . . Those crumbling arches, those falling arches, they remind him of fallen arches, of feet, of boots and shoes, of the old man. Eternal recurrence!

He has fled I. Small down the nights and down the days; fled him through the arches of the years . . . and still the old man bleddies in his ear, flaps at him with the defunct *Globe*—he can feel only the wind of the blow as it passes—and sometimes gets under his skin and, playing funerals, cries for him. Nevertheless, even now, it is perilously easy to gloss over the abuses and remember the day when his father, in the absence of his God-damned mother, became himself, a good if stupid companion, and took him to Kew . . . and it is easy to remember the virtues of his blasted mother who, left alone, among strangers, behaved somewhat like a civilised human being, and became almost tender. God be with her, wherever she may be . . . damn her eyes! Touching the matter of eyes, Charles Small is hard put to know for whom he is weeping—his father, his mother or himself. Perhaps all three. *Tria juncta in uno*—and out comes salt water from the eyes, dribbles from the nose, and a noise reminiscent of hiccoughs . . . and there is another handkerchief for the laundry basket, another pennyworth of soiled life down the drain!

. . . The Night of the Hæmorrhage—how was it possible not to remember it, and the awful grief of the old man, and the queer courage of the old woman who felt the wind of the scythe and heard the clicking of the bony feet of death, sure as Fate. Suddenly it seemed to Charles Small that his mother became noble, and his father became his child, so that suddenly he, Charles, became the master of the house; and as such he had to stay. What else could he do? His parents were become helpless children; he was a man. Does a proper man abandon a child?

But does a proper man abandon and betray himself?

So came that dawn when Charles Small picked up the suitcase that still stood by the umbrella stand, and crept out of the house like a thief, leaving a note; and betrayed himself and deserted Ivy Narwall on that smoky platform, where he left his suitcase rubbing shoulders with hers, and ran. Yes, in the recollection of this perfidy—here is hell indeed. He got back to the house in time to tear up the note he had left. The old man was looking for him. Grey, now, and wrapped in a grey dressing-gown, I. Small appeared like an old shorn sheep. He was pitiful, so agonisingly pitiful that Charles Small was almost relieved when he was confronted with his tormented mother. Attendants were making ready to carry her off, and she was thanking them for their kindness. The old man was going off the deep end again—this time, not with a yell but with a gurgle. What was one to do, oh God, what? Charles Small knows that these people, whom he has always hated, and whose memory he abhors in a half-hearted way, were in his mind at the station. It needed only the appearance of Mrs. Narwall to take the other half of his heart out of him and send him away empty to be refilled with all that he had tried to spit out.

*　　*　　*　　*　　*

He remembers a dreary dream that haunted him through the years; and this was the dream: He was wandering through a park, up and down, over hill and into valley, wandering and wandering, obedient to a blind impulse, step by step into something dark and horrible. And in this dream, at last, he came over the brow of a little hill and saw, far down, an oval house surrounded by trees. He knew that here was his Doom, here was his Weird, and that here he must end. But he had to go over that hill and down and down into the valley, and up a narrow white lane until he found himself knocking at a red door framed in a Gothic arch. He knew that the house was empty; yet the echoing of his knocking sounded like footsteps on the stairs of that hollow house, keeping time to the beating of his heart, and the red door opened and out of the blackness came a hand with a wedding ring, that snatched him into the darkness and dragged him into a black gulf, a chasm without light. This had been a recurrent nightmare until he thrashed it out of himself, remembering that, one day, when the old man had to go out of town, Millie Small, in her turn, took him to Kew Gardens on a summer afternoon, and led him into the place that housed the Victoria Lilies; but was caught short, and had to leave him, so that he was left alone in the steamy half-light. . . . At that moment a horror fell upon him, and later, dreams. Years passed before he knew the meaning of those dreams; and, having learned that they were nothing but trivialities, his own droppings sticking to the heels of his memory, he laughed the dream out of this world to where it belonged, he coughed it into cloud-cuckooland. But then, having rid himself of a dream, he had to lie down at night with the begetter of the dream . . . the pond in which the mosquitoes fecundated, the coil of shit in which the green-arsed blowflies laid their filthy eggs . . . himself, Charles Small. There is no point in trying to escape. He is in a Hall of Mirrors. Consciousness is neither here nor there. Awake or asleep he is whirling in a wild waltz in the arms of the shadow, and when, between dances, he goes to the toilet to make himself decent, his own bones grin at himself with teeth that are his own because he has paid for them by the grace of Solly Schwartz. . . . It is interesting, in this connection, to consider that the work of the dentist, Parmee, will live longer than the three-dimensional work of God that was Charles Small; because his flesh will rot away and his bones will decay, but the gold and the porcelain that Parmee put into his mouth remain. . . . One of these days, a few centuries hence, someone will dig up all that is left of his Shakespearean mouth, and hammer it into an ear-ring, or, more likely, hand it to a Central Committee that will employ the precious metal internationally, secreted underground; or nationally isotopically, for the destruction of the world. And so runs the world away. The wardens of Belsen and Buchenwald knocked the gold fillings out of prisoners' teeth— for gold. Who knows where that gold went? Who knows from where it came? Charles Small's silly little fat-arsed daughter,

Laura, who has recently been given a signet ring, may be wearing part of the diadem of the Emperor of All Men, or a sliver of the misery of the universe; because gold is the only thing Man never throws away. Of all the toys Man treasures, the yellow stuff is the most durable. Put your soul under your hammer and beat it into a gorgeous golden goblet—put your heel on the goblet and trample it into a jagged cake: the gold is there. The dust of Alexander, turned to clay, may stop a bung to keep the wind away. But in Charles Small's teeth there may be something of Ur of the Chaldees, a bit of Rameses, a grain of Karakoram . . . and in the crown of some king a thousand years hence there may be a bit of one of the gold-filled teeth of Charles Small, since no one lets gold go to waste.

Not that all this is worth a blown-out egg; only somehow it is comforting; it smells like philosophy, of which, God knows, Charles Small has desperate need . . . anything, anything, so long as he can get his false teeth into it!

. . . Millie Small died of cancer of the womb and much as everyone pitied her in her agony it was impossible not to be bored by her. Alive or dying, she had a nuisance-value. (Why are Charles Small's eyes wet?) Dying did her good. It made her mind her manners. She stopped saying: "So that's what he is," and "So now we know what you are," and feebly stroked Charles's hand. She remembered a thousand delinquencies which everyone else had forgotten because they were not worth remembering. Her face was almost exactly the colour of her hair, which was grey as ashes; her eyes were wide with agony, and her hands were shrivelled so that they looked like the claws of a fowl. She made a sort of Confession: ". . . I didn't tell the truth about your ribbon at the time of the Jubilee . . . I was jealous, I hid it, I was in the wrong . . . I'll buy you some more ribbon, and I want to give you my fur coat. Srul, give Ruth my fur coat. I can't take it with me. . . ."

"Oh Millie, Millie, Millie!" the old man said, crying like a child. "What *is* this talk?"

"Srul, I'm going home." She never liked the word *Die*. "I'm going home, Srul. If I haven't been good to you, don't bear a grudge against me—I never meant harm. . . ."

"Millie! Millie!"

"Anything I said in a temper, Srul, don't remember it against me. I didn't mean a word I said. You were always a good husband

385

. . . Becky makes good *kreplach*—she'll look after you . . .
I don't want you should marry again, I wouldn't rest easy, I
couldn't rest. Promise!"

"May I bled——" said I. Small, and stopped, gulping, "I
should drop deddy-well bled if——"

". . . Honest, Srul, I was always true to you." (She had got
that out of some novel, probably written by Marie Corelli.)
". . . Give Sarah Mother's watch, the one with the gold pin.
I meant her no harm when I gave her a good smacking that time
when . . . when . . . I forget. Where's Priscilla? Has Prissie
come home yet? At least, whatever she is, she might come home
to say 'Good-night' to her Mummy . . . after all I've been
through for her."

Priscilla had broken her parents' hearts by running off, at the
age of eighteen, with an American millionaire, with whom she
was prosperously living in sin, caring not a damn for her own flesh
and blood. (*Clever girl*, thinks Charles Small, with envy.)

"Yes, Millie, yes, any minute, any minute," moans I. Small,
temporising and lying now as ever.

"Where's Charley?"

He was there, somewhat dazed, juggling with pity and disgust
and tears and laughter—hysterical laughter, theatrical tears,
histrionic pity, and genuine disgust. "Here I am, Mum," he
said. It was impossible not to weep in sympathy with the affliction
of the old man whose blood he had licked off the plate that night
so many years ago; and it was hard not to forgive the Boy's Best
Friend in her last agony. "I'm here, Mummy, here I am, Mum,
can't you see me?"

"I'm going home, Charley . . . I'm done for . . . I'm going
home. . . ."

"Oh, Millie, Millie," cried I. Small, falling on his knees at the
bedside.

Millie Small said, dreamily—she was full of morphine—
"Charley, marry Hettie . . . to please *me*. . . . You've only
got one mother. . . . Marry Hettie, Charley, to please *me*. . . .
I'm sorry I didn't give you the water-pistol I promised you, but
it was dangerous—you could knock somebody's eye out . . .
but you marry Hettie, and . . . marry Hettie. . . ." She
remembered the circulating library, and the works of Marie
Corelli. "Call your daughter Thelma," she said, "but to please
me, marry Hettie. . . ."

Then she began to make a noise in her throat like snoring. "Millie, Millie!" the old man cried. But suddenly, for the first time in her life, she became calm: Millie Small was dead.

Charles went out into the echoing corridor, for he could not bear to see his father kneeling and wringing his hands in his great grief, or hear him whispering, for once: "Millie, Millie, come back, come back. . . ."

A gaggle of uncles and aunts were assembled in a waiting-room, silent. It was Nathan, the Photographer, who asked: "Well?"—as if he didn't know.

Charles Small could not speak; he made a dramatic gesture, drawing a finger across his throat. Millie's sisters, who hated her —not without cause—burst into tears. Nathan, the Photographer, said: "That is Life." The old man came out of the ward, blind with tears, stumbling, and, gripping Charles's wrists, stammered: "Charley—your Mama—you haven't got no . . ." —and let loose a salty rain from his eyes.

"We must live with the living," said Nathan, the Photographer.

"Living . . . schmiving . . ." snivelled I. Small, "Oh Millie, Millie!"

So Charles Small married Hettie.

CHAPTER XXVIII

"It's your Mother's wish," said I. Small; and Charles swallowed it, hook, line and sinker, little stinker that he was. He married Hettie, that sloppy, floppy poultice of a woman, with her absurd nose that was bent in the middle, and her submissive, whimpering voice and—even at twenty-four—her tendency to a double chin. She had five thousand pounds; she was a Jewish girl. Some of Charles Small's best friends are Jewish people, but he knows where they can stick their Yiddishkeit and their pounds. It was Millie Small's wish that he should marry Hettie, and the agony of that idiotic I. Small was intolerable. Charles Small hits himself in the bosom; he takes himself by the right ear and twists it, kicking himself in the ankle with his heel. He punches himself in the jaw, inadvertently biting his tongue, so that he lets out a yelp of pain not unmixed with self-satisfaction.

So he married Hettie, who had five thousand pounds. What the hell did he want with Hettie? He wanted Ivy. And what the devil had he to do with five thousand lousy pounds? He was making a thousand a year, and his tastes were simple . . . a packet of cigarettes, a warm meal, and Ivy. He already had a considerable sum of money in the bank. He wanted Ivy, nothing and nobody but Ivy; and I. Small and Millie Small and the Narwalls had taken her away from him.

Accursed parenthood! And damnable childhood! Dear God, damn and blast both parents and children, because, each to each they add up to dust and ashes, grey ruin.

The memories of fourteen years of marriage run through Charles Small's head like shit through a goose. His wife loved him. He had not the slightest regard for his wife. She had borne him two children, but Laura and Jules had not been begotten on Hettie, but on the ghosts of Clara Bow, Dolores del Rio, Gloria Swanson, Greta Garbo, and Lya de Putti. Not Ivy—he never thought of her like that. Certainly not Hettie; he could not stand her. He could tolerate her only in the dark, and only then if she kept her mouth shut and did not interfere with his imagination.

He remembers a horrid joke: A wife petulantly tells her

husband to hurry up because she is sleepy. The husband replies: "I'm sorry, I can't *think* of anyone."

Yet, somehow or other, he has begotten a couple of brats. Would to God they had been syringed away to limbo!

Ah, well . . . Hettie and he became friends—that is to say, out of pity he became polite to her. And then there were the children. He was determined that Laura and Jules should not grow up tied in knots as he had grown up, so he gave them psychology, which made them so rude that they became intolerable; whereupon he was compelled to beat the boy for spitting in his mother's face and calling her a Bleeding Bastard. He laid on hard, and with gusto; not with a rolled-up copy of the *Sunday Express*, but with the palm of his hand. That knocked the psychology out of the little sods! It put the fear of God into them, the fear of God, their Father—for they were dirty little cowards, just like the father and the mother that brought them into the world.

Charles Small remembers—oh, how he remembers!—the old man died ("passed away" as the family would have it) without too much fuss. He did not kick up a row because he was unconscious. His last words were: "Millie, Millie!" Then he grasped an imaginary copy of the *News of the World*, struck a ghostly blow, and earned the gratitude of his son by getting out of the way and holding his tongue for ever.

And still Charles Small wept, because some kindnesses are hard to forget, and in his ham-handed way the old man was kind, and loved his boychik. So did Millie, no doubt.

Well, the worms had stripped them to the bone, that pretty pair, and here he lay with years and years of life behind and before him, wishing that his too, too solid flesh would melt . . . Shakespeare again . . . working himself silly for the wherewithal to pay the Inland Revenue, and support a couple of brash little loafers whom he wishes he had never fathered and a lumpy, snivelling blonde who gives him the creeps when she touches him. Poor Hettie; she cannot have had too gaudy a time of it, and he feels guilty about this. *Wham!*—he is off again, pitying, pitying, pitying—torturing himself, exacerbating his hateful desire to inflict pain upon those whom he is pledged to cherish. He used to be a gentle fellow, once upon a time. Now, he would walk a mile to find a hair to put in the soup, just to have something to shout about, and would buy the children trumpets and drums to make a pretext for a headache and take the toys away. Oh, what a . . . a . . . a Thingumybob and coward Whatsisname is he! . . . He is forgetting even Shakespeare, now. . . .

His abhorred wife, Hettie, comes up to the bathroom. She sounds like a giraffe; and when she uses the toilet it is as if someone is turning a faucet at a considerable height—*kwiss, kwiss, kwiss, splatter!*—and when she pulls the plug, *whoosh* goes Niagara Falls, and *clunk* goes the seat, and *plonk* goes the lid of the seat and *oink, oink, oink* go the stairs; and *clickety-click* goes a door on the floor below as it opens, letting out music from the radio, carefully kept low. Charles Small wants to dash downstairs and kick the guts out of that infernal wiry contraption; but he knows that if he goes downstairs he will stay to listen, and he will see himself buggered before he will give them—he nearly called them bleddy beggars—the satisfaction. Father is resting. Hell, what bribing and lying and coaxing, and vague promising must be going on downstairs! The very thought of it gives Charles Small a belly-ache just below the belt-line, so that he has to go to the bathroom. Water is still tinkling in the cistern. He is glad of this, because he knows that he is going to make a noise. He imagines that the seat is still warm, and although it cannot be, the very idea turns colic into constipation. So he sits, playing with a bit of toilet paper, an American product, widely advertised. Solly Schwartz has the account. The sales-talk is as follows: Mrs. Ex runs weeping to her mother-in-law, Mrs. Wise, complaining that her husband has a stinking temper. The old girl says something to this effect: "Have you ever considered the importance of a non-irritant toilet tissue?" The little woman dries her eyes, runs out and buys Somebody-or-Other's toilet paper, and husband and wife are in accord at last. Hettie tried even that, the poor girl. Charles Small tiptoes back to the bedroom. There is something like an electric fan spinning in his head, and he touches things including himself as in anticipation of a blue spark and an electric shock. No matter how carefully the kids mute the radio, Duke Ellington shakes the house and blares into his ears—particu-larly his left ear—and a saxophonist blows a great white blast into his left eye and thence, through his neck, into the back of his shoulder, while the drummer makes him waggle his feet in spite of himself, to his intense annoyance.

*　　　*　　　*　　　*　　　*

God is just. Charles Small's heart beats slower and the turbulence of his stomach subsides when he remembers the awful, the inevitable justice of God.

A dozen years after he was married, he had a frightful quarrel with Hettie. It happened one night after the children had been put to bed. Charles was in an expansive mood, in a mood for recitation. He talked his head off and, one thing leading to another, quoted:

> ". . . *Then fly. What, from myself? Great reason why:*
> *Lest I revenge. What, myself upon myself?*
> *Alack, I love myself. Wherefore? For any good*
> *That I myself have done unto myself?*
> *O, no! Alas, I rather hate myself*
> *For hateful deeds committed by myself!*
> *I am a villain . . ."*

And so on and on to:

> ". . . *I shall despair. There is no creature loves me;*
> *And if I die, no soul will pity me:*
> *Nay, wherefore should they, since that I myself*
> *Find in myself no pity to myself? . . ."*

He looked at Hettie for appreciation and saw that she had fallen asleep. He struck her over the head—not with a piddling evening paper, but with a good solid magazine. Hettie begged pardon, and wept. Charles Small wished that he could crack himself between two finger-nails like a louse . . . squeeze himself out of the face of things like a blackhead, pull himself out like a rotten tooth. Hettie went to bed in tears. She looked at him plaintively next morning, waiting for him to say a kind word, but there was a taste of rusty iron in his mouth, and something like cold iron pincers on his tongue, despite his remorse and his heartache.

He left the house without a word. But at eleven o'clock he left his office and went to Goldschmidt's in Bond Street, where he bought a bracelet for three hundred and seventy-five pounds. This would make Hettie happy again; not the gift, as a gift, but the thought behind it. While he was writing the cheque he saw, reflected in a mirror at the back of the counter, a familiar face. It was the face of a woman, dark and sweet. She was dressed very elegantly, and wrapped in mink. He made a kind of double-take, and said: "Ivy?"

"Charles?"

"Ivy!'"

"I was having my watch mended, Charley. How are you, after all these years? You haven't changed much."

"You haven't changed a bit, Ivy. Will you come and have a drink, a cocktail?"

"I don't, I never did. Coffee, perhaps."

They went to Gunter's.

There, they sat and looked at each other, not knowing what to say. At last Charles Small, playing with a coffee-spoon and looking at the egg-shaped reflection of himself in the back of it, said: "Ivy . . . about that time in the station."

"Let's not think about it," she said.

"I . . . I lost my head. Ivy, I've never stopped thinking of it, or of you. You know I always loved you, Ivy, on my honour, and I can give you my word, Ivy, that I paid very dearly for what I did to you. I've been punished. If you bear a grievance against me, set your mind at rest. I've paid, and paid, and paid! I'd give my soul for what I've thrown away. Believe me, please believe me, Ivy, I've always loved you with all my heart, and always will."

Ivy's lips quivered so that she had to put a cigarette between them to steady them, and Charles Small's hand shook so that the flame from his gold lighter flickered perilously close to her chin. Neither of them could drink their coffee; their hands were too unsteady. "I always loved you, too, Charles," she said.

"You did? After what I did to you? After what happened? It's not possible!"

"Don't think of that now, Charles. What's done is done, gone and forgotten. . . . Well, not quite forgotten, perhaps, because I never could forget you. Forgiven, finished."

Incredulously, Charles Small asked: "Do you mean to say that you don't hold it against me?"

"Not a bit. You couldn't help it. I would have run away myself, only I . . ."

"Only you were relying on me to come back and stand by you."

"Please don't let's talk about it now. It's so nice seeing you. I thought we should never meet again. But this morning I had a funny feeling, and when I came out to get this"—she pointed to her wrist-watch, which said that it was noon—"I felt . . . you know, the way some people feel when there's a cat in the room. Excuse me, Charles, I can't think of any other way of putting it. Tell me about yourself. Have you been well and happy? Prosperous? Did you go on the stage after all? I didn't think you did, or I'd have heard of you. We went to all the plays, and I always looked out for you. I always expected, somehow, to see your name on the programme, somewhere. But . . ."

Charles Small laughed bitterly and said: "You'll never see my name on any programme, dear Ivy. I threw it all up donkey's years ago."

"Oh, but why? You were so fine!"

"To please the Old People. They practically threatened to die. I couldn't have been any too damned fine, or I'd have gone my way and let them die. Everybody must die, and so must everybody live. It would have broken their hearts—*hah!*—what nonsense! What if it did? A mercy-killing, better than cancer. What are hearts made for? No, no, Ivy my dear, I did what they wanted, and did well at it; and oh, good God, how I wish . . . It would have been rough work, Ivy; furnished rooms, tinned salmon, hand-to-mouth, and all that kind of thing. But there would have been you and me, and you'd have loved me and I'd have loved you, and if I didn't have a penny to put in the gas-meter, we'd have kept each other warm. But the Old Ones were dying, don't you see, and they had to suck my life. So there you have it, Ivy, my one and only love—and here I am like the shell of a dead crab, stinking to high heaven on a grey beach, covered with flies. Am I prosperous? Oh yes. I have plenty of money. I have plenty of nothing. All I want is Ivy, Ivy, Ivy."

Ivy was silent.

"And you?" said Charles Small.

"If you don't mind, Charles, I'd rather not talk much about that now—not here, anyway. I married someone named Squire —perhaps you remember him?"

"What, that horrible man? Oh no!"

"Yes. I have two children, girls. Would you like to see some snaps of them?"

"No, no. Squire! That one!"

"He died two years ago."

"I hope he's rotting in hell!" said Charles Small. "What business had he marrying you?"

393

"Mother made me," said Ivy. "But I didn't want anyone but you, dear Charles. You married, too?"

"Yes, and my wife isn't dead, and I've got a couple of children."

"That must be nice," said Ivy, sighing.

"It isn't nice. I want you—never wanted anything but you."

She sighed again, looked at her watch, and said: "I must go, dear."

"No, don't—please don't go!"

"I must; the girls. But why don't you come to tea to-morrow afternoon?" she said, giving him her card.

"I will, I will!" cried Charles Small. Then he took the velvet-lined jeweller's box out of his pocket and compelled Ivy to accept it, saying: "I knew I was going to meet you and I got this for you." She took it in a daze, and opened it.

"I couldn't," she said.

"You must."

At last he persuaded her to lock the bracelet on her right wrist, and they parted with a lingering handshake. Charles Small was in high spirits that afternoon, and evolved a good idea in connection with textiles. When the office closed Conscience nudged him. He stopped at a flower shop and bought a pound's worth of red roses for Hettie, over which she ran at the nose with delight.

Charles Small lay awake until three o'clock in the morning, day-dreaming of tea-time to-morrow.

*　　*　　*　　*　　*

Thus Ivy and he were together again, as in the old times. When no one was looking they sat close to each other, holding hands, knee-to-knee, sometimes cheek-to-cheek, saying little, imagining much. Ivy's daughters did not like him, perhaps because he was nervous in their presence. When he recited poetry, or tried to tell a funny story, they exchanged looks of astonishment, as if they were asking each other what the hell this jittering imbecile thought he was playing at. Still, he was happy with Ivy, although he scarcely touched her except with his fingertips, and only brushed her cheek with his lips.

One day in July the girls were sent to stay with their Aunt Enid, who had a house near the sea in Bournemouth. Charles Small's offspring, Laura and Jules, had gone with their mother to spend a week or two with Lily, the wife of Nathan, the Photographer. Lily was far from well; she had a prolapsis, and her womb more or less fell out, so that a surgeon had to put something like what seamstresses call a "tuck" in an unmentionable orifice. Lily was old now, and given to talking about dear, dead days beyond recall. Nathan, retired with more than a modest competence, had arthritis, gout, colitis, and something that felt like a nest of mice in his stomach—to say nothing of hæmorrhoids, corns, wax in the ears, a pain in the neck. He sat by the fire, in the heat of July, shivering and brooding, staring at the embers which seemed to wink at him knowingly, while the smoke hissed and the coals crackled: *Quick, quick, Nathan . . . Pss! What are you waiting for?* He could not eat; he dared not smoke; he had never taken refuge in wine; he could not urinate, tie his shoelaces, or even breathe properly. His false teeth had to be taken away from him in case he might swallow them and choke himself, because his gums had shrivelled. He tried to read an Encyclopædia of Photography, in which there were plates of nudes—one of them undepilated—but his rheumy eyes registered grey blurs, and he could see nothing but the fire, the whispering fire that hissed: *Hurry up, hurry up* over the rasping chuckle of the cinders. Stanley, the gynæcologist with the Ronald Colman moustache, married to the homely daughter of a wealthy builder of shoddy houses, was poking about the private parts of hypochondriacal hags in Harley Street. Old Auntie Lily needed company, and sympathy. All the fight had been knocked out of her. She and Hettie got along like a house on fire, as the saying goes. Laura and Jules played and fought, while the old man drooled at the fire, and the women pitied each other over teacups, brushing biscuit-crumbs from their bosoms, exchanging secrets unprintable except by H. K. Lewis, and in a Limited Edition at that.

It came to pass, then, that Charles Small stuck his elbow into a cream cake and, grasping Ivy's hand, said: "Ivy, my dear Ivy, I love you better than anything in the world! Let's go away, just you and me together. We've missed so much, Ivy. Your mother, my mother; your father, my father—they've taken everything away from us. Together, Ivy, you and me—oh, a devil of a long way away, my darling! Please come."

"What about your wife and children, Charles?"

"They don't need me, they don't want me. They'll have plenty of money. I don't do them any good. I'm a nuisance to them. When I'm out of the house they sing and they dance, and

395

when I come home they go on tiptoe. They don't like me, they don't want me, Ivy; and I don't want them—I want you."

"Enid adores the girls," said Ivy, slowly. ". . . I do love you very dearly, Charles . . ."

"Oh then, Ivy my dear, let us go away, a long way away, right away! I love you, you love me; isn't that so?"

"Yes, Charles."

"Everyone will be looked after. There's plenty of everything for everybody. Didn't you see how glad your girls were to go to Bournemouth, to their great-aunt? They don't like you, honestly they don't And mine—I never saw them so happy in their lives as when they were waving good-bye to me out of the carriage window. Please! Ivy, darling! What do they want us for? What do we want them for? You worry them, they worry you—what *for*? Come away with me, Ivy, a long way away. Yes?"

Ivy shed tears, and replied: "Oh, I do love you, Charles—I do, I do! More than the whole world, my darling. The girls wouldn't really care; they're their father's daughters, and not mine. . . . It's a wicked thing to say, I know, but I never wanted to have them by Jack, and they never wanted to have me. . . ."

"You'll come then? You'll come with me?"

"Yes, I will."

"Oh Ivy, when?"

"As soon as I pack my clothes."

"Thank you, bless you!" cried Charles Small. "I'll pack mine, now. To-morrow? . . . Have you got a passport? . . . Have you? Oh good, good! Portugal, let's go to Portugal yes? Or anywhere. We'll meet at Victoria, eh? And go away, eh? Where doesn't matter—only when. To-morrow, eh?"

Ivy nodded, and said: "To-morrow. At what time shall I meet you?"

"I must pack, and buy the tickets to-day, and let you know first thing in the morning. Be ready very first thing, dear Ivy."

"I'll be ready, dear Charles."

Charles Small had never tasted such spice in life, such happiness. He felt that another little drop of *joie de vivre* would unbalance him, send him off his rocker. He sobbed:

". . . *Entreat me not to leave thee, or to return from following after thee: for whither thou goest I will go; and where thou lodgest*

I will lodge; thy people shall be my people, and thy God my God;
where thou diest, will I die, and there will I be buried; the Lord do so
to me, and more also, if aught but Death part thee and me . . ."

Then, with the taste of her tears on his tongue he hurried
home.

As Millie would have said, he "threw himself about" when he
got home. He stuffed ten suits, twenty shirts, eight pairs of
shoes, fifteen pairs of socks, nine changes of underclothes, a
handful of neckties, and a Panama hat into a cabin trunk and an
immense valise. He forgot his studs, cuff-links, toothbrush,
razor, hairbrush and handkerchiefs; but—he does not know why
—he turned the house upside down in search of an eye-bath, and a
sixpenny tube of yellow eye ointment, for he was subject to sties.
Also, and this was significant, he packed several family photographs which he had never found the courage to throw away:
Millie Small had a superstition about throwing away photographs.
There was one especially repulsive family group: the old man,
dressed in his best, looking at Millie, who was in her prime.
She was holding the two-year-old Priscilla in her lap; even at that
tender age Prissie looked like the uninhibited little tart that she
turned out to be. As for Charles Small, he stood like the *nebbisch*
that he was, in such an attitude that his head seemed likely to
drop off at any moment. (Pity it didn't.) He drove like a madman
to Victoria Station, checked his luggage, and went to the office,
where he told his secretary to drop everything and buy two tickets
on the Golden Arrow to France. After that he went next door
to the bank, just before closing time, and drew a thousand pounds
in ten-pound notes. He was wildly excited; he was alive. He
went to the inner office. A secretary said: "I'm sorry, Mr. Small,
but Sir Solomon says he's on no account to be disturbed"—but
Charles Small pushed her aside and, brushing off a few buzzing
office-boys, burst into the Holy of Holies, Sir Solomon Schwartz's
private office.

The hunchback was grey, now, and almost bald. He was dried
up. The muscles between his neck and his shoulders had shrunk,
and his chin was low on his chest, so that his hump appeared like
Popocatepetl, but his eyes flashed as he growled: "What d'you
want, *trottel*? I wasn't to be disturbed. Who asked you to barge
in? Were you *told*?"

"Mr. Schwartz—I mean, Sir Solomon——"

"—Bugger that for a lark; what's on your mind?"

Charles Small said: "This must be good-bye. I've come to say good-bye."

Solly Schwartz replied: "Out with it, *trottel!* Don't stand there hopping about like a bear with a sore arse. What's your trouble? Look sharp. Sit down. You worry me. Speak up. What d'you mean, good-bye?"

"Do you remember, once, a long time ago, when I told you about a girl named Ivy Narwall? It was the night you took me to dinner. . . ."

"Yes. You took after your old man, another *trottel*—two drinks, and you were drunk as a tinker's bitch. . . . Narwall, I remember him," said Solly Schwartz, laughing in his throat. "He thought he was clever. He wasn't. And Ivy, Ivy? Oh yes. Knew her before her arse was as big as a shirt-button. So? What?"

Charles Small said, simply: "Will you give me the Paris Branch? Or the New York Branch? Or any other Branch out of England?"

"Try and make sense, will you? What's all this got to do with your Ivy? For Christ's sake, man, cough it up!"

"I know I can talk to you in confidence——"

"—You bloody well can't for more than three minutes, you know. Cough it up, spit it out! What about it?"

"Ivy Narwall and I are going to go away together. Please, can I have one of the Continental or one of the American Branches? You know, I——"

"—I know you, *trottel;* I knew you before you were born. Don't make me laugh, I'm not in the mood. You run away from your wife? What, you? Gertcher! American Branches! You couldn't hold down a twig, let alone a Branch. Next time you barge in here you'll be sorry."

"I'm leaving instantly, Sir Solomon. I hand in my resignation."

"Don't want it. I'll see you to-morrow."

"I shall not be here to-morrow."

"You will. You are just like your Dad—you haven't got the bloody nerve to run away. So long, Charley."

"Good-bye," said Charles Small.

Knocking aside his proffered hand, Solly Schwartz said: "I'll be seeing you."

On his way out Charles Small slapped an office-boy for whistling. Then he went to Shortland's and ate cold boiled beef, which he afterwards threw up all over the dashboard of his car . . . there seemed to be pounds of the stuff.

He had had a busy day. For all that, he could not sleep. His secretary came to his house at seven o'clock with the tickets. She gave him a peculiar look. "Will you be gone long, Mr. Small?" she asked.

"I don't know exactly, Miss Appel."

"Shall I——"

"—Yes, yes. Good-night, good-night."

He telephoned Ivy at seven o'clock in the morning: "My dear, darling Ivy—did I wake you?—Are you dressed? Have you packed? Are you ready?"

"Yes."

"Victoria Station, then, at nine?"

"Nine o'clock, dear, in the big refreshment room."

He left an eight-page letter for Hettie. She had a good house, and a good car, all weighed and paid, and enough to support her and the children for ever. When he got into the taxi, Charles Small felt light and free. But when the door of the cab slammed behind him, he felt like a man in a box. There was a weight in his chest, and in his mind an image of Hettie's eyes pink and puffy, and in his ears the sound of her snuffling.

* * * * *

Time would not pass. Twenty times he looked from his watch to the clock and back again. The second hand jumped slowly, like an old toad. He palpitated over a cup of undrinkable coffee and listened to the hissing and the clashing of in-coming trains, and the rumbling of trundled trolleys, and the noise—like a kind of dry, stale rain—of thousands of leather heels tap-tapping on the stones. He was suffocated with excitement, sick with fright, far from comfortable in fact; and he was so tired and all his bones ached. His eyes smarted; he could not stop yawning. He caught sight of himself in a mirror behind the counter, and saw that he looked like a man half-awake after an evil dream. He took his cup of coffee from the bar to a table where he sat smoking cigarette after cigarette, checking watch with clock, clock with watch and watching the seconds flop sluggishly around and around. He closed his eyes against the light, and then a gentle voice said: "Charles?" and he started up as if someone were behind him with a gimlet.

"Ivy! Thank God you've come. I was worrying about you. Have . . . a cup of hot cocoa, have a bun."

She chose cocoa.

"Have you got all your luggage?" he asked, in a whisper.

Ivy shook her head and said, "No, Charles dear. Dear Charles, I haven't, I'm afraid."

"You haven't? Why not?" asked Charles, staring at her.

She did not speak until a waitress had put down a cup of cocoa and departed, and then she said: "Darling, I love you very much; but I *can't!*"

"Eh? What do you mean? What can't you?"

"I can't come away with you."

"What the devil are you talking about? What do you mean, you can't come away with me?"

"I was all packed and ready last night, and I was so excited, I lay awake thinking. I love you, Charles, and always have, and always will, and I'd rather go away with you than do anything else in the world. Dear Charles, I hate to hurt you. Forgive me. I got to thinking, about the girls. Edith is . . . just starting to be a woman. She needs me; it's a critical time in her life—a girl needs her mother then. Charles, truly, it wouldn't be any use. We could never be happy—we'd never know a minute's peace of mind. We'd always be fretting over our children for the rest of our lives. We'd torment ourselves and each other; we'd feel like deserters; if we met anyone we knew we'd have to cross to the other side of the street. We'd never dare to come back home. We'd be wanderers, Charles. We must go home to our children."

At this, Charles Small began to laugh. He couldn't help it. He laughed until bitter bile came into his throat and salty tears ran down his cheeks. "Like flies to wanton boys are we to the gods," he said; and "Oh, the pity of it, the pity of it!"

"We must say good-bye, now, and never meet again, my darling Charles. We'd only hurt each other."

"I suppose you're not hurting me now," Charles said, bitterly.

"Oh my dear, don't be like that! I thought you'd understand."

"Certainly I understand. I give up everything for you"— he waved the tickets at her—"and at the last moment your children come first. If it's not one thing, it's another. If it's not your bloody mother, it's your lousy father, and if it isn't your stinking parents it's your snotty-nosed children!"

"Don't talk like that, Charles—I won't have it."

"Turnabout's fair play, I suppose," said Charles, with a sneer. "First the old cows grab the smeary-arsed little ones by the tail, and then the little ones grab the old cows by the tits."

"Charles!" exclaimed Ivy, rising.

"Oh don't Charles me," he said. "I don't understand it. Just because one of your ill-mannered little bitches is starting to have a monthly period, she *needs* you. A Mother's Care. What are you going to do? Put a cork in her, or something? What the devil do they want you for? To slobber over them? Bah! They don't need you, you need them. You want to take your revenge for what your mother did to you. Well, fair's fair. They eat you now; later on you'll eat them, just as that rotten old witch of a mother ate you!"

"I won't allow you to talk like that about my mother, Charles. I never heard such language!" She was fumbling with the catch of her bag.

Charles Small was eloquent. He knew, now, all about the Irony of Fate. "You and your darling daughters!" and he declaimed:

". . . *Knowest thou the time when the wild goats of the rock bring forth? Or canst thou mark when the hinds do calve? Canst thou number the months that they fulfil? Or knowest thou the time when they bring forth? They bow themselves; they bring forth their young ones, they sast out their sorrows. Their young ones are in good liking, they grow up with corn; they go forth and return not unto them. . . .*"

"Charles Small, I'm glad I found you out in time." Ivy had her bag open and was rummaging with a gloved hand. "I wouldn't have you if you were the last man in the world. You're disgusting. I don't like you any more. I never want to see your face again, never!" She threw down the bracelet he had given her —it fell into his untasted coffee—and walked firmly out of the refreshment room.

How did Charles Small feel then? He does not quite remember. He knows that he suddenly felt dry and hollow, like a mildewed nut, horribly stale. But somewhere, in one of the ventricles of his heart, there was a little light fluttering which might have been relief.

He fished the diamond bracelet out of the undrinkable coffee with a teaspoon, and went home. In the taxi, starting out of a meaningless reverie, he thought that he had had an unspeakable accident; but it was only the little tube of yellow eye ointment. He had sat on it.

He hurried home to get at that letter and burn it. Having done this he had a bath, changed his ointment-plastered clothes, and went to the office, curiously calm. He walked, enjoying the fine morning. He arrived just when Solly Schwartz was limping out of his cream-coloured Rolls-Royce.

"What, *trottel?*" said the hunchback, laughing. "I thought you were in South America already." He hit Charles Small smartly on the backside with a gold-headed stick of tuyia wood. "Go on, *schlemazzel*, back to work. I told you you didn't have the nerve to run away. Come on, *trottel!*"

And the great glass doors closed behind him.

*   *   *   *   *

He is exhausted, now, but calm. He does not know what to make of it all, and he is tired of trying to get any sense out of it. He remembers what an African traveller told him about the scorpions that live in the cracked, sunbaked rocks. The females eat their husbands even in the act of copulation. When the young hatch out, they hop on to their mother's back and sustain themselves by eating her alive, to get the strength to repeat the process over and over again. There is neither rhyme nor reason in it . . . there is family life for you! . . . Poor parents, poor children, thinks Charles Small, dropping tears of pity for his father, his mother, his sister, his wife, his children, himself, and everyone else's children.

. . . At the same time he decides that if, within five minutes, Laura and Jules do not stop playing with that clattering clock-work train, he will go downstairs and beat the Bejesus out of them with a rolled-up copy of *Child Psychology*.

THE END

Barbados–New York City,
1950.